THAT VANDERBILT WOMAN

Philip Van Rensselaer

P♦P

A Playboy Press Book

Trade distribution by Simon and Schuster
A Division of Gulf + Western Corporation
New York, New York 10020

Designed by Tere LoPrete

Library of Congress Cataloging in Publication Data

Van Rensselaer, Philip.
    That Vanderbilt woman.

    1. Vanderbilt, Gloria Morgan, 1904-
—Fiction. I. Title.
PZ4.V2745Th   [PS3572.A528]   813'.5'4   78-17513
ISBN 0-87223-502-5

THAT
VANDERBILT
WOMAN

CHAPTER
1

The stately black Rolls-Royce, its silvered front gleaming as brightly as the white sidewalls flanking the long motor, drew slowly to a halt before the courthouse in downtown Foley Square. It was such a top-heavy car that it appeared to sway and the uniformed chauffeur had had difficulty keeping it on its majestic course.

As soon as it stopped, the crowd that had been waiting for a good hour swarmed about the car. Despite the efforts of the police, some people managed to press their faces against the rear windows and peer into the interior. Seated in the back, erect and still, was a regal figure all in black with lush silver foxes about her shoulders, a veiled hat pulled down over one eye. No trace of anger, disappointment, or fear remained on the face of Gloria Vanderbilt; the face she had made up to reveal to the world was an empty mask that women in her fashionable little set chose to wear. Like a mannequin in a Bergdorf Goodman window, her complexion was marble-

like, her chestnut-brown hair drawn serenely in soft waves
over her ears, the wide lips Chinese red and set in a taut
line. A double strand of pearls rested at her throat on the
lace blouse; a diamond bracelet glowed discreetly below the
cuff of the severely tailored jacket.

The men peering at her were at once struck by her aura of
hothouse femininity and a sense of mystery that put her at
a great distance from them; they remained silent. The women,
on the other hand, resented this air of detachment; the sight
of her in all her splendor enraged them and they began
shrieking horrible things at her, beating at the glass and
making obscene gestures, until the police pulled them back.

The detective who sat beside the chauffeur now opened the
door and Mrs. Vanderbilt stepped tensely out onto the pavement. She was always exquisitely dressed and today she did
not disappoint her audience. Her Paris suit by Schiaparelli
(who also dressed Wallis Warfield Simpson) was a distinguished creation designed to increase her allure and her
air of mystery; it made her, somehow, a divinity, a Garbo or a
Dietrich. Even her shoes, elegant high-heeled pumps delicately laced up her instep, seemed better suited to a goddess,
so thin and fragile were the soles. She wore gloves and
carried a pocketbook tucked in the crook of her arm.

Photographers began to snap pictures and newspapermen
converged on her en masse, pressing close to her gardenia-
scented figure.

The trial, which started September 25, 1934, had provided
the tabloids with a bonanza. The previous week, Gloria
Vanderbilt's only child, Gloria, Jr., heiress to her dead
father's $3-million estate—the income from which was her
mother's sole source of support—had been literally kidnapped
by her paternal aunt Gertrude, the renowned Mrs. Harry
Payne Whitney. Mrs. Vanderbilt demanded that her child
be returned to her. Mrs. Whitney refused. A battery of

famous lawyers was summoned by the warring parties and the case went to the Supreme Court in New York City.

Soon every newspaper in the country was turning out extras. On every street corner from Minneapolis to Mobile, newsboys shouted the latest lurid developments of the trial: "Mrs. Whitney Claims Mrs. Vanderbilt Unfit Mother"; "Prince Rushing from Europe to Defend Lady Love."

The opening testimony by Gloria's discharged servants had given an indication of how scandalous the case would be. They spoke of wild drinking parties at the Vanderbilt mansion, and of Gloria's various titled lovers. The first witness to take the stand told of rat-infested palaces in Paris and Biarritz, filled with cocktail-party revelers like film star Constance Bennett, now the marquise de la Falaise, who danced from twilight to daybreak to the music of three orchestras. The witness also claimed that virile young Prince Hohenlohe, a great-grandson of Queen Victoria and nephew of Queen Marie of Rumania, was seen lying nude on the pink crepe de chine sheets of Mrs. Vanderbilt's French-style bed.

But the most damaging testimony had come from Mrs. Vanderbilt's own mother. A handsome dark-haired woman with a theatrical manner, Mrs. Laura Morgan took the stand and testified that little Gloria was practically an orphan and not wanted by her mother, a woman who devoted herself exclusively to her own pleasures. And when Gloria's ten-year-old daughter swept into the courtroom and past her mother without a word, not even giving her a look, Gloria was prostrate with grief. Dark veils lowered over her stricken face, she had to be assisted from the courtroom.

But today Gloria's composure was admirable. She met the reporters' questions with a set but friendly expression. Her aristocratic carriage, her jewelry, her furs, the splendid suit, all kept them at a slight distance as they pressed around her.

"Will your daughter be coming today?" asked a *Mirror* reporter.

"Perhaps," said Mrs. Vanderbilt, and the crowd pricked up its ears.

"Prince Hohenlohe stated yesterday he'll soon be on his way to testify in your defense," said a *Journal* man. "Will his wife pose any problems for you?"

"Of course not. Why should she?" replied Gloria Vanderbilt coldly.

"What about Lady Furness and the Prince of Wales?" asked a *Herald* reporter.

"My sister has nothing to do with the case," she answered, her lips taut.

"Yesterday the nurse said she stayed in a freezing cold boardinghouse while you visited Lady Milford-Haven in her castle."

"The nurse is a terrible liar," snapped Mrs. Vanderbilt.

"Is Lady Milford-Haven the granddaughter of Queen Victoria?" questioned a *News* man.

"No," said Mrs. Vanderbilt. A dull ache throbbed behind her eyes; her stomach felt queasy.

"Your accent sounds foreign, Mrs. Vanderbilt," remarked a *Times* reporter baitingly. "Are you French?"

"I was born in Switzerland," Mrs. Vanderbilt said. "My father was American consul in practically every European capital."

"So it must be difficult to know where you belong, isn't it?"

"Yes, it is," she said simply.

"Do you prefer European society to American?" queried the *Mirror* writer with an unpleasant expression.

Mrs. Vanderbilt gave him a level glance. "I've rented a house here in New York," she said, trying not to lose her temper. "I intend to make my home here now."

"You'll love the Bronx, lady," cried a man's coarse voice from out of the crowd. The Depression crowds of the Thirties were hungry to tear down the fabulous Vanderbilt family called "America's royalty."

A wave of excitement went through the onlookers. Someone cried, "Here comes Mrs. Whitney's hearse!" A powerful sixteen-cylinder Packard town car pulled up at the courthouse; a dreadnought surrounded by satellite cars containing detectives, lawyers, a maid, and a footman.

Stony silence greeted Gertrude Vanderbilt Whitney as she stepped out of the car. A tall, arrow-thin, middle-aged woman dressed in severe, impeccably tailored black clothes, she carried herself with determination. No one dared hurl insults at her, though the sight of these two women, arriving in their grandiose automobiles, was enough to draw a curious and hostile crowd in front of the columned Greek temple–style building every morning.

Gloria had no desire for a public confrontation with her late husband's sister. She turned to go, but the *Mirror* reporter pushed closer, his face twisting in an ugly way. "Don't leave yet, Mrs. Vanderbilt. I want to get some good photos of you and your sister-in-law together."

Gloria gave him a chilling look and started through the crowd. The husky detective ran interference for her, but he could not block out the hateful and lewd comments hurled at her.

A fat manicurist from First Avenue called out, "I'd rather be under the Prince of Wales too. It's better than hanging onto a subway strap during rush hour!"

"Ever tried living on five dollars a week, Mrs. Vanderbilt?" That from a university student.

"Enough . . ." pleaded Mrs. Vanderbilt, her voice breaking. She managed to meet their eyes, silently expressing to each one of them the pain she felt inside.

Surprisingly enough, the crowd opened a path for her as she moved up the steps to the courthouse where her friend Constance Bennett waited.

"You were wonderful, Gloria," said Connie, taking her arm with admiration. "And fearless. All that pushing and shoving would have exhausted *me*." She carefully smoothed her dress and fur piece.

"Little Orphan Annie said when you're at the end of your rope, make a knot and hang on," said Gloria. "I guess that's what I'm trying to do."

"Well, you *are* brave, darling," said Connie softly. "And you go through it all—those terrible insults and terrible voices . . ."

"I'm glad you can't hear my stomach churning or my heart pounding." She glanced into the courtroom. "Now into the arena, the lions are hungry. . . ."

Gloria would never forget the courtroom that October day. The ugly brown paneled room looked like a church with its rows of benches, and the witness stand under the judge's podium seemed a sinister place of inquisition. She noticed the windows were streaked with months of dirt.

As she walked down to the counsel table, people strained to get a better glimpse of her. Somehow she must manage to hold her head high; she must remain dauntless, mustn't allow herself to dissolve into self-pity. Besides, the harsh words flung at her by her detractors made her see her situation as viewed by outsiders. Things *had* been too easy for her; things had always been done for her. A new and curious feeling went through her: She was not a puppet on a string, she was a person in her own right. Blumenthal and Thaw had wanted to accompany her today, but she had put her foot down. For the first time she was dealing with her own problems; no man was protecting her..

They sat down in the front row; Connie looked around to get the feeling in the room. "I don't know why people stare with such hostility."

"Don't you?" said Gloria with an ironic smile. "I'm rich

and beautiful. I've known glamorous people here and abroad. I have options. These people here have no options. They can't travel; they don't have nannies to look after their children."

"Oh, Gloria, *really*—"

"You seem to feel that money is a sort of passport to exempt us from suffering or sorrow."

"Isn't it?" challenged Connie.

Gloria shook her head. "I hate to tell you, but I often feel that I'm going to end my days in a cheap Broadway hotel."

Connie was shocked. "Gloria! I can't believe my ears, I—"

She broke off as a ripple of excitement went through the room, which usually signaled Mrs. Whitney's entrance. Gertrude Whitney, her daughter, and a group of lawyers were now the focal point of the press and photographers. Gloria didn't dare look at her sister-in-law.

"Is little Gloria with her?" she whispered sideways.

Connie craned her neck. "No, no, I don't see her. . . ."

"Thank God," Gloria sighed.

Nathan Burkan, the celebrated trial lawyer hired by Mrs. Vanderbilt, came and sat next to her now. "Everything will be all right," he reassured her.

"You told me that yesterday," she said.

Burkan patted her hand. "I won't let you down. . . ."

Justice Carew entered, everyone rose. The court was called to order and the room fell into silence. Nervously Mrs. Vanderbilt twisted the enormous pear-shaped diamond back and forth on her finger so that the stone almost tore her flesh, but she couldn't stop.

One of the Vanderbilts' former maids, Maria Caillot, was summoned first to the witness stand. She put her hand on the Bible.

"Do you swear to tell the truth, the whole truth, and nothing but the truth, so help you God?"

"I do," she nodded, then sat down.

Gloria leaned closer to her friend. "That's another one I fired. Gertrude is really scraping the bottom of the barrel with that one. . . ."

Mrs. Whitney's lawyer, Frank Crocker, questioned Miss Caillot about Mrs. Vanderbilt's life in Paris.

"There were rats all over the place," Maria Caillot said with a dramatic sweep of her arm. "I saw them in my room. I saw them all three together on a tray of food in the dining room. They might have bitten the child."

In cross-examination Mr. Burkan asked, "You didn't tell Mrs. Vanderbilt about the rats?"

"No, I didn't think she would be interested."

"Why not?" continued Burkan.

"There were parties in Mrs. Vanderbilt's home that started at nine o'clock in the evening and continued till six o'clock next morning. Often there were three bands, one taking the place of the other as they tired, so that the music would never stop."

Justice Carew stared down at the maid. "Did this happen as often as once a month?"

Miss Caillot smiled unpleasantly. "Oh, more than that; once, twice, three times a week."

"Then she wasn't out every night?" pursued Carew with a grim expression.

"She was out about three nights a week and she gave parties like this on the nights when she stayed home."

"Did it keep the household awake? Did it keep little Gloria awake?"

"Yes, it did," replied the maid, watching her former mistress.

"Didn't anybody complain? Didn't the police stop it?" the judge asked.

"I don't know; *I* wasn't in the drawing room."

Her sarcasm caused some laughter. People leaned forward to see the maid better. Mrs. Whitney, sitting erect with a determined set to her jaw, adjusted an eyeglass and stared.

"Who *was* in the drawing room?" pursued Justice Carew.

"I remember when there were three bands," said Maria Caillot with a knowing expression, "there was Mrs. Thaw and Lady Furness, Mrs. Thomas, whose husband was connected with the American Embassy in Paris, perhaps also Mr. Thomas, a Mr. and Mrs. Donald Mixsell, a Mr. Brooks, Prince Hohenlohe, and there may have been some others."

Nathan Burkan went over to the discharged maid. "Did you see any of them drunk?"

"I saw Mrs. Thomas; she had to be carried upstairs."

"Did you ever see Mrs. Vanderbilt drunk?"

"Yes." The maid stared at Gloria, her eyes unreadable.

"How many times?"

"Two or three times," replied the maid thoughtfully.

"How did you know she was drunk?"

"She smiled and repeated things she said to me two or three times."

Burkan gave her a look of contempt. "So that when a lady smiles and repeats herself she is drunk?" he asked sarcastically.

"She was very happy," replied Miss Caillot.

"So when a lady is very happy you conclude she is drunk, and when she is sad you conclude she is sober?"

"Maybe," she replied, and the audience broke into laughter. Gloria didn't laugh; her stomach was contracting and her mouth felt dry.

"Did you ever see Mrs. Vanderbilt reel?" Burkan went on.

The maid shook her head: "No."

"Was she able to get to her room on the floor above without being helped?"

"Yes."

"In all the five years you worked for her, did you ever see her unable to walk?"

"No," she said.

"Then you have never seen her drunk?"

"Only a little drunk."

Justice Carew interposed: "Did you ever see Mrs. Vanderbilt have champagne served in her bedroom?"

"Yes."

Mrs. Vanderbilt drummed her long nails on the side of the chair.

"When was that?"

"In February nineteen thirty-three," said the maid.

"At what times of day?"

"At six o'clock in the afternoon."

"Did it happen more than once?" asked Justice Carew.

"Five or six times."

"Who was in the room at the time?"

"Somebody," said the maid mysteriously.

The crowd leaned forward as one to catch her words.

"Was it a man or a woman?" asked Carew.

"A man."

"Always the same man?"

"Yes."

"Did you see him?" demanded Justice Carew.

"No, but I heard his voice," Maria Caillot replied smugly.

Nathan Burkan began the cross-examination. "How long did this visitor remain?"

"Not more than half an hour."

"Who served the champagne?"

"The butler. Thereafter Mrs. Vanderbilt rang for me and I helped her dress for dinner."

Justice Carew interrupted. "How was she dressed at the time?"

"In a negligee."

"A housedress, the kind they go around the house with now-adays, I'm told," said Burkan.

"What I call a convenient house garment," said Mrs. Whitney's lawyer, Crocker, dryly.

"It's not known in my house nor the houses I go to," said Justice Carew stonily.

The court burst into laughter. At the counsel table the friends shook with mirth and Justice Carew flushed angrily. Mrs. Whitney kept her stony composure.

"This is a pitiful case and there is no occasion to be funny about it," Carew intoned harshly. He brought the session to a close, stating it was time for lunch. He glanced at Mrs. Vanderbilt, then vanished behind the thick oak doors to his chambers. The sound of the doors slamming shut echoed strangely in her mind.

Connie stood up with a relieved expression. "Well, darling, that wasn't so bad, was it?"

"No, no . . ."

Connie stared at Gloria. "What is it, dear? You're so pale. Some lunch will make you feel better."

Gloria looked up at her with a blank stare. She felt unreal and far away. The terrible presentiment had returned. Try as she might, she could not rid herself of that heavy sense of impending doom. In a blur she found herself moving out of the courtroom with Connie's arm around her. She could not eat a bite of her lunch—and later reflected that it was a lucky thing she didn't, for being sick would have added to the ignominy of that afternoon.

The afternoon session began with Burkan questioning Maria Caillot about Mrs. Vanderbilt's friendship with Lady Milford-Haven. Watching the cross-examination, Gloria started to twist the diamond ring again and glared at her lawyer. Why did he keep harping on Nada Milford-Haven?

Gertrude Whitney's clever lawyer kept bringing the name of Lady Milford-Haven into the testimony, and Gloria wondered what they knew. The throb behind her eyes deepened; the figures of Burkan and Maria Caillot and Justice Carew swam in a sickening blur. Earlier Frank Crocker had grilled Maria Caillot concerning the reason why Mrs. Vanderbilt had been in such a hurry to get back to Europe in 1932 when little Gloria was in a New York hospital for an operation. Now Carew raised the question again with Maria. His eyes were shining with the unholy light of a fierce visionary and Gloria's breath came faster.

"We want to know why a mother left a sick child in New York," repeated Justice Carew, and his words echoed through the large courtroom. "Can you tell us?"

"No, sir," Maria Caillot replied reflectively. Presently she added: "I rushed back to England with Mrs. Vanderbilt to stay with Lady Milford-Haven at her house, at Maidenhead."

"Did anything happen there?" pursued Justice Carew in an ominous tone, and Gloria sat on the edge of her chair.

"No, sir," answered the maid in her quick, alert manner. "But later I accompanied Mrs. Vanderbilt to Cannes where at the Miramar Hotel, a large, expensive hotel on the beach, she met Lady Milford-Haven again."

And as the maid continued, Gloria saw the white steam yachts anchored on the cerulean-blue Mediterranean, saw the violet mist lingering over the mountains of Grasse behind, saw herself and Nada Milford-Haven sipping gin fizzes on the terrace, the sweet alcohol buzzing through their heads.

What a romantic place Cannes was in the springtime. The open touring cars vanishing down the palm-lined avenue; the boutiques with the happy fluttering of canvas awnings; tennis balls striking rackets; the sound of cocktails being shaken beside Rhoda and Freddy Lewisohn's pool at their nearby villa, Corne d'Or, where Lady Sylvia Ashley, Tallulah Bankhead, and the Michael Arlens were discussing the marriage

of Audrey Emery, the Cincinatti heiress, and the Grand
Duke Dimitri, who was Nada's cousin and had the same lean,
handsome, dark look as Nada herself.

Now, remembering Nada, Gloria gripped the arms of the
chair, felt she was slipping away from her body, that she was
losing control. She looked about with a desperate expression,
her pasty forehead dappled with perspiration. I mustn't
faint, she thought with rising panic. I mustn't, I mustn't!
She had to get out of here before something terrible happened.

Suddenly she became conscious of Nathan Burkan's voice
and glancing up she watched him and her former maid.

"Did you ever see Lady Milford-Haven drunk?" he was
asking.

"No, sir."

"Was Mrs. Vanderbilt running about with people there?"

"Yes, with Lady Milford-Haven."

"No, I don't mean that; I mean with men."

"Well, I saw her go out with Lady Milford-Haven."

"You saw nothing improper there?"

The witness took a long time answering. "Oh, yes," Maria
said finally, "I remember now something that once happened that was very *amusant!*"

Her word "amusant" was then translated for the benefit of
the court as "amusing."

Mr. Burkan was already putting away his papers. "Oh,
yes?" he said, looking up. "And what was that?"

"Yes," Maria went on, "there was something that struck
me as very funny when we were at the Hotel Miramar in
Cannes in nineteen twenty-nine."

Gloria wanted to stand up, to scream, to stop the maid
from going on. But she couldn't move, she couldn't speak.

Maria Caillot glanced down at Gloria with a direct glare
from her gray eyes. "Mrs. Vanderbilt called me one morning," she continued, "and asked me to get breakfast. When I
came back with breakfast, I saw Lady Milford-Haven and

Mrs. Vanderbilt, and Lady Milford-Haven was kissing Mrs. Vanderbilt."

You could hear a pin drop. Not a cough; not a murmur. The silence in the courtroom was fearful.

Justice Carew banged down his gavel. "In the interest of public decency," he said, "the press and the public will be barred from the courtroom. Court is adjourned until tomorrow."

Pandemonium broke loose. Reporters and photographers raced to telephones located in the corridors outside. Pushing, elbowing their way, they rushed to get the headline story to their newspapers. This would really push the Lindbergh story off the front pages. It was as hot a headline as last year's suicide of Kreuger, the match king, after his billion-dollar stock frauds were discovered. This was the kind of story that rookie reporters dreamed of, almost an immediate advance to a higher desk—and a raise.

Connie and Burkan exchanged worried looks. Gloria sat there quietly. The diamond was the only thing that showed any life.

"Tomorrow I'll get this removed from the record," said Burkan.

"What does it matter now?" said Gloria dully.

"Come," said Connie, offering her arm to her friend. "Come, dear, let's go."

"Go where?" said Gloria. "My life is finished. Amazing how one can die in three seconds."

Again the lawyer's and Connie's eyes met. They knew Gloria was right. What could they say? In the old days Connie would have suggested a drink at the Plaza's Palm Court. The afternoon tea music had always driven away the blues and excited them about the parties ahead that evening. Now the party was over; indeed all parties were over, and what lay ahead Connie didn't dare think about.

And then she thought, *Oh, what the hell*, and said, "Come

on, Gloria, let's go to the Plaza and have a few martinis. You remember, that's where you first saw Reggie Vanderbilt in that wonderful silver and maroon Rolls-Royce and the footmen on the box."

"A lucky thing Reggie isn't here now," said Gloria.

Finally, flanked by her friend and her lawyer, Gloria walked out of the courtroom and into the street. It was only four o'clock in the afternoon, but it seemed as if night had come. And with the darkness came a whole new legion of phantoms. Her world had collapsed.

Word had spread through the crowd of the terrible testimony of Maria Caillot. Now the mob had increased to over 500. But they didn't attack her this time; in fact they didn't utter a word. The silence was far more sinister than the abuse. How she got down the steps and into the car she never knew, but suddenly she was conscious of lying back against the pearl-gray upholstery of the great car and Connie was lighting a cigarette for her.

"Thanks," she said, as helpless as a little child about to cry; grateful now for any gesture of kindness.

"I was thinking of the Plaza just the other day," Connie raced on. "Will you ever forget the Vanderbilts' fantastic château across the square? And how those enormous gates were thrown open on the Fifty-eighth Street side when old Mrs. Vanderbilt received President Coolidge?"

"Yes—yes, I remember," said Gloria, and to forget today she forced her mind to remember.

"It was wonderful," said Connie trying to shake off the heaviness that somehow seemed to envelop them in the rear of the car. "And I'll never forget how handsome Harry Payne Whitney looked that evening, and goodness, Gloria, what a rush he gave you. I never could understand why you didn't marry him."

"In case you've forgotten," said Gloria coldly, "he was married already."

"Oh, was he?" Connie said nervously. "Well, I remember every woman in her right mind was chasing him—and you were so alluring and *you* got him, Gloria—"

Gloria put her hand over her eyes. "Please, Connie, please stop." She wasn't sure whether a scream would come out or whether she would throw up. "Please, I've had enough."

They sat silently then, both bolt upright, one staring out one window, the other staring out another. In the drizzle the tires of the heavy car made a sorrowful sound. On the streets people stared at the great car going by, but Gloria, looking out, saw nothing. She was remembering the happy times just twelve years ago, although it seemed a century back, when she and her twin sister Thelma were living nearby at 40 Fifth Avenue, when the dozens of towering yellow roses arrived daily, when she was a teen-ager and her whole life lay ahead of her.

CHAPTER
2

It was 1917. America had just declared war and the Morgan family was fleeing from Germany on the last train from Berlin. Harry Hayes Morgan had been recalled and it meant a new consulate post in Switzerland, his sixth assignment in ten years.

His wife and three daughters were trying to make themselves comfortable in the crowded compartment. Laura, her black eyes snapping, was clearly annoyed, as if the war had been his fault. She removed her wide-brimmed hat slowly, taking each pin out deliberately, as if contemplating sticking them in her husband. Disconcerted, he shifted his gaze to his daughters. The eldest, Consuelo, was dark-haired like her mother, but there the similarity ended. She was placid where Laura was fiery. The twelve-year-old twins, Thelma and Gloria, never ceased to amaze him. They were totally alike, dark-haired, with their mother's dark eyes, and constantly full of life. They made the best of every situation; even now they were chatting away.

Their talk ceased when three young German soldiers, blond and brutal, burst into the compartment demanding to see their papers. Morgan stood up and reached into his coat pocket. The German pulled the passports out of his hand and carelessly looked them over. He motioned with his head and another soldier put his hands on Morgan's body, searching for whatever might be hidden there. Finding nothing, they turned to the women.

"Remove your clothing."

The women, standing in a row, froze, as if in a tableau. Laura's mouth was open in shock, while her daughters' eyes reflected fright.

Morgan jumped up. "See here, you can't—" His protest was broken off by a rifle jammed against his chest.

"Outer garments first," one soldier insisted. The English nurse, Edith Cavell, had been shot as a spy in 1915 and the Boches did not want these Americans to be carrying secret documents out of the country.

Laura endured it with dignity, Consuelo without a sound. But the twins cringed in terror, holding one another for support. Laughing and muttering obscenities, the soldiers made a great show of exploring the two frightened girls. It was obvious that if there were no witnesses they would have done more than just paw them.

When the soldiers were satisfied that the Morgans weren't leaving with Germany's most valuable possessions, they laughed, saluted, and slammed the door.

Laura could now have hysterics. "Oh, my God!" she cried, flinging her hands about dramatically. "What brutes! What indignities we must submit to!" Her eyes fastened on her hapless husband. "If you were an ambassador instead of an impotent consul we would have been treated like royalty. It's because we have no money that we must travel this way. Oh, why didn't I marry a rich man?"

Not getting an answer, she slumped to her seat. She'd run

through this same litany at other times, and there was no answer Morgan could give, so in reply he stormed out of the compartment.

Laura sat up straight after he left and turned to her daughters. "You girls don't want to end up like me, do you?" she shrieked. "Married to a second-rate diplomat with no future, traveling second-class over the face of Europe, suffering endless humiliations, forced to scrimp and save. What a comedown for me! From one of the greatest families in the deep South to this!"

She started to sob, hands over her face—but then she stopped and looked at them with a fierce expression. "Now you girls know why you have to marry rich men. I'll make sure you marry well."

Any reply they might have made was drowned out by the shrill wail of the locomotive as it puffed through the night. Underneath them the iron wheels made a loud click-clack, click-clack, and the feeble red light lent the compartment an almost sensual atmosphere.

If there was an easier road to travel, Laura was determined her daughters would find it.

Although the Morgans lived on very little money, mama always saw to it that they moved with the *crème de la crème*. And by 1920 Laura Morgan had skillfully manipulated a brilliant match between her eldest daughter Consuelo (named after the Vanderbilt girl who landed the duke of Marlborough) and the rich count de Maupas. Whether or not Consuelo loved the count was of no importance to mama. For the occasion she had taken a suite at the Ritz in Paris, which she could ill afford, and the wedding was to be held in the Grand Ballroom. *Tout Paris* was expected at the wedding reception.

Consuelo looked beautiful in her white satin-and-tulle

gown with a long lace train held up by two noble pages. The sumptuous rooms of the gilded Ritz were filled with a distinguished throng, made up of aristocratic Europeans and rich Americans.

During the festivities Laura Morgan watched her youngest daughters with a mixture of pride, envy, and fear. Gloria and Thelma, at fifteen, had turned out to be beauties. And now that Consuelo was safely being taken care of by her ardent young count, mama's mind was free to scheme again. Her twin daughters had imaginative personalities, they played the piano, they sang, they danced exquisitely. In short they were the perfect companions for a Rothschild. It was unfortunate that the Rothschilds on the Paris scene were all married. Mrs. Morgan was desperately worried that her twins would run off with penniless European titles, and then where would she be? Gloria had been going out with Grand Duke Dimitri, but since the Russian Revolution he was reduced to a crust. And Thelma was being pursued by a Rochfoucauld—but, alas, not from the branch that married a rich American.

She surveyed the throng with a sharp and practiced eye. No, none of the men here were right for her twins. Then she hit upon an idea that dazzled her with her own brilliance. Why hadn't she thought of it before? Her darlings were entitled to the very best, and they would get it—in America.

Gloria, breathless from dancing, whirled over to her mother's table and sat down. Thelma, who was never very far from her twin, joined them, laughing.

"My darlings," Laura cried gaily, "I have a fantastic treat in store for you both."

"You're going to allow me to marry Dimitri?" Gloria asked, wide-eyed.

"Don't be silly." Mama dismissed that notion with a wave of her hand. "You two beauties should marry Vanderbilts

at least. You should ride in Rolls-Royces and live in those
famous hundred-room châteaus on Fifth Avenue. And I'm
going to make sure you do."

"What are you planning now?" Thelma was highly suspicious of her mother's good intentions.

"Haven't I told you before that you're not going to end up
like your mother with a nonentity?"

"Oh, mama," said Gloria loyally, "daddy is not a nonentity."

"Daddy's introduced us to all the best people in Europe,"
said Thelma.

That was guaranteed to work Mrs. Morgan up into a
frenzy. "It was my connections that got him his first consular
post," cried mama heatedly, "and he should have been an
ambassador by now! I was counting on it! I wasted my brains
and beauty on him. How could I have made such a mistake?
Is it any wonder that I'm half-mad now?"

"Then we're half-mad too," muttered Thelma.

"Well, that's what makes us special," Gloria pointed
out. She was always eager to pacify everyone.

Looking at them, mama thought they *were* special. They'd
been special since they were little girls. Even the press recognized it wherever they went and labeled them "The Magical
Morgan Twins." They'd certainly gotten the best qualities
from their mismatched parents. And despite mama's dis-
paraging remarks, traveling all over Europe resulted in their
speaking six languages fluently and knowing a great deal
about art, music, and furniture. They could even sew their
own clothes in the latest fashions.

"Yes, you are special," said Laura. "And that is why you
deserve special men. Dimitri is not one of them," she added
spitefully. "No, I believe you'll have to look elsewhere—in
America."

"Oh, mama, can we really go to New York?" Thelma, who

yearned to be free, thought of New York as the ultimate in opportunities for adventure. Then she added suspiciously, "Are you coming too?"

"No, I've got to stay here."

"Then who is to be our chaperon?" asked Gloria.

"There's not enough money for a chaperon, thanks to your father," mama added meanly. "In any case, you two have each other."

"Indeed we do!" cried Gloria, putting her arm around Thelma's tiny waist.

"But to make sure someone keeps a proper eye on you, I'm writing to my old friend, Mrs. George Gould. Remember Edith Kingdon Gould? She was an actress and she knows how hard it is to get a foothold in New York society. Tonight I'll pen her a long letter. She will probably let you stay with her. And don't you worry about money; I'll make sure to send you some every month. Maybe Consuelo can get the count to give us some."

She broke off to scan the room for her newly married eldest daughter. Satisfied that all was in order, she continued.

"I'm going to write Richard Bennett, the actor, too. His daughter Constance is a lovely creature—you used to play with her when you were children. But be careful, girls, Mr. Bennett is a great womanizer! So don't allow yourselves to be left alone with him."

"I read that Constance Bennett goes to the Plaza Hotel every afternoon for the tea dancing," said Thelma excitedly. "I would like so much to go there too."

"Well, if she goes there, then she's after money just like the rest of us." Laura fixed a dark eye on her daughters. "So you three can scheme together. And, girls, for heaven's sake, don't dream—*scheme!*"

The girls spun about to the waltz. "Scheme, don't dream!" they repeated, laughing. They danced about, barely noticing that Consuelo had tearfully vanished with her bridegroom and that the guests were leaving slowly. Prince Polignac moved toward them across the parquet floors and nodded, pausing to say his goodbyes and converse with them in fluent German. The Grand Duke Dimitri came by and kissed Gloria's hand.

That set mama off again. "I may not want you to marry penniless noblemen, but a word of warning: Be sure to marry a name as well as money. The money is important, but never forget that a name will carry you through in times of adversity. Think of how far I could have gone as the duchess of Devonshire." Her eyes misted over and her face assumed a dreamy expression.

Thelma giggled. "The only title we'll get is 'Queens of the Plaza Grill.'" That set the twins to laughing, and it snapped Laura out of her mood.

"The *Leviathan* sails in two days, and you'll be on it—no matter what your father says."

The twins had forgotten about their father, which was easy to do. They had thought that their half-mad mama was in one of her many moods, scheming as usual, but began to realize she meant every word. The laughing stopped and they sat down beside her.

All the guests were gone. Laura Morgan and her twin daughters were left alone with the tea roses and potted palms and a rented orchestra restlessly wondering what to play next.

CHAPTER
3

By the autumn season of 1922, millionaire banker and art patron Otto Kahn was including the Morgan twins at his extravagant dinner parties, and Edith Gould and Millicent Hearst granted them social protection. All three of these celebrities knew how hard it was to break into the inner circle of New York society—the ladies had been chorines and Kahn was a Jew—so it gave all three a sort of perverse satisfaction to patronize the twins.

Millicent Hearst's husband had run off with actress Marion Davies. And as for Mrs. Gould, it could be politely said that she had received many black eyes in the social arena. The Gould family had never been accepted by society because old robber-baron Jay had been too ruthless a crook, and Edith's treacherous foothold in society was based solely on her friendship with old Mrs. Cornelius Vanderbilt, Sr.

With the arrival of the twins, to whom Mrs. Gould played mother, the two friends came to share a common denominator: their irresponsible and wild children. Not a day went by that Alice Vanderbilt's son Reggie, a divorced bachelor, didn't make headlines with some new prank. And Mrs. Gould's two charges were also beginning to figure prominently in Cholly Knickerbocker's daily column in the *Journal American*. Indeed she was beginning to wonder if the twins would damage her hard-won position.

Edith Kingdon Gould lived in a sumptuous granite-and-marble palace at Fifth Avenue and 67th Street, a mansion overflowing with Fragonards and French signed pieces and leopard-skin rugs. The twins were delighted to lunch and dine with their new patroness, not only because of the lobster mousse and champagne but because they met Astors and Gerrys and Harrimans—though, alas, no Vanderbilts. Mrs. Gould had guided them through the dangerous labyrinth of New York drawing rooms, told them whom to see and whom not to see; in short, gave some direction to their existence, which these past two years had been chaotic to say the least. However, by the fall of 1922, the twins began to feel that Mrs. Gould did not want to introduce them to the prize, Reggie Vanderbilt; they rightly surmised that she was saving Reggie for her own daughter. And if Mrs. Gould was getting tired of them, the twins were tiring of her patronizing manner and endless complaints of having no money—a common complaint of the very rich.

Mrs. Gould could not be blamed for her change of heart about the twins. First, Thelma had made the ghastly mistake of marrying a man whom Mrs. Gould did not know. A man called Junior Converse—handsome and well born with good connections, but, alas, a ne'er-do-well. They were already planning to divorce, though he still hadn't moved out of the girls' apartment. Secondly, both girls had been lured into the movies by their friend Constance Bennett, a fast baggage in Mrs. Gould's opinion. And her father, Richard, a notorious ladies' man, had seduced Thelma right in Mrs. Gould's house on a leopard rug! Thirdly, Gloria had taken the name Gloria Rochefort and made a movie with Marion Davies, who was being backed by William Randolph Hearst. Gloria, moreover, had committed the supreme indiscretion of making eyes at lustful old Mr. Hearst, which caused irate Marion to throw her off the set.

One damp November day that smelled of autumn leaves and woodsmoke, the girls were sitting in Mrs. Gould's raspberry-and-gilt drawing room. It was a little before noon and they were there to help their tired hostess set the luncheon table and lavish her with praise. Suddenly the gilded doors burst open and Mrs. Gould's statuesque figure sailed into the room followed by a maid and secretary. She swiftly dismissed them and turned a hard eye on her charges. It was gratifying to shriek abuse at them the way people had done to her back in Brooklyn before she landed Mr. Gould.

She touched the avalanche of pearls about her prominent bosom. "Oh, girls, girls, girls!" she moaned. "What am I to do with you? Gertrude Whitney just informed me that you two were doing a tango with Valentino yesterday at the Plaza Grill, and it's all there in the *Journal* today. Don't you realize that you are skating on very thin ice?"

"We meant no harm," said Thelma, pouting.

"Perhaps we have too much energy," added Gloria.

"Too much nerve is more like it," said Mrs. Gould. "Why, Gertrude Whitney says all of New York is laughing about your fortune-hunting schemes. Oh, twins, you'll never get rich husbands now."

"George Brokaw has asked me to marry him," said Gloria with dignity. "And now I shall accept him." Of course it was a lie—George was a tedious middle-aged bachelor and Gloria had no intention of marrying him—but she wasn't going to let this old dragon walk all over her.

"I thought you only went out with Mr. Brokaw when you were hungry!"

"Well, I'm very hungry," said Gloria, which was quite near the truth.

Thelma boldly carried the lie forward. "Tonight Connie Bennett is giving a little tango party to celebrate her engagement; we shall tango like mad at the Plaza Grill, and Cholly Knickerbocker promised to write a whole column about it."

"The tango is an extremely dangerous dance," warned Mrs. Gould; easily distracted, she forgot they were discussing Gloria's supposed engagement. "All that twisting and turning and body contact—"

"It's the danger that I like," laughed Gloria. She winked at Thelma.

Edith wasn't defeated yet. "Furthermore, my dear twins," she went on, "I don't want to deflate your balloon, but your clothes are too daring. Must you wear such low-cut dresses?"

"I refuse to look like a boy when I have the figure of a woman," said Gloria willfully.

"An independent girl puts men off," sighed Mrs. Gould, sinking into her gondola chaise longue of face-powder satin and surrounded by the loot her beauty had brought her.

"Reggie Vanderbilt kept looking at me yesterday at the Plaza," said Gloria. "And he asked Mrs. Hearst who I was."

"Well," sneered Mrs. Gould, "Reggie's handsome brother-in-law, Harry Payne Whitney, lives right next door and he used to follow me on the street. But that didn't mean that he wanted to marry me."

"What *did* he want to do?" asked Thelma mischievously.

"Never mind!" snapped Mrs. Gould. "Frankly I have to confess that I am very displeased with you both. The main reason why I haven't introduced you to Reggie Vanderbilt is that you girls are too conspicuous. This afternoon I feel it is my duty to write your poor mama a letter."

"Don't tell her about our career in the movies!" cried Thelma. "For heaven's sake!"

"She knows already," said Mrs. Gould ominously. "Laura Morgan has the intuition of a witch. I've already had to write to her about your ridiculous elopement."

Thelma flushed hotly, her mouth a tight thin line.

"It's not desirable for a poor young girl like you, Gloria," continued Mrs. Gould coldly, "to be living in the same apartment with that alcoholic husband of Thelma's, threatening you all the time."

"Junior has left," said Thelma faintly.

"Junior Converse's reputation has tainted you girls." Mrs. Gould snapped open her lorgnette. "When Thelma returns to Europe to get a divorce, you should return there too, Gloria— and take up your duties as a daughter."

"Never!" cried Gloria hotly, happy with her new freedom.

"But, my poor girl, what other alternatives have you?"

"The movies!"

"You might have done well in the movies if you hadn't tried to steal scenes from Marion Davies, not to mention stealing old Mr. Hearst!"

Gloria blushed guiltily. "Mr. Hearst chased me all over the Astoria studio."

"It was bad judgment on your part to have surrendered, my dear."

The butler entered and announced that there was a phone call from Mrs. Cornelius Vanderbilt.

"Well, girls," said Mrs. Gould, "I must get ready for luncheon. I'm terribly sorry I can't have you, but, you see, Alice Vanderbilt and her daughter, Gertrude Whitney, are coming here at one, and both of them disapprove heartily of your behavior. If only you had paid attention to me. Now would you kindly go downstairs and see that the luncheon table is set properly? Alice Vanderbilt loves beautiful table settings so put out my best Limoges and gold service. And be sure the African violets have arrived from my greenhouse in the country." The stout older woman vanished into her dressing room and the girls were left alone in their misery.

"Do you think we've made a terrible mistake?" asked Gloria.

"If we'd been demure and quiet, no one would have noticed us," Thelma pointed out. "We don't need Mrs. Gould anymore, we can make it on our own. Besides, I'm tired of making up to her and pretending that I like her when I don't."

"Me, too," said Gloria. She linked arms with Thelma and they danced gaily out of the room.

They weren't in such a happy mood when they got off the bus and walked over to Third Avenue and 51st Street. The elevated trains above them made a fearful noise and Italian fruit peddlers in open stores whistled at them as they passed by. Some midday alcoholics were stumbling out of smoky bars.

"A far cry from Mrs. Gould's," said Gloria ruefully.

"Yes, but we won't be here much longer," Thelma assured them both.

"Let's go upstairs and make some new naughty dresses for our entrance at the Plaza tonight!" Gloria laughed, perking up.

"And," said Thelma, winking, "I'll alert the press!"

CHAPTER
4

The twins' apartment was a fanciful setting of hand-me-down treasures arranged in artistic disorder. There was Mrs. Hearst's Chinese shawl draped over the piano, and a canvas section of an Art Deco Drian screen (also courtesy of Mrs. Hearst) depicting naked boys and girls flying stylishly through palm trees and flamingos. Mrs. Gould's discarded flame-colored taffeta drapes, rich with fringe and tassels, hung at the windows, and a towering Louis XVI armoire, beautifully carved with bowknots and turtledoves, had been painted yellow by the twins and was the resting place of their many dresses. Some were hand-me-downs from their patronesses, the rest they'd made themselves. Staring down into this daring black-lacquered room was a portrait of mama when she was eighteen-year-old Laura Kilpatrick, a flower of the old Confederate South.

Tonight as the girls were feverishly dressing, the Victrola was playing the red-hot Harlem jazz of Louis Armstrong.

Thelma was on her knees skillfully cutting the hem of Gloria's satin dress—a Paris nightgown discarded by Mrs. Gould and cut low in the back and front.

"What a fantastic and original idea," cried Gloria. "This dress will surely shock the staid Plaza crowd."

"That's the general idea, darling," said Thelma. She paused, scissors in midair, at the sound of rapid knocking at their apartment door.

"Hey, girls, how would you like to take a ride up to Harlem tonight?" The usual crowd of eager college boys, who wouldn't take no for an answer, crashed into the small rooms. They gazed at the twins in their satin and crepe de chine with delight and dismay, and Gardner Pell, a lusty lad, planted a kiss on Gloria's lips.

"Felt good," Gloria giggled.

Thelma glanced up angrily. "Just one kiss!" she cried.

"It won't do any harm," said Gloria.

"It's what comes after that causes the harm," said Thelma grimly, remembering her recent honeymoon with Junior Converse.

The dress was finished and Gloria spun about. "How do you like it, boys?"

"Looks like you're going to bed," said Gardner truthfully. "But I wish you would take me wherever you're going."

"You boys can't afford the Plaza!"

"Well, we wouldn't go with you anyway," said a disappointed Princeton swain, Timothy Blake III. "You've got no underwear on. It's indecent!"

"We're modern women," said Gloria proudly.

"Then get into the bedroom," said Timothy manfully, "and show us how modern you are!"

"I play for keeps," said Gloria—which was the currently popular line.

Timothy embraced her roughly and gave her a thrilling kiss. "I've asked you to marry me four times, Gloria, and I repeat the question again. And here are my witnesses. I have a wonderful job in a brokerage downtown and I can give you much more love and satisfaction than those old boys you go out with. Why, George Brokaw is almost in his grave. He couldn't do the things that I could do to you." He planted another ardent kiss on her.

Gloria looked fearfully at his husky body, covered by a raccoon coat and plus fours. His blond maleness reminded her of those terrible German soldiers. On the other hand, his kisses aroused her tremendously. What could she do?

"Come on," said Thelma. "We're off to the Plaza. And, boys, you can drop us off because we don't have taxi fare!"

As they were going out the door Gloria pulled the Chinese fringed shawl off the piano and draped it around her shoulders.

Light snowflakes were fluttering down as they drew up before the ornate entrance of the Plaza. The boys had been drinking gin and they were becoming impossible; the twins could barely tear themselves away from their embraces. Presently, however, Thelma and Gloria were hurrying across the pavement and up the steps.

The doorman greeted the girls warmly and told them that Mr. Reginald Vanderbilt had just arrived. As if they needed to be told! His Hispano-Suiza limousine was almost a block long, with a custom-made wicker body, making it look like Lady Hamilton's carriage in her Nelson days. Two footmen in the red-and-gray livery of the famous family stood by the car. The aura of royalty was heightened by the fact that his mother's 137-room limestone-and-brick Louis XIII palace stood just across the Grand Army Square on Fifth Avenue. The delicate snowflakes falling over the sloping roofs and high pointed windows gave the mansion a sort of poetic sheen so that it seemed to Gloria like the home of Mary, Queen of Scots, her favorite heroine.

"Oh, Thelma," she cried, "I wish we could meet Reggie Vanderbilt. We've tried so hard."

"No other pair has climbed faster," laughed Thelma. "Now cross your fingers and your legs and onward, Christian soldiers!"

The friendly doorman steered them into the revolving doors and they spun into the lobby, snowflakes in their hair and a little breathless. The Plaza was done in the Louis XVI style with majestic mirrors, graceful armchairs with spindly legs, exuberant colored marble, and potted palms. The twins adored such grandeur and rightly felt that they enhanced it all the more. The sound of the piano and drums from the Grill ahead enveloped them, some elegant Italian aristocrats fell on them with delighted cries, and an English duchess said that they were the most astonishing sight she had seen since the tower of the Woolworth Building.

They quickly spun on to another group. Cholly Knickerbocker, Queen Marie of Rumania, and George Brokaw gave them startled looks. Queen Marie was houseguesting with Grace and Cornelius Vanderbilt and she had just been to a grand tea at Gertrude Whitney's.

"Definitely my favorite Vanderbilt is Gertrude!" said the queen, turning her Hellenic profile so that it could be better appreciated by the photographers and reporters who swarmed around her. "Gertrude Whitney is a remarkable woman in these times," she continued dramatically. "She believes men have enslaved women for centuries, and she told me I must make myself independent of them. But it is hard for a romantic woman like myself to think of a business career and a life away from men."

Thelma poked Gloria. "I'd rather have a career in love," she whispered. The twins giggled.

Cholly Knickerbocker watched them curiously. "You girls seem quite happy," he commented.

"We *are* awfully happy," confessed Gloria gaily.

"They haven't made me so happy," said George Brokaw. The tall, distinguished millionaire, middle-aged and balding, bent to kiss Gloria's hand. He was beautifully dressed in gray chalk-striped flannel, sapphire cuff links, and a pearl-and-diamond stickpin on his Sulka cravat. He behaved in a most gentlemanly way toward Gloria, and Mrs. Gould had pointed out that he was dependable. But Gloria didn't want a nice, polite, dependable man, she wanted an exciting man, a glamorous man—like Reggie Vanderbilt. Reggie's life was a gay round of parties, and of course he had buckets of money and was written about in the newspapers every day. Gloria knew she could be quite happy racing his champion stallions, attending the opera and theater openings with his sister, Gertrude Vanderbilt Whitney, and yachting with his brother-in-law, Harry Payne Whitney. The Whitneys were multi-millionaires in their own right. Yes, the Vanderbilt-Whitney tribe was definitely the one to belong to. She glanced through her thick, dark lashes at Brokaw. Still, she could always marry this Brokaw if she couldn't do better. She somehow had the feeling that he would leave her alone and not molest her like those college boys.

Thinking of these things, Gloria smiled radiantly at her suitor and tapped him playfully on the cheek with her fan. "You've made me awfully happy, George Brokaw, and tonight I'm wearing your sapphire bracelet."

Brokaw's ascetic face beamed. "Does that mean you will accept my proposal?" he asked gravely.

"This is the first time I have heard it," she flung back flirtatiously.

"It's not the first time I have thought about it," said George. He continued talking ardently and Thelma pressed her high heel on Gloria's toe, giving her a significant look.

"Gloria," Brokaw was saying, "I've got four of the best tickets for the *Follies* tonight. I hope you and Thelma will honor me with your presence." She seemed irresolute and he added, hoping to win her over, "Afterward we can all go to Texas Guinan's." Everyone who read the society columns knew that was the place where Reggie Vanderbilt and Peggy Hopkins Joyce went every night. "Speak of the devil!" Brokaw exclaimed, glancing over his shoulder. "There's Reggie now, and feast your eyes on those crazy dogs of his!"

Moving slowly through the Plaza lobby was the plump figure of Reggie Vanderbilt. Dissipations made him look older than his forty-two years, but his full drooping lips and sad eyes thrilled Gloria nevertheless. How lonely he must be, she thought.

"I think it's perfectly marvelous the way he dresses those dogs!" cried Thelma, and Gloria's gaze fell to Vanderbilt's feet. Three wolfhounds dressed in leather coats and goggles to match Reggie's attire trotted along regally at his side.

"How adorable!" declared Gloria. "Oh, George, why don't you ever invite Reggie to one of your dinners?"

"Because I would never see you again," replied Brokaw, glumly.

"Really, George! Whatever do you think I am?" she said, though she continued to stare at Vanderbilt. And as she stared at him, he stared back at her. Her heart almost stopped and she no longer could see George or Queen Marie or the photographers fussing around. Here was her goal, her ideal, almost close enough for her to touch.

"Dear Reggie!" called the queen, moving forward to meet her host's younger brother. It was maddening but she did not introduce Gloria to him. Why did everyone seem to conspire to keep Gloria away from him? Again her heart leaped as her gaze met his. Under a chestnut-colored mustache his lips curved slightly in a humorous smile. She adored men who made her laugh and she felt that Vanderbilt would be a fun companion. But her hopes were dashed when abruptly Vanderbilt and his dogs moved away.

"Come, darling," said Thelma, seizing her arm. "Connie is waiting for us in the Grill. And you and I have to practice our tangos!"

"Will you go to the *Follies* with me?" pressed Brokaw.

"Yes, if you take me to Texas Guinan's afterward."

He promised he would and took her other arm. They moved into the marble-columned and stained-glassed space of the Grill which was packed with New York's most fashionable young set.

"Don't worry," Thelma whispered in Gloria's ear, loving the sense of intrigue. "You'll get him."

"How?"

"We'll invite him to our party tomorrow night. I'll hand him an invitation at Texas Guinan's."

Gloria was puzzled. "We're not having a party tomorrow night."

"Yes, we are. And keep quiet," shushed Thelma.

"But who'll pay for it?"

"Someone will. We always find a way," she laughed gaily. Her high, clear voice was drowned out by the music and laughter of other merrymakers as they were led to where Constance Bennett waited with her latest fiancé.

CHAPTER
5

Gilded candelabra with pink-shaded bulbs and heavily veined
amethyst rock crystals shed a soft light on Constance Bennett's table of beautiful people, which was quite naturally the
focal point of the Plaza Grill that evening. The movie star sat
in a tight-fitting gown of shimmery satin, her blonde wavy
hair framing a perfect face. Her auburn brows arched over
sky-blue eyes and her bright red cupid's bow lips curved into
a smile as Phil, her current lover, planted an ardent kiss on
her beringed hand.

In their seminude dresses the twins' skin glowed as if lit
from within. Truly it was their most dazzling asset—Renoir
would surely have loved to have painted them. Constance
Bennett was dazzlingly lovely too, but she resorted to heavy
makeup, jewelry, and hair dye. The twins had natural fresh
coloring and their thick auburn hair glowed with reddish
lights tonight under the candelabra.

George Brokaw was moving Gloria in the intricate steps

of the erotic tango. He was telling her that her mouth was like a rose petal, that her eyes were like mauve pansies, and that her neck was like a swan's. Staring deeply into his eyes, Gloria pretended that Reggie Vanderbilt was dancing with her and saying all those delicious things. Indeed, she even saw herself in her favorite fantasy: Nurse Edith Cavell looking after poor, wounded Reggie; his thick curly head in her lap, she uttering endearing words to him—

"Gloria! You're not paying attention to me," said George with some irritation. "Will you or won't you accept this engagement ring?" He patted his coat pocket.

"I'm too young to get married," she said. "But I'll accept it as a friendship ring," she said sweetly. Both the Morgans lisped and they spoke so many languages that their words had a hint of a foreign accent which was thought most charming by their male admirers and phony by their female detractors.

George pulled her to the side and slipped an enormous, glowing ruby ring on her finger. "Call it what you want. Now, you won't hock it, will you?"

"Georgie, where do you get such crazy ideas?" She held her hand at arm's length and admired the dazzling ring. She wondered how many carats it was.

"I hear Thelma was at Provident Loan pawnshop the other day with all the things Junior Converse gave her!"

"They were wedding presents from Mrs. Gould and Mrs. Hearst!" burst out Gloria, and immediately wished she could eat her words. "Oh, Georgie, she was so disillusioned after her honeymoon in Palm Beach. She's getting a divorce right away."

"Gracious," said George, "what did he do to her?"

"He was an alcoholic beast!" she said, glancing up at him. "Oh, George, sometimes I think every man will turn out to be so different from what he seems to be. Have you any secrets, George?"

"Just money problems," said the multimillionaire.

Gloria broke into laughter.

From their table, Connie and Thelma watched her affectionately. Like Thelma, Connie had made a miserable mistake with a husky football player. He was divinely physical but he proved to be unfaithful after two weeks of marriage. Thelma had had the same problem and the girls were now commiserating. They could talk openly now that Phil Plant had left to chat with old friends.

"The worst part of Junior," said Thelma, "was that he used to beat me up when he was drunk."

"So did mine." Connie took a cigarette out of her gold monogrammed case and lit it, blowing a cloud of white smoke toward the ceiling. "What else did he do?"

"Played around. Gambled." Thelma moaned. "Last summer he borrowed money from all our friends."

"I thought Junior Converse was so rich," said Connie.

"Rich in debts, baby," said Thelma.

"I get the picture," said Connie. "Well, we'll all be more careful next time. I must admit, being a movie star does help when it comes to having offers to pick from."

"Then why are you trying to dissuade me from a career in Hollywood?" Thelma was quite annoyed that her earlier attempts had not gone so well, but she was willing to try again. Marriage to Junior Converse certainly hadn't advanced her the way she'd thought it would.

"Because you won't like the fat apes who'll be grunting over you all the time," said Connie. She tapped another cigarette impatiently on the gold case. "The casting couch doesn't have the kind of rewards you can get here," she added, gesturing toward the many wealthy and bored men who were in the room and jangling the gold and diamond bracelets that were the results.

"Charlie Chaplin said he'd help me get into the movies," pouted Thelma.

"You idiot. Charlie is an awful liar who likes young girls,"

Connie snapped. "Every man's a liar when he wants to go to bed with you."

Gloria and George breezed back to the table and allowed Thelma to inspect the expensive new bauble on Gloria's slender hand. But she was outdone by Connie whose good-looking fiancé, Philip Plant, the playboy son of a doting rich mother, was just returning to the table. He kissed Connie's bare shoulder. Clearly he was dying to marry her. Many of his love offerings—diamond bracelets and pearls—glittered on her arms and neck. Gloria, who was new to this sort of thing, had just begun to acquire her own collection.

George clapped his hands and ordered champagne for everybody. In a few minutes Gloria was sipping the first of many glasses, and with the champagne came a startling change in her. She had always been vivid, now she was wild. She had always wanted glamour and excitement, now she felt she was able to do anything, however reckless, to get it.

"Champagne is magical," cried Gloria radiantly.

"Reggie Vanderbilt couldn't buy you any better," insisted George Brokaw.

"Speaking of Reggie," said Connie, "here he comes again."

"What? But he was just here half an hour ago," said Thelma, "with his dogs."

They all turned to see portly Reginald Vanderbilt move slowly through the marble and crystal entrance of the Palm Court. He was accompanied by Peggy Hopkins Joyce, a blowsy but striking blonde in a low-cut gown, and surrounded by an entourage of about half a dozen people.

"Look at those diamond bracelets Peggy is wearing," said Thelma. "I'd be more than content with just one-tenth of that gorgeous jewelry. I wonder what she had to do to earn them." She lovingly touched her own bare arms in anticipation of such future adornments. In truth she would later accumulate such *bijoux* in exactly the same way, as extravagant gifts from wealthy and celebrated men.

Connie scowled. She was watching Peggy jealously. A striking show girl, Peggy was touted as the greatest siren of the decade. She was famous for the plunder she extracted from various suitors, and she was as much written about in the newspapers as the Vanderbilts, Charlie Chaplin, Gloria Swanson, and the Prince of Wales.

The waiter brought fresh bottles of champagne and served them all. They toasted the future, themselves, and even Cholly Knickerbocker, who happened by at that moment and nodded to them.

"My darlings," said Connie, quite tipsy after more champagne, "here's to gold diggers like Peggy"—she lifted her glass high—"who know how to get the most out of a man. I heard she even went to Vanderbilt and told him she was having a baby. A total lie, of course, and besides, how would anyone know who the father was? But Reggie gave her even more money."

"Reggie really believed her?" asked Gloria incredulously.

"He'd been doing naughty things he shouldn't have," snapped Connie wickedly. "Honestly, sometimes you're too naïve to be believed."

"I wish he would do such things to me," said Gloria, who was quite tipsy herself from all the wine, music, and admiring glances. She felt so reckless that she didn't even care that George Brokaw was growing more and more furious.

To retaliate, George stormed off. He would ask his old flame, Peggy Hopkins Joyce, to dance. That would show Gloria that she couldn't treat him like an old shoe. Goddammit, he was offering her a sixty-room mansion—as big as Edith Gould's! Also a yacht, which was anchored off Newport and manned by thirty sailors, and a secure fortune based on the clothing business that his grandfather had founded.

He greeted Peggy and Reggie warmly. "Well, my dear boy, would you mind if I had a little dance with your lovely girl here?"

"Wish you would," said Vanderbilt in his rather weary British voice. "I'm a lousy dancer myself."

Brokaw led Peggy through the crowded tables and onto the dance floor where they started the slow seductive steps of the tango. Peggy did all sorts of wicked things with her shoulders and rear to excite her audience, though she concentrated completely on Brokaw. He was a big spender and she wouldn't mind having him back in her stable.

"Oh, Georgie," she purred, "it's like old times being in your arms again."

"I'll bet Vanderbilt isn't as good as I am, is he?"

She smiled mysteriously and pushed her pelvis into him, driving him half-mad. He almost forgot Gloria. . . .

Isolated and lonely as he always appeared to be, Reginald Vanderbilt stood watching the hectic dancing crowd. The music and partying no longer excited him, but it filled the endless hours and was a comfortable, pleasurable habit. Instead of watching Peggy dance, he was staring at another table. It had been a long time since he had enjoyed himself the way Constance Bennett and those Morgan girls seemed to be enjoying themselves. He had been reading about the twins for the last few months; apparently Cholly Knickerbocker was taken with them.

Out of the blue, as if Cholly had read his mind, the fat columnist suddenly joined him. "Looking at the Morgan twins? They're certainly an interesting new addition to our scene."

"Wild new addition is more like it. That one in the Chinese shawl and what looks like a nightgown is certainly a standout. I wonder if they dress like that so you can tell them apart?"

"Perhaps you can tell better when they're not dressed at all. Wouldn't twins in bed be a novelty?" Cholly loved playing the role of pimp and he liked having something on the very rich people that he wrote about. Every girl in New York had been chasing Reginald Vanderbilt for years. Wouldn't it be a feather in his cap if he were responsible for Gloria Morgan capturing the millionaire? Then he wouldn't have to worry about his future. And his young boys were growing more and more expensive every year.

Vanderbilt seemed fascinated by Gloria Morgan's lovely profile and mass of reddish-brown hair curling about her face. He ignored Knickerbocker's comment but turned interestedly toward him when Cholly suggested brightly, "I can arrange an introduction."

The two men slowly made their way to Constance Bennett's table where Vanderbilt made a great fuss over Constance and Phil, then spoke formal words of greeting to the twins.

Gloria's legs felt as if they would collapse under her as she stood to greet him. His gentlemanly air suddenly made her feel rather naked. As his slanting blue eyes went over her, she smiled sweetly at him, but received no response. Reggie always liked to conceal his desires behind a screen of indifference; he could have been made of stone for all she knew. She had a terrible feeling that perhaps she had put him off with her clothes and curly, fluffed-out hair. After all, all the other girls wore flat-chested sheaths that were absolutely shapeless and their hair was cut in a boyish shingle.

Her confusion increased when the apparently disinterested Vanderbilt nevertheless said, "My dear Miss Morgan, would you care to dance?"

He moved awkwardly about the floor and it was like pulling teeth to get him to say anything. "I hope you will be at Texas Guinan's later," she said eagerly.

"Hmm," he answered vaguely.

Suddenly she, too, was tongue-tied and couldn't think of anything to say. Finally in desperation she blurted out, "How are your horses, Mr. Vanderbilt?"

"Fine," he said. "Fine. . . ."

"And your dogs?" she inquired brightly.

"Fine too. How are yours?"

Suddenly Gloria began to laugh. She couldn't help it, it all seemed so funny! George Brokaw and Peggy Hopkins Joyce danced by, glaring at them. She could never compete with someone like Peggy.

Reggie looked disconcertedly at the girl in his arms. He knew he was a terrible dancer and his footsteps were becoming heavier by the minute. He'd never been noted for his clever repartee either, and now his tongue seemed paralyzed by her laughter. He covered up his lack of confidence with an arrogant facade and now he said, "I'll take you back to your friends." With dignity he led her back to the table, thanked her for the dance, and moved back to his own table.

"That was awfully brief," said Thelma. "What happened?"

Gloria stared down into her champagne glass perplexed. "I don't think he likes me," she said quietly.

"You'll get another crack at him at Texas Guinan's after the *Follies*," said Connie naughtily, pinching her under the table. "Have another drink."

Gloria sipped it moodily and looked around the Palm Court. A violin, piano, and drum were playing Strauss waltzes, lovers held hands behind potted palms, and white-coated waiters passed bearing trays of napoleons and tarts. Her gaze went back to Reginald Vanderbilt, now seated at a large table with Peggy Hopkins Joyce and various admirers. Still others stopped by to pay court. Although he was constantly surrounded by a thick crowd of fawners and flatterers, he seemed indifferent and kept twisting his mustache nervously. Gloria thought his eyes looked sad. His color was poor and he seemed ill. A fantasy flickered before her eyes: Reggie lying on a stretcher, she in a crisp white uniform with a red cross on the arm stroking his bandaged head. Perhaps he'd be blind like Rochester, in Jane Eyre. Then she could look after him forever up at Sandy Point Farm. . . .

George Brokaw came back to the table. "It's getting late. We've got to leave now or we'll miss the beginning of the *Follies.*"

Everyone stood up but Gloria.

"Gloria, stop that mooning again," Thelma whispered angrily.

"All right," said Gloria dreamily. With reluctance she dragged her eyes away from Vanderbilt, who was now watching her.

The Morgan sisters, Miss Bennett and Phil Plant and their admirers, and Mr. Brokaw made a triumphant procession rather like Vanderbilt's through the marble-columned lobby.

"You don't mind, George, if we go in your car?" asked Connie.

"I have room for fourteen," answered George.

"Heavens," said Gloria, "do you have a truck?"

"It's a new Bugatti," said George proudly. "This one they made for the Romanoffs, but you know what happened to them."

Later, in that marvelous car driving down Fifth Avenue, Phil Plant pointed at a French-style town house at Fifth Avenue and 52nd Street. "That's where my mother lives," he told them. "But alas, she's leaving it next year because she found a string of pearls at Cartier's and Mr. Cartier said she could have the pearls if he could have the house. That's the way it goes."

"Have you ever seen the pearls that Alice Vanderbilt wears?" asked Thelma.

"I'd rather have her house," said Connie. "Jesus, that house, it's five times bigger than your mother's house, Phil, and that poor dame lives there all alone."

"Doesn't Reggie Vanderbilt live with his mother?" asked

Gloria suddenly. She had been staring out at the mauve evening with the yellow lights gleaming through the gray snowflakes.

"He has a splendid town house of his own," said Phil, "and usually has open house there every night until the cocks crow."

Gloria sat up. "If he entertains all night, then when does he sleep?"

"He doesn't. He doesn't have to, silly," said Phil Plant. "He doesn't have a job—no Vanderbilt works. They party and they yacht."

"The Rockefellers and Mellons work. So do the Whitneys and Du Ponts," said Thelma, who was after any one of them herself.

"Yeah," snorted Connie, "but they aren't much fun." She flicked on the lights and combed her waved golden hair in the mirror of her diamond-studded compact—the latest gift from Phil. Her white satin dress trimmed with mink glowed in the half-light.

"How would *you* know?" Phil asked suspiciously.

"Listen, Phil," said Connie, "give me your flask. After another mouthful of gin, I'll tell *anything*. Did you know, Gloria, that a mixture of gin and vermouth is the fountain of youth? Have a swig, toots, and let yourself go. It'll chase those blues away. Promise!"

Gloria put the gold-and-silver flask to her lips, tilted her head back, and swallowed. The gin had an unusual fragrance rather like perfume and the alcohol burned pleasantly on the way down. Her head swam.

"How do you like it?" asked Connie.

Gloria rolled her eyes. "Ambrosia," she sighed, taking another swig.

"It's an acquired taste," said George.

"Like diamond bracelets and chinchilla coats," purred Connie.

"I'd like them, too," giggled Gloria.

"I predict you'll soon have the world," said Connie sagely.

"Let me touch you for luck, Connie!" said Thelma.

"Me too," said Gloria. Her good times had started.

CHAPTER
6

Texas Guinan's club, with its ornate limestone facade and wrought-iron balconies, was reminiscent of Berlin's rococo buildings. The club had once been the old Donahue mansion, an ill-fated house that had been maintained by his wife's Woolworth fortune. Donahue had killed himself by jumping out of an upstairs window when his sailor boy friend deserted him. He was only forty-one. The house had been reduced to a speakeasy in these prohibition days when it was not fashionable to be dry.

Texas herself was a fun-loving blonde in her early forties with a raucous sense of humor and unquenchable vitality. Her club was the most popular of all the speakeasies. The police were forever loading her into their paddy wagon and closing her gin mill, but the next day she'd be out of jail and meeting guests with her customary greeting: "Hi, suckers." Her jazz band would be playing "Sweet Georgia

Brown" while the customers swilled illegal booze smuggled
in by river pirates. You could only enter after someone
checked you out through the peep hole in the iron door.

"Who cares about tomorrow? Think about that when it
comes, baby," she'd say with a lewd wink. "First things first,
and getting drunk is our first priority—right, suckers?"

George Brokaw entered with the "Magical Morgan
Twins," whom Texas was always reading about in the society
columns. She took an instant liking to the girls because they
weren't snooty, didn't put on the dog like so many society
people she saw. She sensed they had the same zest for living
as she did, the same sense of mischief. Also they weren't in
her league, weren't competition. The twins wanted rich
husbands; she wanted a good lover.

"Hi, suckers," she cried, warmly embracing Brokaw—
one of her best customers—and the Morgan twins. Connie
Bennett and Phil Plant had already rushed past in their
eagerness.

Texas was a vivid picture in her flaming red sequined dress
and ostrich-feather boa. She always had a wide grin on her
face, but tonight it was wider than usual. From five o'clock
this afternoon right up until a few minutes ago she'd lain in
the arms of one of the dashing river pirates who had held up
the *Mauretania* yesterday. Her lover, Ralph, had stolen cases
of hooch from the Cunard liner so they could have a terrific
party tonight since George Gershwin was playing the new
score for the *Scandals* and Jeanne Eagels was going to attempt to sing Sadie Thompson. Ralph had given a masterful
performance on her black satin sheets last night and had
come back for more at the blue hour today. He was married
and had kids across the bridge, but what the hell—they'd
had the best sex of their lives. She'd have rough going trying
to explain him to her current steady, Henri, the French heavyweight champion, if he ever found out.

"You look wonderful, Texas," George Brokaw said.

"Ralph was wonderful," laughed Texas with another lewd wink.

"Ralph? Is he the Broadway producer?"

Texas moved her hips in time to the Charleston rhythm coming from the dining room. "The only thing Ralph produces is a lot of babies. Seriously, though," she continued, "he's one of those old river pirates that were in the headlines today—shouldn't be harboring him here because the police will probably be pulling me into jail again, which is where I'm going to end up anyway. And that French boxer will wreck the joint tonight when he catches on. The last time Henri caught me in bed with the trombone player he shot the place down. So be prepared if you hear a big blowout later."

"Never a dull moment," said George.

Texas indicated the next room with a jerk of her shoulder. "That Peggy Hopkins Joyce is in there rolling her beautiful blue eyes at my river pirate, giving him a hot feel you know where. Reggie Vanderbilt stands there, the great gentleman that he is, and watches her carrying on like he doesn't care, even though he and Walter Chrysler are paying for the whole show! Maybe Reggie Vanderbilt doesn't give a damn about anything, but I'm going in there and cool her off!"

Texas sashayed away, leaving them in the vestibule. It soon filled up with a milling crowd of socialites and celebrities. Connie and Phil had disappeared, so the twins and George went into the big noisy room where a jazz band was playing. Behind them Jeanne Eagels and John Gilbert came in; she so blonde and he so dark, they made a dazzling couple. During their brief movie career the Morgan twins had played some scenes with these professionals. John had gone after Gloria, but his ardor frightened her and, like the college boys, she put him off. The truth was, she wasn't the vamp she pretended to be, but was actually a timid virgin. She wondered if he'd guessed. Now, although she waved hello, she was glad it was impossible to stop for conversation.

George and the twins moved into the luxurious cream-and-peach room—once the drawing room of the old Donahue mansion, now crowded with tables about a dance floor. They selected a large table near the band. Overhead was a domed ceiling painted in shades of peach and blue and depicting smirking nude cupids in lustful embraces with nude nymphs. The marble fireplace mantel was supported by two leering cupids and there were still more of them over the many tall mirrors about the room.

Texas joined them again and regaled them with bawdy tales about all her best customers, from Valentino to Harry Payne Whitney, and their various exploits upstairs on her bed. Gloria felt wonderfully sophisticated being in such fast company and listening to such racy dialogue. Still, she kept glancing over at the bar where Reggie and Peggy were, and could hardly believe her eyes when she saw Pola Negri and Valentino join them. Gloria's heart beat faster with the thrill of it all. How marvelous to be a Hollywood siren and sport inch-long lacquered fingernails and onyx-and-gold cigarette holders and trail ermine coats! If only she could be a woman of sin. A kept woman like Peggy Hopkins Joyce. Better still to be like Marion Davies who had hooked a multimillionaire, old Mr. William Randolph Hearst. Gloria had tried hard to ensnare him, but when he pounced on her she got scared and ran away. If only she could enslave Vanderbilt and exchange long meaningful looks with him, the way exotic Pola was doing.

Abruptly, in her impulsive way, Gloria cried, "Oh, Miss Guinan, I'd give anything to be a fallen woman!"

Texas choked on her whiskey. "You're looking at one, darling, and I don't think you would like to play that role."

"But how can I interest Reggie Vanderbilt?" whispered Gloria, leaning closer to the raucous blonde when George was busy chatting with someone else.

"Just be yourself, darling," advised Texas. "Why, don't you know that Peggy and Pola and I would gladly exchange everything we own to be young and fresh as you are. Jesus, if I was a man I would jump on you this very minute and carry you upstairs and give you the time of your life! Not to mention diamond bracelets up to your elbows." Texas held up her plump arm and displayed half a dozen brilliantly flashing bracelets.

A waiter was passing a tray of bootleg whiskey and Texas urged them all to have another glass. Strains of "Do It Again" came from the piano and Texas said, "If you want to meet the man who wrote that divine song, just go over and sit on George Gershwin's lap. Why *don't* you go over and sit on his lap, Gloria? He loves pretty young girls."

"Over my dead body," said Brokaw, rejoining them just in time to catch this latest suggestion.

A tall, handsome, dark-haired man was weaving his way across the dance floor toward their table. "Oh, my God," cried Thelma, "it's Junior! You dance with him, Gloria." Thelma flung herself under the table, leaving a startled Gloria to handle the problem.

Junior was plainly inebriated and he mistook Gloria for her sister. Well, she was in the mood for a good prank. Besides, she and Thelma loved exchanging identities.

"Will you dance, Thelma?" said Converse sheepishly.

"Yes," said Gloria. She stood up and Converse led her drunkenly into the fox-trot.

"I'm sorry I behaved like a heel," he said.

"Have you been unfaithful to me again?" pouted Gloria, moving gracefully in his arms.

"I'm never going to stray again," promised Junior. "And I won't drink so much."

"I've heard that before," complained Gloria, remembering Thelma's details of the honeymoon.

Converse became hostile. "Everybody who's anybody drinks. Why can't I?" Then he turned petulant. "Why, look at Ali Hussein. He's just had his fifth Courvoisier, straight from the bowels of the *Mauretania*."

"I *am* looking at him," said Gloria, turning her head. She stared at a wonderful-looking man in an exotic bedouin costume. She caught his eye and he started toward her.

Junior stopped dancing abruptly. "Thelma, must you make eyes at every man you see?"

Before Gloria could reply, the dark Arab cut in and danced away with her, leaving Junior abandoned on the dance floor. The Arab introduced himself as Sheik Ali Hussein, announced he was staying at Willy K. Vanderbilt's bachelor quarters at 666 Fifth Avenue, and then launched into a monologue that left her breathless.

"Those Vanderbilt houses beat anything we have in the Middle East, my dear lady. My yacht is anchored off Palm Beach. Would you like to come down for Christmas? Tomorrow night we're having a great party for the *Scandals*; it's at the St. Regis and you and your sister must come."

"Can I bring twenty or thirty friends?" laughed Gloria, her thoughts moving as fast as an express train. Here was the party she needed—the one Thelma suggested they have tomorrow so they could invite Reggie Vanderbilt. They would pretend that Ali Hussein's party was really theirs and invite all their friends too.

"The more the merrier!" cried hot-blooded Ali, devouring every inch of her flesh with his eyes. "Al Jolson is going to sing. What can you do?"

"Well, my sister and I will do a dance."

"I've heard about those dances," said the dark-eyed sheik, the veins in his neck standing out in his excitement. "I'm insane for your body, Miss Morgan," he whispered in her ear.

"I'm not Miss Morgan, I'm her twin sister, Mrs. Converse," said Gloria, pretending to be shocked. "You mustn't say such things to a married woman."

"Then where is that delectable Gloria?"

"Under the table."

"You mean that exquisite little creature with the velvet eyes is inebriated?"

Gloria laughed and spun away from him. "We'll talk about it tomorrow at the St. Regis," she said, and blowing him kisses she danced back to the table.

"Come, Thelma," she cried. "I've got some fabulous news for you. We'll talk in the ladies' room about Operation Vanderbilt!"

Some muscular Italian bootleggers blocked their passage as they tried to get into the ladies' room in the hall. They were handsome and charming and Gloria invited them to the party tomorrow night. With that, they kissed her hand and bowed her into the ladies' room.

"You're high as a kite," observed Thelma as they sat down at the dressing table.

"Better that than being down in the dumps," sang Gloria gaily. "Listen, Thelma, everything is working out fantastically."

"Tell!" demanded Thelma.

Swiftly Gloria explained about the sheik's party and his invitation to them including twenty or thirty friends! "And now we *have* to get Reggie Vanderbilt," she said.

"How?"

"You said you'd ask him," pouted Gloria. "Now it's your turn to do some hard work!"

"I'll pretend I'm you," said Thelma, and flew out the door. Gloria let out a scream of glee.

In came Peggy Hopkins Joyce in her ermine coat, orchids pinned onto her bosom with an important diamond brooch. She carried a large half-full brandy snifter. "Hey," she said in her loud voice, "am I having the dt's or did I just hear a female screaming?"

"Yes, I screamed," admitted Gloria spellbound by the blonde beauty with half her breasts falling out of her pink satin dress. Her eyes, Gloria noticed, were the same lavender as the orchids.

"You'll be screaming much louder if you don't keep your stupid lovesick eyes off Reggie Vanderbilt. Don't think I didn't notice you with him in the Palm Court. I'm not sharing my man with any schoolgirl—especially one dressed in those rags you've got on."

"I made this myself," said Gloria, trembling all over.

Peggy regarded her with a speculative look. "Don't tell me you're a seamstress!"

"No, I'm still going to school at the Convent of the Sacred Heart."

"Remind me to use that one," roared Peggy. "Boy, will old Walter C. get a belly laugh when he hears that!" She sipped the brandy that she swirled around in the big snifter, then sat down next to Gloria on a black satin tufted stool and combed out her thick golden curls before the mirror. Dimly came the sounds of piano and saxophones from next door, and Peggy moved her shoulders in time to the music.

Abruptly, to Gloria's surprise, Peggy lowered her dress and smeared rouge on the nipples of her beautiful breasts. She laughed coarsely when she caught Gloria's eye.

"God, I think I've got lockjaw after my afternoon session with old Walter. Well, he gave me my East Sixty-third Street town house so I can't exactly spit in his eye, can I? Although I must say I'd love to." Peggy began to powder her shoulders with a large pink puff, humming a little tune as she did so. "It's an aphrodisiac, darling," she explained when she saw Gloria's puzzled look. "The gents get hard as rocks when they sniff it, if you know what I mean."

"Yes, I do," said Gloria, although she didn't have a clue.

Peggy finished her brandy and smashed the glass on the floor. "Now listen, Miss Morgan, no tricks from you. You just stay with the college boys, get it?"

A shot rang out in the hall and Gloria let out a little scream.

"Don't pee in your britches," snarled Peggy. "It's only the cops, and there's too many famous people here for anything to happen." She stood up and straightened her dress. "Just remember what I told you," she threatened. Then she slammed out of the room on her high heels and left Gloria alone with her racing thoughts.

She was experimenting with the rouge in front of the mirror when Thelma came in. "What on earth are you doing?"

Gloria flushed scarlet and pulled up her dress. "Have the police come to take us to jail?"

"No, thank heaven," answered Thelma. "Imagine if mama read about us in jail too." She plumped herself down on the tufted cushion. "It's just Henri, the French boxer, trying to shoot Ralph, the river pirate. There's a big hole in the ceiling where he missed."

There was a moment of silence between the two sisters. "Aren't you going to ask me about inviting Vanderbilt to the party?" Thelma finally asked.

Gloria's hand flew to her mouth. "Did you speak to him?"

Thelma nodded triumphantly. "He was very polite, even though he was drunk as a lord, and said he would be delighted to come."

Gloria gave a scream of delight and threw her arms around Thelma. "I'll show that Peggy Hopkins Joyce. Maybe I don't know everything, but I'm going to get myself a Vanderbilt too." She added determinedly, "Then we can get you a new husband, Thelma, who can give *you* beautiful things."

"Of course," said Thelma. "That's what we're here for."

The gilded doors of the ladies' room flew inward and Constance Bennett came in breathlessly. "There you are," she crowed. "Come on, Phil and George want to take us to Harlem before the cops arrive. Yellow Peril is going to play the drums for us."

She grabbed them and all three hurriedly made their way through the jazz room and into the vestibule. The party was still going strong, as though gunshots were an everyday occurrence, and the illegal liquor was flowing freely. They got into George Brokaw's waiting car, and as they sped off, the wail of approaching sirens mixed with their uncontrollable laughter. Another party had started. . . .

CHAPTER 7

The next morning the maddeningly buzzing doorbell awakened Gloria. She rubbed her eyes, looked about with confusion. Otto Kahn, who backed the Metropolitan Opera productions, had given the twins the bedroom set from *Aida* and now the carved animals of the Egyptian furniture seemed upside down. Beside her in the swan bed, Thelma was out cold.

"Who is it?" croaked Gloria.

"Let me in," came a female voice. "It's important."

Gloria swiftly put on a dressing gown and dashed into the living room and out into the hall. The plain but pleasant face of a woman in a maid's uniform smiled at her apologetically. "I'm Mrs. Gould's second personal maid," she said in a sweet voice. "My name is Wann, and I'm supposed to look after you two naughty girls." Wann looked about the sitting room with shock. "It looks like a tornado has gone through here, Miss Morgan."

"We were up until five this morning, dancing in Harlem."

Wann nodded grimly. "Mrs. Gould has already heard all about it. And so have I. She was prostrate at the thought of you playing the drums with black men. And I'm supposed to read aloud to you this letter from your mother."

"Can I have some coffee first?" said Gloria, suddenly becoming awake and alert.

Presently the two women were sipping coffee by the window. They took an instant liking to one another, and Gloria, in her bubbling way, was confessing everything about the night before. She was in the middle of describing her lurid tango with Sally Rand's fans when the doorbell buzzed again.

"I'll get it," said Wann, and went into the hall. For five minutes Gloria could hear Wann arguing with two tradesmen. One owned the drugstore across the street and the other owned a grocery shop on Third Avenue. After a time the door closed and Wann trotted back into the room.

"I gave them twenty dollars," she said, "and they agreed to wait for the rest."

"How am I to pay you back?" asked Gloria. "Mother has cut off my allowance."

"And this letter will probably explain why," said Wann. She opened the envelope and started to read mama Morgan's letter, written on stationery stolen from the Hotel Ritz in Paris:

Have you gone insane, Gloria Morgan? Wearing outrageous and indecent clothes at Otto Kahn's and Edith Gould's and God knows where else. To top all the horrors, I hear that you wipe your bottom with the bills from Con Edison, the telephone company and Bloomingdale's. When will all this madness cease? Or are you hell-bent on hitting rock bottom? Wait until I get my hands on you. Am arriving next week on the *Olympic* and will stay with Edith Gould.

Mama

"My God," cried Gloria, alarmed. "She could be here any day!"

"We can spend today getting this place cleaned up and ready for her," said Wann reassuringly.

"But I can't. I must have some decent clothes from Bergdorf's for the party tonight. There's no time to make anything really smashing. And I forgot I also agreed to attend Otto Kahn's dinner party tonight. How will I manage it all?"

"I'll go out and buy you dresses," said Wann. "We're about the same size. And I can alter them for you as well."

Gloria took off the large ruby ring and handed it to the maid. "Here, take this and hock it at the Provident Loan."

"Oh, Miss Morgan, I couldn't. It's wicked!"

Gloria pushed her out the door. "You can't imagine what wicked things I did last night. I promised a handsome Arab I'd go tea-dancing this afternoon, and George Brokaw promised to pick me up in one of his open sports cars. Be a darling and pick up a leather jacket and some goggles. . . ."

Reginald Claypoole Vanderbilt dressed slowly and carefully for the Morgan twins' party. He had some very indecent thoughts about the twins in general and Gloria in particular; yet he was still held back by the Victorian codes of his parents. That straitlaced couple had met in church and were extremely religious; indeed, his mother had recently left St. Bartholomew's because some silly scandal had touched the minister there. Her standards were so high that if her friends did not live up to them, they were dropped. Unfortunately for her, the rest of the family hadn't inherited her strict sense of morality.

The party was to begin at ten o'clock and Reggie had taken a nap earlier. He felt he needed to rest so he could keep up with Gloria Morgan's youthful vitality. He was attracted to her more than to Thelma, perhaps because she seemed somehow naïve and innocent despite her wild ways. Too bad she was only half his age.

When Reggie arrived at the St. Regis at 10:30 the ballroom looked like one of his own thousand-and-one-nights parties. A dozen tents were set up, each containing a table for twenty to dine, and there were rotating bands on the stage and orchids strung through the palm trees.

Ali Hussein had taken over the whole St. Regis roof, it seemed, and decorated it extravagantly with black and silver bedouin tents and tall mirrored columns flashing red and yellow lights. The famous florist Constance Spry had transformed the domed ballroom into a setting for a Babylon orgy and there seemed to be hanging gardens everywhere. The fleet of half-naked boys passing drinks and sandwiches heightened the bacchanalian theme. On the stage Al Jolson was singing "The Sheik of Araby."

Reggie watched the hundreds of people streaming into the festive chamber. For a rare change he had come alone, without an entourage, and he was uneasy. He kept pulling at his brown mustaches and glancing around for Gloria.

Seeing his discomfort, Thelma hurried to his side.

"Gloria?" he asked, relieved.

"No, no, I'm Thelma. Gloria will be a little late; she forgot about a prior engagement." Thelma wrung her hands nervously. Oh, why did the little fool go off at the wrong times? "I'm so sorry she isn't here to greet you. But please, there's plenty of food and drink—please have something while you're waiting." Then she rushed off, not knowing what else to say.

Reggie sat at the nearest table and methodically drank his way through a string of martinis. He nodded to William Randolph Hearst who went by with petite Marion Davies. He chatted dispassionately with an old friend, William Rhinelander Stewart. He watched a hundred more people come and

go, including Valentino and Pola Negri. But still no Gloria
Morgan. And it was after midnight.

"Reggie Vanderbilt, it's absurd of you to give so much
thought to this wild seventeen-year-old girl!" said Bill
Stewart.

"I guess there's no fool like an old fool," Reggie chuckled.

"Well, I heard another old fool, George Brokaw, is going
to get her."

Reggie's mood darkened further. Yes, it was silly to give so
much thought to this popular seventeen-year-old girl. George
Brokaw was dancing attendance on her, and all those athletic
college boys were wining and dining her. He didn't have a
chance. She would merely be another disappointment. In the
old days, of course, he would have dropped diamond necklaces
into her handbag, or taken her off on his yacht to Bermuda.
But now he owed Cartier's $50,000, and his yacht in Newport
was up for sale.

A bizarrely dressed waiter passed him a brandy and he
tossed it down.

Nevertheless, he had an awful lot to offer the girl. He
could give her an almost royal name, a splendid house in
Newport, and show her one hell of a good time. Besides,
he wasn't burned out yet; Peggy could testify to his still
cutting the mustard.

Reggie examined himself critically in a mirrored screen.
He was well proportioned and he still had a lot of hair. A
little overweight? Hmmm, perhaps, but women liked a man
of substance. For himself, he favored women like Peggy and
Gloria with soft supple bodies, so that he in turn could feel
all the more masculine and puff out his chest and light up his
pipe. Peggy hung on his every word, like Gloria, and after
lovemaking Peggy told him he was divine and peerless.
Peggy had been eager to come to this party tonight, but
Reggie had put his foot down and she'd been furious. Indeed,

when he had gone out the door, she had flung a Chinese vase at him.

George Brokaw came up and put his arm around him. "You don't look in very good form, old boy," observed George. "Suffering from too many late nights?" He looked pointedly at the row of empty glasses.

"Where's your girl friend, Gloria Morgan?" said Reggie, forcing a smile.

"Oh, she'll be along. Say, I suppose you've heard Gloria and I are going to be married. I gave her a fifteen-carat ruby engagement ring last night that Mr. Cartier says is one of his finest stones." He slapped Reggie on the back and disappeared into the crowd.

A gray cloud seemed to settle over Reggie. Bill Stewart saw his sullen expression and excused himself. Reggie barely noticed his leaving. He'd show George Brokaw, he brooded. He'd ask Gloria to show him the ring and he'd ask her about her engagement. Of course, all women were deceitful; that was part of their charm. And it created drama, never to know where you stood with them. It was all part of the game, all—

He was startled out of his reverie by an unexpected sight— Peggy Hopkins Joyce making one of her fantastic entrances to the usual oohs and aahs. Even Gershwin at the piano switched to "Lady of the Evening," which Peggy had made famous when she was a *Follies* star. Tonight she was wrapped like a cocoon in a floor-length sable coat, and on top of her golden curls was an astonishing tiara—both loot from her recent British expedition where Bend Or, the duke of Westminster, had been her prime victim. Reggie glared at her and Peggy threw herself on him, sobbing violently.

"What are you doing here?" he cried roughly.

"Someone broke into my house, daddy, and raped me!" she cried.

"I don't see how that's possible," he said coldly. "And don't call me daddy, you imbecile. Get out of here, you weren't invited!"

"Ali says he's dying to have his hard black body squirming over my soft white one." Then she whispered in his ear all the erotic things the Arab wanted to do to her, trying to inflame Reggie with sexual images.

"I'm sick to death of all your lies," he said.

Peggy stiffened; she would have loved to scratch his eyes out. But instead she decided on another try at making Reggie jealous, a bit more subtle this time.

"Reggie," she cooed, "I see Mrs. William Randolph Hearst. Is *he* here? I'd like to discuss journalism with him."

He was about to say no, but then he thought he might as well get rid of her once and for all. With quick presence of mind, he took her arm and spun her over to William Rhinelander Stewart. Bill was in white tie and tails with a white gardenia in his buttonhole, looking very distinguished. With a wink at his friend, Reggie introduced him as Mr. Hearst. Stewart caught on and played the part wonderfully, and all three had a great time. Peggy was convinced that she'd snared the biggest catch of her career and was thinking of the Newport house she had always wanted to have.

Peggy became the center of attention, as she usually was at parties, and to awaken "Mr. Hearst" all the more she crossed over to the piano and draped herself over Gershwin's back. "Darling George," she said, "play that song that Cole Porter wrote especially for Reggie—you know the one, 'Poor Young Millionaire.' "

"I only play my own songs, Peggy," glared George.

"Well, then, play something sexy and outrageous."

Gershwin complied, and Peggy shifted into a low-down strip rhythm, using her beautiful sable coat like one of Sally Rand's fans. Her dress was electrifying white chiffon with a white fox hem that had been a showstopper in the *Follies*.

The two thin shoulder straps seemed on the verge of snapping and her pendulous breasts clearly showed through as she undulated to the music.

Peggy was performing thus when Gloria burst in. Thelma pushed her way through the crowd to get to her sister's side. "Where have you been?" she hissed.

"What an *Abrabian Nights* fantasy!" Gloria cried, her eyes darting about in awe. She turned to her sister, elated. "Otto Kahn's dinner was sensational. Look at the diamond clip he gave me—all the girls at the party got one. He said he wants to manage my career—"

Thelma shook her. "You little fool, listening to such nonsense when Reggie Vanderbilt is waiting here for you. And now Peggy Hopkins Joyce is stealing him back!"

Gloria glanced into the next room. "My goodness, what's Peggy doing here?"

"She crashed," said Thelma furiously, "and she has completely taken over. And in a few minutes she won't have a slip of clothing on. Reggie Vanderbilt is furious that you're so late. He's asked for you half a dozen times. Goodness, look how grumpy he looks. Now hurry over and sit in his lap or something!"

There were easily a hundred guests in the enormous two-story room. All the athletes and actors and actresses who were making news were there, mixed in with the ones like Helen Mencken and Humphrey Bogart who were soon to be married and soon to be featured on the marquees themselves. And of course Cholly Knickerbocker was there, plump and amusing, loving the sense of intrigue that enveloped the crowd. He was with his new boy friend, a pretty lad from Ohio who was dazzled by all the names.

Peggy was definitely the star of the evening, but when Gloria came in, so fresh, so lovely, as only a seventeen-year-old could be, all attention was suddenly focused on her. She wore a simple black velvet dress that was strikingly different from the dresses that the famous and fashionable were wearing. Suddenly Peggy with all of her chiffon and diamonds looked used. Peggy was twenty-eight and she had been on the town since she was fifteen. Her beauty, though at its zenith, had become hard and artificial-looking. The most startling defect was her eyebrows; she had shaved the natural ones off and drawn with a black pencil a high, unnatural arch, meant to be seductive. Between these arches and the cupid's bow lips of heavy scarlet was an inordinate amount of mascara, rouge, and powder, representing hours of studied work.

Gloria's freshness made Peggy appear doubly artificial. Her face had no makeup at all and her eyes had that wide-open trusting look of extreme youth and inexperience. It was wonderfully refreshing, like a cool drink on a hot summer day. You wanted to do things for her, you cared about her. Such was her power.

"We've all missed you, Miss Morgan," said Prince Ali Hussein, coming to her side and kissing her hand. He wore an exotic caftan open to the waist. With such devotion, she could hardly think of Reggie Vanderbilt, but now she glanced over and caught his angry eye. She had a lot of explaining to do. She excused herself and turned to talk to him.

"I hear you're engaged, Gloria," said Reggie coldly. "May I see your ring?"

"She's engaged to me," said Prince Ali drunkenly.

Fortunately, just at that moment an artificial sandstorm was blown in from the stage over the 400 dancers. Gloria grabbed Reggie's hand and spun him into the crowd.

"I don't want to dance," said Reggie. "And where did you get that diamond clip?"

Gloria was thrilled that Reggie was jealous. This evening was working out far better than she'd dared to imagine. In reply to his question she lowered her head and smiled mysteriously, then forced him into the sensual steps of the tango. Reggie could see her finger was bare of any ring. Almost immediately his anger and disappointment faded in the arms of the young girl. He ordinarily hated to dance, but somehow he lost his inhibitions with her and felt his movements becoming confident and masterful.

"You're a marvel, Gloria," he told her as they moved through the desert oasis that Ali had created. Outside the tall arched French windows spread the glittering skyline of New York.

"They don't call us the miraculous Morgans for nothing," retorted Gloria, arching backward gracefully.

"And what other miracles can you perform?" asked Reggie.

"That's for you to discover," she said with a naughty jerk of her hips.

Husky Prince Ali interrupted their dance. Gloria gave Reggie a desperate look because Ali was in his cups, but Reggie went off sulkily. The Arab executed an extravagant display of his virtuosity, sidestepping and turning with marvelous agility.

"I have a present for you," he whispered in her ear.

"Really?" she said, laughing out loud. This was her evening for getting presents, all right!

"A flawless pink pearl," said Ali. "Come, I'll show it to you behind the curtain."

The adventure of it all appealed to Gloria and his daring costume, bare at the chest, excited her imagination. In the tent hidden behind the drapery there was a low red velvet couch and Ali pushed her onto it. "You invited fifty people to my party and now you must pay," he said silkily.

"I thought you were a gentleman," she whispered.

"A man! A man!" he cried, tearing off his robes. Before she had time to think, he had flung himself on her. His eager hands squeezed her small breasts and he writhed over her prostrate body in a sexual rhythm as though he planned to enter her right through the velvet dress.

Gloria tried to push him off, but the muscles rippled in his swarthy skin and he gripped her effortlessly. Gloria moaned in fear and anticipation as Ali's wet mouth slobbered over hers and then moved down her neck and breasts.

He pushed some strange white powder under her nostrils. "Sniff!" he cried. "Sniff, and we will go to heaven together!"

The powder made her cough and her head swam. Her feeble efforts to pound on Ali's chest made no difference— then suddenly his heavy weight was gone and Reginald Vanderbilt was sitting on the couch beside her and holding her hand. Thelma was there too.

"How do all these things happen to you?" complained Thelma. She bent over her sister, concerned and dismayed at the same time. "Mr. Vanderbilt had to save you from a cocaine romance! How can you be so foolish?"

"I love adventure," Gloria whispered.

Vanderbilt shook his head in despair. "Someone's got to look after you, Gloria Morgan. I guess it will have to be me."

CHAPTER
8

Reggie courted Gloria in princely fashion. He had never had any doubts that he was America's royalty—a slogan which all the Vanderbilts believed in and which was to prove self-defeating in the years to come. His sister-in-law, Grace Vanderbilt, was so brainwashed that she told foreigners that she had a position in America like the Princess of Wales in England, and if there was a revolution in America, she would be the first to go. Reggie did his best to live up to the royal image—mainly through lavish spending. Every day he gave Gloria a new present, and every night he gave a new party in her honor—though he could ill afford it.

Naturally Gloria had no idea of her fiancé's financial difficulties. She accepted it all in the unthinking way that teenagers do and lived every day to the fullest. Indeed, every day seemed a brilliant succession of events. Reggie, a lonely man like so many hedonists, caught some of her youthful sense of adventure and began to feel young for the first time. His sordid passion for Peggy Hopkins Joyce was forgotten; he saw New York through Gloria's eyes and started a love affair with that city, a place that had begun to bore him before he met her.

If Gloria brought happiness to her aging flame, it was reciprocated. It was glamorous to ride in his troika on snowy afternoons behind the team of six horses, sleigh bells tinkling, pointed out by all and sundry. It was glamorous to be photographed at all the opera and theater openings, and to see those photos in the Sunday society sections of *The Times* and *Tribune*, which referred to her as Mr. Vanderbilt's fiancée. It was glamorous to go shopping at Bergdorf Goodman and Henri Bendel and to buy whatever caught her eye, glamorous to be carried there in one of Reggie's limousines with a bar setup in the rear and footmen to carry out the boxes. Everywhere she went now she was treated with respect. Even creditors who used to dun her were suddenly delighted to give her unlimited credit.

When Laura Morgan finally arrived in New York, expecting to find her daughter living a life of sin with a rich playboy, she was amazed to see Gloria respectably engaged to the staid albeit wealthy Reginald Vanderbilt. She was thrilled that Gloria was finally realizing her mama's dream for her.

The one sour note was that there had been no formal visit to Reggie's formidable mother, nor to his equally formidable sister, Mrs. Harry Payne Whitney. Gloria often badgered him about this and he would invariably reply gravely, "I'm waiting for the right moment to present you to them." At one point he told her, "Mother will like you, I think, but Gertrude has the wrong opinion of you from all that publicity. They're both fearfully materialistic and have always wanted me to marry rich."

Gloria's face dropped. What could she say? Perhaps the marriage wouldn't come off after all.

"Don't look so worried," said Reggie. "We'll entertain ourselves with friends in the meantime."

Of these there was an endless variety, so that one dazzling scene after another was presented to her. She had tea in Mrs. W. K. Vanderbilt's Gothic drawing room at 666 Fifth Avenue, a jewel of a house designed by McKim, Mead, and White, rich with Persian carpets, marble statuary, and marble columns. There were Sunday lunches at Henry Augustus Coit Taylor's mansion at 3 East 71st Street. Mrs. Sam Barlow had an intellectual salon on Thursday evenings at 11 Gamercy Park, and Mrs. Philip Lydig entertained writers and painters in her Washington Square house. There were conservative dances at the Gerrys' medieval château. Mrs. Gerry had been a Harriman, and although these distinguished people received no publicity, they were as rich as the Vanderbilts, a fact that was most surprising to Gloria.

The biggest of all these residences was of course the sprawling château of Reggie's mother, an endless mass of elaborate stonework and chimneys and wrought-iron gates, the supreme example of Rich Man's architecture. "My old home is bigger than the Racquet Club at three-seventy Park," laughed Reggie. "Mother has the same size reception rooms and libraries and drawing rooms where one can entertain an army of friends."

"When is she going to entertain me?" asked Gloria.

"Soon—soon," he said evasively.

Gloria began to grow distinctly apprehensive. She had thrown over George Brokaw, who was now chasing Claire Boothe, and mama kept urging her to pin Reggie down. Mama now shared the twins' small apartment and was after Gloria constantly. "When are you going to meet his mother and sister?" the hysterical woman kept insisting.

"Mama, leave me alone!" cried the girl. "Reggie is getting furious with your interfering."

This was an understatement. Reggie was raging at Mrs. Morgan's manic behavior. He had hoped to be alone with Gloria amid the palm trees and turquoise sea at Palm Beach, but the old battle-ax insisted on accompanying them. They all traveled down in Reggie's private railroad car, which was decorated like an Austrian hunting lodge with animal heads on the walls, chairs made of antlers, and whimsical wooden bears on which to hang your clothes. Of course the dogs came along too and took an instant dislike to the old dragon. Mrs. Morgan spent the entire trip picking at Reggie, and he spent it thinking of new ways to elude her.

"That madwoman is driving me to my wits' end!" he cried fiercely when at last they arrived in the fragrant warmth of Florida. He comforted himself with the thought that here at least there would be opportunity for escape. And indeed that very afternoon they went off on his cousin Willie K. Vanderbilt's yacht. Their party was having a lovely time on the fantail of Willie's yacht when they spotted Mrs. Morgan trailing behind them in a Chris-Craft.

When they returned to New York, the handsome and dashing Willie K. gave them a terrifying ride over Long Island in his private airplane, a flimsy, single-engine contraption that bounced up and down in the January wind. A big spender like all the Vanderbilts, Willie was in the process of building a new house and later drove them out to Northport to show it off. He had just inherited $55 million from his daddy, so he was in an especially great mood. But their laughter died when they saw Mrs. Morgan waiting by the house in Mrs. Gould's open touring car. What could Willie do? He had to invite her for tea.

Another day ruined.

It looked as though there was only one way Reggie was going to get Gloria alone: Marry her!

CHAPTER
9

In the outrageous Egyptian Art Deco bedroom of their apartment, Thelma lay on the wide swan bed and watched her twin move joyfully about and felt her throat tighten and her eyes fill with tears. They had never been separated before—except for Thelma's honeymoon—and she hadn't realized how dependent on each other they were.

It was an awful thing to need another person so much. Sometimes she even needed Gloria to finish a sentence for her. Yet she had a feeling that when Gloria returned from meeting Reggie's mother, the future Mrs. Reginald Vanderbilt would be a very changed young lady; they would never be close again. Thelma herself was leaving for Europe with mama to get her divorce from Junior Converse. She dreaded returning to her parents' home in Brussels with her tail between her legs. She knew her mother would rub her nose in her failure. But if mama had told her more about men, she wouldn't have made such a fatal mistake with Converse.

Aloud she cried, "If only I hadn't married Junior."

"Really, Thelma," said Gloria, who was trying on several hats in front of the ornate mirror. "How does one know what one wants at seventeen?"

"How can you say that?" retorted Thelma hotly. "You know you want to marry Reggie, and you're only seventeen!" She spun off the bed and paced angrily about the room. "I bet that years from now girls will be sleeping with the boys they like—and living with them too—without the sanction of marriage. And they'll be far better off!"

Gloria turned and gazed at her twin. "But, Thelma," she said, shocked, "that would be scandalous. And it's too degrading a thought. Why, the man would get all the advantages and you'd get none of the benefits. Love without the institution of marriage is cheap."

Thelma laughed. "From now on, my price is going to be high!"

The doorbell rang and a bellboy in a cute blue uniform with gold braid and a pillbox hat entered with two boxes of flowers.

"Aren't I just the luckiest girl in the world?" said Gloria, hurrying to take them. "They must be from Reggie."

Thelma went to her side to see what exotic specimens were in the boxes. Every inch of the apartment was already filled with pink and white azalea plants, orchids, springlike tulips, and fragrant lilacs. Today's addition was two dozen long-stemmed American Beauty roses. The girls lowered their heads and breathed in the fragrance. Then Gloria ripped open the envelope and read the card. "My goodness, these are from Henri, the French boxer."

"When have you had time to see him?" questioned Thelma suspiciously.

"He was dining at the Colony the other night and he kept passing to and fro in front of my table with burning looks.

Thank the Lord, Reggie didn't notice. You know, I don't think he notices very much."

The telephone rang and Wann answered it from the other room. "Yes, I'll tell Miss Morgan," she said. "Mr. Vanderbilt's car is downstairs," she reported to Gloria. "It's the black and maroon Minerva." The message delivered, she went back to her ironing.

Thelma giggled. "It's the Minerva today, Mrs. Vanderbilt," she said, with a little curtsy.

Gloria hugged her twin excitedly. "Do I look properly respectable? Is this hat right?" She put on a gray cloche to match her skirt.

"Imagine," cried Thelma ecstatically. "Imagine the houses you'll have, the servants to look after you, the French chef to make you Cordon Bleu meals, the stable of champion horses so that you can go galloping over the meadows every morning, the jewels that will outshine every other woman's—"

"Wasn't that a gorgeous brooch Reggie gave me yesterday? I just love emeralds." She spun about happily in her incongruously schoolgirlish pleated gray flannel skirt and cardigan.

"And yachts—oh, God, imagine the yachts!" cried Thelma, quite carried away.

Gloria stopped spinning. "Reggie said he's cutting down. He sold his yacht."

"Tough."

"He said we might not be able to stay at the Paris Ritz on our honeymoon."

"I'm weeping," said Thelma, imitating Sarah Bernhardt. The girls fell into each other's arms and giggled. Through the front window they could see the enormous custom-made Belgian Minerva town brougham. There were only ten of them in the entire country. Reggie and his brother-in-law, Harry Payne Whitney, each owned one, which put them on

a par with the Prince of Wales. When Thelma heard that
tidbit of information from Connie Bennett, she couldn't
decide which she'd prefer—the Minerva or the Prince of
Wales; either one would do.

"I'm ready," announced Gloria, wrapped in a gray lamb
coat.

"You look lovely." Thelma walked with Gloria through the
tiny apartment to the front door, and as she kissed her goodbye a frown crossed her face. "I do hope we're not burning
our candles at both ends," Thelma said. At Gloria's puzzled
expression she added, "You wouldn't want to be all played out
at thirty-five, would you?"

"Oh," Gloria tossed back, "I'll be dead at thirty-five!" With
that she was gone.

Thelma went to the window, watched Gloria vanish into
the tufted brocade interior, saw the heavy car with its footman and chauffeur glide away. Thelma shivered, felt a vague
premonition.

She'll never be the same, Thelma thought. The Vanderbilts were an ill-starred family, and Thelma thought of the
towering stern of the *Lusitania* raised high before the final
plunge into the sea.

Not far away, in the Japanese garden of the old Ritz Hotel
at Madison and 45th Street, Reggie and his mother, eighty-
year-old Alice Gwynne Vanderbilt, sat talking of more serious
matters as they waited for Gloria to arrive.

"Reggie," his mother was saying, "do you think it's a responsible thing to do, marrying a penniless seventeen-year-
old girl when you are nearly forty-five and almost in debtors'
prison?"

"Five million dollars is not one step from debtors' prison,"
he pointed out, sipping his customary brandy-and-cream

cocktail. "Why not reserve your opinions about Gloria until you meet her?"

Reggie glanced once again at his watch. Perhaps she had changed her mind—or decided to run off with a younger, handsomer man? Last night at the Terrace Room of the Plaza, Gloria had been ravishing in a pale blue evening dress trimmed with silver and slit up the side. She'd worn her hair Madame Butterfly–style and ornamented with a huge diamond butterfly. Her court of admirers had gone mad and Reggie hadn't been able to complete a single dance with her.

Old Mrs. Vanderbilt watched her son sharply. He was her youngest child and she always treated him like a baby. "My dear friend, the bishop's wife, said she cannot comprehend why you don't marry her Helen, who is your age and available."

"But I don't want Helen. I love Gloria, mother," he said with dignity.

"Well, what about Lord Astor's daughter? Or why not the Harriman girl?" she persisted.

"Mother," he reminded her, "I'm marrying Gloria Morgan."

"You have changed your mind before," she said.

"I'm not changing my mind this time."

"Can you *afford* to marry her?" she demanded.

Reggie sipped his brandy and scowled. "Mother, why do you keep harping on money all the time?"

"Because," said the old lady heatedly, "you have already squandered seven million dollars of your father's inheritance, and now here you are borrowing against that little five-million-dollar trust that your grandfather left you. And I want you to know that Harry Payne Whitney is not going to help you this time."

Reggie's heart sank. "In that case I'll put the touch on Gertrude."

"Gertrude does not approve of Miss Morgan," his mother said coldly.

Reggie smiled charmingly at the small white-haired woman. "Then you'll have to cough up, mother," he said. "Come on, mother, you've always been my best friend. And besides, it's all due to you that I am the way I am."

This remark made her sit up even straighter. She suddenly felt quite warm and divested herself of her sables so that the necklace of pearls and diamonds that were her trademark flashed into full view. She shook her head. What could she do to make the boy see the light? He couldn't go on living in this grand fashion. Gertrude and Harry certainly wouldn't bail him out of this mess, and she herself was not about to part with one of her millions. She'd be dead any day now and then they could enjoy the inheritance.

The fact was that Alice Vanderbilt was feeling the pinch herself. Her eldest son, Alfred, had received the major share of her husband's estate and she had been left a trust fund that barely sufficed to maintain that white elephant on Fifth Avenue and that other white elephant up in Newport. With inflation already digging into her fixed income, she saw no way that she could help Reggie out.

But she hadn't seen Gloria Morgan.

Gloria stopped at the entrance of the Japanese garden. What a poetic place it was, with its fountains sending up sprays of water, its softly glowing lanterns and little curved bridges over the rock pools. She glanced at Reggie's table and crossed her fingers. Sitting next to him was a regal old woman whom, even if she hadn't expected to meet there, she would have recognized instantly as his mother. She had seen pictures of her in the newspapers, aiding various war charities. And today she looked fiercer than ever. Gloria felt her knees buckling, but with a resolute step and holding her head high, she moved toward Mrs. Vanderbilt, the woman whom she hoped would soon be her mother-in-law.

"Here she comes now," said Reggie, his face lighting up. "Isn't she the most exquisite thing you've ever seen?"

"I hear her twin sister is getting a divorce after only six months of marriage," Mrs. Vanderbilt murmured. "Can you imagine what morals the creature must have? Gertrude says they are both—"

Gloria, in her demure gray flannel, lace blouse, and white gloves, stood before them. She felt the old lady's eyes going over her critically and she was glad that she had taken pains with her appearance. She had copied her image from a picture of Mary Pickford and had that "America's Sweetheart" look.

"Hello, my dear," cried Reggie, leaping to his feet and becoming terribly British all of a sudden. "Isn't it wonderful to have mother here? She is most anxious to welcome you into the family—aren't you, mother?"

"Humph!" snorted the old lady, as Gloria sat down.

"Isn't it the most lovely day, Mrs. Vanderbilt?" said Gloria, making full use of her voice which was one of her greatest charms. "The sky was so clear this morning I thought I was in Venice. Do you like Venice, Mrs. Vanderbilt?"

The old lady nodded nonplussed. Edith Gould had told her that the girl was an adventuress—that she did wild things up in Harlem. She wasn't prepared for this fragile and enchanting creature. Reggie was right—Gloria Morgan was the most exquisite thing she had ever seen. Think what children they could have! And the family needed fresh blood.

"Yes, I like Venice," said Mrs. Vanderbilt in a softer tone. "But I don't like foreigners. Look at what the duke of Marlborough did to my niece, Consuelo." She frowned. "You sound foreign, young lady. Are you?"

"My father was an American consul who was posted abroad. So we traveled about Europe a great deal."

"I hope it didn't unbalance you," said the old lady, with a meaningful look.

"Well, I do yearn for a home," sighed the girl. "And Reggie's Sandy Point Farm is a real home."

Mrs. Vanderbilt liked her for saying that. She would have loved to have closed The Breakers and moved into Reggie's cozy house.

"Do sit closer, my dear, so we can chat," she said. "Would you care for a cocktail?"

"I'd prefer orange juice," whispered Gloria demurely.

Mrs. Vanderbilt nodded approvingly. "A sentiment I wish my son would share. My friend, the rector at Saint Thomas's, never touches spirits either—he feels there should be stronger laws to enforce Prohibition. And my dear friend President Harding, who often dines with me in my house, claims that alcohol is the major cause of character degeneracy."

"Oh, I agree completely, Mrs. Vanderbilt." Reggie and Gloria exchanged quick looks across the table, remembering those drunken nights in Harlem and at Texas Guinan's.

"Do you like Newport?" asked Mrs. Vanderbilt. Gloria nodded and the old lady added, "You'll have to come and visit me next summer, my dear. I get quite lonely in that great big house with those seventy cheerless rooms."

"Seventy?" trilled Gloria. "Then how must you feel in your house in New York, which is twice as big?"

"More lonely," muttered the old lady. "And my children hardly ever come to visit me. Of course, Gertrude is sculpting all the time, and Gladys is in Budapest with her Hungarian count."

"I'll keep you company," said Gloria sympathetically.

Suddenly the old lady no longer felt alone. Indeed she found herself looking forward to the summer months when this radiant creature would liven up the monotonous routine at The Breakers. Watching her, Mrs. Vanderbilt began to think of all the things she could do for her. The girl looked so vulnerable and sweet, you wanted to do things for her.

Without a word the old lady clipped off five strands of her pearl necklace and handed them to Gloria.

"All Vanderbilt women wear pearls," observed Mrs. Vanderbilt. "Now, Miss Morgan, you just go to Tiffany's and have them strung together properly. And charge a diamond clasp to my account. They were Catherine the Great's pearls and I don't believe there are any finer. They took eight years to match."

Gloria was absolutely stunned by this turn of events. She lowered her eyes so the old lady couldn't see their triumphant gleam.

At that moment the headwaiter presented them with huge menus with tempting entrees written in French. "I recommend the baby squab," he said, bowing low before the Vanderbilts. "Fresh from North Carolina."

They all ordered squab, and lunch went far better than Gloria had dared to imagine. With her facile social sense she kept the conversation flowing into interesting subjects, as if they had all known each other forever. What really won the old lady's heart was when Gloria said, "I can hardly wait to get settled up in Newport and have dozens of babies! And you know, riding is my favorite sport."

Alice Vanderbilt beamed at Gloria. "You are a dear girl, Miss Morgan, and I must admit that I have quite fallen in love with you."

Gloria took a deep breath. "Thank you, Mrs. Vanderbilt."

The old lady began to talk of her war charities, and Gloria hung on her every word.

Saved! thought Reggie, with a sigh of relief. He lit up a cigar and leaned back on the banquette. It had really gone much better than he'd expected. What a clever girl Gloria was. She had intuitively said just the right thing to his mother—and he knew how difficult it was to please the old czarina. So many other girls had tried and failed. Of course, there was something very frail about Gloria, and that frailty was appealing. He chuckled to himself.

"What amuses you, Reggie Vanderbilt?" asked his mother.

"Never mind," he said. "Just enjoying this lovely get-together."

"Now I must go," said the old lady, standing up and adjusting her furs. "I do hospital work every afternoon. You know, those poor boys who were wounded in the war need so much encouragement. Would you care to meet them tomorrow afternoon, Gloria?"

"Yes, I would," said Gloria, her Nurse Edith Cavell fantasy awakened. She would wear a uniform with a red cross on her sleeve and minister to those poor wounded boys. "It's always been my dream to be a nurse," she added.

"Well, you've got your hands full now, my son!" said Alice. Her wrinkled face lit up behind the veil. "I wish you had known my other two boys. But of course they are dead. . . ." As if on cue a dignified maid appeared and the matriarch moved slowly away on her arm.

"Gloria, you were brilliant," said Reggie, embracing her warmly.

"I loved your mother," said Gloria, watching the old woman in widow's weeds vanish.

Reggie became unusually enthusiastic; the young girl really sparked him. "Listen, Gloria, this is my good-luck day. Mother has taken a great shine to you, so I'm going to roll the dice and gamble that I can pick up a couple of million from sister Gertrude."

"Why should she give you a couple of million?"

"She has a strong family sense—we Vanderbilts must always stay on top of the heap." Reggie led her swiftly through the crowds and put her into the Minerva. "Now, darling, you go to Bergdorf's and then go down to Tiffany's and get yourself a diamond clasp for those pearls."

"Okay," said an intoxicated Gloria.

"And pray for me—pray that tough Gertrude will see it my way. Think what fun we'll have spending that delicious green stuff!"

Gertrude's medieval château at 871 Fifth Avenue was elaborately decorated with stonework—flying buttresses, gargoyles, and dormers. The butlers and footmen made a fuss over Reggie as he entered, as he was a great favorite of theirs.

"Is my sister in?" he asked cheerfully. "And is she in a good mood?"

From behind the velvet curtain of the library came the handsome figure of Harry Payne Whitney. "No, she isn't in a good mood. But she *is* in," he said. He shook his brother-in-law's hand in his charming way. "Good afternoon to you, Reggie my friend, and good luck to you."

"Where are you off to in such a good mood?" said Reggie.

"Mischief," said Harry, winking.

"New in town?"

"Green as only Minnesota makes them."

"I envy you," said Reggie.

"You've got the prettiest girl in New York," said Harry, "and I'm jealous as hell."

The two men parted. Harry went out into the wintry sunlight of Fifth Avenue and Reggie went up the magnificent stone staircase that curved up to the second floor's tapestried gloom. Lucky devil, that Harry, Reggie was thinking. There had always been a sharp sense of competition between the two men and this feeling of one-upmanship had grown over the years. The brothers-in-law had a curious love-hate relationship which they hardly understood themselves.

Reggie opened the door to Gertrude's Renaissance bedroom, a vast cavern hung in sonorous chocolate velvet with a beamed ceiling and a limestone fireplace that a dozen people could have stood in. Gertrude Whitney was seated at a refectory table with her secretary. Now she looked up at her brother and smiled thinly. She was a handsome woman, not yet fifty, with the strong features of her father. Her figure was tall, erect, yet fragile, but there was nothing fragile about her personality. She was always in command and gave one the uncomfortable feeling that she held all the aces.

"Hello, Gertrude. Could you spare a minute alone with me?"

"Of course, my dear boy," she replied in that irritating, patronizing way that she always adopted with him.

"Mother loved Gloria," he began, hoping their mother's favorable opinion might cause her to reconsider her own.

"Did she?" she drawled innocently.

"Gloria is an angel and—"

"A perfect angel," Gertrude swiftly interrupted, "for some rich old man like Otto Kahn or William Randolph Hearst. Mother and I have both decided that you cannot afford the girl."

"Mother has changed her mind," said Reggie.

"Has she?" Gertrude's voice was ice.

"Gloria has charmed her."

"I daresay," said Gertrude nastily.

"Gertrude," he said, swallowing his resentment as best he could, "you've got to help me. I owe everyone, all over town."

She stared vaguely into space. "I find myself strapped at the moment," she said. "Running six establishments that are like grand hotels can be rather expensive."

Better forget the two million, he decided. "All I need is a million to tide me over," he began softly.

"Your irresponsible ways used to amuse me, dear. Now I find them tiresome."

"But you can't be so heartless, Gertrude."

"I can do anything I want," she snapped. She stood up, and such anger distorted her features that Reggie scarcely recognized the usually composed woman. She stared at him with hard eyes. "You dare to come here," she said, her clipped words chilling him, "*dare* to come here and beg for money from me! Why should I support this new little tart of yours?"

"She's not a tart," Reggie flared up.

"You men make me sick," spat Gertrude.

"I'm sorry I came." He turned his back on her and started for the door.

"I didn't give you permission to leave," she said in a commanding voice. He stopped at the door and she added, "I have something more to say to you, Reggie Vanderbilt."

"Yes?" He turned and faced her.

"I hate you and Harry," she said clenching her fists. "I hate your and Harry's constant womanizing."

"Gertrude—"

"How did you ever get it into your stupid head that I would pay for your good times? Why should you pleasure yourself when I have no pleasure?"

Her voice rose to a shriek and Reggie closed it off with a bang of the door.

Back home he was still trembling with rage. Without an outlet, the anger he felt toward his sister eventually turned inward and he felt depressed. Norton, the valet, found him slumped in his library chair by the fire.

"What's the matter, sir?"

"I can't get married," muttered Reggie.

"I'll bring you some tea, sir," the valet told him, not knowing what else to say.

"A double whiskey, Norton."

"But, Mr. Vanderbilt, you remember what the doctor said."

"I don't want to think about what the doctor said."

"Didn't Mr. Harry help you, sir?"

"No," said Reggie, shaking his head.

"But I'm sure your mother will help you, sir."

"Not after my sister fills her with poison!" cried Reggie furiously.

Norton could think of nothing more to say and so he started to make a weak whiskey and soda. Handing it to him he said, "Perhaps it's not a good idea to marry at the moment, Mr. Vanderbilt."

"Perhaps," said Reggie, staring into the flames and feeling cold all over.

"Miss Morgan telephoned, sir."

Reggie raised his eyes like a condemned man who has been granted a reprieve. "What did she want?" he asked quietly.

"She wanted to celebrate with you tonight."

"Well, Norton," chuckled Reggie, "alert the usual crowd. And make a reservation at Sherry's for dinner. And then call Texas Guinan and reserve a table for twenty."

CHAPTER
10

It was a bitter cold night. Gloria stood in the snow wrapped in a black velvet opera cloak and Reggie's white silk muffler, waiting for the peephole to open. Presently, Ralph, the robust river pirate, opened the black door and ushered them into the splendid marble hall.

They joined Serge Voronoff at his table for twelve. Gloria sat next to handsome Dr. Voronoff, who was fifty and looked thirty because he had experimented successfully with monkey glands. Gloria herself was looking particularly stunning in a trailing white satin dress with collar and sleeves embroidered with crystal. A new rock-crystal and diamond bracelet and matching pendant earrings completed the grand Vanderbilt image that Reggie insisted on.

"Just think, Gloria," said the amazingly youthful Voronoff, "you will remain beautiful forever if you take my potion."

"Give it to me," she laughed, "immediately!"

A handsome maharaja turned his fine eyes on her. "Feel like doing something daring, Miss Morgan?"

"Yes!" she said gaily.

"I have four and twenty blackbirds and a pie—and that's where you come in—"

"In the pie?" she asked.

He pressed a hard thigh against her under the table. She looked at him questioningly and he pushed a black pearl and diamond ring into her hand. She shrugged and took it. Every night with Reggie was wild and crazy, so nothing really surprised her anymore. And she was quite adept at taking gifts from men and giving nothing in return.

A stranger asked her to dance and she whirled away. Afterward, swarthy Ralph with his walrus mustache put his large hands on her shoulders. "Listen, Gloria," he said, "how about a tour of the house. You've never seen the *private* rooms upstairs, have you?"

She hadn't, but she knew very well what they were for. "Sounds delicious," she said. She glanced across the room at Reggie. He was talking about his horses to Jeanne Eagels. Gloria tried unsuccessfully to get his attention, then thought better of it; he hated being interrupted and could be very disagreeable when he was. So she stood up and followed the Sicilian river pirate upstairs. Perhaps she shouldn't have gone with him, but she felt in a reckless mood.

Texas's bedroom had tufted black satin walls, and over the bed, which could easily accommodate six, was a canopy of white ostrich feathers. Pink bulbs burned behind pink satin shades and there were white bearskin rugs, with heads, on the floor. The same nude cupids and nymphs that adorned the rooms downstairs adorned this room too. Only these cupids had stiff organs that were poking the ladies, and the ladies seemed surprised.

"They're very stimulating, aren't they, Gloria?" said Ralph, breathing heavily on her neck.

She nodded wordlessly.

"I'll bet I'm the biggest man you've ever seen, Gloria," said Ralph, stretching.

"You *are* very big," she whispered.

"Have you ever wondered what it would be like to have such bigness in you?" he asked seductively.

From the room next door came the sounds of people making violent love. The man was panting loudly as if finishing a long race, and the woman seemed as if she were trying to reach the highest note of a passionate Italian aria, moaning, whimpering, and screaming. Finally both climaxed and both voices cried out together.

"Goodness!" said Gloria, a little embarrassed.

"It's good, all right," said Ralph.

"I'd better go back downstairs," she said, moving toward the door.

The moans continued and Ralph said, grinning and showing some gold teeth, "It's great to come, baby. Helps banish the blues." He seized her waist. "You know something? I don't think you're getting much." He kissed her, sticking his tongue far into her mouth. She felt faint. Then he slapped her hard across the face. She saw stars and felt herself falling. The next thing she knew she was lying on the bed with Ralph's heavy body on top of her. She tried to scream, but his hand was over her mouth. She tried to move, but his great shoulders held her down. Finally she bit his hand and he howled and slapped her again.

In the next room Harry Payne Whitney, putting on his shorts, heard the sounds from next door and was excited by what they brought to mind. He was a carefree man and game for anything, so he opened the door and walked in.

Harry was three years older than Reggie, but tall, athletic, and powerfully made, with a year-round tan from spending much time out of doors, shooting, fishing, playing polo and tennis. He was a great horseman, too, and his massive thighs were thick with muscle. At this point in his life he was still young, his three children were grown up and he could indulge his passion for women. It was his dream to find a great love; he was capable of strong feelings, but he had never found the girl who could arouse them.

Harry moved closer to the bed and to his surprise recognized Reggie's fiancée, the wild playgirl Gloria Morgan. Poor Reggie—cuckolded already! It served him right for thinking he could satisfy such a young and lovely creature. Harry grinned. "You'd better not let Texas catch you, Ralph," he said smoothly.

"Mind your own fucking business," said Ralph. As he turned to face Harry, he removed his hand from Gloria's mouth. She screamed for help, and Harry realized she was not a willing participant. He grabbed the river pirate and pulled him off the satin bed.

A terrific fight ensued, during which two spindly legged gilt chairs were broken, jade lamps were knocked off tables, and a smoked-glass mirror over the bed was completely demolished.

"Stop! Stop!" cried Gloria, who had never seen such violence before. Shielding herself from the flying objects she fled into a corner—the best she could do since the two struggling men were blocking her path to the door. She noticed that Harry was even bigger than Ralph, and the sight of the two brawny men locked in combat sent shivers up and down her.

Hearing the noise from downstairs, Texas burst into the room and fired a pistol at the chandelier. Ralph's attention was diverted and Harry chose that moment to deliver a roundhouse right; Ralph fell back onto the bed, unconscious.

"Your Ralph isn't even housebroken," said Harry, panting heavily.

Texas looked at the almost nude man and laughed. "Gee

whiskers, I never thought I'd see Harry Payne Whitney in my bedroom in his shorts! I'm getting ideas. . . ."

Gloria looked at her savior with wide astonished eyes. So this was the famous Harry Payne Whitney! "You're Reggie's brother-in-law?"

Texas was struck by the ludicrousness of the situation. "Say, haven't you two ever met before? Maybe I'd better leave you two alone so you can get acquainted." She flounced out, laughing.

"I'm Harry Payne Whitney, Miss Morgan," he said with a playful bow.

Gloria made a little curtsy. "How lovely to meet you at last," she said in the same teasing tone.

Harry vanished into the next room and returned fully dressed in white tie and tails. Gloria was sitting at the mirrored dressing table trying to repair the damage to her dress and hair.

"Do I look all right, Harry?" she said, glancing up at the ruggedly handsome man.

"A divinity." He spoke so solemnly that she laughed.

"I really don't know what gets into these men," she shrugged artlessly.

"I do," grinned Harry.

"A maharaja downstairs gave me a black-pearl and diamond ring. . . ."

"I don't blame him," said Harry. "I'd like to give you more than that myself."

Something in his voice made her thrill. He sat down beside her on the stool and started to brush his hair before the mirror. His hands were large and well shaped, and again she felt gooseflesh.

"Please don't tell Gertrude," he said, laughing.

"Is she so jealous of you?" asked Gloria.

"Wouldn't you be?" said Harry.

"You're very naughty to be flirting with me," said Gloria, trying hard to regain some semblance of decorum.

"Reggie flirts with all *my* girls," he said.

"I don't want to hear about them," she said, not liking to think of Reggie in sexual terms.

"What *would* you like to talk about?" asked Harry, turning to look at her.

"I'd love to know why your wife doesn't want to meet me."

"Perhaps she feels you aren't sincere," Harry remarked provocatively.

"What do I have to do, elope with Reggie and live in poverty?" Gloria shot back. She stood up and started toward the door.

"I'd hoped that this was the beginning of a beautiful friendship," said Harry, catching up with her.

"Are you mocking me?" she asked, gazing up at him. The orchestra downstairs was playing the popular tune "I'm Just Wild About Harry" and they began to laugh.

"I hope that's the way you feel," said Harry, all boyish charm.

"Oh, it is!" she said, adopting his tone. "Shall we dance?"

They moved out into the hall and began a fox-trot. Harry was a splendid dancer and it was marvelous being in his arms. She was drawn to him and hoped he would prove to be a staunch ally.

"I wish you'd put in a good word for me with your wife," she pleaded. "It would make things easier for us."

"I promise," he said solemnly.

Somewhere a bedroom door slammed, and soon Gloria heard the same sounds that had come from Harry's room half an hour before. Uncomfortable, Gloria stopped dancing and remained still.

Harry felt her tension and said, trying to keep his voice light, "We'd better go downstairs."

They started down the staircase. Both felt that something

significant had passed between them, but they didn't dare dwell on it.

At the bottom of the stairs a valet brought his topcoat. Harry said distantly, avoiding her eyes, "Goodnight."

"Goodnight," she said coldly, and hurried across the marble floor to the room where there was music, Reggie, and the party.

"We've missed you, Gloria," said Reggie, raising his brandy glass.

Gloria took a sip from his glass, laughed, then swallowed a lot more. She had to forget that incident with Harry Payne Whitney. The memory of his almost nude body disturbed her and she wanted to banish every thought of him from her mind.

The maharaja helped her forget. "Are you ready to do the four-and-twenty-blackbirds act now?" he asked, winking at Reggie. Peggy Hopkins Joyce had danced naked out of a pie at Reggie's house in Newport, and it would be fun for the men to see Gloria do the same thing. Clothed of course. Reggie's feeling for a mistress was very different from his feeling for his wife-to-be.

Gloria agreed to the stunt and went off to change into a costume. After a time, four waiters carried in an immense pie and out she popped, with four and twenty "blackbirds," doing the Charleston. She was dressed now in Texas's spangles and a headdress of towering feathers. The black-birds were twenty-four girls from Harlem's Cotton Club, whom Reggie had telephoned an hour before. Gloria's white-feathered body, surrounded by the "blackbirds," gyrated wildly to the music of Louis Armstrong playing "Bye Bye, Blackbird" on the trumpet. At the end of the number Gloria and the other girls vanished behind the curtain to thundering applause.

Reggie was as drunk as a lord by this time and had almost forgotten this afternoon's failure with his sister. To hell with the ballbreaker! Who needed the old bitch anyway?

He was muttering this when his limousine dropped Gloria at home at six in the morning. "Bye bye, Blackbird," he called, blowing kisses as she vanished across the pavement.

Thelma awoke when Gloria came into the bedroom. "Did you have a good time?" she asked sleepily.

"The usual—but I met Reggie's brother-in-law, Harry Payne Whitney," replied Gloria.

"I hear he's a handsome devil," yawned Thelma.

"Devil he is!"

Thelma sat up. "Don't tell me something happened between you two!"

"It was dangerous—very dangerous," said Gloria, sitting down at the dressing table and taking off her rings and bracelet.

"I knew you weren't really in love with Reggie," said Thelma triumphantly, going over to sit beside her. "You'd rather have Harry Payne Whitney, wouldn't you?"

"I don't want to talk about it," said Gloria sharply. "Tell me *your* news. Tell me about mama! Tell me anything!"

"Well, I'm all packed and ready to go," said Thelma. "Mama is convinced that she can get me an annulment from Junior, and I've got somebody in mind. . . ."

"Who?" said Gloria, beginning to forget Harry Payne Whitney.

"The Prince of Wales," announced Thelma.

The snow was still falling when Harry Payne Whitney arrived home at one o'clock in the morning. The white flakes fluttering over the streetlights caught his fancy and he lingered there on that windy corner of 67th and Fifth. He thought of the seventeen-year-old Morgan girl. How fresh she was, like the new snow. He would have liked to go walking with her through the snowflakes.

He watched the yellow lights of his town car vanish down the endless stretch of Fifth Avenue. The usually busy street was strangely silent after the snowfall. He took one last look at the powdered white trees in the park across the avenue, then inserted his key in the lock and pushed open the heavy oak door.

An old Irish porter was dozing in the vestibule and two footmen were snoring in the hall, sprawled lifelessly over gilded throne chairs. Harry started up the grand staircase. There were no sounds from within, and the walls were so thick and so richly hung with brocade and tapestry that only muted sounds came from without. He heard a radio playing Mozart when he reached the second floor. A bright line of light came from under his wife's door.

"Harry? Harry?" came Gertrude's voice. He gave a start and tripped over the Oriental runner. *Damn!* He was suddenly tired. He didn't feel like discussing the events of the day with her as they usually did. He loved her, but it was a love from which all passion had long gone.

Gertrude Whitney lay in the majestic columned bed of Pope Leo under a portrait of Queen Elizabeth by Van Dyke. All passion had not gone from Gertrude, at least where her husband was concerned. Like Gloria Morgan, she had an obsession for Harry, only hers was much more painful and complicated because they had been married for twenty-six years. She suddenly remembered her coming-out party at The Breakers in Newport that long ago August evening. It had been a joyful event for her, waltzing with Harry who was then a Yale student, but a disastrous event for her brother, Cornelius, who had been caught by that dreadful adventuress, Grace Wilson. Later her brother had married the creature, was disinherited by his parents, and split the family into two sides. Alice, Reggie, and Gertrude hadn't uttered a word to Grace or Neily for twenty-five years; they merely passed one another coldly whenever they met in Paris,

London, the south of France, or even Newport and Fifth Avenue. And now, thought Gertrude, that awful Morgan girl is going to cause another feud in the family.

When her husband stepped dutifully into the room, she wasted little time on the amenities before bringing up the subject.

"But I hear she's adorable," said Harry, suddenly showing an inordinate interest in undoing his tie.

"You men," she laughed scornfully. "Fools for a pretty face."

"I heard at the club tonight that she is a very charming girl and absolutely devoted to Reggie." He flung the tie on the nearest chair and sat at Gertrude's dressing table, unbuttoning his shirt.

"Oh, Harry! Harry!" Despite all the years they'd been married, she still loved to speak his name out loud. "Did you know that Reggie came here today and tried to squeeze some money from me?"

"Did he succeed?" Harry had worked his way through the buttons and started on the cuff links.

"He succeeded in making me furious." She crossed her arms in anger.

"But, Gertrude, you've made so much money in the stock market and you'll make so much more in the boom to come— and after all, he is your favorite brother." The jacket came off and joined the tie.

"Now you're making me feel guilty," she said.

"Don't feel guilty. Just give him a few million."

"Why don't *you?*" she snorted. "You have more money than I."

He turned to look at her with a flicker of amusement. "Why, Gertrude, are we in competition?"

"All men and women are in competition!" she cried. "Especially after they have been married as long as you and I have. Now stop that prolonged striptease and come to bed."

He sneezed loudly.

"Harry," she chided, "you've gone out without your rubbers again. Come, let me feel your forehead."

He sat down obediently on the edge of the bed. "Am I dying?" he grinned.

"You have a fever!"

"Yes, a terrible fever." And again he thought of Gloria Morgan. "Can you cure it, Gertrude?"

She nodded her curly brown head in her positive way and tugged at his belt. "Get out of those wet clothes."

Without modesty or shame, he flung off his clothes and slipped naked between the lavender-scented heavy linen sheets. Gertrude snuggled warmly against him and threw an arm over his massive chest.

The Mozart opera continued to play softly on the radio, and Harry remarked sleepily, "What an invention, the radio."

"Yesterday I bought a huge block of RCA stock," said Gertrude, moving her hand down to rest on his flat, hard stomach.

"Good girl," said Harry. "Sarnoff told me it would triple by nineteen thirty. So will your other stocks."

"You mean I'll be as rich as you, Harry?" she teased.

"You'd like that, wouldn't you, Gertrude?"

"I might be independent," she smiled, "but you will always be my lord and master." Her hand moved even lower. Slowly her teasing fingers aroused him and Gertrude kissed his cheek expectantly.

Harry lay there, eyes closed, enjoying the pleasurable sensation. But his manipulative brain was racing, and right away in his head was born an idea. He could get Reggie in his power. He'd give the poor bastard money. And keep reminding him of his generosity. Then he could begin an affair with Gloria with impunity.

With a groan, he threw himself on Gertrude.

CHAPTER
11

Alice Vanderbilt and her son Reginald were sitting in her second-floor sitting room, which she called her Victorian parlor, a room draped in lavender brocade and rich in Vanderbilt memorabilia. All the tables were draped and there was a portrait of Queen Victoria, whom Alice idolized in the same way that Gertrude idolized Queen Elizabeth and her daughter-in-law Grace worshiped Marie Antoinette. Queens, all, which was appropriate for these Vanderbilt women.

Reggie was examining some family photographs and reminiscing aloud about Aunt Alva and Consuelo, Gertrude and Harry, Alfred and his two sons. He was remembering the yachts, houses, and balls; the shooting parties in Scotland; the races at Cowes; clambakes at Bailey's beach and tennis matches at the old shingled Newport Casino. There was a picture of Reggie and Harry as children, in little sailor suits, coming out of the gates of The Breakers in a pony cart.

There were no photographs of the hated Grace. Nor even a

snapshot of the disinherited Cornelius. But Alice Vanderbilt was at that moment thinking about her banished son, whom they called Neily. Yesterday afternoon she had sent her footman over to 640 Fifth Avenue, the seventy-room brownstone palace in which Grace and Cornelius resided in majestic style. Alice herself had never even been invited there. Now she fell to wondering if the scheming upstart would have the good manners to reply. Perhaps she wouldn't even bother. Grace had become hopelessly grand and insisted on being addressed as *the* Mrs. Vanderbilt, although of course Alice was the head of the family.

"I did something very bold yesterday, Reggie," she blurted out. "I sent Grace an invitation to my family party to meet Gloria the day after tomorrow."

"That *is* daring," chuckled Reggie.

"Do you think she'll come?" asked Alice.

"Not after the way you've treated her, mother."

"It was your father who insisted on disinheriting Neily when he married Grace. It wasn't my fault. As a good wife, I had to go along with him, but frankly I felt it was wrong to cut Neily off and snub Grace." She gave a deep sigh. "I really don't blame her if she doesn't come."

A footman entered with a note on a tray. It was an elaborately stamped letter with the Vanderbilt coat of arms in maroon on a ground of heavy silver vellum.

"It's from Grace!" said Alice, ripping open the envelope excitedly. She put on her spectacles and read:

My dear Mrs. Vanderbilt,

Thank you so much for your kind invitation. Alas, neither my husband nor myself can be with you the day after tomorrow to meet Miss Gloria Morgan. It was good of you to think of us.

Sincerely yours,
Grace Vanderbilt

"It's just as well," laughed Reggie. "They're both such stuffed shirts and climbers."

"What a way to talk about your brother!"

"Well, he is a stuffed shirt, isn't he?"

"And what are you?" she flung at him.

"A ruined playboy," he said with humor, "but eager to repent his sinful ways."

Alice stood up and moved to the fire. "Did Gertrude agree to help you out?" she asked him.

"No. In fact she was quite rude. She said she found my irresponsible ways tiresome," said Reggie wearily.

"Well, they are," snapped the old lady, "and you should take steps to change them."

Reggie was curiously honest and direct; he was not a game player like Harry, and he certainly wasn't able to charm people. The only way he knew to plead his case was to do it in the simplest way. He said, "Mother, if you help me out now, your prodigal son will turn over a new leaf. I've sown my wild oats and I'm going to buckle down to work."

"You? work?" Alice snorted. "You have no business sense whatsoever."

"Well, I've got to do something. Gloria must have the best, as befits a future Vanderbilt."

"Fine values you have!" cried Alice.

"Really, mother, you're a fine one to talk," retorted Reggie. "After all, I got my values from you."

Mother and son fell silent, glaring at each other. Reggie was desperate; he had to have some money to keep the show going. Suddenly he had an idea.

"Listen, mother, I'll make a deal with you. I'll get Grace and Neily to come to your party, if you'll give me five hundred thousand."

She thought for a moment. "It's a deal," she said.

After lunch with Gloria, Reggie dragged her to the brown-stone mansion at 640 Fifth Avenue. A butler stared at Reggie with no sign of recognition and told him that Mr. and Mrs. Vanderbilt were in the midst of a luncheon party for Queen Marie of Rumania.

"Isn't the lunch finished yet?" said Reggie.

"None of the guests is allowed to leave before the queen, sir, and she is still here."

"We'll wait," said Reggie.

"Who is calling, may I inquire?"

"I'm Mr. Vanderbilt's brother," said Reggie haughtily.

With much bowing and scraping, Reggie and Gloria were led into a drawing room on the first floor. It was a memorable chamber with many signed palace pieces made for the sisters of Louis XV, and the walls, curtains, and upholstery were of a dazzling pink Boucher needlepoint. On a massive table desk encrusted with gilded bronze were gold-framed pictures of royalty, all signed with a flourish. They were Grace's pride and joy.

Strains of violin music came to them and Gloria said, "It's Mendelssohn."

"Yes, miss," said the second footman. "Mr. Fritz Kreisler is here to play for Her Majesty."

"How many guests are there?" asked Reggie.

"Sixty, sir," replied the footman.

"That's a cozy group," said Reggie.

"It's the usual guest list, sir."

Gloria began to laugh, and Reggie joined her. She had never felt so close to him as in that moment.

A dignified male secretary entered and said that Mrs. Vanderbilt would see them now, and only a moment later Grace Vanderbilt swept in. She was in gold lamé with water-falls of diamonds from stem to stern.

"To what do I owe this intrusion?" said the queen of American society.

Reggie stood up and smiled ingratiatingly. "Mother is terribly distressed that you can't come to the family party."

"And that's the reason you are here?" asked Grace imperiously. She looked down at Gloria, who remained silent, nervously twisting the pearls that were a gift from Alice Vanderbilt.

"Mother is eighty years old now—" Reggie began, smiling in his most charming way.

"Yes, she's had many years in which to make me miserable," snapped Grace.

"Please, Grace," Reggie said placatingly. "The whole family is coming, and mother wants to end this ridiculous feud. Just a few hours ago she told me that she felt it was a terrible thing that my father did."

"Indeed it was," cried Grace, remembering the endless humiliations.

"So what point is there in continuing it?" he reasoned. "We Vanderbilts must stick together."

"I'm doing very well on my own, thank you very much." Which was a lie, because her husband was an alcoholic and she was tearing through her money. For months she had been brooding on how to capture Fred Vanderbilt, who was the richest member of the family and would soon be a widower since his wife was at death's door. Grace often lay awake wondering how to launch her offensive on the old man and his $120 million. She'd asked him to her dinner party tonight —indeed to the lunch party today—but the canny old geezer always refused.

Just then, by a strange quirk of fate, a butler came in to announce that Mr. Frederick Vanderbilt was on the telephone. Excusing herself, she went to the phone and picked up the receiver.

"Hello," she drawled in an affected English accent, "is that you, Uncle Fred? . . . I'm counting on you tonight, so please don't let me down as I'm seating you next to Queen Marie herself." She paused to listen, then touched the famous headache band around her white hair, trying to swallow her fierce hostility. "Truly, Uncle Fred, I'm *crushed* that you can't join us. It's the most ghastly blow I've received since the day my dear friend the kaiser abdicated. . . . Oh, Alice's party? Well, I'm not sure . . ."

Presently Grace hung up and returned to Reggie and his bride-to-be. Her cold gray-blue eyes went up and down the pair, wondering how they could be useful to her. And then she got it. Fred Vanderbilt had said he'd be at old Alice's family party the day after tomorrow. That would be her chance. And once she got her hands on all that money, she'd really settle a lot of scores.

From long habit she composed her features into a gracious expression, startling Reggie and Gloria with the sudden transformation. "Would you care to join my guests and meet dear Marie of Rumania? She's my dearest friend—we practically grew up together."

"In Tennessee?" said Reggie facetiously.

Grace chose to ignore the remark. Instead she began introducing them to her various guests. Turning to Gloria she very sweetly said, "May I present my future sister-in-law, Miss Gloria Morgan."

Gloria's eyes went wide with astonishment. Reggie was astounded, and even more so when Grace added, "My dear brother-in-law is coming to fetch me for our family get-together the day after tomorrow." She turned to Marie of Rumania. "My mother-in-law's house is the largest on the avenue, and I always enjoy going there." She gave Reggie a fond look that completely mystified him.

What the devil was she up to? he wondered. Whatever it

was, he realized that if they could all get through the next forty-eight hours without a crisis, he'd have half a million dollars.

CHAPTER
12

Alice Vanderbilt's house was brilliantly illuminated for the family party this evening. Every window blazed with light; even the sixth-floor dormers of the maids' rooms gleamed. It had been a balmy Sunday afternoon with the first hint of spring in the air, so New Yorkers were out on the street and in Central Park, enjoying the good weather. As dusk fell, those who happened to be at the Plaza Hotel remarked on the exceptional splendor of the Vanderbilt mansion across the way. There were a half-dozen men posted at the gates in Vanderbilt livery. On the 57th Street side there was such a crowd by five o'clock that the police were called in to keep order.

Alice was the only truly serene Vanderbilt that afternoon. She was the strictest of housekeepers, and seeing that the 137 rooms were spotless was quite a job. Every morning she put on white gloves and ran her fingers over the furniture—and woe to the maids if there was any dust on her fingertips. Now she was in the great hall on the 58th Street side, a tiny figure by the monumental carved-stone fireplace by Augustus Saint Gaudens. The vast hearth had been stuffed with dozens of fat heavy logs that were crackling away merrily in the gloom. It was the first time it had blazed since her favorite son, Alfred, had gone down on the *Lusitania*.

Old Alice was thinking of him now, and wishing he could be here tonight for the family gathering, which would probably turn out to be a family free-for-all. Only charming, handsome Alfred could have kept some order with those raging tigers, Gertrude and Grace.

Gertrude had been here earlier this afternoon and the glitter in her eyes had frightened her mother. "You're going to be sweet with Gloria and Grace, aren't you, dear?" said her mother anxiously.

Gertrude had only laughed, and not very merrily.

So there would probably be a brawl tonight. But what could she do? Grace would probably have one of her temper tantrums, too.

At this very moment, Grace herself was tearing off a silver lamé number and trampling it beneath her gilded Parisian heels.

"Worth has ruined my figure!" she shrieked at her French maid. "Bring me some others, you cretin!"

Grace had always had a difficult time controlling her temper, but because she was so rich she could usually get away with it. Recently, though, she'd discovered that her money was going out at an alarming rate—

The hairdresser came in and Grace threw a clock at her. "You've ruined my hair!" she screamed. "I'm bald as a billiard!" She screamed so loud that the servants downstairs in the sub-basement heard her.

Finally she was dressed—in her usual gold lamé, white fox neckpiece, fringe of diamonds, and brocaded headache band. Her hair was freshly washed, rinsed, and waved; her cheeks and mouth rouged with the skill of an actress. It was still early, not quite five. She dismissed the servants and sat alone in her pink satin boudoir, thinking.

Reggie's remark about her Tennessee origins had bothered her. After all, her brother had married an Astor, and her sister a Goelet. Her niece, May, was the duchess of Roxburghe, and Grace herself had entertained more royalty and celebrities than the White House or Buckingham Palace—two places in which she was most welcome.

It had taken plenty of work and ruthless climbing to achieve that goal. All during her childhood on the Tennessee plantation Grace's mother—like Gloria Morgan's—had told her to push, climb, get to the top. And later when her daughter was a debutante Mrs. Wilson advised, "Every ball is a battle. . . . Get yourself a Vanderbilt!"

And Grace did. She got Cornelius Vanderbilt, who was a brigadier general, a George V look-alike, and a drunk. . . .

Gertrude Vanderbilt Whitney, in her brown Elizabethan chamber, dressed slowly, with care and with thought and some serenity. She was confident in the knowledge that no one was richer and no one was stronger than she.

She smiled into the Renaissance silver mirror on her dressing table, flanked by Cellini candlesticks. Yes, red was a perfect color for her—so rich, so fearful! And the sable sleeves, collar, and hem heightened the effect. Top it all off with diamonds? she debated. No, she decided, the Whitney rubies, blood-red stones that dripped wealth and success and filled one with awe. Tonight she would give Gloria the silent treatment, the most dreaded of all social cuts.

That Gloria Morgan will rue the day she crossed my path,

Gertrude was thinking. And as for Grace, just whom did that faded old "southern belle" think she was kidding? Uncle Fred said she'd been inviting him here and inviting him there, and it wasn't hard to figure out why.

On either side of her the maid snapped on her ruby-and-diamond pendant earrings, then she stood up and viewed the overall effect in a full-length glass.

"Madam looks splendid," said the maid.

"Here is some sherry, Mrs. Whitney" said the butler, entering.

"Get Mr. Whitney," said Gertrude. "I want to drink a victory toast!"

"He's having a massage at the Racquet Club, madam, and said he would meet you at Mrs. Vanderbilt's house."

She was annoyed, since she would have preferred to make her entrance on Harry's arm, but there was nothing for it but to go on without him. As she stepped into her town car and was carried down Fifth Avenue, she was wondering how she could throw Gloria together with Uncle Fred. Then she could save Reggie and wound Grace, all at once. . . .

In his limestone mansion on Fifth Avenue and 83rd Street, the most austere of all the Vanderbilt houses, old Fred was being dressed by his valets. He felt in splendid form and occasionally laughed out loud as the valet trimmed his skimpy silver locks and gentle mustaches.

He was a worldly old man and he knew that Grace was his for the asking. She was making such an effort with him, how could he think otherwise? And it obviously was giving Gertrude apoplexy. He wondered now what delicious ways he could torture them, and after a moment he hit on it. He'd give Gloria Morgan an important jewel, right in front of everyone. That would really stir up a lot of bad feelings. He loved creating an atmosphere of jealousy among women—it amused him to see the expressions they used to cover up their hostility.

"Bring me the Star of Kashmir," said the old man. "The perfect jewel for a young goddess!"

The goddess herself, Gloria, was the only one who dressed with the sweet thoughts of extreme youth—thoughts that would never enter her head again once she became a Vanderbilt. Will they like me? she kept thinking. Is my dress suitable? Is my hair properly done? Will I say the wrong thing? And, oh, how she dreaded a confrontation with Gertrude!

Like the others she had a personal maid—Wann—but there was no gilded paneling, these were no satin walls, no Persian carpets in her fourth-floor walkup, and the crackling of the fire and the strains of the waltzes were periodically displaced by the rumble of the nearby Third Avenue el.

"Oh, Wann, what will I say to Mrs. Whitney?"

"Don't talk about yourself," said Wann. "Let her talk. Everyone loves to talk about themselves."

"But what if she doesn't talk?"

"Then just smile," said Wann, as she propelled Gloria out the door.

Reggie's noble Hispano was approaching his mother's house when police halted its progress on Fifth Avenue. The chauffeur exchanged words with the men in blue, but still they stood.

Finally, Reggie rolled down the glass partition and yelled at his chauffeur, "Drive on, you imbecile!"

The policeman recognized the rich British Vanderbilt voice and bowed. "I'm sorry, sir."

"Don't let it happen again," said Reggie.

Immediately the car began to move slowly through the crowd, which parted in silence, then pressed close as people gazed with awe into the opulent interior.

It was Gloria's first taste of power and she thrilled. She could not possibly have foreseen that just such a crowd would terrify her some ten years later and be hungry for her blood in another part of New York.

A triumphant rocket shot up into the sky, exploding in a shower of colors. Gloria peered out the window with goose-flesh. "Oh, Reggie! You're mother's sending up fireworks for us!"

"We Vanderbilts do things in the grand manner, my dear." He glanced critically at her costume: a severely tailored black velvet suit, his mother's pearls, and his own diamond bracelet. A white satin blouse gave an appropriate air of sophistication and richness. Her long neck, fragile ankles and wrists certainly showed that she was gently bred, and her long fingers with their almond-shaped nails were another sign of good breeding. Certainly Gertrude couldn't criticize her appearance.

Aloud he said, "Weigh your words carefully with Gertrude."

"Is she so terrifying?" whispered Gloria.

"Terrifying," said Reggie, remembering their last encounter. "She's afraid of no one—except, of course, Harry."

Gloria felt uneasy at the mention of Harry's name, remembering his powerful half-naked body. "She must love Harry very much," she murmured.

"She'd annihilate any woman who tried to get Harry from her!"

A long line of Rolls-Royces was drawn up before the ornate side entrance at 1 West 57th Street. One of his mother's footmen opened the door and they stepped onto the red carpet that Mrs. Vanderbilt had had placed over the pavement for the occasion.

The first footman and second footman in maroon britches and black patent-leather shoes, along with half a dozen maids in black uniforms with starched organdy aprons and caps, made a great fuss over them. Reggie democratically introduced his bride-to-be to them and there was a volley of good wishes.

A maid took Gloria's chinchilla cape and Gloria glanced about the two-storied hall. There were enough throne chairs, Venetian torchères, knights in armor, and tapestries to furnish ten palaces.

"What extraordinary-looking things," said Gloria.

"Mother had most of them made in Paris at the turn of the century."

"Are those early Vanderbilts?" asked Gloria, glancing at some of the distinguished portraits.

They stood in front of the darkly varnished canvases in gilt and gessoed frames and tried to read the fading plaques. "I think that one's a great-uncle," said Reggie grandly.

All the Vanderbilts began to arrive together. Behind them, Grace picked up on Reggie's remark and said to Gloria, "My dear, Vanderbilts don't have ancestors like that. The grandfather was merely an old pirate on Staten Island, of very humble origins."

"Look who's talking!" said Reggie in a fury. For there was one thing you couldn't talk badly about and that was the early Vanderbilts. "A farm yokel from Tennessee!"

"Now, look here," said his brother Neily angrily, "you can't talk to my wife like that—"

Fortunately they were interrupted by Harry Payne Whitney's arrival. "My dear chaps! What a way to start the evening!"

Reggie pulled Gloria down the long hall into one of the

drawing rooms. "I don't know what gets into me here," said Reggie, flushing guiltily. He grabbed a whiskey and soda from a passing butler. "This house does hold bad memories for me. Too much was expected of me, you see."

They started into another large drawing room where his mother was receiving with Gertrude. Called the Bird Room, it was all peacock blue with gilt moldings, black Boule furniture with sunbursts of bronze.

"It's the size of a railroad station," said Gloria, wide-eyed at so much splendor.

"Well," said Reggie, "we *are* a railroad family. I'm going to inherit it one day, so you might as well get used to it. It's all ghastly and false, but real antiques were considered secondhand furniture in mother's day."

Old Mrs. Vanderbilt was seated on a Venetian needle-point sofa. On one side of her was her sister-in-law Florence Adele Twombly, *née* Vanderbilt, who lived in a smaller Fifth Avenue château and a castle in New Jersey. She was so isolated she had never heard of Labor Day. On the other side of her was Gertrude Vanderbilt Whitney in her Chinese-red evening dress that showed to advantage her lithe, slender figure.

All ladies adjusted their lorgnettes and peered at Miss Morgan. "Is she a niece of J. P. Morgan?" said Mrs. Twombly hopefully.

"If she were," said Gertrude coldly, "I'd have received her with open arms."

Alice Vanderbilt rose to her feet and kissed Gloria on both cheeks. Gloria was so grateful she almost cried.

"Gloria, you've met my daughter, Gertrude Whitney, haven't you? And this is my dear sister-in-law, Mrs. Twombly."

Florence Adele smiled politely and invited Gloria to tea the following day. Gertrude, however, said not a word.

Alice stepped in graciously by fondly taking Gloria's arm. "Come, my dear, I'll introduce you to some of the other Vanderbilts." And they started across the highly polished parquet floors.

"Really, Gertrude, you're impossible," said Reggie.

Gertrude lit a cigarette and coolly blew out the smoke. Her eyes followed Gloria across the room thoughtfully.

"She's in a foul mood," complained Reggie to his brother-in-law.

"Probably my fault," said Harry. "I haven't been home in two days."

Grace, meanwhile, was having a strategic conversation with old Fred and really getting places with him when Gloria and Alice interrupted her flirtation.

"Hi," drawled Grace, holding up her hand as if she expected Gloria to kiss it.

The old lady glared at Grace; she knew what she was up to. Aloud she said, "Grace dear, how is Neily? His color is so poor."

Reluctantly, Grace left Fred's side and went off with her mother-in-law. "Dear Mrs. Vanderbilt," intoned Grace, "I'm just worried sick about Neily. He's not only drinking now, but he's gambling on the stock market. And he accuses me of all sorts of terrible things. No one has gone through what I have gone through with him. . . ."

"Well," said old Fred to Gloria, "you look blooming, young lady."

"I've never been sick a day in my life, Mr. Vanderbilt."

"Then why do you marry a man who is sick and tired?" asked Fred sharply.

"I can change that," said Gloria, with all the confidence of youth.

"Why don't you try a man who is healthy and strong?" said Fred, puffing out his chest and hitting it.

"Are you flirting with me?" said Gloria playfully. "What a wicked man you are!"

The old man and the young girl smiled at one another. "If you feel like changing your mind, young lady," grinned Uncle Fred, "just ring my doorbell, anytime!"

"I get the strong feeling that you Vanderbilts don't want me to marry Reggie," said Gloria thoughtfully, playing with her diamond bracelet.

"I don't think it would be good for either one of you." Fred was sincere. He'd decided that Gloria needed kindly advice more than she needed gifts of precious gems.

Gertrude was bearing down on them and Gloria said, "Is that what Mrs. Whitney thinks too?"

"Yes," said the old man, whispering in her ear. "And Gertrude called me this morning and said she is going to offer you some money. But you stick to your guns if you love Reggie."

Gloria's whole world collapsed. Really! These Vanderbilts were terrible.

Gertrude breezed up, and Fred introduced them. "You know my niece, don't you?" he said.

Gloria's face froze, but, surprisingly enough, Gertrude smiled at her. "You are so beautifully dressed, Miss Morgan," she said sweetly. "Please excuse me for not speaking to you before. I'm an artist, you see, and the first overall impression of you is so strong that I was a little taken aback. To be frank, I was expecting something quite different."

Gloria relaxed a bit. "I hope that's a compliment," she said.

Gertrude took her arm and said, "Come, dear, let's you and I have a little talk by the potted palms."

"All right," said Gloria and they moved away into the corner.

"You've charmed all of us Vanderbilts," Gertrude began, never taking her eyes off the girl's face.

"Your Uncle Fred just proposed to me," said Gloria with a little laugh.

"I hope you accepted," said Gertrude. "Uncle Fred is the richest member of the family."

There was a silence as Gloria wondered whether or not this was meant as a joke. "Really, Mrs. Whitney," she said finally, "I don't think you have the right impression of me at all."

"I think I do, Miss Morgan," said Gertrude with a nasty chuckle that dispelled any doubts. "So let's get down to business."

Gloria was stunned by her tone of voice. "Business?" she said.

"I came here tonight to offer you a hundred thousand dollars. Now you can return to wherever you came from and marry the boy you love. I'm sure there *is* some handsome young boy at home, isn't there?"

"No, there isn't!" cried Gloria hotly. "And how dare you talk to me in this way?"

Gertrude smiled sweetly. "If you love Reggie, my dear, you will let him marry the Harriman girl, or the Frick. I'm sure you don't want my husband and me to pay for your wedding and your honeymoon and all, do you?"

Gloria fell silent. She didn't know what to say.

"You see, the only money that Reggie has left is a tiny amount in trust. And if he dies it will all go to his daughter by his first marriage. You'll get nothing, Miss Morgan. So what's the point of the marriage?"

"I love Reggie," said Gloria.

"But don't you love George Brokaw as much? He has twelve million of his own and he's not half as difficult as Reggie."

Gloria wet her lips. She felt faint. "Mrs. Whitney, I won't tell Reggie about this distasteful conversation, of course. But I do intend to marry him."

Gertrude gave a false sigh. "What a pretty fool you are. But your prettiness won't last forever, you know. Do you know that Harry Thaw's wife, Evelyn Nesbit, is working on the boardwalk in Atlantic City now, and absolutely stone broke? And she was the loveliest creature I have ever seen, twenty-five years ago. Of course she's a rattled old drunk now, but that's what happens with women of that caliber."

Reggie came over and joined the two women. He didn't like the look on their faces at all. "Well," he said with false heartiness, "how is my wife-to-be getting along with my favorite sister?"

Gertrude stood up and embraced her brother. "I think she is much more intelligent than we give her credit for. We had a most interesting talk, didn't we, Miss Morgan? About you, of course, Reggie."

"Of course," said Reggie. But Gertrude's expression chilled him and he felt acutely uncomfortable.

"Now I must go," said Gertrude. "Harry and I are going to the opera tonight. Thank goodness we are all packed and ready to leave the day after tomorrow." She smiled at Gloria. "My son Cornelius is getting married in Paris next month," she added. "He's a tall, handsome boy—just your age, I believe, Miss Morgan. I'll be sure to introduce him to you when he returns." With that, Gertrude left them.

Gloria began to cry. "What's the matter?" Reggie asked.

"I'm afraid I drank too much champagne," sniffed Gloria, dabbing at her eyes with a handkerchief. "I'm awfully silly, really, but you Vanderbilts are frightening, en masse."

"We Whitneys aren't frightening, are we?" said Harry, coming up to them.

"You're the most frightening of all," said Reggie, putting his arm around Harry's shoulders.

The two men glanced at each other and smiled, and Gloria sensed the deep friendship they shared. It really quite moved her to see that her husband-to-be cared so much for another human being.

"How did you get along with my wife, Miss Morgan?" said Harry in his warm husky voice.

"I wouldn't want her for an enemy."

"Do you have enemies, Miss Morgan?" said Harry with a mischievous twinkle.

"I don't have anything that people should want, so why should I have enemies?" said Gloria simply.

"You have me," said Reggie, kissing her cheek.

"Do I?" she said sadly.

"That's a fine way to talk to your future husband!" grinned Harry.

"After all," said Reggie, "we're getting married in two weeks."

Gloria burst into tears again, and Fred Vanderbilt, who had been watching the girl, now joined the trio.

"My dear," he said, gently touching her hair. He felt an amazingly youthful sensation of love and caring that surprised him. "Won't you make an old man happy by honoring him with this dance?"

Gloria couldn't help smiling and the white-haired gentleman and the young girl floated off. Fred moved in a slow step that was at once dignified and amusing.

The two brothers-in-law watched Gloria's graceful movements. "I've lost her," said Reggie darkly. "Gertrude doesn't like her."

"Well, I like her," said Harry brightly.

Reggie turned haggard eyes on him. "I knew *you'd* appreciate her," he said quietly.

"Listen, old boy," said Harry, "you come to the Racquet Club tomorrow for lunch and I'll give you what you want."

Reggie took a deep breath. "That's white of you, Harry."

"We old New Yorkers must stick together. And you

mustn't lose a girl like that, Reggie. She's special, and I'm all for her. Now don't look so depressed, old boy. You'll have whatever you want tomorrow."

They fell into their old pleasant rapport, talking about polo, tennis, and shooting, like the good sportsmen that they were, and of course about women, another shared interest.

"There's nothing like a seventeen-year-old," said Harry, watching Gloria. "Gertrude can't move that way anymore."

"You're jealous, aren't you, Harry?" Reggie gloated.

Harry made no reply and the two stood quietly for a time, watching Gloria.

The object of their desire was following the careful steps of old Mr. Vanderbilt.

"You were right, Mr. Vanderbilt," Gloria was saying. "Mrs. Whitney offered me money to get rid of me."

"And what did you do, my beauty?"

"I refused." Gloria tossed her head angrily.

"I'm glad," he said. "I want you in the family so I can see you all the time."

Gloria shook her head. "Perhaps Reggie *should* marry the Harriman girl or the Frick girl."

"They're middle-aged, my dear," said Fred. "And you can give Reggie an heir. I shall talk to Gertrude."

Across the room, Florence Twombly joined her niece on the sofa. "You're very quiet, Gertrude. Are you tired, my dear?"

"I suppose I am," said Gertrude.

Florence, like Grace, equated work with social life. So she said, "We society ladies have an existence far more taxing than most people realize."

"No, darling," said Gertrude, "I gave up the party life long ago. Mother's society life is only for imbeciles and pretty young girls on the make, who can use these imbeciles." Her eyes rested on Miss Morgan.

"Look at the way she wiggles her behind!" said Florence. "No wonder Reggie's so besotted."

"And Harry, too," observed Gertrude, suddenly tensing. Her husband had cut in on Uncle Fred and begun a more lively dance with the adventuress.

The only way to get rid of her hostility was to take it out on her old rival. Springing to her feet, she headed toward Grace.

"Well, Grace dear, so here you are! We never see you anymore. I thought you were dead or something."

Grace stiffened. "Hardly, my dear. Just terribly busy. I gave a brilliant dinner for the king of Belgium last night. I would have called you but I didn't have your number."

Gertrude smiled graciously. "I wish I could afford to give so many parties. You entertain a good deal in Europe, don't you?"

Grace nodded. "If you're going to be in London this spring, do telephone. I'm entertaining the duke of York and his bride-to-be, Elizabeth Bowes-Lyon, and then Edwina and Dickie Mountbatten are giving their usual ball for me. And my niece, the duchess of Roxburghe—"

"Grace, do stop dropping names. My head is swimming."

The two glared at one another. "You're handsomer than ever, Gertrude," said Grace nastily. "Perhaps you'd have been happier as a man."

"If I were a man, I'd knock you across the room this very moment."

Suddenly everything went to pieces. Reggie, who didn't like the way Harry was dancing with Gloria, literally pulled the couple apart. "We're leaving!" he commanded, dragging her away.

Eighty-year-old Alice had trouble catching up with them. "Reggie!" she called breathlessly. "You can't leave now; Queen Marie hasn't arrived yet!"

"You know where you can put Queen Marie," he retorted.

"I'm here! I'm here!" cried a dramatic voice in the hall. And in came the queen herself with her nephew, Prince Hohenlohe, and a dozen or so bright young people they had picked up along the way.

Now it was Alice's turn to be furious. "Good evening, Marie," she said. "I suppose there are more friends coming!"

"Yes," said the queen, shaking her tiara. "Darling Leopold promised to meet us here with his retinue. Are you serving dinner?"

"That's at my house," said Grace, rushing to royalty's side with her usual obsequiousness.

"They are dining with *me!*" said Gertrude, right behind her, and the two tigers were at it again with renewed viciousness.

Queen Marie loved every minute of it. "There's nothing like a family fight to clear the air," she said. "Why, it's just like a Balkan revolution."

Meanwhile, handsome Prince Hohenlohe, who hadn't seen Gloria since the old London and Paris days and was unaware of what was happening, asked her to dance. Harry was furious to see a man almost as handsome as himself—and thirty years younger—paying court to Gloria. "Come, Gertrude," he said, "we're leaving!"

"Gloria, I forbid you to dance with Hohenlohe," said Reggie coldly. "Enough is enough!"

"Oh, I feel so at home here," cried Queen Marie. "Now, dear Mrs. Vanderbilt," she said turning to Alice, "I really would like a simple little picnic here for thirty or forty of my dearest friends in New York, to pay them back. I'm such a capricious creature and I love doing things on the spur of the moment. Summon your chefs, my dear, and I'll tell them just what to do," she concluded regally.

Alice had had one stroke already and felt on the verge of another. Her chefs would probably walk out and there would be a horrible scene in the kitchen. Who said that rich people led an easy life?

In the hall, the footman helped Reggie into his mink-collared topcoat. Gloria noticed that his hands were shaking. A strapping yellow-haired footman with tiny malicious blue eyes passed a tray of whiskey and soda before Reggie, who downed one.

"Who is that new footman, mother?" demanded Gertrude.

"His name is Fielding," replied old Alice, "and he's a clever lad."

"I don't like his expression," said Gertrude. "He's a troublemaker!"

As the Whitneys and Gloria and Reggie were going out the door, handsome King Leopold and his retinue were just coming in.

"This party is dreadful," said Gertrude. "Do come and dine with us, Leopold."

Grace raced across the marble floor, drawn like a fly to the oily flypaper in her father's shack, long ago. She hadn't run like this since she'd chased her husband. "My dear Leopold, you're dining with me!" she trilled.

In front of the embarrassed monarch the two women had yet another battle. Somehow, she didn't know how, Gloria found herself in Reggie's car. All of Reggie's town cars had portable bars in the rear and now he fixed himself a strong brandy and tossed it down with his usual speed.

"What a disaster," he laughed, the shakes subsiding.

"Reggie, I can't marry you."

"Now, Gloria, every family party isn't like this one!"

"You must marry the Harriman girl, or the Frick girl, and I shall never see you again." She burst into tears.

Reggie comforted her as best he could. "Harry is giving me the money," he told her. "We're in clover, Gloria!"

But she had a presentiment about Harry and cried all the more.

That evening at home alone, Gloria made up her mind not to marry Reggie Vanderbilt. The sacrifice made her feel noble and she had another good cry and watched the sun rise.

At noon Wann brought in a black velvet box. When Gloria opened it she found the largest and most brilliant diamond she had ever seen. What young girl doesn't change her mind? Ahead lay the wedding, and Gloria began to plan for the future.

CHAPTER
13

For her wedding Gloria wore a classic satin dress embroidered with lace, with a twelve-foot train of tulle. Uncle Fred had sent her a diamond tiara, Aunt Adele had sent a diamond-and-pearl bracelet, and Alice Vanderbilt had sent her a pair of pear-shaped diamond pendant earrings that weighed five carats each. Reggie gave her an important diamond stomacher. She wore all of them at the wedding.

As she moved down the aisle to Mendelsohn's "Wedding March," Gloria saw her girl friends from the Convent of the Sacred Heart, and the college boys, staring at her bug-eyed. And no wonder.

The wedding was simple and quiet—just the family and 300 friends. After the ceremony, the wedding party and family returned to Alice's house where the many gifts had been laid out in a large drawing room for all to see. As Gloria danced with Reggie, the many mirrors told her she looked suitably "Vanderbilt." But Gloria was dreading the moment when she would know her groom in the biblical sense of the word.

Mama had told her that men were swine. And Thelma had said that Junior was a beast on their honeymoon. What would Reggie be like? Gloria glanced at him as they danced and tried to calm her fears, but her mother-in-law stirred them up all over again when they stopped to chat a moment later.

"Have a child right away," Alice advised.

"I'll try, Mrs. Vanderbilt," said Gloria, gulping.

"Be patient with Reggie. He's really just a big, overgrown baby," Alice added kindly.

In the glare of flashbulbs, the couple sped away in a waiting car, to Grand Central Station, where porters recognized the newlyweds and almost instantly a crowd surrounded them. Finally, in royal style, they were led downstairs to the Vanderbilts' private railroad car.

After dinner Gloria got into bed and lay there terrified. When Reggie came in, dressed in pajamas and silk dressing gown, she began to cry. "Oh, Reggie, I'm so frightened," she sobbed.

"Frightened of me?" he asked incredulously, sitting down on the edge of the bed to comfort her.

"Mama said that you men are swine, and Thelma said you are beasts and only interested in one thing."

"What a thing to say!" said Reggie.

"It's true, isn't it?" Gloria blurted out, pulling the sheets high about her.

Below them the wheels turned swiftly. The water glass vibrated on the table and the walnut-paneled coach creaked and groaned as the locomotive gathered speed.

His bride's innocence suddenly dampened his ardor. He rather dreaded deflowering her. "In good time," he said, standing up.

"Oh, Reggie, you are a gentleman," she said gratefully.

"Whenever you're ready, I'm ready," said Reggie, laughing.

He rang for the valet and presently Norton came in. "I've decided to sleep elsewhere," said Reggie. "Could you make up a bed for me?"

Such was their wedding night.

In the following weeks Reggie was very attentive to his bride. Springtime was the loveliest season in Newport, and Sandy Point Farm was ablaze with hyacinths, white and yellow tulips, and later the delicious lavender blossoms on the lilac bushes outside her French windows.

Most of the day Reggie was in riding clothes, talking to his trainers and grooms and watching the champion horses trot around the ring. Gloria spent hours in the library thumbing through her husband's leather-bound volumes of *Country Life* and *Illustrated London News* that spanned a fifty-year period.

"Your husband's a famous turfman," Thelma had written her, "so get interested in his subjects and try to be a stimulating companion for the dear old man."

"The dear old man" himself was growing rather nervous and impatient. By the end of April he was bemoaning his loveless state to Norton, his valet and confidant.

"Patience, sir," Norton replied. "She's only a child. . . ."

So Reggie tried to remain patient and understanding about his wife's fears, although his temper often flared and he sometimes became grumpy and uncomfortable in her presence. And his drinking was increasing, especially when he was alone.

"The time has come, Reggie Vanderbilt," he kept muttering to his reflection in the dressing mirror. "Take the bull by the horns, old boy. It's now or never. . . . My nerves can't stand this much longer. . . !"

So one rainy spring evening when his nerves were raw and his temper short, he strode into Gloria's bedroom after dinner. He stood there in a gray dressing gown smelling fragrantly of Guerlain, with which he'd hastily doused himself, arms folded across his chest in a gesture of firmness.

Gloria was sitting on the bed reading one of Thelma's latest letters. She had changed after dinner into a frilly blue nightgown and matching bed jacket. She put the letter down in surprise at her husband's intrusion.

Reggie gave Gloria a significant look. "It's time, Gloria," he said quietly.

For a moment she was unsure of his meaning. Then she realized he meant to make love to her, and she flushed. But to his surprise she smiled up at him invitingly and patted the side of the bed.

"Sit down, darling," she said, taking his hand. "What a beautiful dressing gown. Sulka? You're always so well turned out—it makes me proud to be on your arm."

Reggie beamed. His heart leapt. This was the moment! "I should have thought to order champagne for this occasion. But I have brandy in my room. Would you like some?"

"You love brandy, don't you, Reggie?" she said softly, glancing up at him.

"Alcohol understands me," he replied, watching her young face with a pang. Seventeen? She appeared much younger, with a ridiculous ribbon through her hair and that girlish baby-blue nightgown.

"I understand you, Reggie dear," she said sympathetically.

"Do you?" There was a melancholy droop to his lips as he begged for reassurance.

Her heart melted. She wanted to give her tormented husband all the love and compassion she could muster. Without a word, but blushing violently, she leaned over and turned off the lamp. Slowly but resolutely she took off her bed jacket and then her nightgown. In the moonlight she could see Reggie disrobe as well. She was glad the shadows did not completely reveal his naked figure as he approached her. Now she would become a woman—perhaps a mother.

When he began kissing her, she kept her eyes open. And later, when he was panting over her and she felt a stab of pain, her eyes were still wide open. Afterward there was an expression of bewilderment and vague disapointment in them, which her husband did not see.

Presently the happy bridegoom rolled over on his side and in a matter of minutes was snoring away. But Gloria could not sleep. And when the light grew brighter at the corners of her curtains, she was still wide awake. She lay there listening to the early-morning sounds: barking dogs, cocks crowing, birds singing. The fragrance of the lilacs drifted through the open windows, but she felt nothing. Indeed she felt a curious emptiness.

Thelma sent a cable from Biarritz: SEND EVERY DETAIL OF HONEYMOON BLISS. But Gloria couldn't write her twin for many weeks. Finally one night in New York, where they'd gone for a *Ziegfeld Follies* opening, she drank a lot of brandy and champagne and the next morning, still tipsy, she sent off a telegram to Thelma. REGGIE TOO THRILLING FOR WORDS. BEING A WIFE IS THE ONLY JOY FOR A WOMAN. SUGGEST YOU TRY IT, DARLING. As she wrote the words, a mocking smile curved her lips.

But if Gloria wasn't always happy, Reggie apparently didn't notice. He was happier, certainly, than he had been before. He became more jovial, improved his appearance by losing some weight, and started taking Gloria on the town again. He continued to shower her with presents and paid the bills that cultivated her taste in expensive clothing. All seemed bright on the surface.

Only Norton, the valet, saw the situation as it really was. Mr. Vanderbilt was drinking more brandy these days, and he kept murmuring, "Why wasn't I born handsome and charming like Alfred or Harry—eh, Norton? What do you think?"

"You cut a very nice figure yourself, Mr. Reggie," replied the loyal valet. "And the downstairs servants agree with the society columns—you two do make a striking couple, sir."

Reggie twirled his thick chestnut mustache. "Well, *she's* striking in any case. I suppose they're all saying that she's far too young for me, and that I'm too old and worn out to make her happy. But she *is* happy, don't you think, Norton?"

"Yes, sir, Mrs. Vanderbilt is a vision," Norton agreed, though in truth he'd often noticed the way she nervously tapped her long red nails on tabletops, and her eyes sometimes had such a vacant stare that it disturbed him. . . .

At the end of May, Reggie grew restless at Sandy Point Farm and booked passage for Europe. Half the fun of going to Europe was getting there, and midnight sailings gave an extra sparkle to the ocean voyage. And so it was on an evening in June that Gloria and Reggie planned to board the *Berengeria*, the most fashionable ship of the decade. A grandiose liner, named after Richard the Lionhearted's queen, it had a distinguished black hull, a white bridge, four towering red stacks, vast public rooms, and elaborate staterooms. It excited Gloria's imagination to think this ship had once been the pride and glory of the kaiser, before the English had taken it after World War I.

As usual they would travel like royalty. Twenty-four Louis Vuitton trunks, sixteen suitcases, hat and shoe boxes, golf bags, and of course dogs. Sometimes, but not this time, Reggie even took along a horse. A fleet of footmen were to be sent down to the docks before sailing, then two Rolls-Royces would carry first Mrs. Vanderbilt and later Mr. Vanderbilt and their friends across town to the Hudson River at the 50th Street pier.

On that June evening Gloria arrived early as planned with two footmen and her personal maid, Wann—who was to share the rest of her life with her, the way Norton did her husband's —to see that the staterooms were filled with fresh peonies and that there were enough crystal Lalique vases to go around. The footmen swiftly hung up some Boucher and Fragonard drawings and scattered some of Reggie's horse trophies about to give the Vanderbilt air of luxury.

When Reggie and the rest of their group arrived he found banners hung from the portholes, iced champagne in silver buckets, and bowls of caviar ready to be passed by the liveried footmen. Rock-crystal boudoir clocks with diamond numerals had been placed on kidney-shaped tables that the footmen had brought aboard so that he would feel quite at home. A portable Gramophone was playing "Who?" when Harry Payne Whitney strolled in.

The sight of her brother-in-law, as always, made Gloria feel a little faint; she found his masculinity overpowering. She busied herself with the flowers so that she wouldn't have to look at him, and Reggie and Harry began talking about the forthcoming races at Ascot and Chantilly.

"Gertrude's with her bohemian crowd tonight," Harry was saying, "so I'm on the town, hoping to get into mischief."

Reggie laughed. "You're the only married man I know who acts like a bachelor, Harry." He left to greet more guests in the the next room. Harry approached Gloria. Her gardenia scent excited him and he fingered the expensive going-away present he'd bought for her: a ribbed gold cigarette case, studded with sapphires. She frowned when he handed it to her, and gave it back to him.

"I can't accept this from you, Harry," she told him.

"Then what about a little goodbye kiss?" he chuckled, moving closer.

"No!" she protested. But he took her in his arms and kissed her deeply.

"What do you think I am?" she gasped, breaking away.

"A young woman who needs satisfaction."

"I don't know what you're talking about," she said coldly, and not untruthfully.

"You'll know what I'm talking about when I satisfy you," he said.

She walked away; he followed. "We'll meet in Paris," he whispered.

"I don't think we're going to Paris."

"We'll meet at Ascot. Reggie always goes to Ascot."

"No."

"Saratoga then?"

"No!" she exploded.

Guests in evening dress came in and Gloria went to greet them, happy to escape from Harry's magnetic presence. Swiftly the sitting room filled with people, and Harry was soon sitting next to Rita Lydig. The aging adventuress had the cabin next door and was, as usual, searching for The Great Love. The champagne flowed and the party was in full swing when the gong rang and a terrific blast sounded through the great ship. The engines below began to vibrate.

"All aboard!" cried the steward. "Visitors must now return to shore!"

The guests were happily drunk, and some daring ones like Humphrey Bogart and Helen Mencken, who had recently gotten married, declared they were going to stay on. Of course they didn't, but it excited everyone to think they might and the champagne bottles popped open even faster.

Gloria always became emotional during these shipboard farewells. There'd been many of them throughout her childhood and the prospect always moved her. Everybody was kissing her goodbye, and again Harry took her in his arms and kissed her on the mouth. She felt weak with longing.

Fortunately, Reggie didn't see the kiss, but Rita Lydig, an old hand at flirtation, did, and Gloria didn't like her expression.

It was the following morning. Reggie was in the pool, and Rita and Gloria were walking briskly about the promenade deck, working up an appetite for the eight-course lunch. Rita was explaining that she had crossed on the *Berengeria* with W. K. Vanderbilt when it was the German liner *Imperator*.

"Willie K. was blissful," sighed Rita, remembering her sportsman lover. "He was like Harry Payne Whitney in many ways: magnetic, charming, boyish—the kind of man that causes women to sit up and feel more feminine, all at once. That Harry's exciting, don't you think, Gloria?"

"Yes," said Gloria, and the pain in her heart grew.

Rita stopped and looked at her. "How was your honeymoon?"

"Lovely."

"You're pregnant?"

"Yes, I think so."

"Tell me about your secret life, darling!" cried Rita breathlessly. "Do you thrill, all through, in his arms?"

"Yes," Gloria replied. But she didn't, and Rita, reading her expression, immediately knew it.

"You're so lucky to have Harry Payne Whitney," Rita said.

Gloria blushed furiously. "You're mistaken," she cried. "I hate Harry! I detest him."

"Come now," laughed Rita throatily. "I saw the looks you exchanged last night. And that kiss he gave you—I felt it myself! God, I'd give my soul to have his lips on me. Every woman I know is madly in love with Harry Payne Whitney."

"I hate him! I hate him!" Gloria trembled with rage.

"You're in for a bad time if you hate him like that, my poor little lamb. Oh, you are in trouble—big trouble." Rita gave her a pitying look and drifted off to change for lunch. Women in first class changed their clothes at least five times a day for those crossings—breakfast, lunch, tea, dinner, and bedtime—elaborate toilets, all.

"Well, my little sparrow," said Reggie, showing up in Savile Row plus fours and tweed jacket, "I'm in blooming health today after a massage and a swim. So let's head up to the bar and have a good dry martini before the smoked salmon."

"Reggie," she scolded, "you promised you wouldn't drink until the sun went down."

"You sound just like mother and those doctors," he teased.

"How else can I treat you?" she said hopelessly.

Reggie raised an imaginary glass. "As a father-to-be! Come, let's celebrate."

Reggie, like all big drinkers, could always think of some occasion to celebrate. The Vanderbilts went inside and started up to the bar.

After his first drink Reggie said, "Harry is green with envy that I'm going to be a father."

"Is he?" Somehow her marriage wasn't going the way she'd imagined. She wondered if a child would make a difference.

"Green with envy that I have a horse running at Longchamps, too. He's always saying he wishes he could afford to live the way I do."

Gloria was struck by the irony of his words, but said nothing.

The summer was spent in grand style. Royalty entertained them in London, Paris, Monte Carlo, Rome, Madrid, and Biarritz. Alphonso of Spain and Victor Emmanuel of Italy took a great shine to Gloria; both put out the red carpet for the newlyweds. She also got to see the interiors of the Massimo and Colonna palaces; it amused her to hear Prince

Massimo say that he was more royal than the English royal family because he could trace his ancestry back to the year Christ was born. The only sour note was Reggie's drinking. However, she and Norton became friends and were constantly trying to find ways to divert him so that he wouldn't get to thinking about his old failures and disappointments.

"I hate Harry!" he broke down and cried one night. "I hate my brothers, too. They were all so good-looking."

That was the crux of the matter. Reggie was a disappointed man. He kept saying that life had defeated him.

In August they returned to Newport. Reggie was good for a couple of weeks and stayed away from his hard-drinking chums at those clubs; only once did something set him off and he was drunk that evening when he came home.

In December they spent the Christmas holidays on Willie K's yacht, the *Alva*, anchored in a Palm Beach lagoon. It was a small family gathering, but, as luck would have it, Harry Payne Whitney was there. Gloria spent much of her time avoiding him—though every nerve in her body cried out to run away with him. A silly thought, considering how pregnant she was. The whole resort atmosphere of Palm Beach added to her temptation—the balmy breezes, heavy with jasmine and freshly cut grass; the romantic lunch and dinner parties in those Spanish patios of the Addison Mizner villas. . . . Harry, moreover, was growing bolder and bolder every day and it took considerable skill to stay out of his path.

She rushed back to New York after the New Year, and in the middle of February gave birth to her daughter, little Gloria. She was a dear little thing with the Vanderbilts' slanted eyes and Reggie's full lips. It was touching to see what pride Reggie took in his daughter. He swore that alcohol would never pass his lips again.

He was fine until the christening, some three months later. It took place at their 78th Street town house, off Fifth

Avenue—a gloomy limestone fortress with the usual Vanderbilt splendors but none of the charm of Sandy Point Farm.

Gertrude was to be godmother to the child, and she arrived
that spring afternoon in distinguished company. Mrs. William Randolph Hearst, Edith Gould, Queen Marie, and Uncle
Fred were there, as was Aunt Adele Twombly, in one of
her rare public appearances. Grace Vanderbilt showed up
too, in a dazzling red lace costume. She was still in hot
pursuit of Uncle Fred.

Harry arrived late, in riding clothes, explaining that he'd
just got off the polo field.

"You look awfuly fetching, Harry," said Mrs. Twombly.

Gloria was thinking the same thing, but she busied herself
with pouring the tea. Shortly, however, Wann came in and
said that Prince Hohenlohe was on the telephone. Excusing
herself, Gloria went out into the hall. Harry followed her at
a discreet distance and stood watching her while she talked
animatedly. How pretty she looked, he thought. Skirts were
higher this year and the pleated pink dress gave an even
more graceful shape to her slender legs.

Suddenly Gloria glanced up and caught Harry's eye in
the Chippendale mirror above her. She hung up abruptly,
her face becoming agitated.

Harry went to her and gazed down at her solemnly.
"You've been avoiding me," he said huskily.

She couldn't speak.

"I'll never get tired of looking at you," he said with such
intensity that she began to tremble. "Your hair, your skin,
your breasts—I always want to put my hands around them."

Her blood was racing.

"You will be the great love of my life," he said. "You know
that. . . ."

They stood there in silence, gazing at one another, and
never noticed Reggie when he came out into the hall. He

watched them soberly, then turned away and went directly to the bar.

The party was ending. It was five o'clock in the afternoon and sunshine streamed into the flower-filled rooms. The guests began to leave, and still Gloria and Harry didn't move. Friends and family embraced her, and out of long habit she responded graciously, but automatically.

Gertrude appeared at their side. "I've quite lost my heart to the little girl," she said.

"So have I," said Harry, staring at Gloria.

"I shall take my job as godmother very seriously," said Gertrude.

"Good," said Gloria distantly.

"At times I might even be disagreeable," said Gertrude.

"Really?" said Gloria vaguely.

"I hope you never see me when I'm disagreeable," continued Gertrude.

Gloria was shaken out of her trance. "I shall try to be a good mother," she said to Gertrude.

"Try to be a good wife, too," said Gertrude sharply. "Reggie's in his cups again."

"Oh, my goodness," exclaimed Gloria, and ran swiftly to her drunken husband's side.

A few weeks later the Vanderbilts sailed off to Europe again, this time on the S.S. *Olympic*, another maritime wonder. Gloria was happy to see the shores of America fade, and the routine on shipboard helped to banish Harry from her mind. Once, Reggie caught her staring at the gulls circling in their wake and he said lightly, "A penny for your thoughts."

"Little Gloria," lied her mother. "I was just wondering if she will like Deauville."

"What does a baby know?" said Reggie, irritated. "In any

case, if she doesn't like it, we can move on to Biarritz or Monte Carlo."

The next fifteen months were spent moving from place to place; it seemed Reggie's favorite pastime. If it wasn't by boat, it was by train. All Gloria heard were the shrill whistles of the locomotives as the luxurious cars of the Blue Train clattered down to the Riviera, or the deep horns of ocean liners.

Reggie was more restless than usual these days when they kept packing and unpacking, but Gloria was happy this way. New faces and new places kept her diverted. There was no time to think. In the casinos, in the speedboats, her mind hardly ever lingered on Harry Payne Whitney.

Yes, traveling was the best solution. She didn't want to think about what would happen when they stopped traveling.

CHAPTER
14

Every morning now Gloria awakened at noon. On this particular morning in Paris in the middle of July 1925, Wann, her maid, entered with her café au lait, pulled back the festoons of yellow taffeta, and flung open the long French windows. The birds were twittering in the garden below, the waiters were setting up the lunch tables, and the sunlight resting on the bowls of gardenias reminded her of the water lilies of Monet.

"Have there been many phone calls, Wann?" she yawned, stretching.

"Six calls, madam."

"Are we going to Berlin or are we going to Budapest today?" said Gloria who was still champagne-high from the night before.

"Mr. Vanderbilt said he wishes to go to London this afternoon," said Wann. "But you know how he changes his mind."

"Where is Mr. Vanderbilt, by the way?" said Gloria glancing about the large room.

"He's at Saint Cloud," said the maid, "with his horses."

"Turn on the music, Wann. Something gay. Oh, those Imperial Russians are something! I think I did a saber dance last night."

"Several boxes of flowers came this morning, madam. Here are the cards."

Between sips of coffee, Gloria opened the envelopes and read the cards. They were blunt and to the point—and divinely erotic.

"My face between your thighs—Hohenlohe."

"Yours—Rothschild."

"Hopefully—Gertrude Stein."

Gloria threw back the covers and moved to the window. The awninged garden below made such a pretty picture, for all the world like a Hubert Robert.

"Really, Wann, the Ritz is the only place to stay in Paris. Could you bear to stay anyplace else?"

"I'd rather stay, madam, where Oscar Wilde spent his last two years, for you know I have literary inclinations."

"I, too," smiled Gloria, "but I'm terrified that Gertrude Stein will throw herself upon me. What would I do, Wann?"

"There are many kinds of love, madam, and for myself I'm sorry that I didn't take advantage of many opportunities when I was your age."

"Wann, you're so wicked! But isn't it marvelous?"

The double doors burst open and Thelma breezed in. She looked more than ever the siren in a large picture hat, flowered silk dress, and ankle-strap high-heeled sandals that the girls called "fuck-me" shoes.

Thelma's scarlet lips were taut in her white oval face. "I've just flirted with Valentino downstairs," she cried. "We made a date for this afternoon, but I'm afraid I won't be able to keep it. Lord, give me a champagne, quick!"

"What's the matter, Thelma?" said Gloria.

"Lord Furness is absolutely insane for me," replied Thelma. "He won't let me out of his sight. I think I'm going to marry him."

"Then you've given up on the Prince of Wales?" asked Gloria.

"For the time being," said Thelma. Wann came in with a bottle of Chandon champagne and Thelma poured herself a glass. "Have one, Gloria, I need company."

"I couldn't," laughed Gloria. "There's no blood in my veins anymore, only champagne!"

"What are you wearing today?" asked Thelma rummaging through the closets.

"I don't know; making a decision is such a problem," sighed Gloria.

"Yeah," said Thelma, "it must be a problem with all the hundreds of dresses here—and you've got more shoes than Queen Marie. By the way, she and Prince Hohenlohe have invited us for dinner, and Connie Bennett is here on a vacation from Hollywood. . . ."

An hour later the twins—Mrs. Vanderbilt and the future Lady Furness—were floating through the long corridors of the Ritz Hotel. They were dressed alike in flowered chiffon frocks, large picture hats, waist-length pearls, and white gloves. Their perfume was so strong that it lingered in the corridors afterward. The little fragile slips of dresses seemed barely to conceal their rounded outlines. The necklines were daring; their skin, for which they were famous, glowed like satin.

As they made their triumphant progress down the corridors of the Ritz, stopping at various jewelry displays in lighted glass cases, Baron Rothschild, the maharaja of

Baroda, and the duke of Westminster kissed their hands. Bend Or, the duke of Westminster, was dressed in tight-fitting breeches, which amused the girls since he was well endowed.

Further along the way they also met up with their old friend Constance Bennett, who fell on the girls with kisses and screams. "My darlings," she shrieked, "just learned that Clara Bow took on the whole California football team and I'm fit to be tied! Got any cocaine?"

Although the girls hadn't seen each other for a year, they immediately fell into their old intimacy.

"How was the honeymoon, Gloria?" asked Connie.

Gloria blushed furiously.

"You mean he's impotent?" asked Connie, misreading Gloria's expression.

"No, but he had to wait *weeks* until I was ready. You see, Connie, I was a virgin."

"You were?" said Connie. "I didn't know such things existed except in *Little Women*—and they were dykes."

"*You* certainly aren't," said Thelma wryly.

"How was Dimitri last night?"

"He's a one-two-three man," said Connie.

"Is that better or worse than an eight-hour man?" said Gloria with a giggle.

Connie put a cigarette in a long holder and puffed vigorously. "An eight-hour man takes his time, if you know what I mean. But a one-two-three man is violently, wonderfully passionate. He explodes in you all at once—one, two, three—with lots of yelling and howling and *Mon Dieu*s and My Gods. What a sweat, and what bites and what bruises! Look at my chin."

"When can we meet this Dimitri?" asked Gloria, atingle.

"Listen, toots, I'd never see him again if he saw *you*," Connie laughed. "Hey, we *are* having lunch together, aren't we?"

"If Reggie doesn't decide to go to England." Gloria made a face.

"Let him go alone," said Thelma. "I need you here for support. Here comes the object of my affection." Thelma gave a hollow laugh.

Lord Marmaduke Furness was striding down the hall with his valet. Duke was a big, florid man, slightly vulgar in speech and action, with a Cockney accent that he thought amusing. His father was a newly created lord, so there was nothing historical about him. He wasn't a descendant of the Plantagenets, no ancestor had fought in the Wars of the Roses; he wasn't even a descendant of Charles II by one of his many favorite whores, as so many titled Englishmen could proudly boast. This lord was just rich and powerful. Like Reggie and Bend Or, he was accustomed to having his own way and was a high liver. The three of them, like the Dolly Sisters, who were also operating around Paris those days, thought nothing of losing a couple of hundred thousand dollars at the gambling tables of Monte Carlo and Deauville.

Lord Furness grinned at the three beautiful women. "How about the old boy staking you girls for a Ritz lunch today? I swear I've never seen such a dazzling trio. Which one will I flirt with?"

"Connie and I are taken," said Gloria playfully. "Alas!"

"Well, Thelma," said Furness, "that leaves you, which suits me to a T. How do you like being wined and dined and jeweled?"

"Silly boy," said Thelma, taking his arm and pursing her lips, as if about to be kissed.

"I hope you all have good appetites," said Furness, beaming. "Most of the girls these days are on these bloody diets."

"I'm afraid we're the same. We just don't eat a thing," said Connie, "but we'll keep you company drinking anyway."

Lord Furness and his party lunched under one of the awnings in the summery garden. Flower beds were bright with zinnias and marigolds. The fountains made a pleasing splash. The ancient limestone statues of the Four Seasons took on a happy sheen; sunlight was screened by the green leaves of the horse chestnut trees.

The headwaiter stood at attention by the mighty Lord Furness. What would milord and ladies enjoy for déjeuner today? Duke ordered like a wolf—a main course, a fish course, and a meat entrée—then waited for the girls to order.

Connie spoke first. "I'd like smoked salmon, then some truffles cooked in champagne, then an entrecote with sauce béarnaise. I'll think about dessert."

"My God," said Furness. "Like a bird!"

Thelma giggled. "Replenishes what has to be replenished."

"I know what you mean," said Furness hungrily, staring at Thelma's cleavage.

The conversation was light and risqué throughout the luncheon. Lord Furness paid fond attention to Thelma, while pressing a hard thigh against her leg. Since her sister was occupied, Gloria turned to Connie.

"Lord Furness here is playing the host so divinely," Gloria said sarcastically. But even Connie's appreciative laugh didn't distract the engrossed couple. Connie shrugged and changed the subject. "How is your daughter? Where is the dear thing, by the way?"

Gloria placed her hand over her heart. "I miss little Gloria so terribly," she whispered. "She's in Deauville now and happy as a clam playing in the sea with her nanny—an odious woman, I hasten to add."

Connie's auburn brows went up quizzically. "Why don't you fire her?"

"Mama loves her," replied Gloria, frowning. "And I guess I still have trouble standing up to mama."

Connie gazed at her sadly. "You're still so young, Gloria.

You're either going to have to grow up or find somebody to take care of you."

Gloria fell silent. She was playing with the chiffon scarf about her neck with a grave expression when she saw a man waving to them. He was in tennis clothes and carried a racket, but the light filtering through the trees dappled his face and Gloria was unable to tell who it was. Both Rothschild and Boroda had similar husky figures so she held up her hand to him. "Good afternoon," she said, with a vague smile.

"Good afternoon," said Harry Payne Whitney, kissing her hand. His deep voice was unmistakable.

"Harry! What are you doing here?"

"I *told* you I'd see you in Paris."

"I didn't think you meant it!"

The others were delighted to see him, and they all joined in a general conversation about the joys of Monte Carlo and Cannes and Bend Or's yacht, the *Cutty Sark*.

"Appropriate title," chuckled Harry. He turned his fine blue eyes on Gloria, lingering on her lips and then wandering down to her breasts. She was disconcerted, and in an attempt to divert him asked, "Are you sculpting?"

"I'm *being* sculpted, by my wife. She just set up a studio in Passy."

"Any particular part of your anatomy?" joked Connie.

The rest burst into laughter. The champagne, Harry's presence, the piano music playing all the popular Cole Porter and Irving Berlin songs suddenly gave the lunch party a new dimension. Abandonment took over. Connie and Thelma couldn't take their eyes off Harry's muscular brown thighs and calves which were gleaming with golden sun-bleached hairs. The impressive girth of his chest and arms hit one like a physical blow.

The girls compensated orally. Connie swallowed more champagne, and Thelma stuffed a creamy meringue ball into her mouth.

Only Gloria met Whitney's large blue eyes with a refreshing openness. He was sitting next to her and she tried not to look at his powerful arms.

"Are you staying long?" asked Harry, making love to her with his every action.

"I'm not sure. Reggie was going to Budapest, but now I think he wants to go to London." Talking about Reggie suddenly sobered her up a bit.

"Budapest is wicked," said Harry.

"As wicked as Berlin?" asked Gloria who had heard the most incredible tales of vice and depravity.

"More so," replied Harry. "It's the Paris of the Danube, you know." He lowered his voice. "I wish we could go there together."

She looked away, and Harry didn't pursue it. Instead he asked, more conversationally, "Have you ever taken a cruise to the Greek islands?"

"Reggie wants to take the Orient Express to Istanbul," said Gloria circling the rim of her glass with her finger. "He's the most restless man I know."

They were interrupted by the sudden appearance of a short, stocky individual whom Gloria didn't recognize. In response to the stranger's greeting Gloria held up her hand as usual. "Enchantée," she said politely.

"My dear Vanderbilt, how ravishing," replied the newcomer.

"Lord Rosberry," said Gloria, still confused, "how lovely to see you."

"My dear pussy, I am Miss Gertrude Stein, at your service."

"Oh, my goodness!" cried Gloria. "I thought you were a man."

"People usually do," said Stein with a sly smile. "I bring you regards from Picasso."

Abruptly the famous lady was gone in her famous tweeds

and crew-cut hair. Gloria and Harry bent double with laughter, tears streaming down their faces. God, it was fun to be in Paris.

Presently Harry asked, "Would you like to see Gertrude's studio in Passy?" He took her cigarette from her mouth and put it between his lips.

"Will Gertrude be there?" Gloria trembled at the thought of finally being alone with Harry.

Harry shrugged, smiling slyly, and Gloria suddenly found she had run out of strength to resist.

A little after three, Gloria and Harry were driving out of the wide open spaces of the Place Vendôme bathed in a cool, violet light. They were riding in an open car, a Mercedes that Harry had just bought in Paris. As they turned right into the noisy traffic of the rue de Rivoli, the park of the Tuileries went by. The fragrance of the horse chestnut trees was heavy in the summer afternoon. Glancing up at the stately gray buildings passing by, with their grilled balconies and shuttered windows, Gloria felt that she had never been happier in her life. The man she loved was sitting beside her, his hand fondling hers. She remembered Anna Karenina running away with Vronsky, forsaking child and home for love. Would she do the same?

They were passing the distinguished Crillon Hotel and the Ministry of the Marine. Down the rue de la Paix she caught a glimpse of the columns of the Madeleine, its Greek temple facade shimmering in a midsummer haze. The horses flanking the entrance of the Champs-Elysées stirred a note of triumph in her.

When they entered Gertrude's studio in Passy, Gloria was immediately struck by the sense of life about the immense pristine white room. French windows opened onto the tree-lined boulevard. Bowls of oranges and apples were on the refectory tables. Yellow and white chrysanthemums overflowed vases. From the Victrola came the sensuous strains of Ravel's "Bolero." Two beautiful heavy-furred chows raced toward them, barking and leaping.

Gertrude was standing on a ladder chiseling away on a stone sculpture of a Herculean figure. She was working with great concentration but shot them a quick look.

"Even my dogs lose their heads over you, Gloria. Be careful or they'll ruin your lovely dress."

"It doesn't matter," said Gloria, bending down and fondling the dogs' heads.

"You look like a fashion plate from *Vogue*, Gloria," remarked Gertrude in an ironic way. "You must spend all your time shopping."

"There's not much else to do," Gloria shrugged. "I don't have an avocation or talent like you. I guess the thing I do best is dance."

Harry laughed appreciatively, but Gertrude's lips thinned in disapproval.

Gertrude was wearing corduroy pants and a man's shirt which revealed her boyish slenderness. Gloria thought she was tremendously attractive this way, so different from the image of the grande dame she presented at home. Looking at her now, it didn't seem possible that she could wear elegant raspberry velvet and egg-size rubies. With her tousled hair and that look of creation in her eyes, there was a freedom about her that Gloria envied. Aside from her brief fling at acting, Gloria had never seriously considered having a career. She wondered now if perhaps she should have.

"Harry's figure is hard to work on," said Gertrude irritably. "His arms and shoulders are so massive. Have you noticed the way his shoulders taper down to his waist? And he has none of those awful ridges of fat that some middle-aged men have—like Reggie," she added with a laugh.

"Reggie is addicted to food," said Gloria.

Gertrude kept chipping away without looking up. "There is a sense of power about Harry that I've never seen in any other man," she went on. "Although his mouth can sometimes be a little bit cruel."

Harry laughed. "That's a fine way to talk about your husband."

"Here in my studio I like to get down to the nitty-gritty," said Gertrude. "It's a welcome change from all that empty small talk back home."

"Well, you girls have a heart-to-heart talk then," said Harry, "and I'll bring you back a surprise."

"I wish you'd known my brother Alfred," said Gertrude after Harry left. "He was built like me, tall and spare, and we were both healthy as horses—hardly ever sick. Reggie envied us terribly when we were children— How *is* Reggie by the way?"

Gloria smiled helplessly. "He's at the racetrack all day, and nightclubs all night."

"And you like that?" asked Gertrude.

"I'm adaptable," shrugged Gloria, moving toward the open French window. Across the way was an awninged café where artists sat drinking their brandies and coffees. Further away was a lush green park where women in white were wheeling perambulators. The greenery and the people seemed in soft focus, as though in an impressionist painting.

"Is it good to be so adaptable?" asked Gertrude.

"It's essential if you've moved around as much as I have," said Gloria.

"Sounds tiring," Gertrude commented.

Gloria laughed. "It is."

"But you're strong?" asked Gertrude.

"Thelma is the strong one."

"Are you very dependent on her? Twins usually are dependent on one another. I find dependency fascinating, like all forms of human behavior."

Gloria wasn't used to this kind of conversation; she liked it. "Sometimes Thelma finishes my sentences for me," admitted Gloria. "Sometimes when I'm alone with Reggie I look about the room hoping to find Thelma there."

"Are you dependent on Reggie?"

"In a way," said Gloria tenderly. "Sometimes I feel I'm his mother."

"Sounds very romantic," said Gertrude.

The fading afternoon light cast large yellow squares on the bare hardwood floor. Gloria felt again what a refreshing change it was—just clean, bare space; no hangings, no carpets, no plush upholstery, no clutter. One felt stripped clean—renewed.

Gertrude had stopped working and was watching her. Gloria wondered if she'd sensed the undercurrent between her and Harry. She thought of Harry now and what Gertrude had said about him. Was he cruel? Was he just playing her along to amuse himself? Uneasiness began to grow in her.

"Thelma's going to marry Lord Furness," she blurted.

"Isn't he much older?" said Gertrude.

"I suppose, in Freudian terms, we're looking for father symbols."

"You're only attracted, then, to older men?" asked Gertrude.

"Friedel Hohenlohe is very attractive to me," Gloria confessed. "He dances so superbly—Reggie doesn't dance, you know. Reggie hates small talk, too—like you, Gertrude."

"Yes, we're outspoken. People know where they stand with us," replied Gertrude. "Frankly, I think Reggie and I would have been happier in upper Bohemia, although he's an art patron rather than a creator."

Just then, Harry returned with a tray of iced tea. "I'm the butler today," he grinned.

"Thank God we don't have those armies of butlers and footmen here," cried Gertrude savagely.

Harry handed Gloria a glass. "I make it with mint and a little whiskey," he said.

"Mind reader," laughed Gloria.

"Isn't it incredible, Gloria? Harry can cook, too! I bet you can't."

"No, I can't," admitted Gloria. "I'm hopeless in the kitchen, and in the nursery, too."

Gertrude chuckled. "I like to think that if the Russian Revolution came here, Harry and I could live in one room and cook our meals over a little flame."

The Whitneys exchanged a look that made Gloria feel jealous. "How romantic," she managed to say.

"Romantic I'm not," snorted Gertrude, "but Harry is. I daresay he's been filling your ear with romantic things on this sublime afternoon. Why, look out the windows. Everything about Paris makes one feel romantic—even that terrible Tour Eiffel in the distance, though I've become rather fond of it now, too."

Under Gertrude's steady gaze, Gloria blushed to the roots of her hair. "Yes, I do feel romantic," she said uncomfortably. "They called me Madame Bovary in the convent," said Gloria, remembering. "I'd yearn for a Prince Charming on a white horse to take me away from it all. I suppose I do live in fantasy a great deal of the time."

"You must have some very interesting daydreams. Tell us about them," Gertrude urged.

Gloria felt hypnotized by this powerful woman standing on her ladder. "Well, for example," said Gloria, "when your mother took me to the hospital where the wounded soldiers were, I cried miserable tears every night when I returned home."

"Were you weeping for all of them, or was there one in particular?" taunted Gertrude.

"The first time, for all them. Later, for one in particular. He brought out a feeling in me that not even little Gloria has brought out. You see, he was blind, and I used to lead this big, tall man down to the lunchroom and as I guided him down the long corridors he'd ask me to describe who and what I saw. . . ."

"My dear—" Gertrude began, touched in spite of herself.

"I felt no one in the world needed me so much," Gloria went on, remembering. "Every day he looked forward so to seeing me. I write to him often and think of him, too. He's my age. His family doesn't want him to come home. His face had been destroyed by fire. What will happen to him?" She began to cry.

She wept for the soldier, in part, but most of all she wept because of Harry, and the knowledge that he had a life of his own with Gertrude and that she, Gloria, had no place in it. She realized she could not, would not, pull him away from Gertrude, although in many of her fantasies she saw herself as the temptress, luring men to their downfall. Her tears came also from exhaustion and strain—the constant, frenetic pace since her wedding day, the baby coming so soon. . . .

The Whitneys exchanged worried glances and watched her in silence. Harry went over and patted her cheek in a fatherly way.

"I'm sorry," said Gloria. "I'm terribly emotional at this point." She stared accusingly at Harry.

"Perhaps you're pregnant again?" said Gertrude, eyeing her figure.

"No, no, no! I couldn't—Reggie doesn't—" She blushed again, not wanting to talk of the details of her married life.

"It's getting late," said Gertrude. "Harry, why don't you take Gloria home?"

"Come, my dear," said Harry. "The car is waiting downstairs."

"I'm so sorry," repeated Gloria.

Gertrude watched her pityingly. "Please don't apologize," she said.

Going down in the tiny elevator, Harry wrapped his arms around her and kissed her passionately.

"Please, not now!" she cried, pushing him away. She flung open the grilled doors and ran blindly through the vestibule and out into the street. It was twilight, which came as a shock to her. Where had the time gone? She crossed the pavement and cried out to a passing taxi.

As she was about to step in, Harry caught up to her. "I'll call you later," he said. He was unable to do more since they were directly beneath Gertrude's window.

"I hate you, Harry Payne Whitney!" she cried violently. "I hate you," she said again, but gazing at his handsome face she felt that terrible, treacherous desire sweep over her. His hands with those long phallic fingers greatly disturbed her. "I loathe you, I despise you!"

As the car moved away, the hurt look in his face filled her with joy.

She was still agitated when she returned to her suite at the hotel. To make matters worse, she found her mother there waiting for her.

"Where have you been?" she snapped when Gloria came in.

"Harry showed me Gertrude's studio."

"I'll bet he did more than show you the studio, Gloria Vanderbilt!"

Gloria stopped dead in her tracks. "How dare you talk to me like that!"

"I'll talk to you any way I want, you whore, you hussy!"

She raced over to Gloria and slapped her face. "I can tell you've been making love!"

"Mama, I forbid you to come here again!" cried Gloria trembling. "Get out of my sight."

"Do you think I'll leave you now when your poor husband is dying?" Mrs. Morgan shrieked.

Gloria froze. "What happened?" she whispered.

"The poor man had some kind of a seizure out at the race-track. It's no wonder," she added, "considering the life he's been leading. They're bringing him back to the hotel; I didn't know what else to tell them, since his loving wife was un-available."

Relief flooded Gloria. "He's been weak for some time," she said. "I can't make him stop drinking."

"I hear you've been drinking quite a lot yourself," snapped Mrs. Morgan.

"Why don't you leave me alone, mama? I don't need you here."

Wann came in and announced that Prince Hohenlohe was on the phone. "Disgusting!" mama muttered as Gloria went to the phone.

"Hello? Friedel?" she said faintly.

"No, it's Harry," came the voice from the other end. "Now don't hang up, because it's urgent that I speak with you."

"Friedel, I really can't speak to you now."

"I want you to know that I love you," said Harry. "Do you know what I'm thinking now?"

"No, please don't tell me," she said, her knees wobbling.

"I'm dreaming that I'm coming to you naked in the bed. You're lying there waiting for me. I turn out the light and—"

Gloria slammed down the receiver and screamed. She took up a Ming vase and flung it savagely at the fireplace. Almost immediately the double doors of the bedroom burst open and Gloria was startled to see Emma Keislick, little Gloria's nursemaid.

"What are you doing here?" said Gloria coldly.

"Little Gloria is very ill," said the nurse.

"But only yesterday you told me she was in splendid form!"

"That was a *week* ago, Mrs. Vanderbilt," said Emma venomously. "The Lord be praised, she's sleeping now."

"You mean my child is *here?*"

"She's in a crib in the next room." The nursemaid stood her ground, almost daring Gloria to push past her into the room where little Gloria lay.

Fortunately Wann came in and announced that Baron Rothschild was on the phone.

"You certainly have a lot of admirers, Mrs. Vanderbilt," said mama sarcastically. "Where did you get that new diamond ring?" Emma Keislick and Mrs. Morgan looked at one another knowingly.

Ignoring them, Gloria crossed the needlepoint carpet and again picked up the receiver. If this was Harry again, she'd kill him.

"Hello," she said sweetly. "Baron Rothschild?"

"I'm in you," came Harry's husky voice. "Deep in you, far deeper than any man has ever been in you, so deep that you're shrieking with joy and—"

"How kind of you, Baron Rothschild," she said formally, "but I must decline your invitation for the time being. Thank you."

She collapsed on the sofa.

"Well, I suppose now Valentino will be calling," said Mrs. Morgan. "Come, Emma, let's check on little Gloria while we're waiting."

Gloria was still sitting on the sofa when Norton arrived with Reggie. He was struggling to support the much heavier man, and Gloria rushed to help him. "My darling!" she cried. "What happened?"

"Our horse lost, Gloria."

"Well," she replied brightly, "we'll win at Saratoga!"

Reggie smiled. Seeing his wife's lovely face made him feel better; she always had that effect on him. But his face was gray and Gloria watched him with troubled eyes. She and Norton led him into their bedroom and he lay down gratefully. He felt at death's door, like an animal who senses it is going to die. He couldn't breathe, there was no air. Even now he felt his heart beating with uneven and disturbing jolts, and the lights were dimming. He broke into a chill sweat.

"It will be nice to get home again, won't it, Gloria?" he said quietly.

"I'm dying to see how that Empire bed I bought looks in your bedroom," she smiled, "and I hope you let me come and visit you sometimes in it."

"A cuddle?" he said lifelessly.

"More than a cuddle." She brought his hand to her lips and kissed it.

The maid entered and lowered the heavy, cream-colored Austrian shades. Reggie wanted to say please, don't lower the curtains, but he was too tired to do so. A blessed feeling of sleep came over him and his consciousness was fading. "I'm so tired, Gloria," he said, his voice trailing away dismally.

She stayed there with him as he slept. Dimly she heard the waiters setting up the dinner tables in the garden below. It had sounded so gay this morning, but now . . .

With a sigh she moved into the drawing room. "He's asleep," she said.

"I wish you'd take him to see my wonderful American doctor," said mama.

"I've tried," said Gloria wearily, "but he won't go."

"Tomorrow morning I'll make him take the cure at Vichy," said mama emphatically.

"We tried that," said Gloria. "Reggie walked out halfway through."

Wann answered the ringing telephone. "It's the duke of Westminster," she announced.

"Tell His Grace that I'm not at home," said Gloria, moving toward the other bedroom.

"I want to talk to you, Mrs. Vanderbilt," said the nurse.

"Please," replied Gloria with dignity, "I want to be alone." She closed the door behind her and went to little Gloria.

Asleep in her crib, she looked so sweet and frail. She remained there by her daughter's side, her chin on her hand, gazing down at the sleeping infant surrounded by all the pretty pink and blue silk pillows, and she suddenly remembered Gertrude's words. Yes, she wished she were pregnant again. It was a beautiful feeling carrying a child. Reggie couldn't give her another child, but perhaps Harry. . . ? What a child that would be!

"Mrs. Vanderbilt, it's almost eight o'clock and your guests are arriving for dinner downstairs," said Wann.

"Ask my mother if she'd be my hostess tonight, would you?"

"But, Mrs. Vanderbilt—"

"No, I can't go out tonight."

She didn't dare see Harry again—didn't trust herself enough to see him. The words her mother had flung at her echoed through her mind. No, she thought, I'm going to be a good mother, a good wife. I am, *I am*. . . .

In the middle of the night Reggie Vanderbilt woke up and entered his wife's bedroom. He was startled to see her sitting there by the child's crib. Later husband and wife slept on his bed. They weren't really asleep; they lay there, their backs touching, she staring at one wall and he staring at another. He was wondering how much time he had left, and she was thinking of Harry's veined arms and his words on the telephone. Both felt sick.

Two days later the Vanderbilts sailed home on the *Mauretania*. The French and English newspapers had headline stories on the multimillionaire and his beautiful wife, traveling with twenty-eight trunks, sixteen suitcases, hampers for dogs and cats, madam's jewel case and dressing case, and the sportsman's golf bags and tennis rackets. It was also reported that Mr. Vanderbilt had lost his passport and had kept the liner waiting for three hours at Cherbourg until the American Embassy could give him another. They did not write that Mr. Vanderbilt looked gray and ill, nor that his wife's eyes were swollen and red behind her veiled gray traveling hat. In the English papers there was also a photo of the couple, and people remarked that he was old enough to be her father.

At Claridge's in London, Prince Hohenlohe gazed at the photo for some time. Something about her touched him deeply; she was so frail, so delicate behind her poetic veiling. He sensed her sorrow.

His aunt, Queen Marie of Rumania, watched him, remembering her early love affairs. "Love will find a way, Friedel," she told him. "And you do move in the same circles, here and in America."

A mile away the Prince of Wales was gazing at the same photo. He was sitting in his mother's sitting room at Buckingham Palace, and Queen Mary stood behind him.

"Is she any relation to that Vanderbilt woman who entertains so splendidly, David?"

"Yes, mother," he replied. "Sister-in-law."

Queen Mary looked over his shoulder. "A rare combination—wealth and beauty. Did you meet her on your visit to America?"

"Alas, no," replied the golden-haired prince. "But I will soon. . . ."

CHAPTER
15

When a man feels that he's going to die, how does he choose to spend his last days on earth? Reggie Vanderbilt spent his last two weeks in Newport, grumpy and anxious. He and Gloria had returned from Europe on August 20, stayed overnight at the Ritz in New York because their house was closed there, and motored up to Newport the following day.

The bells in the steepled churches were chiming five o'clock and it was raining hard as they drove through the old town of Newport. Despite Gloria's best efforts, Reggie remained sulky and silent. She gave up and stared out at the landscape with a growing sense of panic.

"Drop me off at the Reading Room," said Reggie.

She gave him a sharp look. "But, Reggie, those clubs are terrible for you." Reggie had been drinking more than ever, despite the warnings of his doctor.

"I have important matters to discuss about the horse show. We've been abroad far too long."

She gestured helplessly. "I don't know why you can't rest up at the farm and then go about your business tomorrow morning."

"I want to see my old pals," he said.

"And get drunk," she added hotly.

"Why don't you go to The Breakers and wait for me there?" He always got around her like this.

"But I don't want to go to The Breakers," replied Gloria. "I want to be with you, Reggie."

"Do you?" His blue eyes watched her accusingly.

"Of course!"

"Mother and all the family will be there. And Gertrude and Harry."

She could think of nothing to say. Worse still, she felt her cheeks flush. Defeated, she watched Reggie climb slowly up the steps of his club, then she sank back in the upholstery and was carried to The Breakers.

In happier times the pretty little New England town with its salt boxes and shingled Queen Anne–style houses had drawn her interest. Now she could only think of Harry Payne Whitney. Where was it all going to end?

They drove through the towering gates of The Breakers and started up the gravel drive. It was lined with trees and their leaves seemed to droop in the rainstorm. The sounds of the foghorns grew louder and the buoys clanged out at sea. Through the rain-spattered glass Gloria glanced up at the splendid facade of the massive stone structure. The Italianate palace was rich with detail: gargoyles and columns and balustraded French windows. The first Breakers had burned down and Reggie's father had ordered the house rebuilt entirely of stone.

A footman met her at the door. "Mrs. Vanderbilt is waiting for you in the drawing room, Miss Gloria."

The ornate marble rooms were cheerless enough on a

sunny day. In the rain they were a tomb of disappointment and sorrow. Her footsteps echoed gloomily through the four-story-high stone hall and an unpleasant damp smell came from the tapestries and velvet. The footmen standing at attention seemed wardens in some medieval prison. She felt crushed by the heavy grandeur.

"Gloria, my dear," said Mrs. Vanderbilt. Quivering with gold fringe and tassels, she rose stiffly out of a wine-red velvet throne chair. "Come sit by the fire and have some tea."

Gloria sank into a chair and put her hands over her eyes. "This morning I saw blood again on Reggie's handkerchief. The doctor said he'd hemorrhage internally if he continued drinking, and now he's at the Reading Room drinking the way he does at the Brook and the Knickerbocker. He loves to hole up in those clubs with those alcoholic cronies."

Alice Vanderbilt patted her shoulder. "We'll think of something, Gloria."

"I hope so," said Gloria, "because I can't think anymore." She spoke with such despair that Alice was alarmed.

"Then you didn't have a rest in Europe, Gloria?"

"Don't be naïve, Mrs. Vanderbilt."

The front door banged shut and footsteps reverberated through the mansion. With horror Gloria heard Harry Payne Whitney's unmistakable voice.

"Harry can help us," said Alice. "He's always such a help in times of misfortune."

Harry strode into the room in riding clothes, and once again Gloria felt that sinking sensation—the sensation of being powerless before him. She had not spoken to him for weeks and now she avoided his eyes. His Irish Setter jumped up on her and she busied herself with him so that she wouldn't have to look at Harry.

"Reggie has been hemorrhaging again," said Alice.

"Is he still drinking?"

"He won't stop, Gloria tells me."

"I'm worried sick," said Gloria faintly.

"Well, Dr. Whitney's here so don't you girls worry." He spoke with his usual charm and authority.

The butler announced a telephone call and Mrs. Vanderbilt excused herself. Harry led Gloria away to the windows facing the sea, far removed from the footman's attention.

"You've been avoiding me, Gloria."

"I've told you I loathe and detest you."

"In Paris you didn't show up at your own dinner party."

"I didn't dare face you," she said.

"Is that why you were so cold to me in Saratoga? Really, Gloria, you didn't have to cut me dead at Piping Rock."

She studied the face that she saw so often in her daydreams. How different he was in reality. The flesh-and-blood Harry was so warm and attractive—there was no cruelty whatsoever.

"Do you think I have no feelings?" she said. "Don't you know I'm insane about you? Yes, that's the word, because I must be insane behaving as I do when Reggie's so sick. What sort of monster have you turned me into? Now *please*, Harry, you must stay away from me! I'm afraid something terrible will happen if you don't—"

The sound of Mrs. Vanderbilt's footsteps on the stone floor came to them and they swiftly broke apart and started to make small talk. Outside the immense windows was a dreary vista of gray sea and stormy whitecaps. The buoys' clanging was unsettling and those foghorns sounded funereal—terrible reminders of Reggie's illness. But wasn't she as sick as her husband? She suddenly yearned with all her heart to be a girl again—to feel a part of the grass and trees and earth and sky. How she loathed the heavy marble walls, the gilded agate columns and furniture that looked like it came from a Catholic church.

"That was Fred," said Alice. "He wanted to know how you and Reggie were. He's very fond of you, Gloria."

"And I of him," said Gloria.

She spoke so dully that the old woman stared. Alice was wearing her inevitable black and her usual dog collar of pearls and diamonds at five in the afternoon. At least, Gloria thought, she's not wearing diamond bracelets like Grace.

"Is something the matter, dear? You don't look like yourself at all."

"I'm not the debutante I was when I married Reggie."

"We all change," Alice said. "You're a wife and mother now. And speaking of that, where *is* little Gloria?"

"The nurse—Emma—and mama took her up to Sandy Point this morning on the train," said Gloria.

"Your mother has really become part of your life," said Alice, who heartily detested Laura Morgan.

"I asked her to leave, but she's got a skin like a rhinoceros. She acts as though the baby were hers."

A foghorn moaned again and all at once Gloria felt things pressing in on her. It was sort of like waking up with a hangover when all the fears and panics took possession of her. She glanced at her mother-in-law and Harry with bewildered eyes. They didn't seem real, nothing seemed real in this fearful house.

Alice Vanderbilt watched Gloria anxiously. "Harry, why don't you take Gloria upstairs and I'll wait for Reggie here. She looks as if she's going to faint on the spot."

Gloria looked desperately at her mother-in-law. No, please, don't leave me with Harry, she thought.

"Come, Gloria," said Harry in that melting voice, placing his hand on her arm.

Moving away on his arm she felt the sweetness and warmth engulf her, and as they started up the grand staircase with its red carpet and velvet handrail, past dully glowing crystal candelabra, she wondered if she was losing her mind. Harry led her into the room and closed the door. . . .

Years later when she tried to remember this room it seemed like it was something from the sea. The windows were open, the heavy curtains billowing out into the room, and there was a haunting smell of seaweed. The Breakers was situated on a point that jutted out into the sea and through the balustraded windows came the sound of the foghorns booming and now and then the clanging of the buoys like some funeral dirge which she was soon to hear over Reggie's coffin.

And Harry—well, of course she remembered Harry. Harry Payne Whitney naked was quite a memorable sight. For years afterward she tried to find a man of such size and proportions. His lips seemed to kiss her all over, muttering things she couldn't quite comprehend. He was infinitely tender and his hands set her aflame as they unfastened the buttons of her blouse.

"Bed," said Harry. "Bed."

"No," said Gloria. "I can't, I can't. . . ."

He slowly entered her, slowly because of his thickness. And then the warmth she always felt in his presence flooded through her entire being. He seemed to make love to her for hours with great understanding and affection and technique. Presently she became aware of a sensation that she had not had before. She arched her body and clutched his powerful arms.

"Harry," she moaned. "Harry, Harry!"

"Are you close?" he whispered.

"Yes, yes!" She felt such exquisite rapture that her eyes rolled back in her head and she dug her nails deep into the ridges of his muscular back.

"Let it come, Gloria. Let it come."

"*Oh, oh, oh,*" she whimpered.

She felt such joy sweep through her. She twisted, turned, gasped. "God," she cried. "God!"

Her cries blended with his, their bodies tensed together, and they fell back on the bed, bathed in sweat, panting.

"You're a woman now, Gloria," said Harry.

"Yes, I'm a woman," she repeated.

"Are you all right," he asked, lighting a cigarette.

"All right? My God!"

"Do you think we'd have a chance together, Gloria?"

"Oh, yes!" she sighed.

Abruptly the door flung open and Fielding, the tall blond footman, started to walk in. When he saw them he stopped, gave them a long look, and then closed the door.

Harry swiftly got out of bed and started to get dressed. She lingered in bed and he said, "Get dressed, you little idiot!"

"What will we do?" she whispered.

"Nothing," said Harry coolly.

"But what if he tells Mrs. Vanderbilt?"

"He's no fool," said Harry. "Don't you know that these kinds of things happen all the time?"

"You mean millions of other people are committing adultery like this all over the world?"

"They know a good thing," grinned Harry. "It *was* good, wasn't it, Gloria?"

As if on cue Reggie's dogs started barking downstairs. Gloria started. "Oh, my God, Reggie's here! What will we do, Harry? Jesus, my teeth are chattering."

He went over to her and patted her face. "Get dressed," he said calmly. "Fix your hair and come down as soon as possible. And for God's sake, don't look at me; you're in my blood, Gloria." He closed the door and left her alone.

Those terrible foghorns were booming and the mist seemed to be coming into the room. She rushed to the dressing table and tried to brush her hair into smooth waves; heard Reggie's voice downstairs and dropped the hairbrush. She peered at herself in the mirror. "You've committed adultery, you bitch," she cried aloud. "Now there's no hope for you." Yes, it was the hellfires that mama had always promised.

She heard footsteps in the corridor and for a moment she thought Reggie would enter the room. But it wasn't Reggie, it was a sweet nineteen-year-old Irish maid, Mary.

"Oh, I'm so glad you came," cried Gloria on the verge of hysteria. "I can't bear to be alone. Help me get dressed, will you?"

"Yes, ma'am." Her brogue was thick and she gave a shy curtsy first.

"You've just come from Ireland?" Gloria asked gently.

"Yes, my married brothers sent me here to earn some money for them."

"For them?" Gloria said, startled. "Can't they earn any?"

"Times are bad in Ireland, ma'am. They always are, you know. So I send them half my wages."

"That's terrible," said Gloria, getting out of herself and feeling better.

"Fielding says the same. He's the new footman, ma'am, tall and good-looking."

"Is he blond?" asked Gloria with a sinking heart.

"Yes, he is."

"What sort of person is he?" asked Gloria carefully.

"Ambitious, ma'am."

Gloria closed her eyes and put her hand to her forehead. The girl couldn't have said a worse thing.. Now she was sure that Fielding would blackmail them. Aloud she managed to say sweetly, "In what way is he ambitious, dear?"

"He doesn't want to remain a servant, ma'am. He says he's unhappy here."

"I hadn't thought of that," said Gloria slowly.

"Rich people don't often think of us poor people, ma'am."

"But Mrs. Vanderbilt is easy to work for, isn't she?"

"Fielding said he'd rather work for General Pershing." Mary clapped a hand over her mouth, aghast at her own temerity, and added, "Begging your pardon, ma'am."

The maid continued talking about her life at The Breakers and Gloria half-listened while pursuing her own thoughts. That ambitious Fielding boy was going to be difficult to handle. What if he went to Gertrude? Gloria would rather go to the electric chair than face her. And what if she was downstairs now?

Aloud she said, "Mary dear, is Mrs. Whitney downstairs?"

"Yes, she and the countess just came back from a bridge game; the other maids will help them get dressed before dinner."

"You couldn't bring me a little sherry, dear, could you? These gray, damp evenings are strangely disturbing, don't you think?"

"Aye, there's the thunder too," said Mary going out the door. She returned with a small glass on a silver tray and Gloria gulped it down.

Presently Gloria descended the grand staircase, past different-colored marble columns and stupendous marble-topped consoles and the inevitable footmen standing at attention by the inevitable potted palms. As she moved down the red-carpeted stairs she wished that she had someone to protect her. Naturally Harry couldn't stand up for her, and Reggie was now wearing a pair of horns. Her lips became taut and she clutched the handrail.

Viennese waltzes were playing, a custom that Gladys and her Hungarian count had established in hopes of making the place more cheerful. From the billiard room came the sound of Harry and Count Schenye playing pool. From the drawing room came Gertrude's penetrating voice discussing the dangers of publicity and how she wished Reggie wouldn't

be written about so much. "You never read about the Rockefellers, mother," concluded Gertrude heatedly.

"But they aren't in Society," said Alice Vanderbilt.

"Lucky them," said Reggie drunkenly.

In walked Gloria, head high, her figure straight and full
of grace, moving delicately in her high-heeled French pumps.
The lamps had been lit and now her auburn hair shone. Her
suit, like all of her clothes, was draped in a classic line,
elegant and seductive at the same time. This beige classic
was by Jean Patou, who admired Gloria a great deal.

Plain little Gladys stared at her resentfully. She told
people that she detested parties, but in truth she was never
invited to any and was dying to go to them.

"My dear Gloria," drawled the countess. "My maid
showed me an article about you in the tabloids today, and
every day I read articles about you by Cholly Knickerbocker
in *The Journal.* Why on earth are you so written about?"

"I'm colorful, I guess. Both my twin sister and I lead
fascinating lives. Last week my sister had the Prince of
Wales at her ball, and I'm married to Reggie Vanderbilt."
She went to Reggie and put her arm on his in an intimate
gesture.

The thunder was growing ominous now and Reggie raised
his glass in a salute. "Here's to you—and my bootlegger!
This is the best whiskey in town."

"I do wish you'd come to Budapest," said Gladys. "I'd
arrange for Dr. Freud to see you, dear."

"There's nothing wrong with me," said Reggie, "except
life is not at all what I thought it would be."

"We all suffer from that," said Gertrude. She spoke so
spitefully that Gloria met her eyes. Her stomach sank. What
hate she saw written on Gertrude's face. Gertrude couldn't
possibly know what had happened in the upstairs bedroom,
Gloria assured herself nervously. Damn, that grumbling
thunder was giving her a headache again.

"Let's go home, Gloria," said Reggie. "Unless you'd like to spend the night here."

"No," she shivered, "I'd like to go."

Harry strode in. "You mean you're not staying to dinner?" he boomed heartily.

"I'm drunk," confessed Reggie with a wry grin. "Couldn't eat a thing."

"You *should* eat," said his mother, looking at him worriedly.

"I'll make him something so scrumptious that he won't be able to resist," said Gloria brightly.

"You mean the cook will," said Gertrude sarcastically.

Somehow Gloria managed to get out of the drawing room and into the hall. Later they drove for ten minutes to Sandy Point Farm in silence. The rain was coming down in thick sheets and the lightning lit up the landscape. Reggie had reached a point in his drunkenness where all of his old grievances and disappointments were running through his head. This time he regretted not being in the army.

"I wish I could have done one heroic thing in my life," he said. "Otherwise I haven't amounted to a hill of beans. You know, I often think, Gloria, what would have happened to me if I hadn't been born Reggie Vanderbilt? How could I support myself? When you don't work, it's easy to criticize those who do, but I doubt if I'd even be a good accountant or bricklayer. Perhaps I could have been a good footman," he muttered.

"It would have been romantic to fall in love with a footman," said Gloria. "I would have been the kitchen maid at The Breakers and we would have met and fallen in love."

He didn't seem to hear her.

"I would have liked to have done something first-rate—"

His words were interrupted by a flash of lightning that struck a tree in front of them. To Gloria it seemed the wrath of God had struck her and she gave a little cry and nestled close to her husband. Husband? Reggie didn't seem like a husband anymore.

In the middle of the night Gloria awakened in her room. The thunder was so loud it seemed as though it were going to burst right in. Swiftly she put an a dressing gown and trailed downstairs and on into the drawing room.

"You've come down for a drink, too," said Reggie, slumped over a black lacquer table desk.

"I couldn't sleep," she said.

"What demons kept you awake?" said Reggie grinning boozily. "Show me yours and I'll show you mine."

It wasn't the thunder alone that had awakened Gloria; she had had a terrible nightmare about Harry Payne Whitney. She could still feel his lips on her breasts. God! She couldn't very well tell that to her husband, could she?

"Demons?" she repeated. "My demons are all self-in-flicted."

"Aren't they all?" said Reggie.

"Mama's after me, and that terrible nursemaid, Emma, like the furies from the Greek chorus."

"Well," he said, raising a glass of whiskey, "why don't you get rid of them?"

"I—I can't," stammered Gloria.

He shoved a bottle in front of her. "Have a drink, Gloria. Forget all your disappointments—for you are disappointed you know."

"Am I?" she said, and again the image of Harry Payne Whitney came before her.

"First of all," he said, "you're disappointed in me."

She put her hand over his mouth. "Stop that whiskey talk, Reggie."

"Why don't you admit it?" he said. "There's nothing so bad about being disappointed. I think you're disappointed that you didn't marry a man like Lord Furness who has yachts and is full of life. I'm always sick, it seems." He finished the last words with such a sorrowful inflection that she wanted to cry.

"I'll make you well," she said. Her Edith Cavell/Jane Eyre fantasy sprang to the fore.

"Have a drink first."

"All right," she said, "if you promise you'll come to bed with me immediately afterward."

"I think I'll just stay up all night until we go to Saratoga."

"You'll be in fine shape to go to Saratoga," she mocked. She'd been drinking too much herself recently and she didn't like the idea of drinking whiskey at four o'clock in the morning. But she had to admit that after the first glass she felt infinitely better. Even her guilt about Harry seemed to fade. And after she finished her second she became defiant. Why shouldn't she have a man like Harry? Presently she turned on the Victrola and did a little dance. She hoped that her graceful movements would take him out of his dark thoughts, but they didn't.

"I must put my life in order," he kept saying thickly.

"No more whiskey talk," said Gloria, pulling him to his feet. Slowly they moved through the marble-columned hallway and up the curving staircase. They entered his Napoleonic bedroom and she helped him into the mahogany sleigh bed that she'd bought him in Paris. He started to groan when she slipped in between the heavy linen sheets and put her arms around his waist. He seemed to like feeling her close to him, and by the time the light was gray outside the windows and the birds were singing in the trees, both husband and wife were asleep.

A few hours later, at eight o'clock, the French-style manor house with its tall slate roof and four towering chimneys was beginning to awaken and open its shutters. Reggie adored anything English and it was no coincidence that the rambling countryside about his château resembled a Gainsborough woodland setting. The house itself was secluded and private, set at the end of a long drive and shaded by stately elms and oaks and privet hedges. It had thirty-two rooms and was considered by the Vanderbilt-Whitney enclave as dear, sweet, and cozy; but Gloria found it far more beautiful than Uncle George Vanderbilt's house, Biltmore, which was ten times larger and set in sixty thousand acres in Ashville, North Carolina. It, too, was a gentleman's farm with tenant farmers that looked after the place.

This morning the mist was rising from the Seconic River and lingering wetly over the stables full of horses and silos full of hay, both of which gave forth a damp fragrance. Like the army, the maids and footmen were awakened at 7:30, so already they were cleaning the dining room, a finely proportioned chamber with Watteau-type wall panels of misty green and blue, and sweeping up the splendid drawing room which ran the length of the house, some sixty feet, and had eighteen-foot ceilings. Three maids in little dust caps, starched black dresses, and high black stockings were dusting and polishing where a few hours earlier Gloria and Reggie had been drinking and smoking. Upstairs, Gloria's dress was already picked up, pressed, and put away in a closet; she never viewed any disorder, although her mother thought it would have been better if she had.

Mrs. Morgan herself was already up and having breakfast with the nursemaid, Emma. The two had become intimates, a friendship based on their similarly demented thinking, and their conversation this morning was, as usual, intensely critical.

"It's amazing to me," said Emma, "that a fine woman like yourself should have two such wicked daughters. I pray for their souls every day."

"Yes," said mama, chewing on a French brioche, "Gloria and Thelma were always wicked. I tried so hard, but they were completely unmanageable. Now they've both married sick old men. Mark my words, Furness will be done in soon by that vixen."

"Really?" said Emma, hopefully. "I had no idea he was so—"

The cries of little Gloria interrupted their early-morning talk. The child was more holy to them than the child in the manger and now Emma sprang to her feet with amazing agility for so large and heavy a woman.

"If something happened to Reggie," said mama, "I daren't think what would become of our little angel."

Emma nodded her big gray head. "At five she'll probably be swilling gin and dancing the Charleston all night."

"Not while I'm here," said Laura Morgan grimly. "Oh, I bear a heavy weight on my shoulders, Emma, but as long as my baby isn't tainted . . ." Mama sprang up in her high-strung manner, her hands to her sleek black hair. "While you see to the baby, I'll go downstairs and see to my daughter," she said grimly.

Muttering evil things under her breath, mama pushed rudely into Gloria's bedroom, to which Gloria had just returned.

"You might knock," said Gloria glancing up at her mother. She was sitting in front of the vanity examining the dark circles under her eyes.

"You don't look well, Gloria," said Mrs. Morgan viciously. "What man kept you up last night?"

"As it happens, my husband," Gloria retorted. "Satisfied? Does that make me a good and loyal daughter?"

"Good daughter," snorted mama, "the two of you running off without a thought for your poor mother—"

"We didn't run off. It was your idea that—"

"—and leaving me with your father. I'm divorcing him, by

the way. I've wasted enough time on him. Now my duties
lie in South America."

Gloria tried to hide her joy by turning away and starting
to brush her hair. "You're returning to Chile, mama?" she
said, trying to sound sad.

"Soon, soon," mama said. "Now don't bat those big brown
eyes at me, Jezebel. I know what you're up to. Word travels
fast at The Breakers."

To conceal her agitation, Gloria moved over to the fireplace and smoothed the soft waves of her hair. "What do
you mean?"

"Fielding has a big mouth," said mama slowly, enjoying
the look of fear that crossed her daughter's pale face. "Flannel
mouth, they call him in the kitchen. Of course Emma and I
don't like to believe servants' gossip, but in your case I tend
to believe the boy."

Gloria turned around and faced her mother with blazing
eyes. "Mama, you must go! Right away! I cannot take your
innuendos any longer. You're making me quite ill."

"You *are* ill," said mama. "You have an illness of the
spirit. I'm going to say a mass for you today so that you'll
not be eternally damned. A fine man like Mr. Whitney
seduced by your easy charms. I pray for him, too!"

Gloria felt faint. "Fielding's a fool," she said. "If this story
of his gets around, I'll tell Reggie and his mother. They'll
fire him and give him a bad reference, and then where will
he be?"

"Fifty thousand dollars richer," said mama.

"What *are* you talking about?"

"Blackmail," said mama.

Wann entered and immediately sensed the tension between the two women. "Mr. Whitney's on the phone, ma'am."

Mother and daughter continued staring at one another.
Then abruptly Gloria turned and left the room. Her heart
was beating so rapidly that she had to sit down and compose

herself before she picked up the phone. She could feel the veins throbbing in her temples.

"Good morning, Harry," she said.

"You sound strange," he said. "Like an old woman."

"That's the way I feel," she sighed.

"It's that bad?"

"Yes. It's all over for us—you understand?"

"Fielding?"

"Yes."

"I'll come right over."

The sun was burning through the mist at ten o'clock and Harry was sitting on the terrace impatiently waiting for Gloria. There was a bittersweet smell of wet boxwood in the air, and the birds made a charming melody. Presently the sound of high-heeled shoes on the parquet floors came to him and he jumped to his feet and went to the drawing-room doors. He couldn't take his eyes off her as she came toward him.

They embraced and moved out onto the terrace. She was dressed all in white, with a large-brimmed white hat to shield her eyes. The copper beeches looked particularly beautiful this morning and the lilies in her water garden were amazingly fresh and green. The statue of Diana sat in the middle of the pool looking as serene as she wished she felt.

"It's so lovely here," said Harry moving out into the sunshine.

"Alice says she wishes she could live here, and I wish she could too, to help me. Mama and the nursemaid are really going too far now. It was mama who told me about Fielding."

"I'll take care of him," said Harry. "Don't worry about him."

His voice, his masculine presence, reassured her and she felt far happier than she should have. She picked some purple snapdragons and put them in a vase on the terrace. Then they sat drinking iced tea which the butler brought them. Dogs lay sleeping at their feet.

"I feel like we're a couple of old marrieds, don't you?" said Harry.

"I pray for it every day," said Gloria, "and dream about it every night. My heart will break if we can't be together, Harry."

They listened to the fountain trickle in the pool of Diana. Bees made a pleasant hum over the orange and white lilies, and the fragrance of rambler roses drifted over to them.

"Why don't you drive to Saratoga with me now?" said Harry.

"I daren't," said Gloria putting her hand to her heart. Watching his handsome face gave her such rapture it bordered on pain.

"I've got to be with you again," said Harry gravely, taking her hand. "Isn't it awful? I'd like to make love to you right now. I'm best in the morning, as you'll soon discover. Why don't we go riding tomorrow morning at daybreak? We'll gallop over the fieldstone fences and then under some silver birches—in the sunshine—I'll hold you in my arms and devour you. . . ."

By 11 Reggie had bathed and dressed with Norton's help. Gloria joined him, and by 11:30 their car rolled away from the Norman manor and vanished down the avenue of trees. Once out of the gates, the car picked up speed, wine-red cottages and handsome barns and silos passing by. As they passed the cemetery of Saint Mary's Church, Reggie glanced curiously at the tombstones.

"What do you think happens, Gloria, when it's all over?"

Gloria turned to look at her husband anxiously. "Mama says we go to a better world."

"I hope I'll be Harry Payne Whitney in my next life," said Reggie.

Her throat felt constricted but she managed to say lightly, "Well, in that case I wouldn't look at you. Oh, darling, do look at the Queen Anne's lace and wild morning glories. Aren't they just too delicious?"

And suddenly, listening to his wife, the thought of tombstones and death vanished and he was the old fun-loving Reggie Vanderbilt. He even began to hum.

"Oh, you are much better, darling," she cried gaily.

"Yes, much better, thanks to you."

She felt pleased by his admiring looks. "Cook made a picnic lunch," she told him, "so we won't have to waste time and stop along the way."

"Bless you," he said emotionally. "What would I have done without you, Gloria?"

She smiled radiantly under her white picture hat. "We'll make the two o'clock race!"

"Let's hope we don't lose," he said.

"We'll win, darling, we'll win!"

Meadows crisscrossed with fieldstone walls went by. Sunlight lingered in the trees, and cattle were grazing in the fields.

"Is Harry going to meet us at Saratoga?" asked Reggie.

"Yes, he came over earlier and asked if we wanted a lift."

"He's nice, isn't he?" said Reggie, turning to look at his wife. "Women are crazy about him."

"So I've heard," she returned.

"Do you find him attractive, Gloria?"

Amazingly enough, her cheeks didn't flush. "He's very physical," she said, "and I'm not." As she spoke these words she saw Harry's big arms and felt those arms crushing her, felt his lips on her.

"Gertrude knows all about his little flirtations," Reggie continued, "but they're never serious you know, just bits of fluff. He's vain and likes admiration and attention. I often wonder if he really cares for anyone; lovemaking is just a game with Harry."

"How sad," said Gloria, and suddenly the landscape was covered with mist again. The smell of damp marshes filled the car.

"We men are very different from you, Gloria," said Reggie. "We want pleasure, and you want to possess."

"And pleasure is all Harry wants?" How her heart ached.

"He'd tell you the same."

"How charming you make your brother-in-law sound," drawled Gloria, trying to keep her voice casual.

"He's a great fellow all right," said Reggie, lighting a cigarette. "I wonder what juicy damsel the old devil has now. Virgins are his specialty, you know. He likes to break them in."

Gloria leaned forward and rolled down the window. God, she needed fresh air. Her nerves were so taut she had the jitters. I've got to have a drink. I'll kill Harry when I see him—no, I'll torture him first.

Reggie, watching her, leaned back with a satisfied grin. Little did he know that he fanned the flames of her love all the more. . . .

CHAPTER
16

The next few weeks passed in a dream. After Saratoga they'd returned to Sandy Point, and every morning she rose at daybreak, met Harry in the fields, and together they raced over the countryside for miles and miles around. The way he watched her with such love in his eyes awed her.

"Faster, faster!" Harry would say, galloping furiously over the fields.

"I can't keep up with you!" she laughed.

"You can, you must!"

Through thickets full of elderberries, over brooks gurgling over the stones, past meadows full of wildflowers and ancient apple trees, past grazing cows and sheep, past farmhouses with spirals of smoke coming out of their chimneys, and past fields of hay they raced.

"Jump!" cried Harry as he flew over a fieldstone wall.

"I can't, I can't," she cried, but she followed gracefully behind him riding sidesaddle on her spirited chestnut. How exhilarated she felt as the sun started its progress in the sky and the meadows and trees burst with fresh life. Every nerve in her body cried out with happiness.

Every morning they made love in a thicket or a meadow, and once even by a cart full of hay. Today they lay under a grape arbor, their nude bodies lying in the shade.

"It reminds me of Capri," said Harry. "Have you been there?"

"Yes," she nodded. "My mischievous Prince Ruspoli had a villa there overlooking the orange rocks of the Faraglioni, similar to Axel Munthe's poetic villa. It's my dream to return there."

"Did you meet Dr. Munthe?" asked Harry.

"Yes, and I wanted to work with him, become a nurse. It was my favorite fantasy," she said with a smile.

"You're certainly not a nurse now," said Harry.

"I look after a sick person," she said. "Don't I?"

"I hope I have you around when I'm sick," said Harry, "and I promise we'll go to Capri soon together," he added in his resolute way.

"Do you think so?" she said wistfully.

"Sooner than you think, dearest." He rolled over and kissed her and she put her hands through his hair. The birds were singing a song that echoed their sentiments.

A little after ten o'clock they were riding over the fields when a cloudburst drenched them. Finally they stopped at a little farmhouse. They made quite a pair in their elegant riding clothes, both of them with clear-cut features and impressive bearing. A young farmer and his wife let them in.

Gloria went into raptures. "What a delicious cottage!" she cried. "You wouldn't have any milk, would you? I crave fresh milk with such a thirst, you can't imagine. Don't you, Harry?"

"Yes," replied the broad-shouldered gentleman, "I'm famished."

"Are you visiting the manor house?" asked the farmer, thinking they were some of the titled English or French people who were always coming and going.

"I'm Mrs. Vanderbilt," Gloria smiled.

"And I'm Harry Payne Whitney."

"The saints preserve us," said the Catholic farmer, a stalwart, sandy-haired man with freckles and dressed in dungarees.

His wife quickly crossed herself. My God, the sinners themselves, she thought. Her brother had told her the story of the torrid love affair between Mrs. Vanderbilt and Mr. Whitney. But Mrs. Vanderbilt wasn't at all what she expected; she was so gracious and natural, talking to them as if they were old friends. Gloria stood there before the mirror and combed out her thick, luxuriant hair. In a matter of minutes the damp strands were standing out about her face in soft curls. The farmer couldn't take his eyes off her; indeed both husband and wife seemed paralyzed by the radiant pair.

"What's the matter, man? Are you sick or something?" asked Harry.

"We've had sickness in the house, sir," came the sullen reply. "It's my brother-in-law, Fielding."

"Sorry to hear it," said Harry, not really caring if the young man lived or died. "Is he here?"

"Yes, sir. It's his day off and we're looking after him."

"I'd like to speak to him," said Harry, "if I may."

After a time Fielding shuffled in, shifty-eyed and sulky. How he hated these rich people. "What can I do for you?" he asked ungraciously.

"First," said Harry, "take your hands out of your pockets when you're in the presence of a lady." He did so and Harry added, "I'd like to talk alone with you if it's possible."

The farmer and his wife left and the three were left alone.

"Now, what's all this nonsense about you blabbing your big mouth off?" said Harry angrily.

"Nonsense?" Fielding sneered. "I've got eyes in my head."

"Do you think it's right to go sneaking and spying about on Mrs. Vanderbilt's family? It's none of your business, Fielding, and I'm afraid grave measures must be taken."

The young man gulped, but said nothing.

"You don't look happy here, Fielding," observed Harry. "Perhaps you'd like to return to Ireland."

"No," said Fielding vehemently. "I'm here because my grandfather and two hundred other men were hired to come here and build The Breakers. The poor man is old and crippled now and lives on fifty cents a day, but he built that palace where all of you enjoy yourselves. What an injustice!"

"Injustice?" repeated Harry. "They were well paid."

"Well paid?" sneered Fielding. "Grandfather earned four hundred dollars for those two years of work, and The Breakers cost five million dollars to build."

"That was a good wage in those days," said Harry, "and you should consider yourself lucky to get five dollars a week now."

"While you spend ten thousand times that in a week?" cried Fielding.

"Fielding," said Harry pontifically, "there have always been rich people and poor people in the world."

"It's not fair that in this democracy a few should have so much while ninety-nine percent have so little."

"That's the way it is," said Harry, "and you'd just better accept it."

"I don't accept it," said Fielding bitterly.

"Why don't you stand up on a soapbox and preach communism on the streets of Newport?" said Harry sarcastically.

"Perhaps I will," said Fielding darkly. "This is no democracy—we servants know that. Except I'm not going to

be a servant again, am I? You never know what I might say!"
Fielding smirked knowingly.

"What kind of a business would you like to be in?" asked
Harry.

"A business like yours," said Fielding, smiling, and when
he smiled he was surprisingly attractive. So much so that
Gloria looked at him with interest and thought that if he
had the right name, manners, voice, and education she'd
probably be swooning at his feet. God knows he had more
vitality than her little social set in Newport.

After a time it was clear that Harry was going to put
Fielding where Harry could keep an eye on him. He asked
Fielding to come and see him.

"I'll be into your office next Monday," said Fielding. Abruptly, he walked out of the room.

"He's recovered awfully quickly from his illness," said
Gloria, with irony, as they left the farmhouse.

"It left a bad taste in my mouth," said Harry as he helped
Gloria remount. "But it's better than paying blackmail money
outright."

"Perhaps he'll do well in your firm and you'll be pleased
with him."

"He'll do too well," said Harry grimly. "In a matter of
ten years he'll be the president and I'll be the office boy."

"Perhaps the old commodore was like him," said Gloria
dreamily, feeding her horse some sugar. "Strong and ruthless."

"By nineteen forty-five," said Harry "he'll be the president
of General Motors and he'll really give people coming up in
the world a hard time."

"You make it sound so ugly, Harry," she said, depressed.

"Making money is not pretty," he observed, "and it's not
for women's heads."

"Are we such idiots?" she asked softly.

"No, but you've never been in business and you don't

understand how the system works." He spurred his horse forward.

They cantered back through the orchards and fields to the stable, where Gloria and Harry dismounted and grooms led the horses away. As they walked through the garden, Gloria's head was lowered thoughtfully. The scene with Fielding had left a bad taste in her mouth, too.

When they approached the terrace, Wann rushed out. "Mrs. Vanderbilt, your mother-in-law just telephoned to ask if she could bring her houseguests, Prince Hohenlohe and the Dalkeiths, to the ball tonight. And Mr. Gilbert and Miss Eagels just arrived with Louis Bromfield."

"Women's world," said Harry, smiling at her lovingly.

"More attractive than men's world," she observed sadly.

"But our drive creates the wherewithal to pay for it," said Harry, "and there's got to be a lot of money to keep this show going."

"You sound a bit critical," Gloria said.

"Well, what else were you brought up to do but spend money?"

"Then I'm fated to be dependent forever, is that it?" said Gloria.

"Fated," said Harry, blowing her kiss. "Until tonight. Can you tell me what your costume is going to be?"

"No," she said, suddenly feeling happy again. "That's a surprise."

"I like surprises," said Harry, wandering off toward the entrance courtyard.

She turned the bronze bolts of the French doors and stepped into the drawing room. Even on the hottest days like today the high-ceilinged room managed to stay cool.

"The hostess!" cried John Gilbert raising his highball glass.

Louis Bromfield rose to greet her in his vigorous fashion. He wore a conservative double-breasted blue silk suit.

"You've changed, Gloria," said Jeanne Eagels, moving over and making room for her on the deep white sofa. Jeanne, being a sensitive woman, could see a difference in her.

"Perhaps it's my age. I'm twenty now, you know," said Gloria, grinning.

Gilbert was shaking up a fresh batch of cocktails at the bar. "I've never seen so many trophies and cups everywhere. And how many dog and horse paintings can there be?"

"I'm married to a famous horseman," said Gloria.

"Aren't you bored with all these horses?" said Jeanne.

"No, I'm never bored," said Gloria simply.

"And what do you do for fun around here?" said John, a restless soul who was already eager to be doing something or prying into someone's hidden recesses.

"I daren't tell you," laughed Gloria.

Suddenly the three old friends crowded around her, hungry to discover details of her secret life. She confessed she was in love, but the butler announcing lunch interrupted the conversation.

"I'd go crazy with all these servants around," said Jeanne. "My God, what do you do when you want to make love?"

"Close the door," said Gloria, leading her guests into the dining room. Like the drawing room it was filled with flowers and had a dazzling view of lawns sweeping down to the river.

Over their lunch of grilled sole and spinach salad, Gloria looked at her friends and realized that she must always be surrounded by people like this who thought and felt deeply. None of the social people she knew had any capacity for deep feelings. It was all surface and small talk with them; their inherited money seemed to have robbed them of caring or feeling.

"Jeanne," she asked, sipping her chilled white wine, "could you be married, as I am, to a rich man and be dependent on him?"

Jeanne rarely ate a thing and was pushing the food around on her plate. With a chuckle she said, "Men are bad enough as they are, the bastards, but to be dependent on them for everything—no thanks!"

"I wish I had a career," said Gloria. "I wish I had some kind of talent. How I envy you all. Wherever you go, you'll be free and independent."

"Stay just as you are," said John. "You're the type of woman we men like to look after. Isn't that true, Louis?"

"Decidedly," said Louis, raising his glass to her in a salute. "But since you don't have any talent, Gloria, you must do something heroic. You are a heroine, you know. You've quite inspired me to write something about you."

"A love story?" suggested Gloria.

Louis shook his head. "No, I see you more as a figure of tragedy."

They finished their zabaglione and put down their gilded silver spoons and forks. The footmen helped them out of their caned armchairs.

"Tragic . . ." mulled Gloria as the four of them strolled leisurely toward the drawing room.

"Yes, tragic," said Louis, who was much into spiritualism. "All four of us are somehow tragic. We all have so much, but we all have our fatal flaw. . . ."

The gilded French clock held up by the white Meissen elephant chimed three. It was the last lunch that Gloria would enjoy in the house. Indeed the last summer that she would enjoy there. . . .

Gloria's fancy-dress ball that night—or Fete of Roses, as many people called it because of the astonishing numbers of those flowers—was memorable in several ways. There hadn't been a ball in Newport like it since Grace Vanderbilt's Arabian Nights fantasy a few years ago.

First of all, there was the sublime menu. The dinner consisted of chilled melon balls followed by a whole poached salmon brought in with its head on and roast turkeys stuffed with chestnut purée and accompanied by hothouse asparagus swimming in hollandaise. Dessert was a raspberry ice with a rich chocolate sauce that had a peppermint flavor. Gloria was much complimented on the artistic way the fifty oval tables seating ten each were placed about the garden. The Japanese lanterns hanging from the trees, glowing in the darkness, created an atmosphere of enchantment.

Then there were the fireworks at midnight, filling the sky with explosions of color to delight the 500 guests.

Finally, there was Gloria's sensational waltz with Harry, which was perhaps the most memorable thing of all to those scandalized guests who were still there to see it. It was by then two o'clock in the morning, the ball was almost over. The candles were burning low in the chandeliers and candelabra, and the finely proportioned neoclassic rooms were emptying. The orchestra still played, however, for those couples who lingered to dance. Gloria and Harry were among them.

"Of course I love you, Harry," Gloria was saying, looking up at him as they moved to the music. "Who could help loving you?"

"You don't mind having fingers pointed at you?" said Harry.

"Well, there's no doubt you've ruined my reputation, Harry Payne Whitney."

"You're loving every minute of it," he grinned.

"I'm glad you're dressed as Louis the Fifteenth. He had a handsome facade but was rotten inside just like you."

"For your information," he said, "I'm Louis the Fourteenth."

Under the dully glowing rock-crystal and amethyst drops of the bronze chandeliers, Harry looked twenty years younger and exceptionally handsome. He had the carriage of a man of twenty-five and the same vitality and enthusiasm.

"We must stop," said Gloria, suddenly noticing people's expressions. "We've danced enough. You mustn't speak to me again tonight."

"You're not going to go riding with me tomorrow morning?" he said, turning swiftly and drawing her toward him.

"You're holding me too tight, Harry. Stop it!"

"You ate far too much salmon and asparagus," he said laughing. "By next year you'll be a swine if you continue eating like that—and then I won't speak to you."

"Good," she cried, closing her eyes and giving herself up to the fantasy of being Mrs. Harry Payne Whitney.

Reggie came into the drawing room with Rita Lydig. He watched his wife with a frown. He'd been brought up not to express his feelings—the stiff-upper-lip school—and to protect his sanity he only saw what he wanted to see. In his heart he knew what was going on between his wife and Harry, but he told himself it was only a flirtation. So he sat down with the infamous Mrs. Lydig and watched the couple dance, sipping his brandy. Rita Lydig had been an old flame of Reggie's and knew he didn't dance, so she didn't bother him.

The dazzling score of "The Merry Widow" played on and the dancers spun round and round the graceful room. Aware of everyone's stares, Gloria held up a little black mask before her eyes which increased the flirtatious air about her.

When the waltzes came to an end, the remaining hundred guests started to leave. It was way past Alice Vanderbilt's bedtime, but she stayed up to have a talk with her daughter-in-law. She must explain the severity of the situation to her; youth takes everything far too lightly.

Finally she managed to get Gloria alone in the little powder room by the front door.

"I'm so flattered that you stayed late," Gloria said.

"I stayed, my child, because of my concern for your welfare."

Gloria glanced at the little woman with a feeling of dread in her heart. "Oh?" she said, stalling for time and hating the idea of a scene.

"I think it would be a good idea for you to take a little holiday, Gloria. The talk about you here tonight has appalled me."

"I'm sorry," said Gloria, lowering her head.

"I don't wish to criticize your behavior, my dear, but I feel that as your mother-in-law I must give you a bit of advice. I was hoping that having a baby would bring you down to earth, but you're still so up in the clouds."

"I daresay I *am* a romantic," admitted Gloria with a sigh.

"Harry is a very good-looking man," said Mrs. Vanderbilt, "and I can understand your infatuation with him. But you must forget him for the family's sake. It will drive Reggie to drink all the more."

Gloria took a deep breath. The old lady's words brought her down to earth all right. What a romantic little fool she'd been to carry on with Harry in front of everyone. What had she been thinking of?

"I'll try not to see Harry again," she whispered.

The old lady nodded emphatic agreement and, satisfied, stumped off. Gloria stood in the courtyard and watched the heavy black town car carry her mother-in-law back to The Breakers.

"Mother had a wonderful time," said Reggie fondly.

"She never stays up so late," said Gertrude, "unless it's for some remarkable occasion."

"It *was* a remarkable occasion," said Harry. "Gloria and I are going to Hollywood to be the new Vernon and Irene Castle." He kissed Gloria's hand and then said, "Shall we have lunch on the yacht tomorrow before our audition?"

"I'm going away tomorrow," she said mysteriously. She

glanced at Gertrude, who was watching her questioningly, then turned on her heel without a word and walked into the entrance hall. She'd enjoyed the look that crossed Harry's face. Going up the staircase she called out, "Reggie, are you coming up?"

"It's such a beautiful night I think I'll wander about for a while."

He watched her slender figure in the rustling taffeta dress vanish up into the second-floor landing, then he stood there for a moment smoothing his mustache. He was suddenly angry as hell, but it was best not to let the anger take over. In the old days he had gone on some memorable drunks when he tried to drown the anger. Some warning signal inside him told him not to imbibe too much tonight. How tired he was. When you lose your health you lose everything. He'd kept the glow of vitality alive for so long through booze and massage and steam baths and travel, but now there was nothing more to stimulate him. It was all over.

It was around noon when Reggie awakened; he shuffled into Gloria's room in his Charvet dressing gown and silk pajamas. He'd be forty-five in December but looked twenty years older. Yawning and rubbing his hair he said, "I say, old girl, are you going off to Havana to do some gambling?"

Gloria was up and dressed in a traveling suit, elegantly tailored, with a white silk blouse. "No, silly," she laughed. "I decided to go into New York and visit some old friends."

"How long will you be gone?" asked Reggie, feeling a stab of loneliness at the idea of separation from his wife. Was she off to meet Harry? he wondered.

"Just a day," she replied gaily. "Why don't you come with me?"

"My traveling days are over," said Reggie. "I'm all played out."

He spoke so tragically that she went to him and put her arms around his neck. "I'll call you from New York later this afternoon," she said, watching him closely.

"Will you miss me?" he asked with a playful air that he was far from feeling.

"With all my heart," she said, giving him a long kiss.

When he left her, she stood there looking after him. Of course he knows, she thought. And then put her hands to her head as if to block the thought. It was bad enough having to leave Harry, but having Reggie look so ill was truly disturbing.

She left a little after lunch and looked for him everywhere but couldn't find him. The house seemed strangely still; there was no evidence of last night's Fete of Roses. Where had all the flowers gone, by the way? And where did all the food go? she wondered too.

As the car pulled out of the gravel drive, Gloria looked at the manor house. She couldn't get Reggie out of her mind. He'd looked so pitiful with his gray face and pouches under his eyes.

That evening, Gardner Pell, a dear friend, took her to the prizefights. When they arrived in the crowded arena, people stared at her with interest and several asked for her autograph. In those days the Vanderbilts were like film stars and nearly every day she was written about in newspapers and magazines.

"You look pale, Gloria," observed Gardner Pell in his gentle manner when they were seated at ringside. He was a year older than she, well built and good-looking, and many women had vied for his attentions—without success. Gloria was clever enough to know what his inclinations were—the way he looked at men told her a good deal. But it didn't bother her in the least what his private life consisted of; in any case they were close friends and enjoyed each other's company.

"I'm afraid I've been rather foolish with Harry Payne Whitney," said Gloria, who had always felt free to tell him anything.

"Does Reggie know?"

"Yes, and he's very ill besides."

The gong sounded and the two fighters began to savagely punch one another. The harsh overhead lights burned down on the opponents, their heavyweight bodies bathed in sweat. Sitting so close, the sickening thud of fists hitting jaws and noses upset her and she began to feel faint.

"Do you want to leave, Gloria?" said Gardner. "You don't look well."

She shook her head; she didn't want to make him miss it, and anyway it was almost over.

The climax of the fight was particularly brutal, people all around were standing up and screaming for the champion to knock out the contender. Suddenly as the contender was dropping to his knees under the fierce blows, Gloria saw the face of Reggie transposed on the face of the falling man.

"Oh, my God!" she cried, clutching Gardner's arm. "Something terrible has happened to Reggie! *Please*, take me away from here."

With difficulty he led her through the screaming crowd. She couldn't say a word until they were outside on the street waiting for her car.

"Why don't we go to Sherry's and have a drink?" Gardner suggested. "Or the Marguery if you prefer."

"All right, let's go to the Marguery and we'll call Newport and see how Reggie is."

In the Italianate gardens of the Marguery at 270 Park Avenue they drove into the big courtyard and then stepped into the revolving doors. She swiftly put through a call to Newport.

A strange voice answered.

"Who is this speaking?" Gloria asked.

"I'm Mr. Vanderbilt's nurse."

"Nurse!" cried Gloria. "What's wrong with my husband?"

"He hemorrhaged this afternoon, Mrs. Vanderbilt," explained the nurse gently, "but now he's resting quietly."

"He'll be all right?"

"Now don't sound so worried, Mrs. Vanderbilt. Everything will be all right in the morning. The doctor thinks the ball was just a little bit too much for him."

Gloria rushed to the lobby. "Gardner, I've got to go to Newport right away. Reggie's terribly ill."

"Do you want me to go with you?" He put a supporting arm around her shoulders.

"No, thanks, Gardner, I'll be fine." She gathered up her things and called for the car.

She arrived in Newport at five o'clock in the morning. The house looked cold and dark. By the front door was Alice Vanderbilt's black Rolls-Royce. Why was she here. . . ?

Gloria opened the door and ran into the hall. Norton, the valet, was moving like a sleepwalker down the stairs.

"What's happened?" she cried, seizing his arm with a terrible foreboding.

"Mr. Vanderbilt died five minutes ago."

CHAPTER
17

She only remembered fragments of the following days. On that first day she'd slept off and on, roused frequently to take calls from friends. Nights, her sleep was uneasy; sometimes she slept, other times she lay for hours plagued with racing thoughts. Reggie's last words kept going through her head. "My traveling days are over," he had said. "I'm all played out." Had he known he was going to die? She recalled his remark as they had passed Saint Mary's church: "What happens afterward?"

The night before the funeral she awoke sometime past midnight. The house was still. She flung on a dressing gown and began pacing. She went back over their life together, remembering her excitement at their first meeting. She recalled the good times they'd had in Paris and Cannes, London, Palm Beach, New York—not to mention those exciting midnight sailings. . . . When had things started to fall apart—

and why? Was it her youth? Reggie's drinking? Was it Harry?

Round and round she went, confused and bewildered by questions she couldn't find any answers for. She went downstairs and poured herself a stiff glass of brandy. "To you, Reggie," she cried.

At eight Wann entered with her breakfast tray. Mrs. Drexel and Mrs. Van Alen had called to offer their condolences; many other friends had called to say they were coming to the funeral.

"Madam looks tired," Wann observed.

"I couldn't sleep again," cried Gloria, her voice rising almost hysterically.

"Eat something," said Wann tenderly.

"No," said Gloria, "I can't even bear the sight of food."

"You have dark circles under your eyes, Mrs. Vanderbilt, and you shouldn't smoke all those cigarettes."

Gloria lit another one and puffed on it nervously. "It's vile," she said nervously. "Vile and base. Is that my true nature, Wann?"

"You need Father Thomas," said Wann, smoothing Gloria's disheveled hair.

An hour later she was dressed in a simple black silk dress with two strands of imperial jade around her throat. The necklace had been Reggie's last gift and, ironically, she hadn't really liked it; its opulence was too somber, it was too funereal in feeling. Reggie had told her it had belonged to a Manchu princess and that it had taken eight years to assemble the jade in and around Peking.

As soon as she saw the priest's kind face and heard his compassionate words, she wept bitter tears. "I'm no good," she sobbed. "Mama's right, I'm a harlot or worse."

"My dear child, let God be the judge of that."

Between sobs, she told him of her love affair with Harry Payne Whitney.

"And you really love this man?" he asked when she had finished.

She thought for a moment. "I have a ghastly feeling it was all based on lust. Last night I dreamed of his body all night through. It's such a beautiful body, Father Thomas, and it gives me no peace."

He watched her with troubled eyes. "You're distraught, my dear. Lack of sleep and the shock of your husband's death have unbalanced you. I heard you were a very good wife to Mr. Vanderbilt, and now you will have your daughter to give you comfort."

"Yes," said Gloria reflectively, "little Gloria is a comfort to me, although she doesn't need me. My mother and the nurse take care of her."

"And does Mr. Whitney need you?"

She'd had a few sherries in the bathroom and she began to laugh wildly. "I don't know if he needs *me*, but God knows I certainly need *him*! He's the first one who made me feel—all through— do you understand?"

"I understand," said the priest although in fact he didn't; he'd never had any experience of fleshly things.

She held up her tearstained face to him. "What am I to do, Father Thomas? Help me, help me!"

"You must not see this man again," said the priest forcefully. "He is the one to blame, being older and with a greater knowledge of the world."

"And if he comes here today?"

"Send him away."

"I won't have the strength."

The priest took her hand. "I'll pray for you," he said. "Come, we'll pray together. Prayer gives one great strength. Do you ever pray, my child?"

She nodded. "Yes, I prayed last night. Prayed that I wouldn't surrender to him again. You see, I'm so terribly ashamed of myself."

They prayed for fifteen minutes. Later, after he had blessed her and left, she felt calmer and the guilt receded. Before lunch she even managed to receive many friends and acquaintances from happy days at Bailey's Beach and the Tennis Casino. Little Gloria had gone to The Breakers so she joined her there and had lunch in that enormous marble dining room that seated 150. They were served with great ceremony and footmen stood behind every chair. Outside the windows a damp mist floated by. Little Gloria chattered on like a magpie and Emma watched Gloria accusingly. But Gloria had gone beyond caring.

The footmen kept filling her wine goblet and Gloria noticed that Mrs. Vanderbilt was watching her closely. Hell, what did it matter? Nothing mattered anymore.

After lunch little Gloria went upstairs for her nap and her mother was left alone with old Mrs. Vanderbilt.

"Your color is very poor," remarked Alice Vanderbilt. "I'll send over a nurse to help you get through this afternoon. Gertrude and Harry and Gladys and I will be there promptly at five. Grace and Neily will be there too, and Fred. He's a great fan of yours, my dear, so make yourself look your prettiest."

Gloria was grateful to the old woman for speaking to her in such a light vein. It took her mind off the funeral tomorrow and the horror of seeing Reggie in the coffin this afternoon.

"Should I wear a veil in the house, Mrs. Vanderbilt?"

"No, I don't think so. Maybe just a little veil. But for the funeral tomorrow, of course, you must be in deep mourning. Our private train leaves immediately after the ceremony for New York and we'll go from there to Staten Island for the interment. That's where the old commodore was born, you know, and that's where we all go when the Lord sees fit to take us. I'm ready to go any time."

The old woman looked so tragic Gloria wrapped her arms around her and kissed her on both cheeks. "Oh, Mrs.

Vanderbilt, I admire you so much. I wish I could be just like you."

"I wouldn't wish that on anyone," said the old woman, trying to stem the tears. "I buried three children and a husband in his prime."

The two women clung to one another for a moment. Then a nurse in a starched white uniform came in. The old lady drew her aside and whispered something to her, then led her over to Gloria. "Dear, Miss Hartley is going to take you home and give you something for your nerves."

As they drove through the meadows and farmlands to Sandy Point Farm, the Rolls-Royce passed Saint Mary's Church and graveyard. Thinking of Reggie, the tears streamed down her cheeks.

Some Newport tradespeople were waiting for her in the library. "They've come to pay their last respects," Norton told her, "and they'd like to speak to you." She spoke to them for a minute and their condolences touched her. Presently, however, she had a fainting spell and the nurse led her out of the room and upstairs.

"Why don't you lie down for a moment?" said Miss Hartley.

Gloria sank onto the Louis XVI bed under its rich canopy. She swallowed a small pill and lay back with a moan.

In a little while, Wann entered with a small black hat with a veil, and bent over Gloria. "Here is the veil, madam," said Wann, putting the delicate black piece on her head and securing it with pins.

A second maid entered with a tray of champagne. "Norton thought this would help you get through the ordeal downstairs, ma'am. There are about two hundred people downstairs already."

"What time is it?" cried Gloria alarmed.

"A little after five, madam," said Wann.

"Five," repeated Gloria. "Why just a minute ago it was

four. Nothing can be trusted anymore—not even the clocks."

"You can trust me," said Wann, patting her hand.

A moment later Gloria entered the drawing room flanked by Wann and the nurse. Her face looked amazingly beautiful framed by the heavy veiling, which gave her an ethereal look; indeed she seemed almost to float into the room, supported as she was by the two women.

The Whitneys and Schenyes were standing next to old Mrs. Vanderbilt. Gertrude watched her sister-in-law's progress through the room with a mixture of grief and hate.

When Gloria reached the open casket, she stood for a moment without looking in, paralyzed; all the blood seemed to have been drained from her veins. When she finally brought herself to look, she saw that Norton had dressed Reggie in his favorite suit, a blue cashmere one with chalk stripes, and a cream-colored China silk shirt and tie from Sulka. A black-pearl-and-diamond stickpin flashed on his necktie. His hands were folded across his breast and he looked, finally, at peace. That air of disappointment was gone; there was a gentle look about his mouth now with no hint of sullenness or petulance. In death he looked strong, there was a nobility about his profile that was not unlike the last kings of France. Gazing at him she thought how curious it was that this man had been her husband for two and a half years and now she'd never see him again. Father Thomas had told her that they would be reunited in Paradise, but she knew she was going to hell so there was no chance of that.

"He loved you very much," said Alice, her voice breaking.

"I'll never forget him," said Gloria. And to herself she thought, Oh, Reggie, come back. Please come back. Let me make it up to you.

Gertrude wept silently by the casket and Gloria was surprised to see this cold woman display any emotion. Harry

stood gravely by his wife's side. Fred Vanderbilt came up
and kissed Gloria on the cheek and offered his support.

Afterward, as Miss Hartley led her upstairs, Gloria said,
"Why is it so dark? Is it night already?"

"It's merely a summer storm, madam," the nurse replied.
"It will pass like everything else."

"Please leave me alone," said Gloria. She entered her room
and closed the door, but then found she couldn't bear to be
in the huge room by herself. She ran across the hall to
Reggie's room. There was plenty of brandy and soda there.

Reggie's prize stallion, Fortitude, and one of the stallion's
sons, Onward, had been brought from the stables at Sandy
Point Farm to stand as guard of honor as the funeral cortege
left for Saint Mary's Episcopal Church. The little country
church was filled to overflowing with Woodwards, Astors,
Taylors, and all the fashionable Newport throng. The coffin
was a massive bronze one with a blanket of orchids, lilies of
the valley, and maidenhair fern. Following the coffin came
the widow in trailing knee-length black veils, escorted by
Brigadier General Cornelius Vanderbilt. Old Mrs. Alice
Vanderbilt was escorted by Harry Payne Whitney and Mr.
and Mrs. Harry Cushing III. Mrs. Cushing was Reggie's
daughter by his first wife, Cathleen Neillson. All sat in the
family pew in the first row.

The service began at ten and the minister delivered a
moving eulogy. Father Thomas played two hymns on the
organ, "Abide With Me" and Mendelssohn's "Savior, Source
of Every Blessing." Then the bishop began the service, standing on the pulpit with a ray of sunlight streaming in through
the stained-glass window.

"I am the resurrection and the life, saith the Lord. For a
thousand years in thy sight are but as yesterday, seeing that

the past is as a watch in the night. Oh, teach us to number our days that we may apply our hearts unto wisdom. For as much as it hath pleased almighty God in his providence to take out of the world the soul of our deceased brother, Reginald Claypoole Vanderbilt. The grace of our Lord Jesus Christ and the love of God and the fellowship of the Holy Ghost be with us all evermore. Amen."

The words, despite their sense of finality, were nonetheless soothing. Though Gloria's eyes filled with tears, she had a feeling of serenity. Presently, Neily Vanderbilt offered her his arm and they followed the coffin out of the church to the swelling strains of organ music.

Now, whistling shrilly, the blue private train of the Vanderbilts sped through the New England landscape that still shimmered in a summer heat wave. The cars were filled with family and friends, all in dark clothes, many of them weeping. In the rear car lay Reggie's coffin, still covered with its blanket of orchids.

In a luxurious car next to her husband's lay the young widow listening to the monotonous click-clack of the wheels turning swiftly on the iron track below. Across from her on a chair sat her mother reading telegrams and letters of condolence.

She held up a cable from Thelma, in London: " 'Darling, thinking of you at this sad time.' " And then another: " 'Have wonderful plan, darling! Hurry to Europe! Your better half.'

"What does it mean?" asked Laura Morgan in her suspicious way.

"I don't know," answered Gloria dully.

"I'm sure you do," said mama meaningfully. "Your better half is a schemer all right. Now what would you do in Europe with Thelma?"

"I don't know, mama."

"You're certainly not your gay self today," snapped mama. "Now here's one from that prince: 'Dearest love . . .' " Laura read it through, then looked at her daughter darkly. "What caused him to write so emotionally?"

"Friedel's an emotional boy, mama."

"Is he one of your lovers?" Laura Morgan asked nastily.

Gloria was too tired to make a scene. She merely opened her eyes and gave her mother a long, disgusted look. "No, mama," she said calmly. "He isn't."

"Do you like him?"

"He has beautiful manners and wears beautiful clothes. That's all I can say about him."

"Here's a sinister one," said mama evilly. " 'Deepest sympathy, I adore you—Tallulah.' " She fixed her daughter with a dark look. "Where did you meet *that* strumpet?"

"In London," replied Gloria. "Reggie had many theatrical friends there."

"I hear," said Mrs. Morgan, "that she likes women, too."

"How would I know, mama?"

"She didn't try with you?"

"Good heavens, no," said Gloria wearily. "Why don't you just go on and read some more telegrams and stop all this crazy talk? If you can't behave more rationally, I'm not going to permit you to be around little Gloria—and I have sole custody of her now, you know."

"That poor orphan," wailed Mrs. Morgan tearfully.

"Mama, she is not an orphan. I'm her mother."

"No, you're not. *I'm* her mother," replied Mrs. Morgan violently.

Gloria leaned forward and pulled down the blind. The light hurt her eyes and she had a terrible pain behind them. She glanced wearily at her mother. The demented woman had really convinced herself that *she* was the mother of little Gloria. I'll just have to live with it, thought Gloria, lying back on the pillows of pink crepe de chine.

Mama Morgan went through the dozens of envelopes. "Ah, here's a significant one." She held it up wrathfully. " 'At your service—Valentino.' Where did you meet that lustful Italian laborer?" mama cried.

"He flirted with me in Paris last year," replied Gloria.

"And I suppose you're going off to Hollywood to live with him in sin like Pola Negri is doing with Charlie Chaplin?"

"It might not be a bad idea," retorted Gloria.

"You're a slave to your body. You'd run off with a train-man or a coolie tomorrow if you took a fancy to him. Imagine me being the mother-in-law of that immigrant!" She flushed hotly at the thought and fanned herself with a fistful of letters.

"Mama, what do you think I am?" Gloria said tiredly.

"You and Thelma are both adventuresses," proclaimed Mrs. Morgan. "You got yourself a rich old husband, and now that he's up and died on you you're lying there with all your pearls and diamonds prostrate with 'grief' and the wheels of your head are turning with new plots to get another victim. I bet next year you're going to be Mrs. Fred Vanderbilt. That's a logical choice. I saw him ogling you at the funeral service."

"Mama, he's sixty-eight years old!"

"It doesn't matter," said mama. "They always want the same thing."

Her eyes veiled over and she was silent for a moment— but just for a moment. When she spoke again, however, it was in a different mood.

"Your friend Ilka Chase of *Vogue* says the ultrafashion-ables go to Biarritz these days. Remember when we used to go there and to San Sebastian when you were children, Gloria? The Basque country has such a special feeling with those lovely fertile farms and mountains. And will you ever forget when we went to Lourdes and you wanted to help the poor crippled people? I still think you are basically good, Gloria, and have the right instincts. I was watching you at the church when the bishop was reading the Resurrection and the Life—"

She was interruped by a knock at the door. It was Harry. "We're coming into New Haven," he said, "and some people from Yale will be at the station to say a few words, so get ready."

Yale had been Reggie's alma mater—Harry's too, for that matter.

Gloria stood up and put on her hat, adjusting the heavy crepe veils that went almost to her ankles. She avoided looking at him. His voice, as usual, gave her a quiver of excitement but she said nothing. And Harry, of course, aware of her mother's eyes on them, was polite and respectful.

"Reggie's older brother, Bill, died here when he was twenty," Harry was saying courteously to Mrs. Morgan. "Reggie's father built a library here in memory of his son."

"We're all well versed in the family history, thank you very much," snapped Gloria. She moved swiftly out of the compartment, carrying herself with her usual dignity and grace. The train came to a stop and the conductor lowered the steps.

"Let me help you," said Harry, offering her his arm.

"You can never help me," she flung back at him.

"But you need help badly now, Gloria," he reminded her ominously. "In case you don't know, you're not rich anymore."

Gloria stepped down to the platform. Some faculty members from Yale presented her with a beautiful blue wreath from the class of 1902. They praised her husband's virtues and she nodded mutely. Then dabbing her eyes she boarded the train again. The whistle shrilled, the locomotive hissed and grumbled, and they were on their way again.

The rest of the journey she lay inert, her eyes covered with a handkerchief doused in cologne, but she didn't sleep. When

the train raced past 125th Street she sat up and stared out
the window. Row after row of dreary tenements passed by.
Windows were open and black women stared out at the train.

"I wonder what it would be like to live here, mama," she
said.

"Don't worry your pretty head about it," came mama's
reply. "I'm sure you'll feather your nest again soon."

The mourning train pulled slowly into Grand Central Station and a throng of reporters and curiosity seekers surrounded the cars. "Help me, mama," said Gloria. "These
veils are so heavy." She glanced in the mirror fretfully. "I
look so thin. Do I look fearful, mama?"

"No, darling, you look beautiful and I love you." She spoke
so tenderly that Gloria turned and embraced her. Such
moments were rare, but when they occurred Gloria was
swept with feelings of ambivalence. What could she do with
her?

Reggie's mother moved through the large car that was like
a drawing room with sofas, lamps, and festoons of curtains.
"Harry will escort you to the car."

"I don't want Harry to escort me," replied Gloria sharply.

The old lady was too grief-stricken to notice. "Come, we'll
face the press," she told Gloria.

Gloria stayed close to her mother-in-law on the ferry ride
to Staten Island. Gertrude and Harry tried to talk to her, but
she ignored them.

"The family mausoleum is very grim," said Alice. "But
the interment service will be short. We'll be back in New
York for tea."

The gulls were screeching wildly, swooping low over the
ferry as it made its way over the choppy water. By the Statue
of Liberty the great hulk of the *Mauretania* with three majestic red funnels rose up on the horizon. The smell of the
salt water was invigorating to Gloria and she gave old Mrs.
Vanderbilt's arm a squeeze. The tugs made a joyous sound

as they flanked another huge liner going out to sea, and all at once Gloria thought of all the fresh adventures ahead of her.

"I'll miss Reggie so much," said Gloria, putting her arms around Mrs. Vanderbilt.

"He'll miss you, too."

At the huge marble-columned Vanderbilt mausoleum, gravediggers were preparing the casket for interment. The rector of Saint Thomas Church spoke the final words, concluding, ". . . The grace of our Lord Jesus Christ and the love of God and the fellowship of the Holy Ghost be with us all evermore. Amen."

The little group of mourners turned away in silence and were carried back to the ferry.

"It's all over," said Gloria. She sighed with relief.

"Do you want to come home with me and have some tea?" her mother-in-law asked.

"Thank you, Mrs. Vanderbilt, but I don't think I'm up to it."

Gloria and Mrs. Morgan drove home to the limestone house on 78th Street. The butler opened the door and the usual fleet of maids surrounded her with little cries. It was a bright sunny day, but inside the heavy jade lamps were burning dimly through the Chinese pagoda shades.

Depression settled over her.

CHAPTER
18

New York was like a Florida swamp in midsummer and the people seemed listless as the drooping trees in Central Park. The radio forecast thunderstorms every afternoon and more humidity in the days to come. The bad financial news didn't come right away.

That curious feeling of anticlimax that had so plagued her husband all his life now visited Gloria. Time lay heavy on her hands. She missed Reggie. It was sad, she reflected, that Reggie was more on her mind dead than when he was alive. At odd times during the day she'd turn her head and imagine his voice, languid and jolly and sometimes peevish, saying, "Well, old thing, what have you got planned for tonight?" And in the mornings she'd awaken and wonder if he would want to go to Saratoga or Newport or motor out to Meadowbrook or Belmont, or perhaps even get on a yacht and go to Havana or Cairo or maybe Tahiti.

The diamond hands of the agate-and-rock-crystal boudoir clock Gertrude had given her, from Black, Star and Gorham, seemed to jump queerly and at other times to remain on the same numeral for hours. Sometimes she'd glance out into the garden and it would be dark when she thought it was mid-afternoon.

It was all very odd.

Jeanne Eagels came to visit her one afternoon, and after she left, Gloria thought, Perhaps I, too, will take to drugs and go mad. She had no household duties to perform, her engagement book was blank, little Gloria was with Reggie's mother in Newport. It was thought prudent for "the delicate child" to remain by the salty breezes from the sea as long as possible, although Gloria could never understand why mama and Emma insisted the child was so frail and sickly, for little Gloria was strong and healthy as could be.

If she missed Reggie, she missed Harry too: missed his voice and the hundred shades of color that went with his voice, missed their early-morning rides over the meadows and the sense of security he gave her; she never felt she could completely take care of herself. When after a few days mama left for Newport and she was left alone in the house, she even came to miss the abnormal scenes with mama. In her whole twenty years she had never before been alone. She wished Thelma were here to give her some incentive, some goal to rouse her interest. She sent off a series of urgent cables to her twin.

Sometimes in the early-morning hours she lay in a half-sleep, in a kind of voluptuous reverie, and fantasies of Harry and herself flickered through her mind: the feel of his powerful shoulders and arms as they tensed and shuddered during orgasm, and the throaty satisfied cries that came from him later; the pungent smell that came from him while she lay on his large chest. Sometimes her mind wandered back to that morning in the flower arbor in Newport when Harry had kissed her breasts so violently that she'd complained they were sore to the touch afterward.

"Good," he'd cried, "you'll remember me better till the next time."

The next time! God, would it ever come again?

In the late afternoon she'd sit by the telephone in the drawing room and pray that it would ring. She had transformed the space in the rear of the house into a lovely garden with junglelike plants and shrubs and flower beds. At twilight she'd sit there looking out at the pretty zinnias and campanula and pray that Harry would call. "Dear God, please make him call," she whispered.

But she never heard a word from Harry. September deepened and she grew desperate. She took to taking tea with her mother-in-law on 57th Street, hoping to catch a glimpse of Harry, but he never appeared. What had she done wrong? If only she'd resisted him longer. Now at night she was plagued by insomnia; the "if onlys" and "whys" went through her head till daybreak as she tossed and turned on the rumpled damp linen.

Prince Hohenlohe came to call one afternoon. He'd telephoned in the morning, said he was at loose ends, and she'd invited him to tea. Afterward she wondered if it was proper to receive him alone with no chaperon, but she had never paid much heed to convention, and, besides, she was in too listless a state to feel even a quiver of desire; she doubted seriously that she would ever take a lover again or indeed be capable of love.

Nevertheless, when the butler announced Prince Hohenlohe and the tall, distinguished, dark-haired young man entered, she was struck by the beauty of his face, the modeling of his features. In contrast to Reggie and Harry, Friedel was just her age and looked incredibly clean and fresh. Right away they spoke the same language, and for the first time in weeks she found herself talking animatedly, prattling happily together about this and that, mostly about people in their little circle. Yes, he flirted with her, but in a less physical way than Harry

They had tea at a small wicker table in the rear garden. It was sunny and delightful. "New York is marvelous," Friedel was saying in his enthusiastic way, his hands fumbling for some pipe tobacco. "The Metropolitan Museum is marvelous too; far better than anything we have in Berlin or Vienna. Have you been to Vienna or Berlin?"

She gave a playful laugh, at once warm and seductive. "No, but I long to go to Vienna."

He smiled eagerly in return. "We'll go now if you like!"

Before she could reply, the butler came in with a large white box of flowers and handed her a card. Guessing that it was from Harry at last, she tore open the envelope and read, "Yours, Harry."

Yours? Oh, my God.

Hohenlohe was a sensitive man and saw the look of agitation cross her face. Abruptly he stood up and walked over and kissed her hand. "Is there some problem, Gloria? Can I help?"

"No—no, thank you." Gloria hastily folded the card.

Friedel kissed her hand again and made his goodbyes. He blew her a last kiss and was gone.

That evening Gloria spent another sleepless night. And the next day there was no word from Harry, or Friedel either, for that matter. What was wrong with her? Had her looks fallen off already? She would have to start living again—with a vengeance.

From then on, Gloria made sure the phone never stopped ringing. Many college boys—swains from the Plaza Hotel period a few years ago—came to call bringing her new records and new books. Many of Reggie's middle-aged and older friends came to call, too, and she was on her best behavior.

One afternoon the butler ushered in Gardner Pell and Prince Hohenlohe together.

"What a lovely surprise," said Gloria, smiling at her friends. She gave a special look to Friedel, whose good looks were beginning to grow on her more and more.

"You've become a celebrity, Gloria," said Gardner, handing her the afternoon tabloids.

"Goodness," she replied, looking at the picture of herself. "Where did they dig this up?"

"It says that you've inherited seven million dollars," said Gardner teasing, "so I've come to propose marriage to you."

"I too," laughed Friedel.

They had iced tea—made like Harry made it, with mint and whiskey. They were drinking it when the butler came in to announce that gentleman himself.

"So the pretty widow is receiving her admirers already," observed Harry sarcastically.

Her smile faded and she glared up at him. How crude and brutal he looked, she thought, gazing up at him. His chest was too big and his shoulders too broad. Really a brute! She decided he didn't really dress well at all; his clothes were too tight and fitted him like upholstery, were too young for a man his age. Also, she found his mouth too big and his nose too fleshy. He had a double chin too! Two creases ran from the end of his nose to his mouth. God, she thought, he's half a century old—almost in the grave!

"Would you care for some iced tea, Mr. Whitney," said Gloria with mock formality, "or perhaps a gin and lime?"

He shook his head. "Neither, thank you. I'm here on business." He gave the boys a withering look and they promptly got to their feet and left.

Gloria felt uneasy in his presence and avoided his eyes.

"I'm sorry to break up your party," he said scornfully, sitting down in a chair near her and stretching out his long, powerful legs.

"It's no party," she replied. "I've been lonely, and they were kind enough to keep me company."

"I'll bet," he said, chuckling, but he did not take that opportunity to explain his long absence, despite her pointed remark. The fact was, he had tired of her, decided she wasn't his Great Love after all. And Harry, once he wearied of a woman, could be cruel.

His eye fell on the newspaper Gardner had brought. "I'm glad you've seen the afternoon papers," he said, "because that's what I'm here to talk to you about."

"Am I to be so rich?" said Gloria.

"No. But now that people think you have seven million dollars, every fortune hunter will be after you."

"Prince Hohenlohe is not a fortune hunter," said Gloria hotly.

"Just a word of warning, my love."

Their eyes met, and despite her attempts only a moment before to deny the attraction he still held for her, the old sexual tension sprang up.

"Am I to be on the street then?" she asked, trying to keep her voice casual.

"You will be if you don't stop spending," he replied. "Dozens of cases of White Rock and beer, caviar, and pâté. How many luncheon and dinner parties do you have every day? Of course I realize the staff is padding all your bills, but even the staff will have to be cut down to a skeleton crew."

"So I'm to be the poor Mrs. Vanderbilt," she said with irony.

"Yes, the poor Mrs. Vanderbilt you are, and it's no laughing matter." He stood up and stretched. "Do you mind if I take off my jacket and loosen my tie?"

"You've already done so," she pointed out.

"Your daughter," he continued gravely, sitting down once more, "is now heiress to two and a half million dollars. The other half went to Reggie's other daughter, as you know. You, my dear, will live on little Gloria's bounty until she is twenty-one. Afterwards—who knows?"

"I think it's rather unfair," said Gloria.

"Reggie's debts are staggering," said Harry, unbuttoning the top three buttons of his shirt, "and you as the widow are responsible for them."

She gulped. "How much are they?"

"There's a fourteen-thousand-dollar bill to the butcher alone. They all add up to about a hundred thousand."

"What am I to do?"

"You're young and good-looking," he said with a cynical smile. "You'll marry again."

"I'd better sell my jewelry," she said, touching the necklace of black pearls at her throat.

Harry relished her dilemma. "Since you're under age, you and little Gloria will be appointed wards of the court and your guardians will grant you a suitable income so that you can live comfortably." He glanced about the luxuriously furnished room. "Not as comfortably as this, of course, but you can manage in some small apartment nicely."

She clenched her fists; that patronizing tone of his was like fingernails on a blackboard. "Any other good news for me, Harry?"

"Tomorrow when I go down to my office I'll see how things are and perhaps I can forward you some money."

"Please don't put yourself out on my behalf," she said sarcastically.

He stood up and put on his jacket and adjusted his tie. "I'd invite you out to Westbury," he said in that patronizing way, "but we have a dozen guests from England and we're in the process of building a new and larger house."

She gave him a cold smile. "Are you thinking of having a seraglio for your mistresses?"

"Good idea," he growled, the lines on either side of his mouth deepening.

"How's Gertrude?" Gloria nonchalantly lit a cigarette.

"She's sending her cast of Buffalo Bill out to Wyoming."

"I daresay she was inspired by your manly physique," Gloria remarked dryly.

"Oh, you remember it then?" He moved over to her and his face was dangerously close to hers. "I was hoping you'd forgotten. Family involvements are never wise. Don't you agree?"

She knew he was trying to torture her. She said nothing, merely blew a cloud of smoke in his face. How conceited and vain he was.

"By the way"—he stopped at the door for the last word—"I wouldn't sell any of the furnishings here, because they belong to the estate."

The next morning George Wickersham, the attorney, and Thomas Gilchrist, who would play an important part in her trial some eight years later, came to call with heavy briefcases. "Uncle George" was with the famous law firm of Cadwalader, Wickersham and Taft and had been one of the most famous attorney generals of the United States. Mr. Gilchrist was a younger man and really quite attractive.

"The estate's in bad shape," said George gloomily.

"We think that your mother-in-law will pay all your husband's bills," Thomas Gilchrist put in, watching the widow with fascination. He drank in her gardenia perfume, eyed her pearls and pear-shaped diamond. A perfect victim to be fleeced, he thought.

"Your husband," said Uncle George, "had a life interest in

the Fifty-seventh Street house and he would have inherited
two or three million dollars if he had survived his mother.
But now the property reverts back to his sister, Gertrude
Whitney."

"And she really needs that money," observed Gloria
ironically.

Gilchrist could hardly take his eyes off her—to the point
where she was quite embarrassed. Now he spoke up again.
"We've also applied for forty-eight thousand dollars a year
from the trust for the support and maintenance of you and
your daughter," he told her. "Now just sign here and everything is going to be all right."

She knew nothing of legal matters and signed away merrily. From that moment on until the trial nine years later, the
Sword of Damocles hung over her head.

The next week, on Wednesday it was, she went down to
see Wickersham and Gilchrist about settling the estate.
They used a lot of legal jargon she couldn't comprehend, but
she nodded her head and signed whenever they wanted her
to. Presently they led her out of the office, all smiles and
obsequiousness.

Out in the street, she paused a moment, irresolute. The
humidity was frightful, but she was restless after sitting
for hours and wanted to stretch her legs. Park Avenue was
dead so she strolled over to Lexington, which at least showed
some signs of life. Shops were open and doing business. She
peered into Bloomingdale's windows, gazed into a shop
selling Japanese kimonos and wondered how she'd look in
one. (She was quite looking forward to a stay in Peking as
she'd heard much about the Chinese men from Madame
Wellington Koo.)

By the time she reached the seventies she was dripping.
She stopped at a fruit stall, bought some green seedless

grapes, and began eating them on the spot. The owner looked at her, intrigued. Despite the heat, she made a smart figure in her mourning dress, veils, and gloves. He recognized her from the pictures in the newspapers and handed her a glass of water.

"It's from Saratoga Springs," he told her. "Why aren't you up there, Mrs. Vanderbilt?"

"If you know my name, you know the reason why I'm not there," she said. Refreshed by the water, she mopped her brow. "I had no idea a summer in New York could be so hideous."

"I've spent thirty-six summers here," he laughed.

"You never go away?"

"Poor working people need money, Mrs. Vanderbilt. Ninety-nine percent of the people never see Newport or Monte Carlo. You're lucky," he told her, "and lucky to be independent."

"Yes, I know," she said, "and I'm very grateful."

She moved away eating a delicious peach, a rather incongruous image. People stared, but she didn't care. It was nice to break away from the strict confines of the Vanderbilt world. She never would have been able to eat a peach on the street like this if Reggie had been alive. It was nice also to be free of those heavy cars and the chauffeurs and footmen that went with them.

Head lowered thoughtfully, she made her way home. Yes, the majority of the people lived hard lives; she knew that from her blind soldier friend whose family lived in Flushing Meadows in a semiattached house—whatever that meant. And she'd certainly escaped the woes and problems that beset most of the people in the world. She suddenly understood why she and Reggie were so talked about and written about; indeed this very morning she'd heard a radio broadcast about the fabulous way that Reggie Vanderbilt had lived, and they'd compared him to a Renaissance prince. She and Reggie *had* escaped the dull routine that kept most people enslaved all their lives. They'd been able to have an exciting life, free of responsibilities. Reckless? Well, that's what her detractors were always accusing her of being, but how indeed did one make one's life "worthwhile" and "meaningful"? Children? Career? Love?

Well, a child she had; a career she wasn't interested in; and love she wanted most of all but couldn't find it.

Walking west on 78th Street now, toward Central Park and home, she noticed how tired and brown the leaves were on the trees. She turned the key in the lock of the grilled entrance door and went in. For a moment she stood in the hall and looked about in confusion. Where was she? It was her first attack of disorientation, which was to occur again in her life many times during periods of stress. Then she recognized the portrait of Commodore Vanderbilt over the mantelpiece, and the Vanderbilt coat of arms in the stained-glass window.

She started up the stairs to the third floor where her bedroom was. The lawyers had given the servants their wages, and most of them, save Wann and the cook, had vanished. The house was strangely still and rather disturbing; she got the same feeling when she entered the gloom of The Breakers or the Whitneys' Gothic château on 68th Street that had more the feeling of a cathedral than a home.

She opened her door and gasped. Harry was lying asleep on her bed. His arms were folded behind his head and the sheet only covered him to the waist. In the half-light she gazed at the naked chest and gulped. She tiptoed over to the double bed and sat next to him. Gently, she touched one muscular arm, then stroked it caressingly until he opened his eyes.

"Gloria," he said huskily, not fully awake.

She put her head on his bare shoulder, waiting.

"I had to come to say goodbye," he said after a moment.

"You're going away?" She glanced up fearfully.

He stroked her hair. "No, you are," he said gently. "Your dearest Thelma is in London and your father is in Paris. Now that your financial arrangements have been worked out—well, it would be best for you. You'd be happier there."

They watched each other in silence a moment.

"You want me to go, don't you?"

"Yes," he said. "It's better that way." And as he spoke the words he thought it was the most honest thing he'd ever said to her.

She stood up and went to the fireplace. Presently she said, "You'd better go, Harry. Servants talk, and we don't want another Fielding episode."

"Don't you want to say goodbye properly?"

"No, I don't dare. I care for you too much. Please don't make it harder than—"

He flung back the sheets and went to her, nude. Kneeling, he pressed his face against her, his arms tightening around her. The old sweet warmth filled her.

"Darling," he said tenderly, standing up. He lifted off her veil and cap, then the pearls, kissing her neck as he did so. He unbuttoned her dress slowly, then lowered her slip until finally she stood before him as naked as he was.

In a frenzy she pressed herself against him. "Oh, Harry," she whispered. "Please don't leave me. I love you so much."

He didn't reply, but kissed her passionately on each breast.

"It was a ghastly joke!" she cried. "You aren't really leaving me, are you?"

"Down," he said, pushing her head firmly. "Down and around. . . ."

Much later, at five in the afternoon, Harry was getting dressed. All thoughts of love had vanished from his head now that he was satisfied. He could only think of going to the Knickerbocker Club and having a couple of drinks with the boys and later a good dinner at 871 Fifth.

Wann knocked at the door. "Mrs. Vanderbilt, Prince Hohenlohe is downstairs."

"He's a persistent fellow, isn't he?" Despite himself, Harry suffered pangs of jealousy.

"He loves me," replied Gloria quietly. She slowly zipped up her dress.

"Implying I don't?" Harry flung his jacket on angrily.

"You only love what we do together in bed—like dogs or pigs." She turned away and lit a cigarette.

"You and Hohenlohe will be happy in Paris having a platonic relationship," said Harry disdainfully. Later as he strode through the hall he shot Hohenlohe a contemptuous look.

Gloria was left behind, confused and upset. This disturbing love-hate relationship was bad for her, she realized. She decided to pay more attention to Friedel.

Weeks passed. The trees in Central Park turned copper and the leaves started to fall. Hohenlohe came every day now and they took long walks and held hands. He hadn't kissed her yet, but she felt it was coming any minute. It was a refreshing change to be with Friedel, who hung on her every word and laughed at her every joke. Being with him gave her some measure of self-confidence again.

Not a word from Harry. Gertrude telephoned one day; she'd heard Gloria was leaving for Paris and asked her to come by for a farewell drink. So one afternoon near the end of October she pulled the bell at 871 Fifth Avenue.

The butler greeted her. "Mrs. Whitney's in the ballroom, ma'am."

"Oh? I was about to go to her drawing room upstairs."

"We're redecorating the ballroom, ma'am."

She was ushered into the immense cream-and-gold chamber with its painted oval ceiling in rich pinks and blues. Louis XV and Louis XVI garniture in the inevitable needlepoint stood about the parquet de Versailles floors that had been torn from a château in Normandy. Gertrude was surrounded by interior decorators, she introduced them to Gloria, and presently the two women were left to themselves.

"What does one do with a room like this?" sighed Gertrude. "The ceiling is something special, but all this space—Harry's father used to have dances for the Four Hundred here. Can you imagine my sending out four hundred invitations today? Although my secretary is dying to, as she says she has nothing to do. . . . That tapestry you're admiring depicts Philip the Second and the armada. Harry is wonderful about history and can tell you about it. And speaking of Harry, it was he who told me you're leaving us for a while."

At the mention of Harry's name Gloria felt a slight sickness in her stomach. "Yes," she managed to say. "I'm going to make Paris my headquarters."

Gertrude put her arm around her and beamed. "My dear, I'm so happy. I never really thought you'd adapt to Fifth Avenue and Newport, and despite all of Reggie's bohemian talk, he was chained to mother and The Breakers and everything that went with that."

"Yes," said Gloria nodding, "I suppose you're right."

"One gets accustomed to something and doesn't like to change," Gertrude went on.

"Yes," said Gloria, suddenly aware that they were talking about something totally different.

The butler came in and asked if they would like to have something to drink. Gertrude said she'd become wild for Pernod and would Gloria like to try some on ice. "It's rather like ouzo," she said.

"Heavenly. We can sit here and pretend we're in Athens."

"It doesn't bore you to sit here in this great big barn, does it?" laughed Gertrude. "I told Harry I'm going to use it as a studio, which amused him no end. He's a good sort, you know. We're used to one another, we speak the same language. That's why our marriage has lasted." She looked at Gloria, but Gloria couldn't read her expression.

"How fortunate you are, Gertrude."

"Harry has little flirtations, but he always comes home to me. You see, I leave him alone and I have a life apart from him."

"I wish I were independent."

"But you're a dependent type, darling."

"That's what everyone always says," agreed Gloria sadly.

The butler brought them their drinks and they sipped them appreciatively.

"You'll find the right man, my dear," continued Gertrude. "I hear Hohenlohe is very taken with you."

"I do like him," Gloria confessed.

"You'll be a Serene Highness and will be better seated at table than anyone else, which will make Grace furious. And someone told me his castle in Germany is extraordinary."

"You make it sound too exciting for words, Gertrude," she said, tipsy now on the strong drink.

"And little Gloria—what of her?"

"I'll bring her back here when she's seven or eight and enroll her at Brearley or Miss Chapin's."

"Admirable. That's where Gladys and I went to school."

"My father's going to retire now to Paris, and Thelma travels backs and forth from London to Paris with great regularity. So I won't be alone," said Gloria. She drained another small glass.

"I didn't think you'd be alone," purred Gertrude. "But Harry and I will miss you, my dear. You've been a bright spot in our lives and given us much to talk about."

"I'm sorry to deprive you of your entertainment."

The two women's eyes met and they both knew they hated each other.

Gertrude's eyes darkened and Gloria swiftly stood up. "I must leave—there's so much to do. Will I see you in Paris?"

"If I can't, your guardians, Wickersham and Gilchrist, will keep me posted on your activities," Gertrude said in a meaningful tone.

Gloria felt a shiver of fear. She held out her hand and said goodbye; the two women didn't embrace, and each one parted from the other with a feeling of envy and ill will.

On December 5, Gloria with her retinue sailed for France on the *Aquitania*. This time, because of her mourning, there was no farewell party—only that ill-starred duo, Jeanne Eagels and John Gilbert, came to see her off.

Later Gloria and Prince Hohenlohe stood on the deck and watched the skyline vanish behind them. She looked so sad that he put his arms around her protectively and said, "It's all behind you, and ahead lies a new life."

She looked up at him trustingly. "Yes, I think so."

The great propellers churned up a furious wake of foam and the gulls screeched noisily. This time, Gloria reflected, they sounded happy, unlike that day of Reggie's funeral. . . .

CHAPTER
19

She took a house at Biarritz in the summer of 1926, and little Gloria and mama liked it so much that she took the same villa for three subsequent summers. She had such horrible fights with mama, however, that mama never returned to the villa after the summer of 1928. What a relief it was to have that woman out of her hair. She caused everyone in the household to fight and be at each other's throat, so the atmosphere was always chaotic.

Gloria's home in Paris, at 14 avenue Charles Floquet, overlooked the Champs des Mars by the Ecole Militaire in the 16th arrondisement. She had three lovely floors with large, well-proportioned rooms whose balconies and shutters overlooked a charming vista of trees and gardens. She and Hohenlohe often went off together to his beautiful *Schloss* and she grew fond of his mother who was in many ways like old Mrs. Vanderbilt. Sometimes they went off on trips to the south of France or Venice or Le Touquet on the English

Channel, but she never returned there after she nearly perished in an air crash.

It was the night after this crash that Hohenlohe proposed to her again, and this time she realized she loved him as much as he loved her. He was a charming man, sweet-tempered and never dull to live with because he had an active, inquiring mind and the same love of traveling that she did. "I feel in such a holiday mood today," he would cry, throwing open the shutters of their bedroom. Every day was like that with him. Once, on a dare, they even got on the Orient Express and went off to Istanbul.

One morning in the villa in Biarritz, Hohenlohe brought her her breakfast in bed. There were yellow and pink sweetheart roses on the tray and a lovely little card saying, "Three years mine and so much love." He was always bringing her cards and bunches of flowers.

"Gloria," he said firmly, "I know you hate to be pinned down to things and make a decision, but I want a definite answer. Will you marry me or won't you?"

He sat on the edge of the bed with a lock of his dark hair falling over his forehead. His red dressing gown was open and the thick matting of hair on his chest gave her the usual quiver.

"Well . . ." she sighed.

"Yes or no!" he said distinctly.

She gazed at him for a moment. The bright Basque sunshine was streaming through the French windows into the room overflowing with yellow roses. Outside the gardeners were raking the gravel walks between the flower beds and pruning the acacias. The fragrance of pink and white oleanders, mixed with the fresh, salty smell of the nearby sea, was exhilarating to the senses, and he seemed part of all this joy. He was so young and sweet and she couldn't bear the idea of ever losing him.

"Yes," she said happily. "Yes, I'll marry you, Friedel."

He was overjoyed. His face was so radiant she was moved.

"Then you must go to America immediately and tell your guardians your intentions and what a wonderful papa I'll make for little Gloria."

"Oh, I will," she cried, "and I know they'll see it our way."

"Even the Vanderbilts will approve of my castle. It's as big as any of theirs."

She arrived in New York on the *Ile de France* and took a suite in the Hotel Netherlands at 59th and Fifth Avenue, a location she knew only too well. But how sad to look out of her window and no longer see the great hulk of the Vanderbilt house—the mighty red and gray Blois château—but Bergdorf Goodman in its place! So many of the Vanderbilt palaces had been demolished and skyscrapers put up in their place. Only Grace and Neily continued their grand social existence at 640 Fifth, and old Alice told her that he was gambling recklessly on Wall Street "to keep the show going."

One morning she was surprised to hear from Harry Payne Whitney. "It's urgent I see you," he said. "Come down to Wall Street because I can't get away. The catastrophe is coming any minute."

In 1926 Sandy Point Farm had been sold to Gloria's neighbor, Moses Taylor, and in May of that year she'd had an auction on the premises and sold all but two of the twelve cars. Now the chauffeur was driving the old Hispano-Suiza down Third Avenue under the El which grumbled furiously with the trains above. The chauffeur had been with Reggie's father and he drove maddeningly, sometimes pressing the accelerator to the floor so that he almost hit a pedestrian, and at other times creeping along at ten miles an hour so that there was a long line of impatient drivers honking behind them.

In a highly agitated state she arrived at Harry's office. She was dressed in a fashionable beige suit from Patou, the cuffs and collar bordered in silky lynx, and she carried a muff of the same fur. A veil went to the tip of her nose. Most of her jewelry she'd sold on Harry's advice and invested in blue-chip stocks, but today she wore the sapphire ring Harry once gave her and of course Reggie's beautiful marquise diamond.

Gloria was ushered into the walnut-paneled office and Harry rose from behind a massive desk to greet her. She was shocked to see how he had aged.

"You're a welcome sight in all this Wall Street gloom," he said, making a big effort to seem the way he used to be.

"Are things so bad?" she said, sitting down in a chair across from him. She took out a cigarette and he lit it for her.

"My chum Harrison Williams believes the bull market will last forever," said Harry, looking gray and tired. "Harrison has got a billion dollars in the market at this very moment. I begged him to sell, but he's stubborn as hell. Ferd Eberstadt and I sold most of our holdings last year, and now I'm trying to convince Gertrude to sell hers before it's too late. She's made an enormous killing but like so many people she's greedy for more."

"So am I," said Gloria, with a little laugh.

"Gertrude's parlayed it up to forty million and that's a nice sum for a woman, don't you think?"

"Definitely." Damn that bitch, Gloria thought.

"I hope you've sold out."

"I haven't."

"How much do you have now?"

"Around seven hundred thousand, all due to you, Harry. RCA and General Motors have done brilliantly, and Electric Bond and Share—"

"Jesus," cried Harry, "sell, sell!"

"Oh, but I hate to sell them, they pay me such good dividends," she said helplessly.

"But they won't pay any more dividends, Gloria. I think they're going to be taken off the boards in a few weeks. I'll call your broker, if you want me to, and put in the sell order."

"All right," she agreed. "God knows I need cash. I'm spending far more than my income."

"As usual," Harry smiled. "How much did you pay for that outfit you're wearing?"

"Patou gave me a special price."

"Why did he give you a special price?" The old insinuating, seductive tone came back.

"He's very fond of me," she said with a mischievous smile.

"I hear he's a great womanizer," said Harry.

"He is!" said Gloria.

They both laughed and looked at each other affectionately. Their grand passion had faded to only a memory. Now they were like two old friends.

The secretary came in and announced some important calls, and while he was on the phone Gloria looked about the room. She was touched to see a picture of herself on a library table, taken in an ethereal chiffon dress with gardenias at her bosom. Across from it was a photo of Gertrude looking regal and austere. Looking at the pictures, Gloria felt there was much unfinished business between them.

After a short time Harry hung up the phone and turned his attention back to Gloria. "Is Thelma here with you?" he asked.

"My dear," she said with a Mayfair intonation, "Milady is riding high with His Royal Highness Prince Edward David George Windsor—in Biarritz."

"I read in the paper they stayed with you last month."

"Yes, everyone was beating at our doors—the press was terrible, following us everywhere, mistaking her for me and vice versa, until I had to flee to Lourdes."

"With Edward?" said Harry with a playful wink. "Now listen, Gloria, we're old friends. I want to hear what the boy's like. Don't bat your eyes at me, I know you've had him."

"Really, Harry, what do you think I am?"

"The best lay in town," he said, puffing on a cigar. "Come on, old girl, tell Uncle Harry what the prince is like in bed. Out with it. What did Thelma tell you?"

She lowered her head and giggled. "Well, Thelma says it takes a lot of work to get him—excited, if you know what I mean."

"And does he have a whopper like Chaplin?"

"Oh, Harry, you know Thelma and I don't talk about things like that!"

"The hell you don't."

It was nice to be with Harry. Nice and relaxing to be with an old friend, for really she had become deeply attached to him and he to her.

"Harry, what is the urgent matter that you wanted to talk to me about? It wasn't just about stocks, was it?"

"No." He stubbed out the cigar and his face became serious. "I hate to be a killjoy but your mother is all over Gertrude every day and filling her head with a lot of poison."

"That troublemaker!" Gloria slammed her hand down on the desk in frustration.

Harry nodded. "Gertrude has never liked you, for reasons we know all too well, and now your mother's played right into her hands. And I can tell from Gertrude's remarks that she believes all of her lies."

"She wants to believe them," said Gloria bitterly.

Harry shrugged with a weary gesture. "You must protect yourself somehow, Gloria."

"What can they do to me?" She nervously lit another cigarette.

"Prove you're an unfit mother and take little Gloria away from you."

"My God!" she cried, all the breath leaving her body. Such a thing had never occurred to her. "Why would they want to do that to me?"

"Gertrude hates you, and your mother is envious and hates you too, and you know she's a very disturbed woman; she resents your having her 'little precious darling.' "

"What can I do?"

"Return here to live and give up Hohenlohe. He's not only a foreigner but a German, and the family will never relinquish Reggie's child to him."

"But I'm going to marry Friedel," she said. "That's why I'm here."

"You can't marry him," said Harry quietly.

"Am I to have no happiness?" Tears filled her eyes.

"You'll find another man here," Harry told her. "You're so young and pretty, and you made an enormous impression on Gilchrist. He's always reading me and Gertrude articles about you and showing us pictures of you by Cecil Beaton and photos of your parties in *Vogue*."

"I'll bet Gertrude has plenty to say about that." Gloria dabbed at her tears with a lace-trimmed silk handkerchief.

"You can imagine what she thinks, with your mother filling in the lurid details. Sounds like the worst Somerset Maugham melodrama."

He watched her sadly. The future didn't bode well at all for her, but he didn't want to tell her that.

The secretary came in to announce that lunch was ready in the club next door.

As they were going out the door, he took Gloria's arm and squeezed it. "Did I tell you about that sinister devil, Fielding? He's become a millionaire working for J. P. Morgan and married some very rich girl—I can't remember her name."

She smiled. "You did predict it."

The club dated back to the old Dutch days of New Am-

sterdam. A warm fire was burning in the Delft-tiled fireplace
and maps of old New York decorated the dark, smoke-
stained walls. With its beamed ceilings, it was just what she
imagined an old Revolutionary tavern to look like.

"George Baker and J. P. Morgan often come here." Harry
had spoken the bad news and now he just wanted to pretend
for a few moments that everything was all right. He didn't
want to think about his failing health either.

"Harry, dear," she said softly, "you don't have to make
small talk with me. Tell me how you are. You don't look
yourself."

"I'm fine," he lied, "but I'm worried about you. Will you
promise to dump all your securities like a good girl? Then
I won't be anxious about you, you'll have a good income to
get you through the bad times ahead. Call me tomorrow and
tell me that you've sold them." He put his hand on hers. It
felt cold and gave her a nasty turn. She knew in her heart
that Harry wasn't well, but that he was too much of a stoic to
speak about it.

When they left the restaurant they found the rain pouring
down in torrents. Gloria glanced up at Harry. In the gray
light he looked ill and she hated to let him go. She tenderly
put her hand on his arm. "Why don't we dine tonight and
catch up on all the news?"

He glanced about apprehensively. "There's too much business to take care of, Gloria, and very little time left." He
spoke with such resignation that she stared at him, frightened by his tone. The all-powerful Harry was fading before
her. Who could she turn to if he was gone?

Suddenly an elaborate town car with wicker doors drew up
and a handsome, beautifully dressed man with a blond
mustache and bowler hat jumped out. It was Fielding! And
looking for all the world like Mayor Jimmy Walker, elegantly turned out in a double-breasted cashmere overcoat and
highly polished Peal shoes. He was a man of importance

now, with a town house on 64th Street and a country estate
in Locust Valley. His wife was social and fashionable and
much written about. He'd arrived.

"Hello, you sinners," he cried gaily. He spoke with such
charm that they laughed. "Listen, can I give you a lift?" His
voice and manner were still rough and crude, but she felt a
strong physical attraction to him.

"My office is right around the corner, but I wish you'd
give my sister-in-law a lift," said Harry.

"Delighted!" Fielding spoke the word with such zest that
Gloria almost forgot Harry's gray face.

"Get in, Gloria," said Harry, pushing her into the car.
Fielding jumped in beside her and the heavy car started forward through the crowded streets.

Gloria rolled down the window and tried to signal Harry.
"Take care, darling, and call me later," she cried. But her
voice was lost in the traffic noise and he didn't turn and see
her. That was the last time she saw him.

"I have three of these automobiles now," said Fielding,
turning to look at her in the gray suede interior. "The purr
of the engines is like music to my ears, and the way the doors
close is a work of art."

"I know only too well," she said, thinking of Reggie.

"Where are you staying?" he asked.

"At the Netherlands."

"Why don't you move to the Ambassador? I'm part owner
of the hotel, you know, along with a lot of other real estate.
My biggest killing was in RCA. There are eight hundred
and fifty million radio sets in America now, you know. . . ."

He went on relating his various triumphs in the financial
and social scene, but she no longer listened to his words. She
felt horribly depressed by what Harry had told her. Mama
and Gertrude teaming up was really bad news. Could they
really take little Gloria from her? And if that wasn't bad
enough to think about, there was Harry looking so strange.

And what did he mean that she couldn't marry Hohenlohe?
All her supports were being pulled out from under her. . . .

Fielding had noticed that she was staring out the window,
not listening. "These rainy days make you feel blue?" he
asked.

She nodded quietly, then she burst into tears. "Everyone's
against me," she sobbed. "I'm finished, finished."

"That's a fine way for the most beautiful woman in the
world to talk," he said, taking her hand.

The next thing she knew, they were stepping out of the
elevator upstairs at the Netherlands and she was turning the
key in her apartment door.

An anxious Wann met her. "I couldn't get rid of your
mother," she whispered. "She's been here for hours."

Gloria and Fielding stepped into the drawing room and
there indeed was mama. Mrs. Morgan gave Fielding such a
knowing look that Gloria blushed. Embarrassed, she introduced her mother to him.

"Fielding, did you say?" said mama in her sharp manner.

Fielding caught the uneasiness between mother and daughter and gracefully made his exit.

Laura Morgan turned on her daughter.

"Such a powerful-looking man, and what extraordinarily
hard blue eyes! I daresay you just picked him up in the lobby
downstairs, didn't you?"

Gloria took off her hat and flung herself into a chair. The
same old mama. Aloud she said, "He's an old friend—he
owns hotels and real estate."

"He's no gentleman," observed Mrs. Morgan darkly.

"Did I say he was?"

"That diamond ring on his pinkie and those diamond cuff
links!" she snorted. "Really, the mother of a young child
should be more circumspect about the garbage she consorts
with. This one is worse than that Boche, the uhlan, that
German swine, Hohenlohe."

"Fielding is an old friend of Harry's and we bumped into him after lunch," Gloria said wearily.

Mrs. Morgan smoothed her sleek black hair. "Harry, eh? So you're up to your old tricks with him again! Any new presents to show me? You'll never change—but then, a leopard never changes its spots."

"Why are you here, mama? What do you want?" Gloria was getting tired of these endless scenes.

"I want you to sign over little Gloria to me," Laura Morgan replied silkily.

"That's insane," said Gloria.

Laura Morgan watched her daughter with a triumphant air. "The Whitneys and Vanderbilts are in back of me," she declared. "They know what you are; the whole world knows what you are."

"Knows what?" said Gloria.

"Knows your fast and reckless habits," retorted mama. "I could tell when you walked in here just now that you were dying to jump into bed with that common hotelkeeper!"

Gardner Pell, who was now Gloria's stockbroker, called just then, and she was so rattled by mama's accusations that she couldn't make head or tail of what he was saying to her. Even Harry's advice completely slipped her mind. Later she would bitterly reflect that mama's scene had cost her over $700,000; the enormous profits she had made last year were completely wiped out.

"So you've taken to gambling on the stock market, too," cried mama after Gloria hung up; then abruptly changed her tack. "Well, I daresay you do need Hohenlohe to look after you—you're so sweet and impractical." She gave her daughter a long look. "You want Hohenlohe, don't you?"

"Yes," said Gloria.

"You'll be a beautiful princess and everyone will bow and curtsy to you," mama continued, her black eyes unblinking and hypnotic. "Hohenlohe is a strong man, and you need

a strong man. And I'm certain you'll have many boys to in-
sure the line."

"I hope so," said Gloria.

"You see? Your destiny lies in Germany, my darling, and
mine lies here in America with my little Gloria."

"You're insane, mama."

"Little Gloria is mine!" insisted Laura Morgan, her voice
rising angrily again. "She's always been mine. You have no
true feelings for her—all you want is her money."

"That's not true, mama. You know I care for her, and
Friedel does too."

"Well, Gertrude doesn't like him, and she's her godmother.
Look," said Mrs. Morgan logically, "she has money and
power and political influence behind her. You have nothing,
so give us the child and take your prince. Don't you see it's
the only way out for you?"

Gloria turned and went to the window. The rain was still
coming down in heavy sheets. She remembered Harry's
gray face. No, he couldn't help her anymore. Only one person
could help her now—Friedel. But he was in Europe.

When she turned around to tell mama her decision, Mrs.
Morgan was gone.

At seven that very evening, husky, blond Fielding, looking very handsome in his midnight blue double-breasted topcoat, appeared at her door.

She opened the door a crack and said, "What do you
want?"

"I have some wonderful tickets for Mae West in *Diamond
Lil*," he told her enthusiastically.

"I can't, Fielding, I've just come out of the bath." It was a
lie, but Gloria was too distraught to think of going out.

"Well, let's just stay home then." He pushed the door open
and went in.

The door closed and didn't open again for days. No one saw them in the hotel except the chambermaid and the man from room service who brought them their meals. Fielding's cruel, powerful body completely enslaved her and she reached new heights of passion. It was the most physical experience she'd ever had and it kept her mind from dwelling on terrible things. Harry was like a choirboy compared to Fielding. She was haunted by his enormous sex to such a degree that her disturbing dreams were filled with obelisks and erotic vegetables.

Black Tuesday, October 28, came and went. Frantic calls came from Gardner saying that sixteen million, four hundred and ten thousand shares had changed hands. General Motors alone dropped from 72¾ to 36, and New York Central plummeted from 256 to 160. John D. Rockefeller and Andrew Mellon said they believed the economy was basically sound. Richard Whitney, known as the Morgan broker, who had been a friend of Reggie's, kept placing enormous orders for U.S. Steel and Eastman Kodak. Gloria put through a phone call to him and he assured her that everything was going to be all right; this "little liquidation" was just a "sell-off" and everything would soon bounce back. Poor Gloria blindly believed him.

One November day when Fielding had gone out, Wickersham and Gilchrist arrived. She ignored Gilchrist's stare and his obvious infatuation. The only thing that got through to her was that they did not approve of Hohenlohe, and nothing she could say would alter their opinion. They could not allow a German to be the stepfather of little Gloria Vanderbilt. Looking at their faces, she found herself wondering if they'd joined Gertrude's camp. Everyone did have his price, as Fielding often told her.

"But Prince Hohenlohe is such a good man and he loves little Gloria so much," she pleaded.

"It's out of the question," said Gilchrist sternly.

"Besides," said Wickersham, "Mrs. Whitney would never give her approval of a Vanderbilt child being raised as a foreigner."

"And Mrs. Whitney has so much to say about this matter?" asked Gloria.

The two men looked at one another. "I'm sorry, Gloria," said the fatherly Wickersham. "If you insist on marrying Hohenlohe, you'll almost certainly forfeit the child."

The two men put on their coats and left her alone with her dark thoughts.

That evening when Fielding arrived, she started to tell him the verdict of Wickersham and Gilchrist. "Darling," she said, "my guardians tell me I cannot—"

But then his brawny arms were around her and his mouth was on hers. They fell onto the bed and again they lost track of time. . . .

In the blurred days that followed she couldn't even write Friedel her decision, although finally one day at the end of November she did send him a vague and rambling letter: "My money is all gone due to my stupidity and the Wall Street collapse, and my guardians will not give their stamp of approval to our marriage. Missing you dreadfully—so lost and empty without you—Your heartbroken Gloria."

By now her relationship with Fielding had reached the point where he told her he couldn't abide his wife any longer; she was grumpy and peevish all the time, he said, and her stuffed-shirt friends bored him to death. Was he thinking of marriage? Gloria wondered. Apparently not. They had a drink one evening and went to see *Porgy and Bess*, then he dropped her home and that was the last she ever saw of him. She read in the papers in the following days the stories about "The Fielding Stock Swindle" and then learned that he was in Havana.

By early December she knew she could no longer stay on in New York; these drifting days must come to an end, she had to make a decision even if it was the wrong one.

Thelma's cable on December 5 caused her to pull herself together and make a plan. "Darling," the cable read. "David [as she called Prince Edward] and I want you to spend Christmas with us here at Fort Belvedere—so cozy and informal with the duke and duchess of Marlborough and the marchioness of Bath and a divine Russian, Nada Milford-Haven. Hurry, hurry, hurry, my soulmate! Here's to 1930 and the best years of our lives! Peggy Hopkins Joyce, if you can bear it, is with Furness now in her villa in Monte Carlo. Good riddance. Much love, Milady."

She sent off a quick cable to Thelma asking if she could bring Friedel, and the next morning received an affirmative. Then she sent off another cable to Friedel telling him that Thelma and the Prince of Wales expected him for Christmas at the fort and asking him to meet her there. She received no reply from him, and two days later she and Wann sailed on the *Berengeria* where she had the royal suite to cheer her up. She'd just lost $700,000 and knew she should be cutting costs—but what the hell. . . .

CHAPTER
20

Belvedere truly was a fort, with cannons on the battlements and round towers with pointed windows and a moat complete with drawbridge. Here the most famous man in the world, the young and pretty Prince of Wales, played at the simple life the way Marie Antoinette had done at the Little Trianon. The slender, golden-haired prince greeted Gloria in a kilt with scores of dogs yapping at his feet. Thelma was hanging onto his arm, and Gloria noticed many new pieces of jewelry blazing on her.

"Welcome, my dear," said the blue-eyed heir apparent, and she was struck by the winsome handsomeness of his face. "My goodness, you two really are identical."

"Does it bother you, dearest?" said Thelma playfully.

"It gives me food for thought," said the future Edward VIII.

"No hanky-panky with Gloria!" ordered Thelma gaily.
"You Americans are smashing," declared David. "My
grandfather loved Americans too, you know."

"Yes, he had a wandering eye that wandered over two
continents," observed Thelma dryly.

It was three days before Christmas and the fort was
decorated in the old-fashioned style with mistletoe, holly,
and a ten-foot Christmas tree topped with an angel. It was all
very festive, and Gloria didn't have time to talk to Thelma
privately until after dinner and bridge.

At a little before midnight the twins finally found time to
be alone. They were in Gloria's tower room with its black
lacquer and mother-of-pearl furniture, a gift from the
maharaja of Baroda. Gloria had gotten into a silk-and-lace
nightgown made specially for her by nuns in France.

"What a chore," sighed Thelma, "but of course goodness
has its reward."

"But you love him, don't you, darling?" said Gloria.

"I'd rather have an Arab chieftain who'd carry me off into
the desert," chuckled Thelma. "As it is I have to carry the
bonny prince off to bed—and what work, my dear, in the
feathers!"

"But he's so sweet," said Gloria. "And he loves you so."

"That's just the trouble," said Thelma.

Gloria slipped into bed between thick, heavily coroneted
linen sheets and lay back against a pile of downy pillows
also monogrammed so thickly that they left an impression
on her face.

"Thelma," she said thoughtfully, "where is Friedel?"

Thelma looked uneasy. "I have bad news," she said. "He
cabled that he couldn't join you here."

"Oh," said Gloria faintly. "Did he say why?"

"Well—" Thelma hesitated. "Gloria, he said he's going
to marry Princess Marguerita. She's a plain little thing,"

Thelma hastened to add, "the daughter of Prince Andrew of Greece, and he's marrying her for dynastic reasons. Marguerita's sister is married to the grand duke of Hesse, and Theodora, the other sister, is going to marry Berthold, prince and margrave of Baden."

Gloria was stunned. Another failure. "I seem to be doing everything wrong," she cried.

"Nonsense," said Thelma brightly. "I believe everything happens for the best. And my David has a divine younger brother who is pining to meet you. Prince George is arriving Christmas Day. He's going through a playboy period now, but you know how to handle playboys, don't you, darling!"

Thelma was so confident that Gloria laughed in spite of herself. "Tell me more about this paragon."

"Very horsey, darling. Always off to the hunt—he shot fifty-six pheasants last week in Scotland. His tweeds smell frightfully gamy!" The twins laughed together and soon they were scheming again.

On Christmas day they had a large party with a stuffed pig, wild game, and the most delicious vegetables Gloria had ever tasted—except perhaps at Alice Vanderbilt's. Prince George was supposed to have arrived at lunch but still hadn't appeared, and his brother was becoming angrier by the minute. Watching him, Gloria thought the Prince of Wales was similar to poor Reggie: so petulant, so sullen if he didn't have his own way.

Soon, however, they heard a commotion in the hall.

"Jingle bells!" cried Prince George, bursting into the room with his aide de camp, Lord Norton. Both men were so good-looking and high-spirited that Gloria warmed to them at once. They were only a few years older than she, and she liked being with people her own age now.

George sat across from her at lunch and kept pressing his foot on hers under the table, which rekindled her self-confidence a bit. "I've never seen skin like yours," said George. "It has a look of El Greco, and Titian would surely have given his soul to paint it!"

"How do *you* feel about it?" said Gloria, falling into her old lighthearted mood.

"I'd give my soul to touch it, too," said the blue-eyed athlete, "although I'm only a prince, not an artist."

She liked him for saying that. What a lovely man he must be—a perfect Christmas companion, and very attractive, too. . . .

The next morning the twins were lounging about Thelma's sitting room. It was all hung in cheerful red-and-green Scottish tartans and a wood fire was crackling in the marble fireplace.

"You may have lost one prince, darling," Thelma was saying philosophically, "but now you have another!"

"The law of averages," laughed Gloria, her gray New York mood completely gone by now.

"How was he?" cried Thelma, trying on new luncheon costumes that had just arrived from Paris, and settling on a dazzling Chanel.

"Sweet," said Gloria. "Like a schoolboy. And so grateful."

"These English royals are rich as Vanderbilts, you know. Not like so many of our friends jumping out windows in Wall Street. David will have an income of over ten million a year, you know, when he becomes king."

"Do you think George is interested in marriage?" asked Gloria thoughtfully, staring into the flames.

"I think he's just out for a fun time," replied Thelma. "But of course, Napier Norton is another matter. He's frightfully attractive, don't you find? But there's something brutal about him, as if he'd like to kill you."

This aroused Gloria, and at the lunch table she looked at Lord Norton with fresh interest. However, he was cold and silent most of the time and spoke only when spoken to. Gloria decided he was a complicated, profound man—which further fascinated her.

The days passed pleasantly. The men were out riding in the morning and shooting in the afternoon. Sometimes Gloria accompanied them and sometimes she didn't. George was hungry for American slang and her words amused him no end. Norton, however, never cracked a smile.

"Let's go to the Embassy Club for New Year's Eve!" cried the Prince of Wales in his boyish way. "They have a new jazz band there and Gloria can teach me the new steps from New York."

The Embassy Club was a fashionable nightclub in London, so they trooped into a caravan of Rolls-Royces and, like the old Vanderbilt days, proceeded to get drunk in the rear of the cars. The club was all black velvet and chromium and mirrored columns, with a huge dance floor surrounded by tables. It was really exciting to be in the company of the Prince of Wales and his brother. And needless to say, they were treated like royalty.

George was a sublime waltzer and he and Gloria whirled about the dance floor, the cynosure of all eyes. Lanvin had made her a black velvet evening dress and the full skirt billowed out romantically as they spun about. Her luck was changing! Gloria thought tipsily about how wonderful it would be to be a royal princess. There would be no end of triumphs for the Morgan twins!

George was wonderfully attentive to her. "You know, I've been hearing about you for years, Gloria," he said.

"Disappointed?" she said flirtatiously.

"God, no!" He kissed her neck and drank in her heady gardenia perfume.

At midnight everybody blew whistles, and a cloud of red and white balloons was released.

"The Thirties will be our time," cried Thelma, kissing her prince tenderly.

Lord Norton suddenly leaned close. "Nineteen thirty will be our year, Gloria," he said.

Gloria was taken aback by the unexpected remark from this usually uncommunicative man. "Why, Lord Norton," she said, recovering, "I do declare! What will George say?"

"You're just a glass of champagne to him," said Norton.

"Let's drink to that," said Gloria, raising her glass and clinking it with his. Like Reggie, she was forever thinking now of ways to celebrate which would give her an excuse to drink. When she was tight, all of her guilt and self-hatred faded and she seeemed to become the person she'd always wanted to be.

Prince George decided he wanted to escape the winter doldrums of London and bask in the sun of Egypt. It was a bad move—leaving Gloria behind with the big red-haired Norton.

Napier was with her all the time now and his big brutal body gave her something to look forward to. Indeed it thrilled her to think that perhaps she had met the man who would destroy her. His gray eyes were so tormented and her fantasies of him grew more erotic.

They boarded a yacht and set sail for the green palm trees and violet shores of Monte Carlo. Every night they were in the casino, and Gloria gambled recklessly and compulsively —the way she did everything these days. When she was seventeen she had had goals, but then these goals had been realized, and had proved disappointing. Now there was no goal, only drifting. Somehow she was unable to sit still long enough for moments of introspection. Like most women, she was terrified of being alone, and like most romantic women, found it necessary to have a man look after her.

"You're always escaping, Gloria," Thelma would say.

"Escaping what?" Gloria would gaze off into the distance as though in a trance.

"Escaping yourself and your responsibilities. You must think, Gloria Vanderbilt."

"I don't want to think, except of Napier." He was the only man in her life now that Friedel and George were gone and the love of her life, Harry Payne Whitney, had just died. The news had prostrated her for days.

"And what about little Gloria? You hardly ever see her."

"Does any mother in our little set see her children?" asked Gloria.

"That's true," admitted Thelma. "They all have nurses and governesses to look after them."

"Little Gloria has Wann and Emma," said Gloria with a sad smile. "And I'm there when she needs me."

"Do you have any rapport with the child?"

"Did mama have any rapport with us?" cried Gloria, a little angrily.

"But, darling, what I want to find out is, do you have any feelings for her? You seem so hostile every time I bring up the subject."

"I don't want to talk about it," said Gloria with a stubborn expression.

Thelma gazed at her twin reflectively. "You resent her, don't you?"

"Resent?" cried Gloria. "Why should I resent my own child?"

"Because she has the money and you're living off her income, that's why."

Gloria winced. "What an awful thing to say," she whispered.

"It's the truth, isn't it?"

"I don't want to hear it. Ever!" cried Gloria.

"Then run, run, run!"

And run she did. Napier was in some ways like Reggie—
he was bitter from disappointments and early hurts. Unlike
Reggie, however, he took pleasure in punishing her, with the
result that they had a strange and passionate sadomasochistic
relationship.

They returned to Paris to spend Christmas of 1931 with
little Gloria, but every minute that she was with the child she
kept hearing Thelma's odious words. It was true—she did
resent little Gloria. It was horrible to have to admit it, but
there it was.

Norton flew back to England the next day and Gloria
pulled the sheets over her head and didn't stir out of her bed
until twilight. That evening she dined with Connie Bennett
and her new husband, the French marquis Henri de la
Falaise. They all went on to the grandiose apartment of the
Match King, Ivar Kreuger, a legendary billionaire and
notorious Swedish swindler. They dined in his apartment
at avenue Victor Emmanuel, and the celebrated tycoon
took a great fancy to Gloria.

Although she did not find him physically attractive, she
accepted an invitation to his New Year's Eve party the next
evening at Maxim's.

For New Year's Eve, the Swede had invited a party of
twenty and Gloria found herself seated between Kreuger
himself and a short, cocky man named A. C. Blumenthal, who
was a sort of cross between Charlie Chaplin and Edward G.
Robinson, violently sexual and a famous swordsman. "A
great dancer," Thelma would have said.

"What do you do here in Paris, Mrs. Vanderbilt?" asked
Blumenthal over their pheasant mousse and champagne.

"What I do in New York, London, Biarritz, Rome, and Monte Carlo."

"And what's that, may I ask?" he said in an insinuating tone. All the time his evil eyes never left her mouth.

"I don't think I know you well enough to tell you."

"You'll know me well enough by the end of the evening," he said.

What a nervy creature he was! She turned her back on him and started a conversation with Kreuger, though you couldn't exactly call it a conversation because Kreuger hardly ever spoke. Indeed he didn't look in the best of health. She babbled away anyway so she wouldn't have to turn back to Blumenthal.

Gloria was talking animatedly to Kreuger, thus, when Napier Norton strolled in.

"Napier," she exclaimed, "you're back sooner than expected." She held out her hand to be kissed.

"Your nursemaid, Emma, told me where you were." He was surly and reeked of gin.

"Delighted," she said coolly, although her heart was beating in uneven spasms. "Mr. Kreuger, you know my friend, Lord Norton, don't you?" she said, introducing them casually. "We've just been to Monte Carlo and it was divine!"

Norton hated her social facility. It was so easy for her to cover up her thoughts and actions with this superficial blather.

"You bitch!" he said, and brutally pulled her out of her chair. "As soon as my back is turned you're out with other men."

Blumenthal sprang to his feet and the two men exchanged heated words. But nothing really bothered Gloria too much these days. Drifting and drinking gave her a curious detachment. So she simply excused herself and left on the arm of her jealous beau.

"A fine cavalier *you* are," she said to Norton as they stepped into his Mercedes.

"You're going to pay, and pay dearly, for this," cried Norton.

The way he spoke suddenly filled her with fear. "Where are you taking me?" she said, not wanting to go home and have a scene in her house.

He said nothing. At an alarming speed he raced through the boulevards of Paris, yelling at other drivers, and once he banged into another car that was stopped at a red light.

"Napier, do go easy," she cried.

"Look who's talking!" His eyes blazed with such fury that again she was filled with dread at the prospect of a scene at home. Emma loved to cause trouble and God knew what she would do if she saw them brawling.

The car screeched to a halt before her building. Swiftly, without a word, she opened the door and raced across the pavement. But despite his heavy body and muscle-bound physique, Norton moved with incredible speed. Catching her before she could reach her door, he struck her, ripping her sable cape off her shoulders. "I'm only gone a few days and you are off with the richest man you can find!" he shouted.

"Shut up, you fool! You'll wake up the whole house." She snatched up her cape and kicked him. He slapped her again and shouted curses.

A door was flung open and a concierge ran out. "Ah, Madame Vanderbilt! What is happening?"

"Lord Norton has had too much to drink," she said. "Please see that he gets home all right."

She ran up the stairs to her apartment. She was turning the key in the lock when Napier sprang up behind her. She gave a little cry and he flung her violently into the hall. A small table overturned, making an awful racket.

"Napier, for God's sake! You'll awaken little Gloria!"

His answer was to take her in his arms and kiss her roughly. She was struggling in his arms, thus, when the huge figure of white-haired Emma appeared in the doorway. Her expression was cruel and gloating as she watched the lovers.

"You've had too much to drink, sir," said Emma coldly. "It would be wise to return home."

Her expression sobered him and he stared at her dully. Without a word he turned on his heel and left.

"A fine way to behave," muttered Emma.

"Why did you tell Lord Norton where I was?" snapped Gloria, eyes blazing.

"I didn't want your friend to be disappointed, Mrs. Vanderbilt. And I wanted him to see you as you really are."

"And how do you see me, Emma?" asked Gloria icily.

"You are merely a gay widow," said Emma coolly, "living off the income of a child."

"How dare you!" She wanted to strike the odious woman.

"Little Gloria will be eight this year; the years go by awfully quickly when you party the days away. And then she'll be twenty-one and you'll be on the streets, where you belong."

"You're fired!"

"Mrs. Whitney wouldn't like that, Mrs. Vanderbilt. She wants me to be with the child." Emma folded her meaty arms and stood her ground, a smug look on her face.

"You're in correspondence with Mrs. Whitney, then?" A sinking feeling hit Gloria.

The big woman nodded her gray head. "I write her a detailed letter once a week."

Gloria turned and went down the hall to her room. So Gertrude Whitney and Emma were in contact. She felt somehow that a net was being thrown over her. Tomorrow she had to pull herself together and get up early. When you stay in bed all day, until five in the afternoon, nothing is accomplished.

I *must* pull myself together, thought Gloria as she slipped into bed. My life is becoming messy, and I don't like messiness. For the New Year, I need a new life and a new man.

Part of her wish was answered the next day. She didn't get a new life, but she did get a new man.

As she was in her gardenia-scented bath, the phone rang. It was Blumenthal on the wire. "I'm at Cartier's," he said, "and there's a diamond rose here that made me think of you."

"What a sweet thing to say!" Gloria was thrilled.

"I'm not sweet," he said darkly, "as you'll soon discover."

"I can hardly bear the suspense!" she laughed.

"Nor can I," he said. "Lunch?"

"We'll have to go someplace unfashionable where Kreuger won't find us."

"He'll find us," said Blumenthal. "I'll bet he has detectives on you this very minute. Why, look out your window!"

"I can't," she giggled, "I'm in the bath."

"Stay there," he said. "I'll be around to join you directly."

"No, no, no, no!" she cried hysterically. "You mustn't!" But he had already hung up. What could she do?

She and Blumenthal saw each other constantly over the next few months. He brought her the diamond rose as a gift to cement their relationship.

On the morning of March 12, 1932, Kreuger fired a bullet into his heart and ended his life. The Match King's suicide rocked the world. Gloria was pretty stunned, too, by the news; he had given her some Kreuger stock and she wondered how it would fare.

She and Blumenthal were having their usual cocktails in the Ritz bar, before lunch, discussing this turn of events. It

was five days after the suicide and Blumenthal was worried
sick by the New York news.

"Kreuger stocks are being dumped on the Wall Street
market," said Blumenthal, "and I think the firm that spon-
sored Kreuger stocks is going to collapse. Gloria, I've got to
return to New York."

"What will I do?" she said, for as usual she had grown
dependent on him.

"Come with me," he said, fondling her cheek with his
warm hand. For such a small man he had abnormally large
hands and gazing at them she felt a little shiver of desire.

"All my Kreuger money is gone then?" she asked sadly.

"You'll have plenty of Blumenthal money now, baby." He
chucked her under the chin.

She pulled her head away. "Please don't call me that,
Blumie. It's too humiliating."

"You love humiliation, baby."

He had her number all right. "I'll return with you to
America," she said quietly, placing her fate in his hands.

She wrote her daughter's guardians and told them she
wished to return with the child to New York. They wrote
back telling her they thought it a good idea. "Little Gloria
can now go to Miss Chapin's school," wrote George Wickersham.

So Gloria booked passage on the *Mauretania* and Wann,
Emma and little Gloria were thrown into the customary disorder that packing entails. Gloria began having attacks of
disorientation.

"Blumie, you mustn't come on the same ship with us,"
Gloria said.

"Who'll love you like I do?" he said.

"I can't think of love now." She wrung her hands in dismay.

"You'll always think of love, baby," he laughed knowingly.

"I forbid you to come on the ship with us!" she told him as
strongly as she could.

The day before she sailed, a letter came from Alice Vanderbilt:

My dear Gloria,
I am shocked to see a picture of you at the Match King's funeral. Emma is in constant communication with Gertrude and she said that you were often in this swindler's company. My dear, what has happened to your sweet character? And Emma wrote that you pay hardly any attention to poor little Gloria, that you spend all your time in nightclubs and casinos with violent men. I feel responsible, dear Gloria, since Reggie introduced you to this kind of life. So please hurry home before Gertrude gets quite out of control. By the way, your mother is here and spreading the most horrible false stories about you. I say false because I can't believe you could have fallen to such depths! I long to see your lovely face so I can reassure myself that all the stories about you are not true.
Much love from your anxious mother-in-law,
Alice Vanderbilt

The letter unsettled Gloria. Now she'd have to give up Blumenthal, too.

When the ship set sail and slowly moved out into the choppy channel and into the wintry horizon, she discovered that Blumenthal had the cabin next to hers on A deck.

"I can't see you anymore," she told him coldly.

"Silly girl," he said huskily, kissing her so ruthlessly that she felt his teeth.

"But I can't be seen with you!"

"Then I'll see you in my cabin," he said slyly.

"I'm so frightened!" She felt on the verge of hysteria.

"I'll frighten you even more, baby."

There had been a storm at sea and the violent shakings

of the poor ship seemed to match her own feelings. Thelma was always accusing her of having no feelings, but she certainly had feelings for the muscular little gangster. He was always saying that he would kill her if she was unfaithful to him, and one evening after a third brandy stinger, she danced with Blumie and thought how nice it would be to die in his arms.

By the time they arrived in New York she was even more madly in love with Blumenthal than ever. This man would be the death of her.

CHAPTER
21

Old Alice Vanderbilt and her daughter, Gertrude Whitney, were standing in the wooden Customs shed. It was chillingly cold and damp. As she moved down the long gangplank, Gloria saw Gertrude's eyes watching her and wished her sister-in-law hadn't come.

Later, as they drove crosstown in the Whitney Rolls-Royce through the dreary West Side streets with Depression crowds glaring at them on Broadway, frail, white-haired Alice in black broadtail and pearls clucked her tongue: "Those poor people. I wish I could do something to help them."

"Why don't you turn your house into a soup kitchen, mother?" suggested Gertrude, sarcastically.

"Are things so bad here?" asked Gloria, who was swathed in mink. The hungry faces staring at her from the sidewalks seemed less real than a movie.

"I can't conceive of being hungry," said the old lady, touching her diamond dog collar.

"Is no one doing anything to help these poor souls?" said Gloria. The wan gray faces were haunting; she identified with their despair.

"I am," cried Gertrude forcefully. "You must come tomorrow, Gloria, and see my museum in Greenwich Village that aids new artists."

"We'll lunch tomorrow at the Colony Club, Gloria," said her mother-in-law, patting her hand affectionately, "and discuss your future."

Gertrude watched her sister-in-law with a wry smile. Future? she thought. What future does this woman have? Gloria was always beautifully dressed, beautifully made up and manicured, but going nowhere—except down.

They drew up smartly before the revolving doors of the Savoy Plaza Hotel, and porters immediately swarmed about the powerful car.

"Until tomorrow, dear," said Alice Vanderbilt, blowing a kiss at Gloria.

"You look enchanting, Gloria," said Gertrude, "like Anna Karenina."

Gloria smiled. "She's my favorite heroine."

"Naturally, my dear," said Gertrude, smiling sweetly. "Now call me if I can be of any assistance to you getting settled. Perhaps you'd like to come round and have tea later."

Gloria just wanted to get to bed early—it had been a hectic day. But despite her good intentions, she wound up spending a raucous evening spinning through the new night spots on West 52nd Street. Blumie introduced her to a whole new cast of characters, Broadway ones, of course. He flirted outrageously with every pretty girl and Gloria became incensed. Finally, at three o'clock in the morning she started to put on her wrap.

"Where are you going?" Blumie demanded.

"Home," she replied coldly.

"No one walks out on me, baby." He grabbed her arm cruelly.

"Gloria Vanderbilt does."

"Try it," he sneered.

She didn't.

The most horrible part of the evening was meeting up with an aging Peggy Hopkins Joyce, who was loud and boisterous.

"Hi, toots," said Peggy, flashing her customary diamond bracelets. "Come and join the old bag. All the old gang's finished, you know."

"Really?" said Gloria, sitting down at the table next to her old rival.

"Yeah, and your chum, Jeanne Eagels, kicked off with an overdose of morphine."

"No!" said Gloria, shocked.

Peggy nodded her waved blonde head. "Yup. John Gilbert is dying of booze on the Coast, and Louis Bromfield is trying to go straight and find himself way off in India. Cheers!"

The two women clinked their glasses of Irish whiskey.

"I'm on my last legs, myself," shouted Peggy in the noisy dive. "But at least I've still got good legs. When a woman's legs go, she knows she's finished. How are your knees, baby?"

"Fine," said Gloria, who as yet had no tell-tale signs of age.

"I go to Jeanne Eagles's health doctor on Park Avenue," cried Peggy in her rowdy way. "He gives me a jab and I'm soaring over the rainbow again!"

"He sounds dangerous," said Gloria.

"That's what we want, isn't it, darling?" said Peggy.

"I suppose so."

"Besides, he's good-looking, and what a lay!"

"Give us the scoop," said Blumie, sitting down at their table.

"Well," giggled Peggy, "the first time I went in to him, he gave me a 'miracle shot' of 'vitamins' and I blacked out. You can imagine what happened next!"

"What?" said Gloria.

"When I opened my eyes the good-looking doctor was on top of Miss Peggy! I was hooked after that."

"On the vitamins or his dick?" said Blumie.

"Both, you fart!" cried Peggy.

Blumie's attention was caught by a platinum-blonde Jean Harlow type in seductive white fringe and he pushed his way through the smoky dimness to join her.

"Are you hooked on him, Gloria?" Peggy asked her.

"Yes," said Gloria, although she hated to confess anything to this woman.

"Blumie's a great help when you're going down," said Peggy, finishing her Irish whiskey.

"What do you mean?"

"He gives you the final push!"

A young, on-the-make actor, Peggy's current flame, dragged her brutally to her feet. Gloria started to intervene, but Peggy laughed and rolled her head drunkenly. "He's the Marquis de Sade, himself," she whispered in Gloria's ear. "And what a zeppelin he has, the bastard! If you can believe it, I'm paying for him. How do you like them apples?"

Her drunken laughter as she staggered off rang in Gloria's ears disturbingly. Onstage, show girls were kicking up their legs and a torch singer was moaning, "Love for sale, appetizing young love for sale. . . ." Blumie was dancing with the platinum blonde. It was the first time she had ever been left alone at a table in a nightclub. It was an odd sensation. A bit scary, too, in a low-down dive like this. It was a tough crowd and she didn't like the looks she was getting from the

adjoining tables. She wore a lot of good jewelry and her chinchilla wrap was draped over the back of the chair.

An exotic black-haired woman came out and started to do
a belly dance with a boa constrictor around her shoulders.
Gloria was terrified of snakes and she gave a little cry of
alarm.

"Don't worry, baby," cried Peggy, returning to the table
again. "That fat boa is as drugged as I am. And did I tell you
about that Indian princess what's-her-name who sleeps with
a pet python? You can imagine what they do—"

Gloria didn't stay to find out. She ran blindly toward the
door. A table of black men tried to detain her, but she managed to get by them. She hailed a taxi and arrived back at
the Savoy Plaza at daybreak.

All the Irish coffee she had drunk made sleep impossible;
and when she finally did doze off, she slept badly.

At nine in the morning she awakened from a terrible nightmare and screamed out loud. The boa was coming toward
her face, its head all swollen and its eyes glittering like
Blumie's—

On her bedside table the phone rang and of course it was
Blumie. What a way to start the day! "I hate you," she cried.
"You're common, cheap, and vulgar!"

"I'm coming up," he said.

The manager called her a minute later and asked if Mr.
Blumenthal could be sent up. She said, "No!" and apparently
there was a terrible fight downstairs. Finally she managed to
fall into a kind of drugged coma. Halfway between sleep and
consciousness, in a kind of sensual daydream, she saw a lost
little girl running away from the wolflike Blumenthal. . . .

Wann awakened her a little before noon with a breakfast
tray. She couldn't touch a thing. There was a dull ache in the
back of her head and her reflection in the dressing-table
mirror seemed queer and distorted. She had to pull herself

together. She was supposed to meet her mother-in-law at the
Colony Club for lunch and mustn't be late.

She bathed and dressed swiftly, then reached for a huge
bottle of perfume that Blumie had given her. As she took the
stopper off, the bottle slipped out of her hand and spilled
down her blue suit. Her nerves were in such a bad state that
she asked Wann to make her a daiquiri.

The phone rang again and Blumenthal's voice came over
the wire. "I'm downstairs, baby. Let's have lunch and a long
matinee."

Suddenly he seemed the cause of all her trouble, and she
screamed at him so savagely that Wann stared at her
anxiously. "You detestable womanizer! Don't you dare ever
telephone me again!" She banged the receiver down. Her
head reeled; she felt she was losing control.

"Should I order a car to take you to the Colony Club,
madam?" asked Wann, concerned.

"No," said Gloria, "I'll walk. The fresh spring air will
clear my head." She smiled. "It is spring, isn't it? Do I need
a coat? No? Anyway, what does it matter. . . ?"

She walked unsteadily across to Park Avenue. The early
spring sunshine hurt her eyes and the pavement was dirty
and covered with newspapers. Reaching the club, she made
her way up the steps and into the dignified marble hall. It
was a womens' club, a fashionable place for conservative
ladies of impeccable background to lunch, play cards, swim,
read in the library, and gossip. The building itself was a
stately red brick Georgian mansion with cream-colored
marble trim; every inch of Elsie de Wolfe's rooms reeked of
respectability, old money, and genteel behavior.

What a contrast to that smoky dive and Peggy's drunken
lipstick-smeared face, Gloria thought, beginning to feel
better.

Dowdy matrons glanced at young Mrs. Vanderbilt's slim

figure in her beautifully tailored Paris suit. She was too flashy for this crowd, with her startling good looks, auburn hair, and—worst of all—the large flashing diamond rose pinned between her breasts. The diamonds were baguette and far too large for the daytime.

With ceremony, Gloria was ushered into the dining room. It was a large room with fine proportions, painted pea green with a large Louis XVI fireplace and shaded sconces. The fire was burning quietly and the ladies' voices were subdued and barely audible. Aristocrats like these rarely raised their voices.

As the major domo led her to her mother-in-law's table, Alice Vanderbilt was struck by the young woman's pallor and the air of sadness about her. A fast life never brought anyone happiness, Alice thought, but perhaps she could open some new horizons for Gloria.

"You make us all look so dowdy and unfeminine," said the old lady, smiling as she greeted her.

"I feel like an outsider here," sighed Gloria, sitting down.

"That's for you to change," said Alice calmly. "You must live here now, and establish yourself in New York society."

"Yes," said Gloria, who always agreed outwardly with everything that everybody said, but never paid any attention.

"Would you care for a cocktail, Gloria?" Alice signaled are waiter.

"A brandy," said Gloria faintly. "I'm getting a cold."

"I think I'll join you," said the old lady. "The doctor told me it was good for my heart."

Presently they were sipping their brandies and talking of family matters. The old lady had always had a soft spot for Gloria, and now in her presence it was hard to believe the terrible stories she had heard from Gertrude. Surely Mrs. Morgan and that nurse, Emma, had exaggerated. Despite her worldliness, Alice Vanderbilt was still taken by charm. And charm was one thing that Gloria had in abundance.

"What pleasure it gives me to have you here," said Alice. "Your voice is so French and your clothes so Paris! You look so fresh and pretty."

"I wish I felt that way." A vision of Blumenthal swam before her eyes. "I'm drifting, Mrs. Vanderbilt. Once I had a goal, and now I don't."

"Gertrude is going to change all of that for you," said Mrs. Vanderbilt, starting in on her shad roe and bacon.

"Is she?" Gloria was startled by that piece of information.

"I think you started your adult life on the wrong foot, Gloria," said the old lady, watching her with compassionate eyes. "Reggie wasn't a very good influence for an impressionable young girl of seventeen."

"Well . . ." What could Gloria say?

"How old are you now, dear?"

"I'll be twenty-seven in August."

"Still so very young," sighed Mrs. Vanderbilt. "Think, dear, you have your whole life before you. And Gertrude and I will find you a distinguished young lawyer or banker who will settle you and little Gloria down. Gambling casinos and nightclubs went out with the Twenties. Reggie's irresponsible sort of life-style has all vanished. And just as well, too. Where does it all get you?"

"You're so right," said Gloria. It was nice to think that perhaps she could lead a subdued and balanced life, like the women in this room.

"Gertrude is going to give you a great big pep talk about what she calls 'terminal adolescence.' That's what she says those bright young things forever flitting about are suffering from."

"Terminal adolescence! What a fearful term. It sounds as if I'm dying."

"Well, you *are* dying," cried Gertrude Whitney in her vigorous fashion. She kissed her mother's cheek and then

Gloria's and sat down. "Aren't you dying of boredom in those European resorts, Gloria?"

"I suppose I am," said Gloria, fondly remembering those nights in Cannes and Monte Carlo and Biarritz with her carefree companions.

"I can tell just by looking at you, my dear, that you feel lost and out of place here in America," said Gertrude. "What's lacking is a sense of purpose, direction. . . ."

"Direction? I haven't heard that word for ages."

"High time you did," said Gertrude. "Your whole life is going to have order and form now," she went on, "because I'm going to take over the reins."

Gloria had always liked the idea of being told what to do by a dominant person and she warmed to Gertrude. Pulling herself together she thought, I must make a good impression on Gertrude. It's the only chance I have left.

At three o'clock they got into Gertrude's car and started down Park Avenue. As they passed Grand Central Station, Gertrude remarked sadly, "There's the last monument of the Vanderbilt family in New York. Do you know, Gloria, that all of us have given up our private railroad cars?"

"Things *have* changed," observed Gloria.

"Socialism will take over here if we're not careful," said Gertrude.

"Goodness!" said Gloria with much concern.

Her enthusiasm caused Gertrude to turn and look at her. "That's why it's important for people of our class to set a good example. Why, I never wear a fur coat, and Grace is the only showy one left in the family—poor leftover from the Gilded Age!"

"I'm afraid," said Gloria with a self-deprecating laugh, "I'm afraid I'm a bit overdressed today."

"Well, darling, that's your stock-in-trade, I suppose. It always seemed to me that you were dressed as if you were on your way to Ascot, or to be presented at court. Of course, my artists will all fall in love with you when they see you, because you *are* an inspiration, my dear! And you'll take to my museum like a duck to water, I think. . . ."

The car drew up before the Whitney Museum at 10 West 8th Street. It was a nice turn-of-the-century brownstone and inside were etchings, paintings, and nude statuary. Gloria stood a long time before the Georgia O'Keeffes, de Koonings, and Jackson Pollocks. Her favorite was an erotic flower by Miss O'Keeffe.

"I'd give my soul to know Georgia O'Keeffe," said Gertrude. "She has such independence and strength of character. I've always loathed weak, dependent people, you know."

"I hope that remark isn't aimed at me, Gertrude," said Gloria softly.

"No, my dear, it isn't," said Gertrude, putting her arm around her. "I know it's bad to change horses in midstream, but I did a lot of thinking last night after we left you. I haven't been fair. You know why."

Gloria nodded. "You must miss Harry very much."

"Yes, I do. Love and romance have all died for me."

"I wish I could say the same," said Gloria sadly.

Gertrude then proceeded to introduce her to a half-dozen painters in wool shirts and dungarees. One of them was a strapping youth called Larry and she admired his pictures of the Dali school.

"He's homosexual," whispered Gertrude.

"I know," said Gloria, "but many of my friends are."

"You don't mean the Prince of Wales and Prince George are pansies?"

"No, silly, but Gardner Pell is and we are great friends. I don't care what anybody does."

"Behind closed doors, you mean," said Gertrude.

They were standing in front of a Georgia O'Keeffe painting of a cactus and Gloria remarked, "They can do it on a cactus as far as I'm concerned."

"Why, you're as broad-minded as I am," said Gertrude. "I never would have thought it."

A little later they had tea in her office, a sunny yellow chamber with gray corduroy curtains. The only link with her Vanderbilt background was the collection of Boldini, Sargent, and Helleu drawings of elegant ladies and gentlemen from the early 1900s. But, thank God, no gilded French furniture, only early American Chippendale.

"Why don't you come down for lunch tomorrow?" Gertrude asked. "Come at twelve, if you like, and I can find some things for you to do."

"That would be nice," said Gloria quietly. She liked the creative atmosphere of the museum.

"A good steady routine will give you the zest for life again."

"I hope you're right," Gloria said. "My spirit is somewhat frayed."

"It's never to late to change," said Gertrude with a gentle smile. "Listen," she added, sensing Gloria's loneliness and isolation, "drop by the house anytime and have a meal with me, if you care to. I rattle around in that big old barn by myself just like mother does in her hotel. They should tear all those houses down and put up skyscrapers."

"You don't feel any sentiment about those houses, Gertrude?"

"I live in the future, my dear. Not in the past, like Grace Vanderbilt. Why, do you know, Gloria, that Grace and Neily turned down nine million dollars for their Fifth Avenue house? Imagine what madness! And neither one has anything left. Pitiful, when you come to think of it."

"How is the rest of the family faring?"

"Uncle Fred carries on at Hyde Park and Fifth Avenue in the grand manner, and Aunt Florence Twombly's still making news with her entrances at the Metropolitan Opera openings. Of course, they're in their seventies, so it's too late to change, Depression or no."

Gloria smiled. "But not too late for me," she said. She hoped Gertrude was right—that it wasn't too late to begin a new, more orderly and meaningful life. Anyway, it was nice to think so.

"If you'd like to dine and go to the opera tomorrow night, I'd love to have you. They're playing Mozart's *Magic Flute*."

"That would be lovely. Thank you." Gloria was touched by Gertrude's concern.

"I've a charming extra man. Frank Crocker is his name. And he's a brilliant lawyer. Rather like Harry—so rather your type."

The two women smiled, as only two women can who have loved the same man.

CHAPTER
22

The following weeks passed happily. The hours flew by at the gallery. New vistas were opening up for Gloria, and even stuffy people at the Metropolitan Opera, friends from the old Fifth Avenue and Newport days, greeted her with consideration. Gertrude Whitney, of course, had a formidable position, and Gloria, as the favored sister-in-law now, benefited from this.

She spent most of her time learning to catalogue the art books in the library and having gay lunches with Gertrude or the artists. Her new life was quite nice, so different from the fast, high style of before. She wondered how long it would last.

One morning in April Gloria breezed in, humming a tune, and Gertrude exploded. "My dear, don't you have any *simple* clothes?"

"I haven't led a simple life!" said Gloria gaily.

"Vionnets and Molyneux are all very well, my dear, but don't you have simple, everyday clothes?"

"Mainbocher did whip me up some dear little things that are copied from workmen's clothes. . . ."

"Wear those tomorrow," said Gertrude. "And how much did Mainbocher charge you, by the way?"

"Seven hundred per outfit," replied Gloria.

"I can't afford that," said Gertrude, and the two women shared a laugh.

There had been some urgent phone calls from Blumenthal, but Gloria hadn't seen him—in fact she'd avoided him like the plague. It came as a shock one afternoon when his muscular little figure strode cockily into the gallery. She was standing on a stepladder adjusting the paintings and nearly fell off.

"What do you want?" she cried ungraciously.

"You know what I want!" Blumenthal stood defiantly at the foot of the ladder.

"Get out of here. And take your hands out of your pockets when you're talking to a lady."

"I have to keep my hands in my pockets when I see you," he joked.

Actually, he was a little startled by the change in her—the workman's outfit, the scrubbed face with no makeup. He glanced at a good-looking artist.

"You're screwing one of these bohemian studs, is that it?"

"Don't be vulgar."

"Well, what role *are* you playing here?"

"I'm working for my sister-in-law, if it's any of your business."

"Everything you do is my business, baby," grunted Blumenthal, his eyes going up and down her slender figure. "Now come down off that ladder and take those ridiculous spectacles off."

The way he looked at her, his manly swagger, gave her gooseflesh. Yes, he was in her blood. Such longing swept through her that she wondered how she could have gone without him all these weeks.

She climbed down and stood before him like an obedient child.

"Kiss me," he demanded.

"Stop it," she said, pushing him away. "Not here!"

"I said kiss me! . . ."

And so the dreadful liaison with Blumenthal started up again. As with Harry Payne Whitney, she felt powerless before Blumenthal.

He took her back to the Savoy Plaza that afternoon in his yellow basket-weave Rolls-Royce. Thank God, Gertrude wasn't there to see him. She was supposed to dine and go to the Philharmonic tonight with Gertrude, but at six she telephoned Gertrude and said she had a headache.

"God, I've missed you," said Blumie, lying naked on her bed.

The next morning she called the gallery and said she couldn't come in. That evening Gertrude called her and asked what was wrong.

"I left so many—loose ends in Paris," Gloria stuttered, with Blumenthal lying in the bed next to her.

"Do you mean you are returning to Europe?" Gertrude's voice was incredulous. "You were doing so well here, I thought. When are you leaving?"

"The sooner the better," said Gloria, watching Blumenthal fearfully. He was making gestures for her to end the telephone conversation. And then he began kissing here where he shouldn't.

"What a capricious creature you are, Gloria," said Gertrude disapprovingly. "I'd like to keep little Gloria here this summer, while you get all your business matters sorted out in Paris. But you should hurry back here. Frank Crocker is most taken with you, by the way."

"And I like him, too," whispered Gloria. Blumie glared at her.

"Let me know when you are leaving," said Gertrude, "and we'll have a farewell dinner if it suits you."

Gloria hung up and Blumenthal made a terrible scene about Frank Crocker. "You're the most dishonest female I've ever met," he sneered, twisting her arm up into her back so that she cried out in pain. "Why didn't you tell me about this telegram from Norton?"

"What do you mean?" she gasped, stalling for time. She'd forgotten about the telegram; she hadn't answered and left it lying about.

"I'll give you a black eye if you're thinking of going back to that red-haired bastard!" He shook her angrily.

As always she was both appalled and thrilled by his language. "I don't care if I never see Norton again," she said, trembling. "I'm all yours, Blumie." She threw herself across him and nibbled hungrily on his ear.

He lay back with a smile. "Well, I've got news for you, baby. We're not going back to Europe. So put that in your pipe and smoke it."

"As you wish, my lord and master. . . ."

The next morning she got up early and rushed to the travel agency downstairs. "Get me on a ship that's leaving today," she said in a jittery voice.

"But, madam," said the pleasant young man, "the *Ile de France* and the *Britannic* are the only ships sailing today and they are all booked up."

"I am Mrs. Vanderbilt," cried Gloria, "and I must get on the *Britannic!*"

Heads turned to look at her, and the travel agent was a bit alarmed by the glitter in her eyes. Of course these rich people led such wild, crazy lives. And he had heard about this one.

So at five that afternoon Gloria and Wann sailed down the Hudson River, past the Statue of Liberty, and out into the open sea.

"You made this decision so quickly, madam," said Wann, unpacking the wardrobe trunks in the stateroom.

"I had to. Blumenthal was becoming a threat to my sanity —you understand?" Gloria was puffing anxiously on a cigarette.

"He is very violent, madam." What else could Wann say?

"Yes, and I'm terrified of him," confessed Gloria. "Terrified of what will happen to me if I surrender completely to him."

"Now, madam, lie down and have a little rest before dinner." Wann pulled down the bedcovers and helped her into bed.

Gloria closed her eyes and slept. She had a terrible dream of Blumenthal and Norton fighting and little Gloria and Gertrude breaking up the fight—

At seven she awakened in a sweat.

Wann watched her mistress worriedly. She was on her knees taking some evening dresses out of blue tissue paper and asked the inevitable question: "Would you like a drink, madam?"

Even after her third chilled martini upstairs in the bar, the images of Blumenthal and Norton would not fade. How could she escape them? She had run away from Blumenthal, but now Norton was waiting for her. What had she done? Why couldn't she just say no? Was her life always going to be measured by the men who pursued her? . . .

Norton was waiting for her at Le Havre, and they had a passionate reunion in Paris. He was in a splendid mood, having sold some family pictures and silver from Norton

Hall. He had money now and they could go back to the
night life.

"You're brilliant, darling, and I adore you," she cried
happily, flinging herself into his arms.

"Love me," he said, unbuttoning his shirt. "I need your
love."

The sight of him was too much for her. They spent the
weekend together and never saw the light of day.

On Monday morning, the butler announced Lady Furness
was on the phone. "Dearest," Thelma cried, "I'm giving a
costume ball in London to amuse my little prince. Come the
day after tomorrow and bring a Marlborough House set
costume with bustle and sweeping trains and—you know,
darling! You can either stay with me or at Somerset
Maugham's. . . ."

Gloria and Norton boarded the boat train for London,
Wann carrying a huge hoop which was to serve for Gloria's
costume. They could barely get it into the compartment and
had a good laugh over it.

They stayed at Thelma's distinguished town house in
London, and one morning when Norton went off to White's
Club, the sisters let down their hair.

"Norton must be a heavenly dancer," Thelma said envi-
ously. "What a physique! It gives me quivers." She flung
some tea roses into a vase and smiled over them. "How's his
bank account, dear?"

"He has hopes," Gloria shrugged.

"Don't we all! But who can live on hopes when bills have
to be paid?"

"You're so practical, Thelma."

"You've got to be when you're balancing on a tightrope
like I am—and like you are. My little prince isn't really very
generous, and I'm getting a divorce from that promiscuous
beast, Furness, so I'm in a terribly vulnerable state."

"Join the club," laughed Gloria. She linked arms with her twin and they went down the hallway together.

"What happened to that rough diamond, Blumenthal?"

Gloria tossed her head. "Blumie is a thing of the past. I never want to hear his name again."

"Sure," said Thelma, knowingly.

Gloria threw herself into a round of festivities. Every night there were balls, and every afternoon there were horse races at Ascot. There's no show equal to the one the English aristocrats put on, and the brilliance of the scene served as a further distraction from her responsibilities to little Gloria. The letters from Gertrude lay unanswered on her desk. How could she find time? And indeed, what could she say?

It excited her imagination to dance with the duke of Devonshire, the marquis of Bath, Lord Londonderry, and Lord Suffolk. And the flames were rekindled when she danced with Prince Hohenlohe.

"I've never seen you look so radiant," said her former lover. "Your dresses are memorable. . . ."

Indeed they were memorable; she kept them in trunks until the day she died. Glorious tulles, satins, laces, chiffons that floated over the body, velvets that gave such richness. Her Edwardian Marlborough House dress was plum velvet draped in white lace with a train that she had to gather up in her hand when she waltzed. Her favorite was a white lace caught up with pink roses. Norton's favorite was a hundred yards of green tulle with satin panels and a tiny satin sash around her waist. These dresses were really works of art.

The London newspapers wrote much about the twins. They described Mrs. Vanderbilt as the daring waltzer with a long neck and heavy coils of hair, glittering with Vanderbilt diamonds. There was one photograph of her with Hohenlohe and she hoped mama didn't see it.

Of course she did, and of course she showed it to Mrs. Whitney.

"She's a woman who devotes herself completely to her own pleasures, Mrs. Whitney," said Mrs. Morgan in Mrs. Whitney's house in Old Westbury, Long Island. "Imagine gadding about Europe with those cheap four-flushers, when she has an eight-year-old daughter waiting for her in America."

Napier bought a convertible and they roared off to France and Spain. In Seville she hired flamenco dancers for her party and later performed the complicated dance herself. On to Italy, where she hired tarantella dancers for her party in Capri. They hired a yacht and went up to Venice, then his valet met them there with the car and they went up to Austria. She had a gypsy party in the mountains of Kitzbuhl and the guests all dressed in *lederhosen.*

Then, of all things, she bumped into Blumenthal in the Sacher Hotel in Vienna.

"How about lunch and a matinee, baby?"

"You swine!"

Their dialogue hadn't changed.

The next day she and Norton rushed on to the music festival in Salzburg, and it gave extra excitement to their love affair to have Blumenthal in hot pursuit. In such a way, the rest of 1932 and the first months of 1933 passed.

The fun of it all began to wane in Deauville in May. Norton's money had run out and he was gambling like a devil. Any fool knew that you never won at those casinos and she lost her temper with him many times.

They sold the car and took the train to Cannes. It was June 1933, a time that would come back to haunt Gloria until the day she died.

It so happened that Norton was losing heavily at the Palm Beach Casino at Cannes and his losses amounted to over $40,000. Her pleas to stop went unheeded; he continued to play—and lose—like a wild man. Finally one evening he actually pulled the diamond necklace from her neck and flung it onto the green felt chemin de fer table. "That's worth more than a hundred thousand," he told the croupier.

The place was scandalized and crowds of people suddenly surrounded them. With as much dignity as she could muster, Gloria trailed out of the huge marble gambling rooms, down the steps, and into a taxi.

Back in the Miramar Hotel on that palm-lined avenue, the Croisette, that ran along the beach, Gloria ran into an old friend, Lady Milford-Haven. "Nada, darling," she said, "I've had the most ghastly ordeal!"

"Come to the bar with me and we'll have a drink," said Lady Milford-Haven, a lean and beautiful Russian, the daughter of Grand Duke Michael. She had the highest position since her husband was Victoria's grandson.

They went to the bar and had pink ladys.

"I've never seen you so *distrait*, cherie! Is it that brute?"

Gloria nodded. "Yes, he's gone quite mad. I don't know what to do." And she began to cry. She cried so hard that Lady Milford-Haven was worried. Gloria was such a delicate little thing; men would destroy her, of course.

"I can't go home to Norton," gasped Gloria.

"Stay with me, darling," said Nada, putting an arm around her.

The next morning Gloria woke up and stretched in the large bed they had shared. It was noon, and Lady Milford-Haven had been awake for an hour. She was sitting by the balustraded French window looking out at the Mediterranean. The sun sparkled brightly on the water, and she could see little white sailing yachts skimming along the horizon. The smell of oleanders drifted up in the heat.

"Oh, Nada, what am I to do?"

"Call your maid, darling, and have her bring you over

some morning clothes. Then we can plan what to do with Norton. . . ."

When Gloria's other maid, Maria Caillot, entered the bedroom, she found the two women laughing gaily on the bed. This was nothing new to Maria since Mrs. Vanderbilt had many lady friends and they were all affectionate and easy in their ways.

"Order me some breakfast, would you, Maria dear?" said Mrs. Vanderbilt.

Ten minutes later when Maria returned with the usual fresh orange juice and coffee, she found Mrs. Vanderbilt crying and Lady Milford-Haven kissing her and telling her everything was going to be all right. Both women were in nightgowns and the maid felt an eerie sensation: There was something strange between these women.

Maria said nothing to Mrs. Vanderbilt about the incident, but she wrote to Emma, in Old Westbury, Long Island. You can imagine the furor the letter caused. Mrs. Morgan didn't even show the letter to Mrs. Whitney—she was waiting for the right moment.

Gloria returned to America shortly afterward, found a house at 49 East 72nd Street, and was about to settle down in it when Blumenthal appeared.

"I'm going back to Europe, baby, if you want to come with me," he said.

"Yes, I do," she said, watching him as if he were her executioner. It was terrible. She had no control over her emotions anymore.

And so she returned to Paris and resumed her party life there. When Blumenthal became too insufferable, Norton would move back in, and vice versa. There were constant trips to London to see Thelma, and she often bedded down with Hohenlohe there. They had to be careful since he was a married man, but Gloria had never covered her tracks very well. Indeed, she was becoming so careless now that often she would make three luncheon engagements in the same day, with different people. She was now like a juggler in the circus: trying to keep all the balls in the air; trying to please a half-dozen people and be all things to each one of them. It proved to be a great strain. Her nerves were raw. She often had fits of hysterics. She felt driven. It was as if she felt compelled to destroy herself.

She spent Christmas with Norton in Paris, and New Year's with Blumenthal in St. Moritz.

Paris has as brilliant a season as London, and the midnight race at Longchamps in 1934 was the climax of the glittering social activities. Nine different orchestras played, and the Paris corps de ballet performed on a platform in front of their box in the grandstand. Prince Aly Khan, who was in love with Thelma, rode in the midnight race. In the box with the twins was Aly's father, the old Aga Khan, whose guests they were, and Daisy Fellowes, whose mother had been a Singer of the sewing-machine family. Gloria had just been off on Daisy's yacht in Monte Carlo with Norton, and the temperamental red-headed man sat beside her now. Gloria was flirting with a handsome Italian count in the next box, and Norton was carrying on with the beautiful wife of an ambassador.

It was all very racy and exciting. All around the Aga Khan's box were the most handsome and promiscuous members of the European aristocracy, most of them involved in amorous intrigues. Gloria had become accustomed to this way of life; indeed it was an occupation that drained all of her time and energy.

Arthur Rubinstein played Rachmaninoff on the illuminated stage. When it was over, Gloria trailed out in her lilac chiffon and egret feathers and amethysts set in diamonds. She was on the arm of the fat old aga and was amusing him with stories of her torrid affairs with Hohenlohe and Norton. And of course Blumenthal.

"I'd love to meet a gangster," said the old aga. "Al Capone and Edward G. Robinson are so much in vogue!"

"Blumie is a combination of both, darling," laughed Gloria.

As they were having their midnight supper of cold lobster and champagne, the little devil himself turned up, and Gloria introduced them with a humorous inflection.

Presently Gloria and Blumenthal found themselves alone in the crowd. "What are you doing here?" she asked coldly.

"Ending a love affair, like you."

"Norton is very devoted to me," she drawled.

"Everyone tells me he is madly in love with that Brazilian beauty."

"We have our ups and downs."

"Talking about ups, how about lunch and a matinee tomorrow?"

She had to laugh, in spite of herself. "I'll kidnap you in my Rolls," he went on, "and we'll drive down to Monte Carlo. We'll arrive just in time for breakfast."

She went off with Blumenthal.

In the great columned lobby of the Hotel de Paris atop the cliffs of Monaco, Gloria found herself alone in August. Blumenthal had left her the week before for an eighteen-year-old, and the humiliation still rankled.

And then Friedel appeared out of the blue! He was always there to pick up the pieces, it seemed.

"You look rather drawn, Gloria," he observed. "Why don't you come back and visit me in Germany now?"

"Would we be peaceful?"

"Far more peaceful than Monte Carlo," he laughed. "And my schloss is like a second home to you."

What better way to escape her complicated love affairs? Except that in Germany she found herself falling for Hohenlohe again, and things became so difficult there, too, that Thelma had to rush in and smooth oil over the troubled waters. Marguerita Hohenlohe was a worldly woman, but she was in love with her husband with the same strength of feeling that Gertrude had had for Harry Payne Whitney.

"You must terminate this liaison with Hohenlohe, Gloria!" cried Thelma. "Things are getting very bad in New York and I think you must return there, to protect your interests."

Gloria was a little taken aback by the urgency in Thelma's tone. "What have you heard?"

"They're very upset over your gallivanting," said Thelma. "And mama, of course, is absolutely out of her mind with rage. She wants to knock you out of the picture so she can get little Gloria. Now sit down immediately and write your child a letter. . . ."

That afternoon Gloria scribbled off a series of postcards and notes to her daughter. But Thelma didn't think that was enough. She kept urging Gloria to go back to America.

"Oh, all right," snapped Gloria. "I'll go back. But first I must stop in Paris to tidy up my affairs."

"Don't use that word," shrieked Thelma. "You fool— you've probably ruined everything already."

At the end of August Gloria and Blumenthal sailed back to America. She had met up with him again in Paris and decided to throw in her lot with him. For better or worse.

Her fate was sealed when Mrs. Whitney's detectives observed the pair moving down the gangplank together. "Now you have her," said mama Morgan. "And now you must destroy her, Mrs. Whitney. Sin must be abolished."

Gertrude Whitney hesitated. Queen Elizabeth had been reluctant to sign the death warrant of her cousin, Mary, Queen of Scots. "Gloria is still my sister-in-law," said Mrs. Whitney, "and part of the family."

With that Mrs. Morgan flung the letters of Maria Caillot on the writing table. Gertrude read them and paled.

"Yes," said Mrs. Morgan, "Gloria is involved with women now. Men aren't enough for her."

"Imagine carrying on with Lady Milford-Haven!" said Gertrude. She was utterly shocked, and then she remembered Gloria's remark in the museum and her carefree attitude toward different types of sex.

"All those idle aristocrats are tainted," said Mrs. Morgan. "Why, look at Marie Antoinette. She tried with her son!"

That did it. Gertrude picked up the telephone and called her lawyer, Frank Crocker.

"Hello, Frank? Something has to be done about my sister-in-law, Gloria. . . . Yes, she's back here in New York with that Blumenthal man. What can we do to prevent her from having the child? . . ."

CHAPTER
23

Every day, every week, every month, the Whitney lawyers relentlessly hammered away at Gloria. Frank Crocker handed her a photograph when she took the stand.

"Would you look at this photo, Mrs. Vanderbilt? Whom do you see in this picture?"

"Myself and Mr. Blumenthal," she replied, frowning.

"And yet you said yesterday that you didn't know Mr. Blumenthal."

"We were acquaintances—shipboard acquaintances, you might say. I was traveling alone and Mr. Blumenthal was kind enough to keep me company."

"Did you see Mr. Blumenthal often during the voyage?"

The sarcasm in Frank Crocker's voice made Gloria furious.

"No," she said angrily.

"Are you quite sure, Mrs. Vanderbilt? Then your memory isn't very good." The burly lawyer handed her another photograph. "This is a picture of you and Mr. Blumenthal in a

Paris restaurant. May I ask when this photograph was taken, Mrs. Vanderbilt?"

"After the trip." Oh, Lord, they had her now.

"Then you *did* see him, quite often?" Crocker smirked.

"It would seem so."

The audience tittered and Justice Carew glared at her. "Mrs. Vanderbilt," he said, "I must remind you that this is not a cocktail party."

The lawyer took up his questioning again. "It would seem, Mrs. Vanderbilt, that Mr. Blumenthal was more than a shipboard acquaintance."

"He was a dear friend; a woman such as I has many male friends."

"I daresay." Crocker gave her a knowing look.

"I resent your implication, Mr. Crocker. How dare you talk to me in such a manner!"

"It's the only way to talk to you, Mrs. Vanderbilt. Because you refuse to take this trial seriously."

Fifty-nine-year-old Justice Carew, father of five, looked pained. He was sorry he had been called in on the notorious Vanderbilt-Whitney trial. Being a father himself, he'd had a talk with little Gloria Vanderbilt and learned from her own lips the sort of life she had lived with her mother. Of course, he had read about resorts like Monte Carlo, Cannes, and Deauville, but he had no idea they were such corrupt places. His puritan soul was shocked by the testimony of Mrs. Vanderbilt's servants. Drinking and fornicating and dancing seemed to have taken up much of her time.

She's a bad number, he thought, watching her now. And like Norton, he despised her charm and social graces which she used so cleverly. The way she looked at men from those dark glittering eyes made him believe the accounts of amorous interludes and drinking parties he had heard in the courtroom.

The stern judge shot a look at Mrs. Whitney, sitting in

the front row of the courtroom. She looked every inch the great lady. Wise, serene, in command of herself and others. A woman of ability and talent. He had read that she was called the first lady of the American art world. Certainly she was in every way a more suitable guardian for the child—and she was, after all, her grandmother.

His shrewd gray eyes returned to Mrs. Vanderbilt. She was too pretty, too smart in that elegant gray flannel suit. She wore too much perfume, too, and her lips and nails must have taken hours to paint. Her whole character was a complete mystery to him. How could a woman gifted with so many physical endowments lead such a self-destructive life? Yet, sometimes when she looked up at him with those heavy-lidded eyes painted a shiny blue, he felt his heart melt. What a seductive creature she was. He thought of Greta Garbo as *The Temptress* and Marlene Dietrich as the jewel thief in *Desire*.

Now his eyes, as if hypnotized, watched her slim ankle nervously moving. He had never seen such a lovely shape. Then he fell to listening to her foreign voice that was at once warm and seductive to the ears.

"What else did you do with Mr. Blumenthal?" Crocker asked.

"We dined at various places." Gloria paused. "We danced. He drove me home."

"In a Rolls-Royce?" Crocker asked.

"Yes." Gloria was annoyed at this line of questioning.

"And you like Rolls-Royces, don't you, Mrs. Vanderbilt?" Crocker's voice purred.

"Every woman does."

The audience tittered. They found the trial vastly entertaining and fought each morning for the best seats.

"What else did you and Mr. Blumenthal do together?"

"Really, Mr. Crocker, I forbid you to talk to me in such a manner." Gloria turned from him and paid an inordinate amount of attention to smoothing down her elegantly cut Molyneux suit.

Crocker tried a different approach and asked sweetly: "Who gave you that huge Rolls-Royce that carries you here every day?"

"The income I receive from my husband's estate is quite large enough for such an automobile," Gloria replied.

"But how is it possible when you only receive forty-eight thousand dollars a year from your husband's estate, and a Rolls-Royce costs half that or more?"

"I'm a clever manager," Gloria said flippantly.

The judge shot Mrs. Vanderbilt a reprimanding look. "Mrs. Vanderbilt, I must remind you that this is a serious matter; I might even say a tragic matter. And you mustn't make light of it. Now please explain to the court how you managed to afford such an expensive car."

"It was a secondhand car, you see, and only cost four thousand dollars. Then my chauffeur put in a new motor and that was another thousand, I think, but you'll have to ask him as I'm not very good at those kinds of details."

Crocker put his hand heavily on the witness chair and paused for effect. "I've already asked your chauffeur, and he told me the car cost twenty-five thousand."

Silence fell over the courtroom, and the crowd stared at Mrs. Vanderbilt. Gertrude Whitney, in the front seat, did not remove her eyes once from Gloria's face. Several minutes went by while Gloria groped for a reply.

"Have you thought about who gave you the car, Mrs. Vanderbilt?" Crocker pressed. "We've given you almost five minutes to think."

"My husband was a very rich man, you know, and I received a great deal of valuable jewelry while I was married."

"So you sold some of this jewelry to pay for the car?"

"Yes. Yes, that's it."

Mrs. Vanderbilt's leg began to move more swiftly and the judge watched the fragile ankle, fascinated.

"You were always selling things, weren't you, Mrs. Vanderbilt?" said Crocker nastily.

Justice Carew interrupted the lawyer. "I think we'll have a little recess now. It's been a long morning and I'm sure we've all worked up a good appetite for lunch."

Relieved, Gloria stepped down from the stand. Her eyes met Mrs. Whitney's. Then the older woman turned away and started out of the courtroom. Constance Bennett came up and took Gloria's arm.

"What a shit that lawyer is!"

Gloria looked around nervously. "Did Friedel hear that testimony about Blumenthal?"

"I'm afraid he did, darling." They walked slowly down the aisle, ignoring the curious crowd.

"There's going to be hell to pay. In fact, I've probably lost both men."

"There are plenty of other fish in the sea," said Connie, philosophically. "I'm just your age, darling, and I've had three husbands already. . . ."

There was a nice old-fashioned lunch place around the corner, by the Catholic church. When the girls walked in, Hohenlohe was sitting at a table waiting for them, and he was clearly upset.

"I had no idea you were so friendly with Blumenthal, Gloria," he said sulkily.

"I'm not," she returned. She sat down and carefully removed her gloves.

"Well, it would certainly seem so, after the testimony I heard!"

"My dear, you know how lawyers make mountains out of molehills. Why, I just danced with Mr. Blumenthal a few times. I couldn't very well cut him when he had the cabin right next to mine on the *Mauretania*, could I?"

"Jealous lover!" sang out Connie gaily, and groped Hohenlohe under the table.

"You know I care only for you, Friedel," said Gloria, patting his cheek.

"I guess you had to do something to keep yourself busy when I wasn't around," he said, his long upper lip quivering.

"My darling, I've been thinking I might even return to Germany with you. Unless those dreadful Nazi people cause trouble for you."

"They aren't dreadful, Gloria, They are the salvation of Germany. Why, Hitler is our savior. You don't remember how Berlin was ten years ago. He has pulled us all together."

"That's what I need," said Connie, downing her martini.

"I thought you told the newspapers you didn't drink," said Hohenlohe to Connie.

"I don't," she said, tossing down the rest.

So Hohenlohe's fears were calmed a bit and Gloria felt that she could use him if all else failed. Now that she was pushed up against the corner, trapped almost, she had to constantly think of exits. Hohenlohe was still the best way out of this mess.

They returned to the grim, dusty courtroom in higher spirits. But the Whitney lawyers were more relentless than ever.

As she took her place in the witness chair the tension pains in the back of her neck started again. Frank Crocker approached her to begin the second round of questioning.

"Can you describe for us a typical day in Paris, Mrs. Vanderbilt?"

"Paris?" Gloria was puzzled. Why Paris in particular?

"Paris, Biarritz, Cannes, Monte Carlo—any one of those. How did you fill your days?"

"Well, luncheon parties, cocktail parties, dinner parties, and sometimes we would go to a Russian boîte." What on earth was he getting at?

"And you managed to see your daughter in the midst of this busy routine?" Crocker's eyebrows went up. "Did you take an interest in her schooling?"

Carew leaned forward and looked at Mrs. Vanderbilt. "Did you ever read to your daughter or tuck her into bed?"

"Yes, Your Honor," Gloria replied indignantly.

"Pray continue with your cross-examination, Mr. Crocker," Justice Carew ordered.

"And what were your expenses for little Gloria during this period, Mrs. Vanderbilt?"

"She was in a growing period so she needed new clothes constantly. She loved pretty clothes, like me, so I bought her a white fur coat and matching hat." There, that should do it, thought Gloria triumphantly.

Crocker was puzzled. "But Emma, the nursemaid, said that there was never enough money for little Gloria's expenses."

"Emma must have spent the money I gave her on something else!" Oh, that awful woman. If only she could get her hands on that dreadful nurse, she'd kill her!

"Could you list your other expenses, Mrs. Vanderbilt?" Crocker asked. "Your apartment in Paris was pretty large, wasn't it?"

"I had a cook and a butler and a chauffeur, and of course a secretary and a footman." Did they expect her to live like a pauper?

"And were your household expenses very high?"

"I served the best food, naturally, at my table." Gloria was indignant again. "And the best wines and whiskey. After all, if you have Winston Churchill to dine, you have to have the best brandy. Likewise champagne with Queen Marie of Rumania."

Crocker changed his approach again. "Did you often stay up very late, Mrs. Vanderbilt?"

"Only if there was something special to celebrate."

"But wasn't every day a kind of celebration, Mrs. Vanderbilt?" His knowing smirk reappeared.

"I don't think so," Gloria replied carefully. Oh, what
an odious man!

"And when you slept until four or five in the afternoon,
when did you see little Gloria?"

"She was brought in before dinner. Otherwise I saw her
before lunch. It is the accustomed European tradition for the
aristocracy to have children taken care of by a governess."

"And rich American children are brought up in the same
way?"

"Of course," Gloria retorted.

Crocker turned away and stood with his back to her. "And
you think European resorts, casinos, and nightclubs are the
right places to develop a child's character?"

"I never took her to a casino or nightclub!" Gloria cried.

Crocker whirled and pointed an accusing finger at her.
"But the nurse testified you showed your child how to make
a good dry martini."

"It was merely a joke!" Gloria protested. "I was having
a party. Larry Thaw and some friends were there, and I
thought it would amuse them!"

"Didn't Mr. Thaw send you flowers and expensive presents?"

"Rubbish! His wife is an old friend of mine. Why, my
sister and I knew her in our early New York days."

"Ah," said Crocker. "Your twin sister, Lady Furness, was
divorced from Lord Furness last year, was she not?"

"Yes." Now what was he getting at?

"But Lady Furness has been traveling around Europe with
the Prince of Wales since nineteen twenty-nine. Can you
explain what kind of marriage she had with Lord Furness?"

"In the higher echelons of English society, couples go their
separate ways and have their separate lives. It's considered
quite civilized," Gloria replied coolly.

"Ah, so you favor the European mode of marriage, is that it, Mrs. Vanderbilt?" Crocker's voice was triumphant.

Mrs. Whitney, sitting in the front row, stared hard at Gloria, and Gloria felt her stomach quake.

"You make everything appear so sordid," she finally snapped.

"But wasn't everything, in point of fact, sordid, Mrs. Vanderbilt?" His nasty leer had returned to mock her.

"Never! I forbid you to utter that word again." Gloria clutched at herself in alarm.

"It was *your* word, Mrs. Vanderbilt."

Crocker's voice was so insinuating that the judge banged his gavel. "You've made your point, Mr. Crocker."

There was a pause as Crocker paced to his desk and back.

"And your clothes, Mrs. Vanderbilt—in the old days you made them yourself, but surely you didn't make the outfit that you have on now?"

"No, it came from Captain Molyneux in Paris." Gloria sat up straighter to show off the suit's elegant lines.

"And how much does a suit like that cost, Mrs. Vanderbilt?"

"Five or six hundred dollars."

"And your hat. How much did that cost?"

"It came from Reboux in Paris and I suppose it cost a hundred dollars."

"And your shoes?"

"A hundred dollars or more; they are made by a great artist in Florence." Inwardly Gloria fumed. The lawyer was deliberately making the Depression crowd hate her even more.

"So you must spend an enormous amount on clothes, Mrs. Vanderbilt."

"I'm very selective," Gloria carefully replied, "and travel with very little."

"But you arrived here with fifteen trunks a few months

ago, Mrs. Vanderbilt. Were they all filled with your Paris dresses, hats, and shoes?"

"No, of course not," Gloria explained. "I was moving from my Paris house to my New York house. So they were filled with china and porcelain and silver."

Crocker stroked his chin, as if puzzled. "But your maid testified earlier that all those things arrived months before."

"She'd say anything to malign me!" Gloria snapped.

Crocker smiled at her as though she were an idiot and again changed his tactics. "Now, Mrs. Vanderbilt, can you explain your relationship with Prince Hohenlohe?"

"He is a good friend," Gloria said wearily. "I have a great affection for Prince Hohenlohe and I'm very grateful that he is here to help me. His wife is a dear friend of mine, too."

"Like Mrs. Thaw?" Crocker asked nastily. Then he said quickly, "How about Mrs. Blumenthal?"

"I don't know any Mrs. Blumenthal. I wasn't aware of her existence." The first part was true. The second, not quite.

"Your mother says that you were more than friendly with Prince Hohenlohe before you were married," Crocker stated. "But you didn't really become *intimate* friends with the prince until after your husband's death? Is that correct?"

"Yes. That is correct." Gloria nodded.

"How does Mr. Blumenthal feel about Prince Hohenlohe living in your town house now?"

"I couldn't care less what Mr. Blumenthal feels about it," Gloria snapped. How dare he!

"But isn't Mr. Blumenthal helping out with expenses?" Crocker pressed.

"I don't know where you got such a fantastic idea," Gloria retorted, her voice trembling.

"From the nursemaid. And the butler." Crocker was almost shouting now.

"It's ridiculous! Absurd and outrageous!" Gloria shrieked. She stood up and started to cry.

The judge brought down his gavel. "That's enough, Mr. Crocker. We'll reopen the case tomorrow. That's all for today."

Constance Bennett and Hohenlohe escorted Gloria down the endless flight of steps from the Supreme Court. The crowd's jeers echoed strangely in her mind.

Gloria fell into the car, raging. "It's vile that that Crocker man asked me those questions! And Gertrude sitting there gloating. I tell you, I'm not going through another day of this!"

"Now, Gloria," said Hohenlohe comfortingly.

"No!" she cried, lashing out at him. "I'm *not* going back in there tomorrow!"

"But, darling," soothed Connie, "you have to go back."

"I won't," she cried, "I won't!"

"Then you've lost the case," said Hohenlohe.

"I've lost it anyway. Or are you so *stupid?* Yes, you *are* stupid! I can see it in your eyes. And I hate you! Hate you! It's all your fault that I'm in this terrible mess. If you had married me in nineteen twenty-nine, none of this would have happened." Gloria cried even harder, ineffectually dabbing at her tears.

Hohenlohe took her in his arms. "My dear," he said tenderly, "I'd been asking you to marry me for five years. And finally you said yes and returned to America to get the verdict of your guardians. It was negative, and that was the end of our love affair. So don't blame me."

"I do!" she cried. "And I hate you!"

"Well, I love you," he said gently, drawing her closer to his warm chest. "You definitely must come back to Germany with me."

"What will Blumie say?" asked Connie, unthinkingly.

That bitch, Gloria thought.

"I'll fix his hash tonight," vowed Hohenlohe.

"Oh, good," said Connie. "A fight! God, I wish I could get my marquis so excited. . . ."

Of course Friedel was too dignified to get into an argument with Blumenthal. They never even met, because Gloria decided to avoid everything and leave town for the weekend. She knew the faithful Hohenlohe would be waiting, and so she planned a trip to Hyde Park to see old Uncle Fred— *wealthy* old Uncle Fred, who had an eye for the ladies. . . .

McKim, Mead, and White, architects and creators of palaces, had designed a stately and classical Louis XVI mansion for Fred Vanderbilt in Hyde Park, combining the glories of Bourbon France with the dignity of ancient Greece. The four facades of this imposing structure had columned porticos, and sitting in the shade of these great Doric columns, Gloria was telling Uncle Fred of the more amusing aspects of the courtroom drama being enacted at Foley Square.

As she talked, old Fred drank in the vision sitting across from him. Gloria, in her blue silk dress, silk stockings, and white hat, looked spring-fresh despite her ordeals.

"*Alors*, my dear," she said, falling into French. "From all over America I'm receiving letters of sympathy from mothers. Imagine! They're only addressed to Gloria Vanderbilt, New York, and they get to me! Such is the power of publicity and the Vanderbilt name, *mon cher*."

"I've always hated publicity and shied away from the limelight," Fred said in his cultivated voice. "Of course, I'd like to testify on your behalf, lovely Gloria, but Gertrude would kill me. And, too, the doctors tell me I must avoid any excitement—although having you here is giving me palpitations!"

Gloria laughed and impulsively leaned forward and took

his hand. "Dear Uncle Fred, you've always been a friend, from the very beginning."

"A lot of water has gone under the bridge since then," he remarked sadly. "And the Vanderbilt family has gone downhill; soon they won't have any position at all."

"Nonsense," protested Gloria, "why—"

"Roosevelt will be the downfall of all the rich families," Fred said with a gloomy expression.

The president, thought Gloria. Why hadn't she thought of him before? Perhaps he could help her!

"Uncle Fred," Gloria said, smiling prettily, "do you think you could take me over and introduce me to the Roosevelts? Do you think the president would help me?"

"My dear child, what could he possibly do?" Fred patted her cheek. "Besides, Eleanor Roosevelt is a friend of Gertrude's."

Gloria pouted.

"Times are changing," said Uncle Fred. "Perhaps you would be better off today if you'd been born poor."

"But I *was* born poor," cried Gloria. "That's why mama brought me up to please others, and especially to please men— to be popular at parties and dance all through the night. . . ." She took out a small lace handkerchief and dabbed at tearful eyes.

Fred rose slowly and took her arm. "Come, Gloria, let's go in and have something to eat. Perhaps you'll feel better."

They walked slowly to the dining room, a cream and gold chamber of immense size and imperial proportions. They sat at an oval mahogany table and ate Maryland soft-shell crabs and drank vintage white wine from the Rothschild cellars. The Sèvres dinnerware came from the Marquise de Pompadour, no less, and two sisters of Louis XV by Nattier gazed down at them. Through the twenty-foot-high windows framed in masses of gold brocade was a vista of lawns, shrubbery, and stone urns and statues from monsieur's château in Normandy.

After many years, Gloria had become accustomed to such extravagance, and the realization that she might soon have to grow unaccustomed to it was what had led her here in the first place. Oh, well, now that Uncle Fred had said he would not testify in her behalf, it still wasn't the end. He was quite elderly now, and there was always the possibility he would remember her in his will. . . .

Fred's voice brought her out of her reverie. He was talking about something that struck fear in her heart.

". . . your age, I had two very old uncles whom I hated visiting because they were wrinkled and feeble. But my mother insisted I call on them, for they would leave me a great deal of money." He chuckled. "And they did."

There was a terrible silence. The butler and second footman cleared their throats. The Boule clock struck the hour. Gloria felt at a loss for words, since Fred had just articulated her latest scheme. The situation needed a lot of charm and energy; if only she didn't feel so tired.

Aloud, with all the vitality and grace she could muster, Gloria said spritely, "My dear Uncle Fred, *touché!* I'm here to steal all your gold and your Fabergé collection, and that's why I came with such big suitcases. Your Gobelin tapestries may pose some problems, though."

Fred chuckled. "I'm sorry, my dear, but it will come as a shock and a surprise to everyone that I am leaving my estate to another pretty woman—my wife's niece, Daisy Van Alen. Perhaps you know her, Gloria?"

"Yes, from the old days in Newport," she replied, her brain racing frantically. "And she is indeed very pretty!" And an operator, Gloria thought bitterly.

"Daisy's been very kind to me," he said. "My own family hardly comes to call. You never even wrote me from Europe.

Of course, you had many young admirers and it would probably be boring to come and see me. . . ."

He stood up slowly. "I'm quite tired and must go to my
room for a while." He took her hand in his own and patted it.
"Thank you for coming to see me today."

His valet assisted him, and Gloria watched him leave the
room. He climbed the broad staircase slowly on the arm of
the valet; Gloria stood there in the vast circlular hall and
watched the thin old man vanish up into the second floor.
Then she went home, in Fred's maroon and silver Rolls-
Royce, sitting rigidly in the back seat with her head high.
A terrible sense of failure penetrated so deeply she could feel
it in her marrow, but on no account would she lose face.
She would go down with all guns blazing.

Thelma, who had recently arrived and was staying with
Gloria, was waiting for her return. She received the news
about Uncle Fred with a little laugh. "Dear me, wives and
girl friends do pose such a problem these days. That's why
Connie had to leave, and that's why I'm here from Europe,
hoping my prince will follow."

Thelma was upset because the Prince of Wales had
taken a fancy to another woman. No one's plans seemed to
be going well these days.

"While you were having a quiet weekend with old Fred,"
said Thelma sarcastically, "mine was equally peaceful. A
beggar threatened to throw acid on my face as I stepped out
of your car last night. And today, lunching at the Ritz, a
woman made a pass at me."

"Thelma, how dare she?"

"The old lez probably had read what you and Nada
Milford-Haven were doing in sinful Cannes."

"We did nothing," cried Gloria hotly.

"You look awfully pretty when you blush, darling. I'll have
to remember to put on more rouge."

"You're terrible, Thelma."

"That's nothing," Thelma smiled wickedly. "While you were gone, I tried to invite the Hohenlohes and Blumenthal, and your old friend Captain Jeff Cohn, to an intimate dinner party for tomorrow—just the six of us. A perfect number: three men and three woman. I loathe dinner parties where there are extra women, although Somerset Maugham often chides me—'Thelma, darling, a dinner party is not a mating game.' But of course to me it is!" She fussed with her coiffure. "Anyway, it fell through because Blumenthal decided he'd had enough publicity. I think he's left town."

Gloria collapsed in the nearest chair. "Blumie's gone. Uncle Fred won't help me. What will I do?" Tears started to course down her cheeks, streaking her makeup.

Thelma ran to her and patted away the tears with her own handkerchief. "Oh, please, Gloria. Try to control yourself. Your face is one of the few assets you have left. . . ."

CHAPTER
24

The momentum of the Foley Square days accelerated. At night the nightmares grew more intense. Black express trains collided and burst into flames, she in one, and Gertrude Whitney in the other, and she had no control over the racing locomotive. Sometimes she entered a dark tunnel with no sign of light at the other end. The heavy double wheels of the locomotive ground vengefully into the iron track as if they wanted to punish her and reduce her to smithereens. By November another horror was introduced into her subconscious: She was on the *Lusitania* with Reggie's brother, the handsome and dashing Alfred whom he had envied so, and like she and Hohenlohe on the *Aquitania* ten years before, they began a love affair at sea. Then she saw a submarine below the surface—Emma, Gertrude, and mama were watching the great hulk of the *Lusitania* through a periscope.

"Fire away!" cried mama.

A line of torpedoes, long, fat, and tubular, raced through the water toward her. In her stateroom Alfred's hard, brown, naked body was on top of her frail white one and he was thrusting masterfully; with each thrust she gave a sob and gripped his powerful arms and shoulders. Then came the explosion, and the water poured into the hole, the great ship shuddered and listed.

"We're being punished," cried Gloria.

"There's no punishment in this world," said Alfred.

"What of the next?" said Gloria.

And then such terror of the unknown, of what was to come, gripped her and she screamed.

On the morning of November 15 she awakened with a cry of terror from this terrible dream. She was lying in her four-poster bed with its scalloped pillows and bolsters in disarray about the floor.

Wann held her in her arms and rocked her. "Mrs. Vanderbilt, Mrs. Vanderbilt!" she cried. "It's only a dream."

But memories of the nightmare lingered on, coloring the day. And as the black Vanderbilt town car rolled into the wide spaces of Foley Square and stopped before the sinister Greek temple of justice over which was written, "The true administration of justice is the firmest pillar of good government," the roar of the angry mob came to her and she remembered the cries of the dying and drowning of the *Lusitania* nightmare. In panic she pressed her hands to her temples.

"What's the matter, darling?" cried Thelma worriedly.

"The end of my life—I saw it! In a dream! And now it's here."

"Nonsense," said Thelma, for she was not superstitious like her twin.

"You must keep calm, Mrs. Vanderbilt," said the nurse, glancing at the white misery of her face in the dying autumn sunlight.

The shrieks of the crowd were louder and more vicious today; they had no money in their pockets, and a long week-end stretched ahead. Added to this were the newsboys shouting her name on the street corners. The *Daily Mirror* headlined: MRS. VANDERBILT HAS ALLEGED EROTIC INTEREST IN WOMEN. The *Daily News* and *Journal* were more graphic and sordid.

As the sisters stepped into the mob before the courthouse, the low roar became a din and the mob became even more unruly. Gloria shrank from all of their abuse; the nurse had to fairly drag her through the crowd. The noise was terrifying. Even the bodyguard, a hefty 250-pounder, sensed danger.

She moved slowly up the steep flight of thirty stone steps and under those ten thick towering stone columns. The corridor was depressing and dirty. The painted ceiling depicting justice being carried out seemed a hideous mockery. In that gloomy all-marble place their footsteps echoed loudly and she felt the same chill in her heart as she had when she entered The Breakers long ago. Even the newspaper people seemed to stare at her accusingly, and their questions were more personal and probing.

Today Gertrude Whitney's lawyers were even more ruthless. They asked her vile questions, the sort of questions that no one had ever dared ask her before. They insinuated horrors about herself and Blumenthal. She put up a tremendous fight, but she collapsed just before the lunch recess and the nurse had to revive her with some smelling salts. Later the nurse and Hohenlohe led her out into the corridor.

"I must have some fresh air," said Gloria weakly.

Hohenlohe glanced at his wife. "I'll take Gloria for a walk," he said quietly.

She took his arm and they stepped out into the daylight. The fresh smell of the sea from the nearby Hudson and East rivers carried a pleasant freshness that reminded her of Newport and Sandy Point Farm. On Reade Street, a 1900 structure of grim, gray stone with a Mansard roof was another Vanderbilt reminder. Had she ever worn that Gainsborough

costume? Had Harry Payne Whitney ever really been in love
with her? Strangely enough, it had come as a shock when
she read in the obituary columns that Harry had left $70
million and his brother Payne had left three times that much
in 1927.

Presently they were walking through the graveyard of
Saint Paul's Church. It had been built in the eighteenth century and had a New England dignity about it that she liked.
It was peaceful here, with the dying leaves falling about their
feet. The inscriptions on the tombstones made them realize
how fleeting one's stay on this planet was.

She looked at Friedel tenderly in the half-light. "What are
you thinking about?" she asked.

"Money," he said.

"That sounds odd coming from you."

"As I grow older, I think more about it," he replied sadly.
"I never used to think about it in the romantic, golden days
ten or fifteen years ago. I was idealistic then, and you were
my ideal."

"Was I?" she said, looking up at him wistfully. She had
lost fifteen pounds and had never looked more frail.

"I fell in love with you at that London ball in nineteen
twenty-two. But I think I loved you best at the Vanderbilt
reunion in that fantastic old château, and it was torture for
me to know that Harry Payne Whitney was so mad for you."

"Yes," she said, as if to herself. "Yes, I had everything
and didn't realize it." She smiled sadly.

"You were careless, spoiled, and irresponsible," he said,
kissing her hand.

"I'm not anymore," she said bitterly.

"I think you'll always be," he replied. "A lovely child of
seventeen—frozen in that age and unable to grow."

They walked on with their arms around each other's waist.

"The tide has turned," said Gloria. "I'm afraid I've lost
the case."

"You always have a home with us in Germany," said Friedel gently.

She gazed up at him with irony. "What would you do with me there?"

"I'd give you my love and protection."

"I'd be your mistress, you mean. Your wife might have something to say about that. And how long would you love me?" she asked. "You told me the whole political scene is changing so swiftly in Germany. What would you do if Hitler took everything away from you?"

"Well," he said, "if things became too unpleasant, which I doubt seriously, we could go to Switzerland. I have cousins and family in Geneva."

"It would never work," she said quietly, "and you know it. Tell me truthfully, Friedel, was it me or the Vanderbilt money that you loved?"

"It gave you an aura," he admitted.

They moved thoughtfully back to the courthouse.

The sense of serenity that had come over her in the grave-yard quickly ended when she stepped into the gloom of the judicial chambers where her fate was being decided. Somehow she got through the afternoon. Afterward the drive uptown was fearful. The shrieking trains rumbling noisily over the El seemed a vengeful spirit. From tenements in Hester Street, the Bowery, and Chinatown, Gloria imagined that people stared at her with hatred. Back on 72nd Street she could hardly bear to look at Friedel.

The weekend dragged. Her lawyer, Nathan Burkan, told her the verdict would be reached Monday or Tuesday. She and Thelma played bezique for hours at a time, other times backgammon. The nurse gave her large sleeping draughts so that she fell into unconsciousness, and she awakened in a torpor with a heavy sense of defeat and failure.

On Sunday something happened which stripped her further of her illusions. Thelma and Wann took her to see some small apartments. Everyone seemed to be pushing her to live poor—to "cut down" and "face your situation."

"I think it's lovely," said Thelma, glancing around a three-room apartment at Southgate at 415 East 52nd Street.

"I could never live here," cried Gloria hotly.

"Why not?"

"My position," said Gloria.

"*What* position?" said Thelma in a mocking tone.

"I'm Mrs. Reginald Vanderbilt," she said proudly.

"A Vanderbilt with no money means nothing," said Thelma realistically. "And poor widows are just a drug on the market."

"Oh, is that what I am?" said Gloria. "A poor widow?"

"It's time to reevaluate your position," said Thelma more gently. "Things have changed in ten years, you know. You were something special with Reggie's support on one side and Harry Payne Whitney's on the other. But now that's all over."

"What about Blumenthal?" she said desperately.

Thelma laughed. "What about him? Last I heard, he's gone back to his wife like all the others. Well, here am I preaching to you and I can't even accept the fact that Wallis Simpson has probably got my David. That's one blow I'd never recover from."

The sisters returned to the house in a black frame of mind.

By Monday afternoon there was still no news and Thelma suggested that they go and pay mama a visit. Laura Morgan was living in a fashionable small hotel on 60th Street off Madison. Gloria didn't want to go, but anything was better than waiting around the house—especially now, when they were being plagued by obscene phone calls and kidnap threats.

"Mrs. Morgan is receiving no visitors," said the desk clerk as they entered the lobby.

"Tell Mrs. Morgan," cried Thelma imperiously, "that her

daughters, Mrs. Vanderbilt and Lady Furness, are here."

The elevator operator bowed them into Mrs. Morgan's suite and mama rose up with a hard look in her face. "Why are you tormenting me? Haven't you brought me enough sorrow?"

The mother and daughters didn't embrace.

"Why did you do it?" asked Gloria.

"I couldn't let you and the German squander my darling's money."

"How much did Mrs. Whitney give you?" said Thelma.

"A hundred thousand," the old woman answered triumphantly.

Without another word the twins departed.

Nathan Burkan was sitting in the drawing room when they returned. His expression told them what they both had sensed—Gertrude Whitney had won custody of little Gloria. Justice Carew had signed the court order that made Gertrude the child's legal guardian.

"We'll appeal," he said.

"Yes," said Gloria faintly, "we'll appeal."

"Well, now that it's all over, I must pack and return to Europe." Thelma headed for the stairs. "Elise! Elise!" she called out for her personal maid. "Hurry, hurry and place a call to the Prince of Wales in London!"

Gloria followed Thelma into her bedroom. "So you're abandoning the sinking ship," said Gloria, trying to keep her voice light.

"Darling, I'm a drowning man myself," cried Thelma frantically. "I've probably lost David to that awful Wallis Simpson. And to think that I stupidly introduced them!"

"Why did you?" asked Gloria, amused.

"Bad judgment—I got too big for my own britches." Thelma threw open the closet doors and rummaged through her dresses. "And that's what you suffer from too, my puss."

"What do you mean?"

"You think that being Mrs. Vanderbilt makes you something special," laughed Thelma. "Well, I hate to tell you but you don't have any value anymore. Blumenthal, Larry Thaw, and your host of admirers will drop you like a hotcake. You wait. The phone's not going to ring at all anymore!"

"What shall I do?" cried Gloria, sinking onto the bed and falling into her old dependent role.

"Take stock, you idiot, take stock! We're almost thirty years old, and our thirties are going to be a lot different from our twenties." Thelma began to throw dresses on the bed.

"How so?" said Gloria faintly, with a sinking feeling in the pit of her stomach.

"There will be less people to love you," said Thelma, giving her a long sad look. "You're no longer a sweet, vulnerable little girl of seventeen—although I know you think you are."

"Yes, I suppose I do," sighed Gloria, sitting forlornly on the bed.

Elise announced a call from the Prince of Wales and Thelma flew to the phone. Before she picked it up she cried, "Scheme, don't dream!"

Gloria fell back on the pile of dresses, laughing and crying at the same time. . . .

The Hohenlohes departed the next day, after Thelma left. Most of the servants were let go or gave their notices; the vast house became silent. Gloria wandered about aimlessly.

She sat by the window, a forlorn figure in that immense bay, and tried to find some answers to the questions that went round and round in her mind. But her concentration was hazy, dulled by ten years of dissipation. It seemed a grayness covered her now.

She had never been a strong character; never sure of her identity; never could figure out where she belonged in life.

In truth, she had taken on the identity of whomever she was close to. Like a chameleon, she had worn the gaudy colors of Reggie's life, and then become enslaved by Harry Payne Whitney. When Harry suggested that it would be better for her to go to Europe, she had gone. Now she realized that it had been a fatal mistake, cutting herself off from the Vanderbilt family who, after all, buttered her bread; her living abroad had really lost her the trial. It suddenly occurred to her that all her problems were due to her own stupidity, that she and she alone was responsible for her predicament today. There was no one she could blame.

She picked up the needlepoint canvas that lay in her lap and tried to make sense of it. The design was a complicated flower and bird. Finally she cursed out loud and flung it down. She sprang to her feet and began pacing like a tiger. To hell with taking stock! To hell with introspection!

The grandfather clock chimed eleven and she thought, Time to go back to bed and pull the sheets over my head. What better idea?

Instead, however, she wandered down into the deserted kitchen and butler's pantry. She hadn't been in a kitchen for eleven years and looked at the stove with curiosity. She went into the servants' sitting room and picked up first one thing and then another, without interest.

Finally she had a glass of White Rock, lit a cigarette, and started upstairs. She began pacing in the drawing room and started an inner dialogue. Her questions and answers resembled the staccato questioning of the Whitney lawyers.

Q: Gloria, why have you ended up this way?
A: Because I'm stupid.
Q: I guess you didn't think very much.
A: I surely didn't!
Q: Can't you use your brain now?

A: What brain is there?
Q: Can't you work?
A: What have I been trained for?
Q: Helpless?
A: Helpless.
Q: Hopeless?
A: Hopeless.
Q: So. . . ? Do what you're best at, darling.
A: Men!

The hallway phone rang and she was grateful for its sound; she ran to it as if a pot of gold lay there waiting. It was the first time in ten years she had picked up the telephone without having the call screened first by a butler, secretary, or maid.

The voice over the wire was friendly. "This is the man from El Morocco calling. I talked to you the other night, remember?"

"Yes, I remember," she said brightly, although she didn't.

"How would you like to have lunch today?"

Suddenly her spirits soared. "I'd love to," she gushed.

"One o'clock? At Twenty-One? I think we'll get along," he said. "I'm like Blumenthal in many ways."

"How marvelous!" she said gaily.

"I don't know if I'm that marvelous," he said with a little laugh.

The conversation was getting a little out of hand—he was really becoming too familiar. "I'll be there at one," she said somewhat coldly. "And I'll pin a gardenia on my muff so you'll know who I am."

"Oh, everyone knows who you are, Gloria Vanderbilt. . . ."

All of her vitality and high spirits returned as she raced up the stairs. She would wear her black Mainbocher suit with sable muff, scarf, and hat—Anna Karenina–style. Thank

God she still had her mother-in-law's pearls! And Reggie's diamond ring of Mazarin. Not to mention Harry's emerald-and-diamond brooch.

Her dressing-table mirror told her that the line of her cheek was still clear and her neck was like sculpture. However, she had to do a bit of work on her complexion so that the gardenia freshness, for which she was famous, would be overwhelming. She glanced at the Fabergé clock; she was late. She left her lipstick-smeared cigarette smoldering in the onyx-and-gold ashtray, a remnant from Sandy Point Farm, soon to be disposed of at her bankruptcy auction.

As she was about to go out the front door she decided she didn't like the sable hat and raced back upstairs for a change. Her new creation was an off-the-face romantic black picture hat with egret feathers curling about her face.

She went over to Park Avenue to get a taxi—she who had always had a chauffeur and footman to aid her, and a town car at her disposal. Luckily she spotted one almost at once, and in just a few minutes she found herself before the familiar facade of "21" on West 52nd Street. The major domo and hatcheck girl all greeted her with customary politeness (Were they perhaps too polite?) and she was led to a table. She suffered a bad moment of anxiety when she passed Cholly Knickerbocker's table filled with people she knew. She smiled in their direction, but no one smiled back; the host himself was careful not to meet her eyes.

She waited and waited at the table. Minutes passed like hours. Every stare seemed a nail hammered into her defenseless body. Her presence at "21" caused such a sensation that people came from upstairs and peered in at her. The hum of conversation was terribly loud. The rich and arrogant society women at Cholly Knickerbocker's table were particularly unpleasant. They had all had lovers and been careless with their children, leaving governesses to look after them

while they pursued their own pleasures, yet they felt contempt and hatred for that Vanderbilt woman. Because she
had allowed herself to be caught. Worst of all, she had ex-
posed their life-styles for the whole world to see.

That was unforgivable. For her stupidity, she must pay.
And anyway, who could blame them for not wishing to
associate with such a dreadful woman who had been branded
a whore and a lesbian in court?

Sitting there, stared at, pointed at, Gloria finally understood that the stranger was not coming. He was merely
playing a cruel joke on her. What to do? The best thing to
do was just to pretend that nothing had happened. So she
ordered a daiquiri and a filet of sole with grapes. The daiquiri
warmed her, and somehow she managed to get the food
down. With her coffee she ordered a brandy which would
give her the courage to get up and walk down the whole
length of the room.

Presently, without a word, she moved through the crowded
tables and out into the hall. She held herself erect, her head
high, her eyes straight ahead. In silence, Gloria moved out
the door, a frail figure in her exquisitely tailored black suit
and hat with the quivering feathers. Then, with lowered
head, she started toward Fifth Avenue, a strange smile
flickering across her lips.

By the ornate limestone facade of Cartier's, the towering
figure of William Randolph Hearst was watching Gloria.
Surely she was one of the sights of New York, walking up
Fifth Avenue in the afternoon. She moved with a dancer's
grace and allure, and he liked the mysterious modeling of
her lips. He stepped forward and stopped her progress.

"Gloria, my dear, aren't you going to say hello to an old
friend?"

"Mr. Hearst! I'm so happy I could cry," she said sincerely, and her eagerness brought the old sparkle back to her cheeks and the upward curve of her lips.

"Marion and I have been meaning to write to you—" he began.

"Let's not talk about that," she said. "It's all finished and done."

He watched her closely. He noticed things, unlike most rich people, and he didn't like her expression. He hated to think what she'd gone through. Nobody wanted their child taken from them, or their income. She mustn't be defeated.

"What are your plans?" he asked.

"I don't know," she shrugged helplessly. She looked at his mouth and wondered what it would be like to make love to him. She knew he wanted her. But could she kiss a sixty-year-old man? Of course, he was strangely fascinating—and extremely wealthy. . . .

"How about flying out to sunny California with me?" he invited.

"Well . . ." she said, pouting her red lips and feeling alive for the first time in months.

"San Simeon is like Shangri-la," the gray-haired tycoon said. "You won't have to shoot dice with your sanity there, the way you do here." He gazed down at her lovely face. "How about it, Gloria?"

She threw her arms around him and kissed him on both cheeks. "What better place than Shangri-la for me! You adorable, wicked, *handsome* man! I could eat you this very minute!"

Mr. Hearst gulped. "You could? You would?" He offered her his arm gallantly and the doorman ushered them through the portals into Cartier's. "Would you care to help me choose some Christmas presents, Gloria? I've always admired your style and taste tremendously. . . ."

And so the enormously tall multimillionaire publisher,

one of the richest and most powerful men in the world, and the frail and elegant woman in Catherine the Great's pearls and seductively quivering egret feathers, vanished into the gilded French rooms of Cartier's—once the home of Phil Plant, and "pure Vanderbilt" in feeling.

Yes, Gloria thought, Thelma had been quite wrong. She *was* still Mrs. Reginald Vanderbilt. People could never take that away from her. Everything else, perhaps, but never her name. . . .

Her jewelry eventually went. Reggie's diamond ring was sold ten years later, when her daughter refused to support her. Thirty years later her pearls were gone, too. Harry's emerald-and-diamond brooch was sold when she died—appropriately enough in the land of dreams: Hollywood. The ghosts of yesterday came out of retirement—Mary Pickford and Buddy Rogers—to attend her funeral; they had known her in her heyday when she was the legendary Mrs. Reginald Vanderbilt.

Gloria remained Mrs. Vanderbilt until the day she died—a title which gave her much comfort in the days of her decline.